THE POWER THAT SHAPED A NATION.
THE LOVE THAT DESTROYED
A KINGDOM.

KING ARTHUR—The bold adventurer. Lustful and violent, brutally torn between his loyalty to the Britons and his fierce devotion to the ancient tribe of the woman he loved.

MORGANA—The beautiful leader of Britain's Faerie-folk, whose love for the king threatened her people's very existence.

GUENEVERE—Proud, defiant, ambitious. Consumed with an intense jealous hatred of the woman who endowed upon Arthur the treasure she herself could never give him: a son.

MODRED—Burning with rage and an unquenchable thirst for vengeance. Sworn to destroy the man he considered his greatest enemy—his father, King Arthur.

FIRELORD

"Godwin is a major find; a convincing researcher and a master novelist."

—Algis Budrys, *Chicago Sun-Times*

Firelord

Parke Godwin

BANTAM BOOKS
TORONTO · NEW YORK · LONDON · SYDNEY · AUCKLAND

*This low-priced Bantam Book
has been completely reset in a type face
designed for easy reading, and was printed
from new plates. It contains the complete
text of the original hard-cover edition.*
NOT ONE WORD HAS BEEN OMITTED.

FIRELORD
*A Bantam Book / published by arrangement with
Doubleday & Company, Inc.*

PRINTING HISTORY
Doubleday edition published October 1980
Bantam edition / May 1982
3 printings through June 1985

A Kind of Dedication

To Quackenabush and Diavolo, who suffered with this, believed in it, read, cared, cheered and encouraged, stuck pins in sinister dolls, heard confessions, gave absolution and usually paid for lunch. With Love.

Acknowledgments

Firelord is a fantasy, though I've attempted to stretch an elastic legend over the bone of historical fact regarding the reigns of Vortigern, Ambrosius and Arthur. For this, I'm deeply indebted to John Morris's lucid and fascinating *The Age of Arthur* (Scribner's, 1973) and Jean Markale's unorthodox *King Arthur, King of Kings* (Gordon & Cremonesi, 1976), translated by Gordon Cremonesi.

For the picture of Morgana and her people, I drew heavily on the pioneering work of Dr. Margaret Murray, whose books *The Witch-Cult in Western Europe* and *God of the Witches* (Oxford University Press, 1971, 1973) retrieved the fairy folk from moonlit legend and restored them to history where they belonged.

Arthur is as historical as Lincoln or Julius Caesar, merely less documented. Almost certainly he succeeded Ambrosius as overlord of the Britons. Geraint was indeed Prince of Dyfneint, Marcus Conomori was overlord of Cornwall. Trystan appears to have been his son, though I have kept the usual form of the legend. Peredur was actually a prince who ruled at York. Guenevere is probably as historical as the rest; like them, she is remembered with kindness or severity, depending, as Arthur notes, on who is telling the tale.

That they didn't all live at the same time is beside the point. Very likely some of them did. Assembled on one stage in one drama, they make a magnificent cast. It should have happened this way, it could have, and perhaps it did.

P.G.

Contents

Celtic/Roman Site	Modern Site or Vicinity (where known)
Astolat	Imaginary seat of power, Dyfneint
Avalon	Imaginary
Caer Legion	Chester, Flintshire
Caerleon	Southern Wales, near Llandaff and Cardiff
Cair Daun	Doncaster, Lincolnshire
Camelot	Imaginary
Camlann	Near Carlisle, Cumberlandshire. No precise site. Legend says Arthur received death wound here.
Camulodunum	Colchester, Suffolk
Castle Dore	Southern Cornwall, near St. Ives
Cathanesia	Caithness, Scotland
Cilurnum	West of Corbridge, Northumberland. No precise site.
Corstopitum	Corbridge, Northumberland
Dyfneint	Modern Devonshire
Eburacum	Modern city of York
Kaelcacaestir	About seven miles southwest of York
Leinster	Territory of southeast Ireland
Mount Badon	No precise site
Neth Dun More	Imaginary. On the River Neth between Cornwall and Devon.
Taixali, Venicones and Votadini	Pictish tribes inhabiting the central and eastern lowlands of Scotland. The Attecotti were inhabitants of Cathanesia (Caithness). The Faerie (Prydn) were nomads with no fixed home.
Verulamium	St. Albans, Buckshire
The Wall of Hadrian	Erected by the Emperor Hadrian in the second century; it stretched across Britain from Solway Firth in the west to Tynemouth on the North Sea.
Ynnis Witrin	Glastonbury, Somerset

The King Lies at Avalon

Damn it, I haven't time to lie here. Whatever comes, there's more for a king to do than squat like a mushroom and maunder on eternity.

Dignity be damned, it's a tedious bore.

Even when he was wounded, Ambrosius told me he hated being carried in a litter like a silly bride. Slow, uncomfortable, and the wounds open up anyway. Mine are rather bad. The surgeons tell me to prepare for their ministrations—Jesus, spare me professional gravity—and that priest looks so solemn, I think God must have caught him laughing and made him promise never again.

So tired. So many miles from Camlann, where nobody won but the crows. And some time to spend here at Avalon listening to the monks chant in chapel. No complaint, but one does wish the love of God guaranteed an ear for music. They do not speed the hours.

So, this testament.

Young Brother Coel who writes it for me is very serious about life, but then no one ever told him it was a comedy. He thinks I should begin in a kingly manner at once formal, dignified and stirring. I was never all three at once, but to take a fling at it:

I, Arthur, King of the Britons, overlord of the Dobunni, Demetae, Dumnonii, Silures, Parisi, Brigantes, Coritani, Catuvellauni—

> *—am disgusted and out of patience, being up to my neck in bandages like a silly Yule pudding. I'd write myself if I had an arm that worked.*

1

Let's be simple, Coel, let's write as it was. Then there's a letter you may deliver for me.

Why, to Guenevere, lad. To my queen.

A king should write his own story, especially a Briton. We are a race of musical liars, and who you are may depend on who's singing your song. Many's the tree-spirit come tripping out of yesterday to find itself a saint today and rudely surprised by the change. I've been called Artos and Artorius Imperator, but it seems to stick at Arthur, the way the monks write and the bards sing. That's unimportant; what matters is who we were and what we did. I want to write of us the way we were before some pedant petrifies us in an epic and substitutes his current ideal for ours. As for poets and bards, let one of *them* redecorate your life and you'll never be able to find any of it again.

It's an insult to freeze men like Bedivere and Trystan, Gareth, Geraint and Lancelot into a legend. How Tryst would laugh at that and send an epigram searing down the centuries more potently than anything I could write. We were never that still or complete, always moving between the end of one thing and the beginning of another. Guenevere wouldn't sit still while Time painted her in serenity, and God *knows*—Morgana? Catch the lightning, friend. Chain the wind.

No legend then. I give them their world as it was and let them stride.

From my casement, I can see the apple orchard blossoming and remember another May. Let me begin with spring, then. Spring in the earth, in the blood, young and green as new grass that knows nothing of winter.

Spring at home and being ten years old. The spring when I met Vortigern and the mad boy called Merlin.

Merlin and a Sword

The hills near our villa were long and low and made for children to run over. So we ran that day, Kay and Bedivere and I, up one rounded height and down the other, straining for the highest ridge where we could see east and west for miles and the flash of sunlight on the eagle standards of the approaching cohort. We panted up to the topmost rocks and hung there gasping, me and my half-brother Kay, while Bedivere scrambled up onto the crag edge, shoved the sweat-lank red hair out of his eyes and pointed to the east.

"There he is! Ambrosius!"

When we climbed up beside him, Kay gasped: "He's brought a whole legion!"

"Only a cohort," I corrected him. "I heard father say so."

Bedivere pointed again, to the west this time. "And there's old Vortigern."

We didn't understand much of what was to happen that day, only the rough shape of it. The Emperor Vitalinus was come to give up the imperial sword to Ambrosius Aurelianus, commander of the Roman legions in Britain. Vitalinus was his real name, but in the west where his support was strongest he was called Vortigern, the over-king. I rarely heard him named anything else. And yet that picture stuck in my mind, Ambrosius coming like a god with the flash and thunder of horses and the blare of horns—and the old emperor slipping down the valley with a few men and a little dust like a tired memory. That seems the way with kings: we go out quieter than we come in.

They were to meet at the villa of my father, Uther, chief magistrate of the Dobunni. We were boys and didn't understand

3

much. We saw the great shimmering force and the little cloud of dust and called one strength, one weakness and let it go at that. Bedivere and I were ten. Kay was nine.

"It's time he gave up the sword," Bedivere growled.

"Why?" asked cautious little Kay.

"Why? Isn't he the cause of all the troubles? Didn't he bring the foreigners in? My da says he sold us out."

Bedivere's father was Uther's master of horse and a man who spoke freely what mind he had.

Kay looked to me for judgment. "What does father say?"

"Just that Vortigern did what he had to."

"What's that mean?"

"It means I don't know. Now leave me be."

We watched the great, shining snake of the cohort coil across the eastern plain toward the white square of the villa. By the time we got home the courtyard would be jammed, the house a confusion of officers and servants, the baths full of soldiers. Flavia had warned us to be back before they came. A shiver of excitement went through me, lifting my arm to squeeze little Kay's shoulder. He was a solemn, careful child who looked like Flavia. I didn't, but even then I knew I wasn't her son. My real mother was just a name, Ygerna. I never knew her. My da Uther said she died.

The war horns blared in the afternoon, the sun glinted off the eagles. Kay jiggled with wonder and excitement.

"Oh, *look* at them!"

I looked, I yearned.

That's when it began, that very moment—the buzzing in my ears I've known at odd times through life. My eyes squeezed shut against the suddenly intolerable glare of the sun. When I opened them, I found myself looking through a blur down the western valley and hearing, faint but ever stronger, a host of voices.

Ave! Ave, Imperator!

Hail to the king.

I blinked. The hills were deserted, yet the sound grew and swelled into thunder, one high boy-voice singing over the rest—

Ave!

Something beyond self propelled me, jolting me down the western slope of the hill. Bedivere and Kay called to me, but I warned them back in a voice barely my own: "Leave me alone. Go away!"

I didn't know if they followed, but ran until the ground

leveled out under me, drawn toward that high-singing voice, not caring that I was out of breath and running uphill again, brambles tearing at my legs and ankles.

Ave!

Now in that thunder of voices I heard a name, not Vortigern's. The boy-voice still sang over them, nearer than ever. I struggled to a jutting ledge. As I collapsed on it, the thunder faded away until the air was still as stopped time in the late afternoon, but the stone beneath me trembled under the pounding of my own heart.

Ave, whispered the rocks.

Then the soft, near sound of a shepherd's flute.

A gay song, and though my ears still rang with the buzzing that had summoned me, no single note of the flute made discord with it, but blended with the other as harmony. I seemed to know the melody note by note before the wood flute sounded them. The song spun out while my heart slowed and breath came easier. Then it ended, leaving a perfect, filled silence trailing after.

"Arthur."

The young voice was full of verve and laughter.

"Who—where are you?" I called.

An impertinent run on the flute. "Round the other side of this rock. Come up, Arthur, and see the emperor ride."

"Bedivere, is that you? Are you fooling me?"

A chuckle. "They're so far they can't hear you. Look back and see."

I saw them across the vale, Bedivere and Kay, coming slow as a dream, like running under water, their arms floating out from their bodies like seaweed drifting in lazy current.

Frightened, I edged along the narrow rock face, rounded its point and found myself on a wider shelf that looked out over the whole western valley.

"Hail, Arthur."

The boy was seated on a flat rock, the flute in his lap. The finespun gold of his tunic caught the sun's glare like Ambrosius' eagles. Over it he wore, thrown back, a long cloak dyed the color of new grass, caught at the shoulder with a great bronze clasp. A strange place to meet a king's son, but he couldn't be less. He looked maddeningly familiar with his shock of blond, curly hair and gray eyes glistening with secret excitement: things to do and tomorrows that couldn't be caught up fast enough. He *shimmered* all over, he made me tingle with the energy that came from him in the flash of his gold. I couldn't breathe. It was no king's son I'd come on, but a *boucca*-spirit such as the Dobunni speak of, a shape-changer. But even as I thought it, the boy laughed again.

"Don't you know me, Arthur?"

I didn't want to show my fear, but kept my distance. "N-no."

"No matter, you will. If not now, tomorrow." Another quick run on the flute. "I met you tomorrow among the Faerie. There was a woman you loved, and here you don't even remember me."

"Woman?"

"Oh, but you were older then. How should you remember? Why do you shut your eyes?"

"My—head hurts."

"So it does, so it does. But how can you be of the Dobunni and not know Merlin?"

The fear lessened; it was hard to focus my eyes on his shining. I became bolder, even angry. "Merlin's dead. He was an old man if he ever lived at all. Who are you?"

The boy rose, only a little taller than me and not much older, but he talked in grown-up riddles. "I am called Merlin. I'm called a lot of things. There's not a stone or leaf or life that men won't put a name to. It gives them a nice safe box to collect things in. They get in the habit of collecting things and end up surprised at the weight they're carrying. A dream they thought might fit someday, something bright and sweet like a woman, picked up for her shine and somehow never left or at least never forgotten. Or an ambition! There's a fine item in any man's bag. A great, glowing ambition. They never fade, never wear even when you've outgrown them. Always there to look at and remember and play might-have-been. A while ago in real time you saw the eagles. And you wished, Arthur."

I knew nothing of women then, they were only a bother with their tucking you in and kissing good-night and finish-your-supper and go-take-a-bath. And ambition was a word I didn't know. But I had seen the eagles and for a moment thrilled with a wish so vast and secret I couldn't breathe it even to Kay or Bedivere. It was as if the golden boy read my thoughts, as if his hair and tunic glowed and shimmered with all my own bright boy-hopes. He laid his hands on my shoulders.

"Look where the emperor comes."

His hands were strong. I had to obey. The late sun was in my eyes and the ringing in my ears grown to a roaring again, a hundred thousand voices from unseen throats. *Ave!*

"See!" Merlin commanded.

Down the valley rode a golden-haired king on a great war-horse. Beside him the dragon standard swayed in the grasp of another man maddeningly familiar as the king himself, and behind them surged the shining hundreds. Not Vortigern, that king, but a young man whose gilded breastplate caught the sun and hurled it back at the sky while the valley and hills and my poor head rocked with the name they hailed.

My aching eyes bulged. "What—what *is* it?"

Idly, Merlin produced three colored balls, red, white and green, tossing them aloft like a skilled juggler. "Only bright tomorrows you carved out of wishes and painted with dreams. See the horses, each a hand higher than cavalry's ever known. See the *men*, how they ride. Such men ride for love, not Roman pay."

I was frightened; none of this could be true. "Are you a *boucca*-spirit? Have you cursed me?"

Merlin laughed tenderly. "Cursed and blessed all in one, Arthur. Blessed with the power to make this be. Cursed with an eye to see too far. You still don't know me? Or that man who carries the standard?"

"Bedivere! But he's *old*, he's—"

"And that other on the king's right hand? He was part of those tomorrows. Such men come when kings dream them."

A man straighter and prouder than any of the rest, but with the eyes of a sad priest.

"This is the beauty of it," Merlin said in a different tone. "There's that part not half so fair. But now the gold still glitters, the men have not grown lean with age nor know of bitterness or regret. The standard is new and proud. Hail to the king!"

The roar filled my head and buckled my knees under me. I clutched at my pounding temples, tried to stop the thunder from my ears. I cried to Jesu and all our household gods to help me, and they brought me kind darkness through which the cheers still echoed. *Ave, Imperator*, and Merlin's voice whispered:

Did you hear the name?

"I don't believe it."

No matter, that was tomorrow. See me again where we met before, at Cnoch-nan-ainneal.

I tried to open my eyes. "The hill of the fires? Where?"

Not where but when. At Beltane, remember?

No, I didn't remember. I was ten years old, run foul of a *boucca* and gone mad. "How can I find you?"

How can you not? Though you never catch me, how can I escape you? At May Eve on the hill, remember? The Faerie woman, the one you loved . . .

Bedivere and Kay found me on the ledge, staring out over the valley where the dust was settling after Vortigern's passage. They were hot from running, puzzled and cross with me.

My eyes focused better now. "How long have I been here?"

"Just this moment," said little Kay. "We ran right after you."

Bedivere punched me on the arm. "We called and called. You ran like daft, wouldn't stop."

"You didn't see him?"

See who, they wondered.

"Him, the boy in the gold tunic. Merlin."

Bedivere laughed. "Merlin, is it? Come to fright your dreams?"

"And didn't you see the men come down the valley, the hordes of them?"

They were more mystified than ever. They'd seen only Vortigern's guard, not more than fifty all counted.

Kay pulled at me. "We'd best get home. We'll catch it if we're not there when they come."

We started for home, myself trailing behind. My head wasn't clear yet, though the ringing was gone. I spoke no more of what happened, but now and again I looked sideways at Bedivere. No mistake: people grow and change, but the set of the eyes remains. He was the man grown who carried the dragon beside the king, but who was that strange other who rode with a doom on his shoulders? I knew him, would know him, and the name was on the tip of my tongue. As we hurried on, I realized numbly in my ten-year-old head that the Merlin-*boucca* had indeed cursed me to see too much and too far. "Blessed and cursed," he said. Many years later I knew what he meant.

Why do men strain at the curtain that hides tomorrow? Why do seers grow rich pretending to pull it aside for a blurred, distorted view? It is hardly a blessing.

Our villa lay a day's ride up the Severn valley from where the river widens into the sea channel. This has always been the land of our tribe, the Dobunni, and our cousins, the Silures. For a hundred years before I was born, we Pendragon wore the Roman toga fastened over our left arm and the enameled gold armlet of tribal chieftainship on our right. By the year of my birth, father called himself Roman more out of habit than fact. It had been fifty years since Constantine went into Gaul with the last of the combat legions, leaving only the thinly spread auxiliaries from which we tried to build an army again. Suddenly we were defenseless, a prosperous people used to four centuries of unbroken peace and order. When the Romans left, we crowned a new emperor in the imperial name and others in quick succession as the separate tribes dissented from one another and rose up to slay the leader they themselves might have hailed a year before.

And the wolves waited outside our walls and grinned and watched: the Irish across one sea, the Saxons across another, the Picts in the north. Their envoys came and saw the lush lowlands poorly defended and went home to sharpen their swords. Out of the confusion of tribes came a Council of Magistrates, sub-kings with their own people's interests at heart. They raised one of their own to the purple, a Silure called Vortigern, and he stopped the warring for a time.

In some ways it's marvelous to be old. You have years of hindsight to play with. Grandfathers sit by the fire rumbling sagely of what should have been done at a certain time and place to prevent a certain thing. Trust in this or pray to that god, life has a way of bringing the right man sufficient to the time, though the time may not know it. So with Vortigern—inglorious, ignoble street squabbler, the petty bargainer in the marketplace, the cold, suspicious face of a losing gambler, the peasant shrewdness, the small man's need for endless self-explanation, the veneer of courtesy and court rhetoric quickly dropped for street vulgarity among cronies or in moments of stress. Not a hero, not a man to remember.

But I say he came to power against the wall and ruled with his back to it, until that day I saw him in our house. He inherited the empty shell of Roman form and power, half-trained, ill-equipped legions that would not fight outside their own province. He inherited the threat of invasion from three sides, and when these threats became real, he faced them with timorous chieftains not yet imperiled enough to rise above self-interest, an empty treasury and letters of refused help from a Rome that could no longer repel the barbarians at its own gate.

What would you have done?

If you were a hero, beset with three vicious dogs, you might fling yourself on one, but the other two would destroy you. You could guard against all three, but how long before one or all charged? The bargainer in Vortigern threw a bone to the worst of the dogs and set it loose on the others. He invited the Saxons as mercenaries, fed them and gave them a kennel.

But the dogs grew too numerous for the kennel, always more of them, always greedier, demanding where they used to ask. Soon the whole east of Britain was theirs and the treasury empty again. Then people said to old Vortigern that he was a compromised, humiliated fool and it was time for new blood on the throne. "A leader!" they cried (they always do), a fighter, a name that rings with the glory of Rome. And they turned to Ambrosius Aurelianus, commander of Vortigern's armies.

Thus this one day at Uther's villa, the high men of the west gathered to hail a new emperor while the grubby street peddler slipped away to oblivion. In the glow of hope, few will recall the lesser man who bought the new heroes time, carved out with pitiful, broken tools.

I say this so that you might understand that battered, bartered old man—Vitalinus, called Vortigern, Emperor of Britain. He had the soul of a tax collector. I would not put such at the head of a mounted charge, but to bargain on wile and an empty purse, I would send Vortigern before Lancelot. Bards, when you shape a song to heroes, drop in a verse for Vortigern and let it begin: "Each man in his time."

Our villa was built in the old days of the long peace. You couldn't defend it for an hour, but never since, not even in Camelot, have I so loved a place.

The plan was the usual Roman square with the villa itself built around three sides, the fourth closed with a low, white-washed wall that formed a wide courtyard. The baths and kitchens ranged down one side, with the slave quarters opposite; family chambers joined them to make the base of the square, and the whole stretched out room by room at ground level to catch as much sun as possible. Stables, smithy and auxiliary kitchens and quarters were outside the wall. Floors were mosaicked, well warmed in winter by hot air blown from ample stoke holes. The imperial engineers built it to last forever. I remember nothing earlier than this house, no other mother but Flavia.

We raced into the courtyard bare minutes ahead of Vortigern's

party. Flavia was standing on the portico, small and plump,
dressed to receive royalty and definitely impatient. Bedivere left
us to go home; Kay and I slowed apprehensively as we approached
our mother. Before we could speak, Flavia beckoned the house
slaves, Scipio and Aulus.

"Both of you to the baths with Scipio, and don't dawdle.
Aulus, lay out clean tunics, tell the women to feed them in their
room tonight."

Scipio whisked us away, and precious little time we had to
splash about. He herded us through all three baths for a quick
dip, oiled and scraped us efficiently, then toweled and trotted us
back across the courtyard. Already the emperor's guard milled
about, rattling down from mounts, grooms leading the animals to
the stables. The officers were of high rank, few lower than
tribune. We had only a quick, wide-eyed glimpse of them before
Aulus had us under his fussy wing for dressing and combing and
Flavia's special orders. We weren't to go near the triclinium
while our parents were dining with Ambrosius and the emperor.
We would be brought in later to pay our respects and say good
night. This would be a polite signal that dinner was over. The
business and protocol of the accession were then to be discussed.

The dinner dragged on. We stretched out our own meal,
played some knucklebones on the floor, bored and vaguely
excited at the same time. I listened to the faint voices, distin-
guishing between them. The quiet, cadenced reason: Uther. The
fluttering laugh like a startled bird, mother. There was another
heard less often, clipped and precise. The fourth spoke often and
long, monotonous as the beating of a hammer, rising above the
others or boring through them, a voice like a toothache.

"That's Vortigern," said Kay. He peered close at me. "You're
squinting again. Does your head still hurt?"

My ears rang faintly and the golden boy Merlin danced through
memory to the piping of his flute.

The moment arrived. Flavia came for us, ushered us solemnly
down the hall with whispered warnings: "Arthur, don't slouch.
Kay, keep your finger out of your nose. Salute as your father
taught you and answer clearly. It will just be a minute."

We had to stand politely in the doorway for some time,
waiting to be acknowledged. Even as we approached, that dogged voice droned on. Father and the gray, compact man who
must be Ambrosius still reclined on their couches, but the emperor
paced about the room, fat, rumpled, sparse hair uncombed. He

looked sweaty and disagreeable even though our slaves had pampered him through the baths only three hours before.

Flavia said you could tell a Roman of equestrian rank by the cleanliness of the napkin spread over the end of his dining couch to catch the sauce drippings. Father's had a dab here and there, the like for Ambrosius who was used to a rough table in camp. Mother's napkin barely needed washing, but the martyred linen crumpled over Vortigern's couch might have been used to wipe down a horse.

"Don't trust the Council!" He was saying that as we came down the hall. "Get the army behind you—if you can call it that—and keep it there, don't ask me what you're going to pay them with. Land or turnips, I guess. Haven't been any new mintings for a hundred years and most of what there was is buried. One whiff of danger and those—*princes* buried it deep as they could. Fat lot of good, most of them got their throats cut anyway. Well, they deserve it."

The emperor paused to drink noisily, then grinned at father. "Ironic, isn't it? Anywhere you go, you could be walking on a fortune, and not enough silver above ground to paint a button. 'Where's the army? Why aren't we protected?' I tell them, cough up, an army costs. Where in Christ's name do you think it's coming from? Where are your audit rolls, your tax schedules? You're the Council of Magistrates, I tell them, the assembled princes of Britain, and you don't even know where your money is. They're so used to dodging taxes, they think it's a right. They squeeze it out of the tenants. I tell you I've got no use for monks, but the buggers are right in screaming about the way the bloody landowners lay the taxes on their tenants and then can't find five *anas* to support the army they whine for. Oh, one magnanimous fellow told me he'd let go two stableboys and his peacock keeper. Really tightening his belt. I flicked away a tear.

"And they say *I* betrayed them. *I* let in the Saxons. You're damned right I did. Because your noble peers, Uther, or their fathers at least, couldn't agree with each other long enough to pay the troops. Because *your* father, Ambrosius—bless his memory, he was a good soldier, enemy or no—but he wouldn't move his troops out of Eburacum when I needed them in the south."

Unruffled, Ambrosius answered levelly, "That would have left the Wall with nothing but a few guards. The Picts—"

"The Picts came by sea." Vortigern sagged down onto his couch as though tired of the whole subject. "I said they would and they did. And I used sea raiders to stop them. It was bargain or deluge, fight one enemy or two. So I bargained. Now . . . now they say the old man's no good anymore. Down Vitalinus, up Ambrosius. Well, I told them. I was right. I'll write my recollections one day and remember every mother's one of those bastards. I told them: mend a broken sword with sealing wax, don't be surprised it breaks in half again.''

Vortigern hunched on the edge of his couch, staring into his wine cup, his train of thought lost or not worth continuing. My father cleared his throat.

"Sire, my sons wish to pay their respects."

The old man's head came up. He stared blearily at us. "Oh. Of course."

Flavia led us forward. We saluted jerkily. "Artorius," Flavia presented me. "We call him Arthur. And baby Caius. He's our Kay."

Vortigern gave us a weary smile. "Good lads. You're a husky one, Arthur. What does your father have planned for you?"

"We hadn't thought too much of it yet," Uther said. "He fancies military service."

Vortigern took a drink. "The legions? I think Ambrosius could find a place for the son of Uther Pendragon."

I became aware of Ambrosius studying me closely. Not for years did I understand that scrutiny. "Perhaps on my own staff," he ventured.

"Arthur's a fine rider," Uther volunteered with audible pride. "Thinks he'd like the *alae*."

"The cavalry? Rot!" Vortigern snorted through what began as a belch. "Stay with the legions, boy, that's where the rank is. Cavalry's an afterthought. Socially it's scum, no place for a man of birth. Damn, Uther, that's our *problem*! Not a good Briton in the lot. Iberians, Goths, Persians, Thracians, and they all smell like sick camels. Ride half naked, most of them, and a good thing. We couldn't afford clothes. I wouldn't send anyone to the cavalry except my first wife. Well then, young Kay, where's your heart set?"

Unsure, Kay saluted again. Vortigern returned it gravely. "Well?"

Kay writhed. "Go with 'torius, I guess. Sir."

Flavia ruffled his darkish brown hair. "Kay's tutors say he has a fine head for mathematics. That may be a good thing some day as it is."

"Um." The emperor seemed to forget us entirely, head drooping, elbows on bony knees. "Ambrosius, remember what I said. Don't trust the Council."

Ambrosius exchanged a tolerant look with Uther. "I wouldn't, but we need them."

"Rot. Force is what you need, a force that moves fast when they're told. Men loyal to you alone."

"Sire, with your permission." Flavia bent her knee slightly to him and shepherded Kay and me to the door.

"Flavia Marcella," Vortigern called after her. He extended his hand in a fatherly blessing. "For this hospitality, we are in your debt."

"The Emperor of Britain graces our house," mother returned the courtesy. "May he find his chambers adequate."

Father asked Vortigern, "Will you return to Caerleon tomorrow or rest here?"

Vortigern sighed. "Will it make any difference? Do you know what the late emperor plans to do after tomorrow? I think I will ride west until I hear the sea breaking on some quiet beach with no one around except oysters. Then I'll sit and watch the sun go down. It always does, you know, and I want something simple to rely on for once in my life. That should keep me busy for years. Good night, Flavia."

That was my farewell from Vitalinus, Emperor of Britain. To me he seemed a little drunk and shabby next to the dignity of my father and the taut manliness of Ambrosius Aurelianus. The next day he went through the ceremony of accession, spoke too long, passed the sword to Ambrosius, shambled away to obscurity, and the world forgot him.

But that night, as I floated closer to the soft edge of sleep, I remembered his words: "Gather a force loyal to you alone. A force able to move fast when and where you need them."

The war-horses clattered through my dreams, the flute sang softly, Merlin laughed and threw and caught the colored balls, and over the shoulder of his green cloak, I thought I glimpsed the dark Faerie girl.

And my pillow whispered to my ear: "*Ave Artorius, Imperator.*" Hail Arthur, King of Britain. Mad as life and as true. The moon rode its arc toward morning and I dreamed no more.

*　　*　　*

Even for impatient boys, the years have a way of passing. Ambrosius proved an energetic ruler. He wrangled with the tribes constantly for money, pouring what he squeezed out of them into the army. We lost no more land to the Saxons, but we gained none back.

On Uther's death, our home went to Kay along with the *magisterium* of the Dobunni. I had no cause for jealousy, being old enough to understand it by then. Kay was Uther's lawful son while I was begotten in the wrong bed. Beyond that, the Dobunni wanted a Pendragon loyal to them before the emperor, one who would rule from home. They saw very little of me but the hind end of my horse. I was off at the first opportunity with an appointment to Ambrosius' military staff and a modest patrimony to supplement my positively humble pay as an officer-elect. At my side rode Bedivere, my aide, grown tall and hard as myself. He got his red hair from his mother, who was of the Belgae, and from his father the self-convinced stubbornness and loyalty that marked him all his life. Not that he always agreed with me; more often he didn't and I'd have to argue. But once Bedivere saw a thing was common sense, he would ride into hell for it. There was one infallible trinity to his world: God, Arthur and Bedivere. My right arm would desert me before he did.

We learned the army. We ate and quartered with the officers out of minimal courtesy, carried dispatches and ran errands. Everyone outranked us, though most of the centurions were only auxiliaries who grudged as little time as possible to their duties before hurrying home. Many of them were incompetent; they mocked my seriousness.

There are two senses you shouldn't look for in youth: proportion and humor. Bedivere and I raged privately over the laxness of what passed for an army. I grew increasingly vocal, even arrogant, as time passed. When a promotion to centurion came down from Ambrosius himself, even Bedivere noted the swelling under my helmet. It must have been infinitely galling for a veteran tribune or legate to hear a boy in new harness glibly dismiss four hundred years of a fighting force.

"In a word, Centurion—if that is possible—what do you find wrong with the imperial legions?"

"In a word, sir; top-heavy and obsolete."

A prolonged silence which I later found to be terminal.

"You may go, Pendragon."

Next day I was posted to the Second Legion at Caerleon. The imperial staff had decided to blunder along without me.

A frustrating situation: a centurion without command, still a fetching boy who'd never fought a battle. But I had eyes. The day of the legion was past. The forces that threatened Britain would never stand still for pitched battle. They hit our coasts in lightning raids, sailed deep inland in shallow-draft keels, struck and got away. The legions, even if they could be coaxed from home, were not mobile enough to cope with such tactics.

But gradually, patiently, Ambrosius was remolding our remnant army. A new generation was growing up with little memory of Rome, contemptuous of its now ineffectual name, determined to preserve for themselves what country remained. Men like Geraint of Dyfneint in Cornwall, where his father Caradoc held some minor sway.

The Dumnonii had little contact with Roman custom. This was evident in Geraint, who could not wear military gear with any consistency. At first sight he looked like a brigand interrupted halfway through the robbery of an officer: sky-blue cloak over a homespun yellow tunic and loose trousers tied at the ankle. To this was added a battered breastplate, *cingulum* and baldric from which hung a sword longer by a foot than my own.

Geraint's errand to us was simple and urgent. He was one of Ambrosius' new breed, given army status to form a squadron of horse from his own tribesmen that might eventually be built into a cohort. The men had their own land to look after, had not been paid and didn't trust Romans anyway, and couldn't be kept together at Neth Dun More without silver.

Nonplussed by this sunburst apparition, our legate Trajanus passed Geraint along to a tribune with instructions to find an idle centurion, issue the necessary silver, let them escort this what's-his-name home and report on training progress. The cavalry-mad Ambrosius might be interested.

"And teach that overdressed barbarian what an officer is supposed to wear and how to salute and speak to a superior, and—oh, just get him out of here."

The good tribune consulted his *notitia dignitatum* for the most expendable officers in camp and issued the orders. We would not even have a complement of men, but Bedivere and I were used to being homeless now and rather liked it.

"I'll pack us up straight after supper," he said after bringing the colorful Geraint and our orders to my tent.

Geraint placed one foot on a stool, threw back his worn cloak and surveyed us as if he were not sure he would remain in our company. I waited for his salute. When it didn't come, there was nothing for me to do but sit down and look military.

"May I ask your legion rank, Prince?"

Geraint had no tact, but an innocence to charm the harp out of an angel's hand. "Do you know, they told me and I've forgot, sir." His Cornish drawl turned *sir* into *zor*. "I'm half in, half out of the legions, you might say. Don't like to leave home that much."

Bedivere grunted. "None of them do."

Geraint's brow went up. "Well now, perhaps more of us would if some legions we know would be about the decent paying of the squadrons, and if we could leave home with a reasonable—a *reasonable* hope, look you, of finding it whole and unburned when we got back. I've three months' service and have been told to provide my own gear and mounts, so I found what was available, and that's not much, and here I'm come on the simplest mission to your tribune, and he said to come straight to you, sir, and here I am."

"I am Centurion Pendragon. My aide, Bedivere ap Gryffyn. Bedivere, tell the kitchen we'll dine here tonight, the three of us."

He saluted with familiar ease and left the tent.

Geraint folded down onto the stool with a weary exhalation. "Ah, God, was I supposed to salute? Mother of Jesus, I'll never learn it all."

"I suggest you do, Geraint."

He clawed at his long, tousled brown hair and thin beard. A first beard by the look of it. I made him a year or two younger than me. He appraised my uniform; this was my first official visit from a subordinate officer, and I gave thanks to the god of vanities that my tunic was fresh from washing and the *phalerae* of my breastplate was shined. Geraint took it in with a sigh before turning to business.

"Do you know what the Saxons call us? Welshmen."

"What does it mean?"

"A horrible word in their horrible dog-bark of a tongue, sir. It means foreigners. Foreigners in our own country, look you. That's how Mother of God sure they are it will all be theirs someday. I've seen them come, I've seen what they leave behind. And here's myself with only a few good men to guard poor Neth and unpaid at that, so—with one coil and another to make life hard, and since I'll never remember the ranks and titles—do you suppose I might clepe you by your Christian name?"

There was no slyness or craft in Geraint and absolutely no sense of respect due to rank. He was a king's son, voluble, serious, passionate, his acquaintance with table manners as vague as his notion of military courtesy. The food was slung rapidly in the approximate direction of his mouth, bones and scraps more or less toward his plate. But he had ideas and opinions akin to mine. We believed in the future of cavalry and warmed to each other through the bond of arrogant youth. We would overhaul the army, bring the cavalry to the fore. We would change the world and even dazzle it, given the chance.

The wine went round and round between us. We agreed with Geraint's basic complaint: he wanted his cavalry attached to no legion, free to move on their own. As he spoke of this, pounding the table for emphasis, I heard again the ghost of shrewd old Vortigern, saw behind my eyes the fleeting glimpse of the golden king coming out of the west.

A force to move swiftly when they must.

We shouted at each other, proposing, counterproposing, opinions breaking across one another like waves in a crosscurrent, but we knew one truth for sure. The Saxon would meet his match one day when Britain could field a force to match their swift-raiding keels.

"You're a good man, Arthur Pendragon," Geraint toasted me a bit unsteadily. "And no less Bedivere ap Gryffyn. When you command for the king, when you become Count of Britain, put Geraint at the head of your horse—ah dear, yes, let me do it, and I'll give you deeds to sing about!"

No . . . no, I wasn't dozing, Brother Coel. Just thinking, dreaming, an old man's privilege. Those were the good times, so young, so long ago. They did come to sing about him, you know. Oh, yes. "At Llongborth where Geraint's sword ran red . . ." Aye, it was that Geraint. And he never did learn to salute.

We three were so unimportant the quartermaster stowed us on a merchant vessel bound out of the Severn for Irish ports. The master took half an hour to put us ashore at the mouth of the Lyn. From there it was an easy two days to Neth Dun More, keeping the sea in view all the way.

I'd never seen the country of the far Dumnonii: wild, stark cliffs clawed out by the restless sea, occasional monks' cells perched like lone gulls on bare promontories. Geraint's strong-hold was a monastery far in decline when he commandeered it for service. Some of the younger monks took off their habits and joined him, but (he owned proudly) they were still Christian men and heard mass every day. As we rode, he talked of his squad-ron, his family and his hopes. They were too far from Caerleon to expect timely help in the event of a sea raid, hence this clumsy start of a home force. His father, Caradoc, signed him-self King of Dyfneint though the emperor insisted on referring to him as magistrate. Things were changing a crumb at a time. Even Kay was called prince by our own people now.

Geraint chattered on, a simple man displaying his accom-plishments without false modesty, but I noticed his eyes were never long off the sea: all his life the Saxon had come from there.

He learned of us, too. Unfortunately, the wrong things first. It led to a misunderstanding that might have become ugly. Bedivere and I were soldiers of some service by this time, shuttling from camp to camp as couriers, barracks-rowdy, famil-iar with every army brothel between Bath and Eburacum. They were few now, but how often had we awakened groaning with full heads and empty purses next to two beasts whose names we couldn't remember. And laughed and gotten up to ride all day, knowing we would feel fit as ever by noon. You have to be very young for that. Young enough to stand it, green enough to call it pleasure.

I grew up among men, without a sister. Woman's honor was something vaguely connected with Flavia. All others were fair game. Sometimes in wine or a woman's bed I caught a ghost-glimpse of the dark Faerie girl, her face near mine, the musk of her brown skin heady in my nostrils. Then she was gone, and the woman would see the drunken puzzlement in my eyes and laugh: "You're stone mad, Artos."

Aye, mad. My soul was never my own. The girl and all of them were part of the tomorrows Merlin put in my head.

Bedivere and I knew few such shadows in our morning sun. We sang more than we thought. No sweeter voice than Bedivere's was raised in the west of Britain, nor was my own so bad, a little deeper, though not as pure. We tossed the songs between us like Merlin's juggling balls, army songs that jingled like saddle gear and shortened the miles. You wouldn't trot them out before a well-born woman, but we hardly expected Geraint to take offense.

Our favorite ditty was "Good-bye to the Ninth," about a

pliant lass who loved the whole outbound legion and undertook
to say a bedridden farewell to the lot of them from legate to the
last stone-slinger, with a verse for each. We'd worked our way
down to the centurions when Geraint suddenly pulled his horse
aside and trotted a few paces to the cliff edge. When we joined
him, he was red and rigid, staring out to sea. I thought he'd
spied longships.

"What do you see, Geraint?"

His mouth disappeared in a tight line. "Do you have a sister,
Pendragon?"

"No, why?"

"I do, and I'm sick to think of you in the same room with her.
You would sing such a song about her if you could. My father
said it would be like this. The army comes with its orders and
money and whores, and will it not dirty us as it has all else?"

"It was a song, that's all. No one said a word about your
sister."

Geraint turned toward me, hot, angry tears in his eyes. He drew
the longsword. "If you are fortunate enough to meet Eleyne, you
will treat her as a saint."

Bedivere reined up on Geraint's off side, drawing his own
blade. "The centurion outranks you," he said carefully. "Put it
up."

Geraint flashed at him. "I deal with lords, not grooms."

"So do I," said Bedivere. "Put it up or lose an arm."

"We are not boys!" I turned my voice hard as I'd heard
Ambrosius do when he was crossed and wouldn't allow it. I was
angry. No man likes to be called a pig for his mere laughter, but
Geraint was a simple cut. Honor was a fragile thing to him.
From somewhere inside, I dragged up the beginnings of humility
and perhaps a little wisdom.

"Our fooling offended Lord Geraint. We apologize." I caught
Bedivere's eye. "Don't we?"

Bedivere sheathed his sword, the disgust silent but eloquent.
"So we do."

"Geraint, may your sister find a lord as honorable as her
brother."

He blinked and looked away; my apology left him nothing to
strike at. "Well. Well enough. It's just that . . ."

"I know. But you have schooled us. Let's ride on."

Geraint led out ahead of us, wanting to be apart for a time, I
suppose. Bedivere gave him a sour appraisal.

"Full of honor and a few other things I could name. He'll never make an officer."

"But a fighter he is."

Sage words from men never within hailing range of a battle. We cantered after Geraint, keeping a little distance, letting him choose the time to join us again. After a mile or so, he began a song himself in a voice pure as Bedivere's. There's nothing like music to melt a Briton. We grinned at each other.

"And a singer," I decided.

"That he *is*."

Geraint waved us forward, the cloud gone from his brow. "Come you up and sing a good man's song. Do you know 'Bronwen in the Vale'?"

We touched heel to flanks and galloped forward, already in harmony with him. For the rest of the day, we sang well-laundered lyrics and knew we must be the soul of gallantry when we met the sainted Eleyne.

"There!" Geraint pointed ahead to a finger of bare cliff poked out at the sea. "Neth Dun More."

My own eyes were sharp but could see at first nothing more than the raw rock. A few minutes later a subtle regularity of line became a low wall along the top of the cliff.

By Geraint's design, we had kept the sea in sight all the way. When he pulled away from us suddenly and rode to the cliff edge, we wondered had we insulted him again. Not so; this time he pointed far out to the southwest. The word was like a low snarl.

"Keels."

Weak sun struggled behind clouds. Bedivere and I saw our first Saxon longships, two of them, low and black in the water, the gracefully upswept sea-serpent prows making rapidly for the river mouth.

"Toward Neth," said Geraint.

"The fort?"

"The village just south. They don't know the fort's there."

"Nor does Dun More." Bedivere squinted toward the promontory. "No smoke. This time of day, wouldn't there be a cooking fire at least?"

Geraint went pale. "Dear God, they can't be gone without a watch at least. It will take hours to bring them. No. No, listen!"

Faint in the morning air shimmered the tiny sound of a frantic bell.

"The alarm." Geraint lashed his horse into a gallop. "They are there. Hurry!"

We dashed after him along the cliffs, across a small valley and then up the narrow path cut out of living rock that was the only entrance to Neth Dun More. The bell went on clanging as we clattered into the main enclosure and saw what Geraint called a fort: a scatter of low-domed beehive monks' cells, an oratory, a tiny chapel and several newer buildings of wattle and thatch, a middling timber hall and makeshift stable. But no men. The only living creature in sight was a saddled horse. The bell ceased as we reined up and a slight figure appeared in the chapel door, a young girl of thirteen or fourteen with a brown hooded cloak over her plain kirtle. She ran to Geraint, who leaped with a shout from the saddle to embrace her.

"Sister!"

"Geraint, I was in the village when I saw them, and—"

"Where are the men, Eleyne?"

"Gone home. They waited and waited for you to come back."

Geraint exploded. "Gone home, is it? Did I not have to contend with the legate and the tribunes and the God knows what? And here's the centurion with the silver to pay them. Oh God, God: there's not time to gather them all, those that heard the bell."

By my calculations, we had perhaps half an hour before we must be riding again. Tired mounts would do us no good.

"Bedivere," I said, "walk the horses, give them a fast rub and see if there's feed in the stable. Not too much."

I ran to the seaward wall and looked for the two keels: they were just off the river mouth, near enough to see the men laboring at the oars. Geraint and his sister joined me on the parapet. Geraint's courtesy was hurried but not without grace.

"Sister, this is Lord Arthur, the brother of Prince Kay who visited father last year. My sister, the Lady Eleyne."

"My lady."

"God save you, sir."

Eleyne had the same tawny brown hair as her brother without his high skin coloring. The child looked frail and ill, a brave little mouse of a woman and plain as a boot. I turned to Geraint.

"I've counted oars. No more than forty to a boat. Any sort of a force could stop them."

Geraint studied the keels. "That's true."

"Have you met them before?"

"Since he was fifteen." Eleyne took his brother's arm. "At Astolat, we hang their broken shields on our walls. We heard six ships raided at St. Petroc. Maybe these are two of them."

"Very like." Geraint's lips worked over his teeth as he thought. Stores, he judged at last; that's all they wanted. Two small keels were too light a force for raiding. Probably hit by a storm and separated from the other boats, short of supplies. A fight was the last thing they wanted. Geraint laughed and swung his sister toward her horse with rapid instructions.

"Cross the ford, tell the folk to quit the village until they hear our bell again. Then ride to my nearest men, tell them to come. Let each man tell two others and so on. But the first of them must be here within an hour—dear God, no longer, killed horses or come what may—and say Lord Arthur's here for the paying of the silver. Haste you now."

Geraint watched her go with a zestful rubbing of hands. "Got them, by God's Blood, got them fair!" With his dagger, he etched his plan in the dirt. "They won't beach the boats, there's not time. They'll anchor shallow, ready to move before anyone can get here. But, by Jesu, the filthy boats won't be there. We'll cut them loose, and those heathen who never heeded Gospel or Christian prayer will be caught between the squadron and ourselves."

He glanced from Bedivere to myself, waiting for our enthusiastic approval and perhaps a word of praise for his tactics. Bedivere stared at Geraint as if he had just dropped from the moon.

"We can burn the boats, set them adrift," Bedivere said with considerable restraint. "But if your men don't get here in time, we're three against eighty."

Geraint laughed aloud, ran to a small cell and emerged with three long boar spears. He tossed one to each of us. "Do you not see the glorious mathematics of it? That's twenty-six apiece!"

From the cover of a stand of trees, the three of us watched the men splashing ashore. At this distance, a good bowshot, Geraint recognized the flag flying over the sails: a coiled serpent.

"Cerdic."

I knew the name. Cerdic was a very young son of a war chief out of the island of Gueid Guith, which the Saxons call Wight. The men were all young and lightly armed. Besides the necessity of stores, this was probably a prestige raid. Younger men became war chiefs when they proved their leadership and gathered loyal *gesith*-companions to their personal service. This Cerdic pup was out to make a name for himself.

"And it pains me to think what that name will be after this day," Geraint chuckled. "Jesu, you lumbering sods, get ashore. I've work to do."

Bedivere counted the men pattering up the beach. "Seventy-five, Arthur, not an archer in the lot. Swords and axes only."

"And none left aboard. The boats will be easy." I tried to keep my voice level. My stomach fluttered with a mixture of excitement and terror. My hands sweated on the spear haft.

"Watch out for the small axes," Geraint cautioned. "They throw them."

We waited a hundred heartbeats after the last of them disappeared through the trees toward the village, then dashed forward along the shore and out to the anchored boats. Geraint was to watch while Bedivere and I each took a boat. The keels would have braziers of live coals ready for cooking and other needs. For good measure, each of us had an ample skin of lamp oil. I tethered my mount to the boat hawser and hauled myself up over the side.

She was a beauty, built on a concept that made her the fastest, finest thing in the water. Even as I tossed the oil about, I tried to remember everything about her. Ambrosius should build boats like these. With such craft we could meet them on the sea, even carry their war home to them.

The smoke rose from Bedivere's keel as the flames lapped over the deck and up the square sail. He waved to me and grinned: frightened as myself, Bedivere still looked ten years younger at that moment, thick in the middle of our old boy-mischief just before we got caught. He pointed to the shore: Geraint paced his horse back and forth, restless as a leashed hound straining after quarry.

I fired a piece of kindling from the brazier and dropped it on the oil-soaked deck. The greasy flame rolled along the boards, grew, crept up the mast toward the sail. When it was roaring healthily in the river breeze, I leaped overboard, floundered to the shying horse, mounted, cut the hawser and coiled the loose line under my arm.

"Let's pull them out!"

As we spurred the horses up onto the beach, there were two

doomed craft swinging about in the current that caught at them and nudged them faster and faster downstream.

Geraint chortled. "Trapped! You dear men, one on each side of me now."

Bedivere scanned the hills nervously. "How long since we left the fort?"

"About half an hour," I judged.

"My men will come," Geraint promised. 'When they move, they move fast."

The first sharp cries reached us from the village, startled and angry. Geraint couched his spear. "Jesu, I can hardly wait."

Bedivere licked his lips. "I could."

And looking up one last time at the empty hills, I could, too. Ten more minutes, at least five, I begged whatever spirits had helped me live this long. The first running figures appeared among the trees. I swallowed hard; our count must be wrong, there must be a hundred or more. I glanced at Bedivere, saw him white as myself, but Geraint sighed with pleasure.

"Are they not a lovely sight? Be not afraid, Bedivere."

That was too much for Bedivere, catching his heart midway between fear and courage. He answered through clenched teeth. "Geraint, if I die today, which seems a good wager, I wouldn't want to go off without letting you know my opinion of your abilities as an officer."

Alas, Brother Coel will not write what Bedivere called Lord Geraint—pungent and colorful as it was, impugning his intellect, his judgment and, most of all, his sanity. Then there was no more time for talk or thought. They'd seen us. The big fellow in the lead, blond as myself but shaggier, broke into a loping run, shouting at his men.

With a cry, Geraint kicked his horse into a gallop, Bedivere and I behind. We had agreed to stay in a close wedge, not to be encircled and dragged from our horses, but Geraint forgot that now. It was too late to close with him. He charged straight into the nearest of them. Bedivere and I couched our lances tight against our bodies and, close together for protection, galloped after.

Faces snarled up at me, bodies toppling, until the lance stuck in something and wouldn't come free. A blurred picture of Geraint's sword hewing like a thresher, Bedivere's horse wheeling round and round, then that hated face.

"Cerdic!"

I spurred at him, sword whirling in the air. A dull, distantly

painful jolt somewhere in my body and the face was gone. A
great, cold rage had taken me, part hate, part fear. Cold it was,
though, and I could still think with terrible clarity. Geraint was
beyond saving now. It always seemed he was surrounded and
doomed; then, impossibly, he was free again to plunge back into
the dodging Saxons. Time after time Bedivere and I tore free of
the men who reached for us to form together and charge back in
as a two-horse wall, scattering or crushing them underfoot. None
that I met were good swordsmen, but their shield work was
brilliant. We had to watch that their wounded didn't hamstring
our horses, whose lathered flanks already bled from a score of
small wounds.

Then Geraint's horse went down. I closed in to cover him,
give him time to mount again, but he refused, swinging the long
sword two-handed. Cerdic's men joined in a circle around us,
tightening, clogging movement. I felt my own mount stumble,
begin to fall, and leaped clear, shield up and sword at guard.

"Back to back, Artos!"

Even as I felt Bedivere's wet bulk against mine, the horn cut
the air, and through a stinging curtain of sweat and blood we saw
the shining line of Geraint's horsemen break over the hill with
the battle roar deep in their throats. Geraint saw them and swung
his sword so viciously, it sang as it cut the air.

"Now, Cerdic!" I dropped my shield, gripped the sword with
both slippery hands and dove for him. He knew he was trapped,
but evaded my weakening blows, backing, yelling to his men. I
lunged again as he stumbled over a body. My sword should have
cut off his arm. It merely floated powerless, a mile from its
mark. Without knowing how, I was down on all fours, staring
stupidly at churning legs and hoofs, hearing that rich-singing
rally of Geraint's over it all: "Now for God and Christ, after
them. After them!"

Where did he find the energy to roar like that, a bundle of red
and rags like myself and another like him close by, the three of
us suddenly alone like shells on a beach, the tide of battle
swirling away from us. The riders wore flowers in their helmets.
That was my last clear sight before Bedivere's arms went around
me. The tears streaked his dirty, bloody face.

"Artos, look at you!"

It seemed a great effort to talk, much less to smile, but the
absurdity was too much. "Flowers in their helmets."

"You're killed, man."

"Silliest thing I ever . . ."

"Lie back, lie down, damn you."

"Flowers . . ."

We were alone. Geraint's company pursued Cerdic, who had the canny sense to splinter his men into twos and threes that some might escape, and most did. Geraint would have none of his squadron stay to help us. By ourselves, on hacked, suffering horses, we forded the river and stumbled back into the stronghold. Inside the gate, we slid out of the saddles and simply fell where we lighted, too spent to move. Breathing. Silent.

We were blooded now, no longer boys but tried soldiers. And for all that happened that day and would happen a hundred times again, we would never understand it. No man knows the face of battle. You go through it like a dark room, you sweat, you fear, the fear passes, you come out of it and utter nothing but meaningless words about what you saw or felt.

Geraint struggled to his feet. "The bell. I must ring it to bring the village home. And then we can go to chapel, three good men that we are, give thanks for the luck of this day."

Bedivere nodded, dragging a filthy paw through blood-clotted hair. "I didn't look to be alive now. That's worth a month of masses, right, Artos? Artos. . . ? Oh, good Christ, look at—"

From far away, I felt him fumble at my armor buckles, felt suddenly cool air on the sticky mess of my body. Bedivere sobbed. "His chest, it's—are there bandages? Are there. . . ?"

He floated away in the darkness.

My eyes opened to evening, the clear sky at dusk and its first timid stars winking down at me. I lay under my cloak, body tight-wrapped in linen bandages, not far from where I had fainted. A little figure in white stirred a pot over a brazier nearby. I blinked the haze out of my eyes and recognized Eleyne.

"Where's Bedivere?"

She turned to me, relief in her eyes, quickly knelt and put her hand to my forehead. "God is good. Awake at last with no fever, and here we thought what with one wound and another that we scarce had linen for—"

"Bedivere, girl. How is he?"

"Now don't move. Here's the good thick soup and myself just

waiting to offer it. We were graced it didn't rain as it does so
often in the spring, because we dare not move you. Now raise
your head—''

Like her brother, Eleyne couldn't cry for help in a fire without
a page of prologue. My weakness made me foul-tempered.

''And eat this good—''

''Damn the soup and damn the bloody rain. Where's my
lieutenant!''

She drew in as if I'd struck her. In an instant I was ashamed
and sorry. I saw how spent she was, ridden weary that day to
warn the village and summon the men, then returned to care for
us and even brew the savory she waited humbly to serve me. I
knew little of woman's mind or soul. All I saw in her was a
naïve girl who would never be even middling comely. Saintly,
perhaps; we ascribe virtue to a woman when instinct can offer
nothing more personal. That's a well-turned epigram, worthy of
a Roman table, witty in its truth, impoverished for its ignorance.
I learned more from Eleyne than ever I taught her.

''Please forgive me. I was only worried about my friend.''

Resilient, she shrugged it off and fed me the soup. ''He and
Geraint are asleep in the hall, where I should be before I fall in
my tracks. But I must pray first.''

I tried to make amends with an attempt at charm. ''Pray me
some manners, then.''

Alas, her smile was less subtle than prim. ''We pray for what
can be, not for miracles.''

''I deserved that. You must be tired. It's been quite a day.''

''A fine day. My brother always said the answer to Saxon pig
was British horse.''

''Things are changing, Eleyne. There'll be more horse soon,
the gods willing.''

Eleyne stared at me with open curiosity. ''Why say you 'gods'
as if there were many? Are you not Christian?''

I had to think about it. ''Well, I don't know.'' It seemed a
simple admission, but her astonishment made me embellish. ''At
home we sacrificed to all sorts of gods. I've received the bread,
drunk the wine. Some of our folk have been baptized thrice over
just for the linen shirts they give out. I've sacrificed to Mithras,
Mars, Jupiter, even Venus in . . . certain places. I guess, all in
all . . .''

What, all in all? What to say on the subject of God from the
Olympus of my twenty years and one brief battle? Now I was

through it, already healing with youth's vigor, age too far away to imagine. The young are truly immortal. My arms would never tire, my loins never lose their hunger. God? I *was* God, my body the earth, my brain the cosmos. *Do you see the joke now, Brother Coel?* I said at the first that time was the traitor. The day comes when the seething beds can cool and not matter, when love means something beyond a reflection of ourselves, when there is more behind than ahead and the house of mind is haunted in every chamber with old songs, old ghosts, old hopes. And youth, though they see every day the cradle and grave shaped so alike, never believe death will happen to them. I told you it was a comedy.

"All in all, I've never seen the face of God. Unless it was a magical boy named Merlin, a glimpse of other faces, a girl I'll know. A man I've never met and almost remember. No, truly, I don't know what I am."

"Then God bring you an answer and His peace. Let it be your quest as I have mine."

"You're worn out, Eleyne. A little more of this soup, then off to bed. Leave the prayers till morning."

She filled the bowl again. "If I let go all the others, there is still the Grail prayer."

My knowledge of Christian protocol was admittedly faint. "Pardon, the what?"

She looked me straight on with that ponderous innocence. "Geraint did not tell you?"

"We were very busy. He must have forgotten."

"Oh." She settled herself beside me. "It's a grand tale fit for a bard, but that it's every word true. Before we were chiefs in Dyfneint, we were still appointed folk with a charge on our souls. The Hebrews were the chosen of the Lord. Their blood is in Geraint and me."

"How's that?"

"On the night of the Last Supper, Christ Jesus used his bowl to say the first mass. Or some say the bowl brought here was that of a Hebrew tinsmith, Joseph of Arimathea, who stood high with Pilate. At Jesus' crucifixion, he caught the Holy Blood in a cup which later he and his family brought into Gaul and then here to Cornwall. Some say one, some the other." Eleyne turned to me, her eyes large in the dusk. "But there *was* a cup, Lord Arthur. Joseph brought it here to the mines he visited so many times as a young man in the tin trade."

That much could be true; the whole world bought its tin from Cornwall.

"While Joseph and his family guarded the Grail, they were specially graced of God and could heal as Christ did. Folk came, multitudes on pilgrimage to see the Grail and the spear that pierced Christ's side. These things were passed down from father to son until one of them weakened and sinned."

I finished the soup and handed her the bowl. "Whatever your sense of history, Eleyne, no one can fault your cooking."

"But this is history," she protested. "It happened. It is my own family, not a word changed or forgot. Why is every king of Dyfneint called the Sinner King?"

That was also true; somewhere I'd heard it and never connected the meaning.

"This man, my ancestor, fell from grace. A young woman pilgrim came to him. It was hot summer, her robe was loose. He gazed on her—in less than a brotherly fashion, look you. The spear upon the instant pierced his side with a wound that would not close, and the Grail disappeared from the sight of men and has not been seen by mortal since."

It occurred to me that a man sensible enough to enjoy a woman's body might have lost the cup in a manner less than mystical, but Eleyne was rapt in her story, so I listened on.

"That was many generations past, but the charge stands. Our blood lost it, our blood must find it again. If not Geraint and I, perhaps our children. It will be hard, even though I feel it is still in Holy Britain."

As gently as possible, I asked, "Have you any notion where?"

"Where the heart is, Lord Arthur; and when we are sworn to regain the grace we lost. When we are again wise enough, pure enough to see what other men are denied. We or our children or our children's children. So every night, sick, well or weary, each of us prays—oh, not to be given the Grail as a gift, but the grace to be worthy of it."

She seemed so grave and serious hovering over me in the dusk, I tried to lighten the mood a little. "There'll be other things, Eleyne. Don't pledge away your life before you have the handle of it. A fine girl like you will be married soon. Were I landed and settled, I might speak to your father myself."

But Eleyne was light as lead. "Oh no, you are unsuitable. You are much too ungentle, Lord Arthur. And inclined to lewdness, my brother said."

Had I felt better, it might have tweaked my vanity to be

discarded so out of hand, but my body suddenly weighed a thousand stone and had to lie down. Eleyne covered me carefully.

"Sleep now," she murmured, "and I will pray for you."

"Fine." I tried to stretch, but it hurt too much. "And if I find a man of sufficient grace, I'll send him to Dyfneint."

"I would thank you for that, Lord Arthur."

She took my meaning as she took all, in deadly earnest. For all her father's "kingdom," she was only a Cornish tribeswoman, unused to equality with men. I've said somewhere else that proportion and humor are the mellowing gift of time, but some souls will always be passed over. Still the gods must have a sense of humor or at least irony. There was a worthy, gentle man for Eleyne. You see, it was I who sent her Lancelot.

Few of the Second Legion even knew of my going to Dyfneint; my return caused no large ripple. I submitted my report to the imperial staff and waited for my chest to heal. I was still unable to wear harness over it when the whole camp suddenly snapped and bustled to attention with the arrival of Ambrosius. The emperor gave little warning of his arrivals anywhere, but moved with the speed of the cavalry he dreamed of. Some time had passed since we'd last spoken. It was a surprise when my tribune sent for me.

A thirty-year veteran, the tribune had little use for dead weight in the legions. He considered me a royal pet, one of those myriad lordlings trickling into service for whom a safe, comfortable place is always found near the top of the promotion list.

"The emperor has asked for you, of course. He seems fascinated by your little holiday in Dyfneint. Those scratches about closed?"

"Still a bit raw, sir."

"Pity; nevertheless suffer your way into proper harness before you see him. And shave, damn it. You and Gryffyn look like a pair of failed mountebanks."

"When am I to see the emperor, sir?"

"Now, my lord. If it is *not* too much trouble."

I got the breastplate over my linen tunic with Bedivere's help. Carefully he slung the baldric over my right shoulder and sheathed the longsword Geraint gave me. It seemed glaringly unmilitary. Bedivere suggested a short ceremonial sword for lightness.

"No, I want Ambrosius to see this blade."

Bedivere cursed over the straps and buckles as he did me up. "God fry that rutting trib, making you square off like this. You'll open those wounds again. You're sweating already."

"I think Ambrosius read my report. Got to go."

"Na, how do you feel under all this harness?"

"Like I've been dead two days. Rest easy till I get back."

The Via Praetoria, central street of the legion camp, was crowded with soldiers, singly about their business or in small detachments. The armor already caused me a good deal of discomfort. To avoid returning salutes the whole way, I shunted behind the first line of tents. As gingerly as possible, I started across the Via Principalis, giving way for a small group of mounted tribesmen in tartan trousers and dark hooded cloaks, barely noticing when they turned to stare at me.

"Lord Artos!"

The Dobunni accent halted me. One of the riders shoved back his hood, jumped down and ran for me with open arms.

" 'torius!"

"Kay!"

With his beard and rough leather tunic, my brother looked less a prince than the country horse breeder he was. But Uther's gold armlet shone on the worn sleeve. Before I could stop him, Kay hugged me to his chest: "By the gods, we've missed you so—"

"Don't squeeze me, Kay—"

"What's the matter, you're white as milk."

"Easy on, lad. I'm half bandage under all this."

The smile vanished from my brother's round face. "Then you were hurt. Your letter said it was only—*och*, mother will be sick with it."

"Unless she doesn't know. It will be well, Kay."

His dark eyes welled and glistened with tears he wouldn't let fall. "They didn't honor you for Dyfneint? Not even a word of thanks?"

"A day's work in the army, Kay."

"Is that what they call it, then? Well." Kay breathed deep. "Well, then. Emrys, take my horse, I'll walk a bit."

"I can't," I told him. "The emperor is waiting for me."

My brother made a face. "Don't I know. I'm bringing my taxes. I'm one of the few that pays regularly." He brightened quickly. "Where's Bedivere?"

"In my tent; any officer will direct you. Will you wait for me? There's much to talk about."

"There is. I'll wait for you." My brother cast a disgusted look at the camp around him. Then, agile as a monkey, he vaulted to his saddle, pointed to me with fierce pride and roared to every ear on the Principalis, "Who was it routed Cerdic at Dyfneint's Neth Dun More?"

His men bellowed back, "Artos ap Uther!"

Passing soldiers and officers stopped to gape at him, but Kay faced them straight and stern as a sword. "And who was his right arm?"

"Bedwyr, son of Gryffyn," roared the men.

Now Kay's voice must have carried to half the camp. *"And are they not of the Dobunni?"*

"Aye!"

Kay wheeled round to me, eyes shining. "I just thought someone should know."

Ambrosius' guards saluted as I approached his tent. "Centurion Pendragon on the Emperor's command."

"You're to go in, sir."

Ambrosius was alone, working at a plain table. He was grayer now, near white, and the compact body had gone lean and stringy. I knew for a fact he was not well, that he drove himself too cruelly, that he had not seen his family for months, but he still wore full harness as if born in it. The gaudier toys of kingship, the heavy purple robe and jeweled circlet, hung in the corner out of his busy way. Ambrosius looked like a harried officer of the line. I saluted sharply: *"Ave, Imperator."*

He returned the salute, then came forward to grip my arm in friendship. "Welcome, Artorius. I wish you found me in better health, but . . ." His eyes narrowed as he perceived my pallor. "You're not healed yet either."

"Well enough, sir."

"The hell you are. Sit down."

I sank gratefully into a chair. Careless of ceremony, Ambrosius filled his own cup with wine mixed with water and squeezed fruit, and offered it to me. "I've heard your tribune's opinion of those he considers royal favorites. He has his point; thirty years is a long climb, and men don't take readily to change. When change comes in the form of capable young men, they sometimes regard it as walking impertinence. Nevertheless, I plant for fruit, not flowers. You're part of my harvest. Tired of being the trib's messenger boy?"

I swallowed some wine. "Heartily, sir."

Ambrosius smiled thinly. "It's done you no harm, but I think you're about ripe for picking. There's a command if you want it."

My heart leaped with a hope and fell again with the prayer that stepped on its heels: Jesu-Mithras, not the line, not the bloody infantry.

"Your own squadron of horse with the sixth north of Eburacum."

More relief than joy: "Thank you, sir."

Ambrosius changed tack abruptly. "I read your report on Dyfneint. Three against eighty is damned reckless, don't you think?"

For that carnage reckless was a wanting word. "Not my charge, sir."

"You were the ranking officer."

"Only by chance. Geraint was on his own land. He knows it and the Saxons. I would have been a fool to assert rank, and there was no time to argue."

Ambrosius nodded, pacing in front of me. "Do you think Geraint a good officer?"

I weighed the answer. "In a fight, Prince Geraint is a divinely inspired butcher."

"So is a boar hog. I said an officer."

"He has no tact and only one tactic: close and kill. Fine in a charge, but to maneuver or follow precise orders . . . no. Sir, his squadron's not an army unit, but a lord's levy with personal loyalty to him and Caradoc."

"So are most of them," Ambrosius observed. "And so we must use them. Tell me how it went."

"We burned their boats; that was easy enough. We should build craft like that—"

He waved it away. "I saw your drawings. Get on."

"They were on foot. We were mounted with boar spears."

A spark of particular interest: "What length?"

"About nine feet. We couldn't keep Geraint with us, but Bedivere and I stayed together. We hit them again and again as a wall. When they finally unhorsed us, we closed and worked together still. That's what saved us."

The emperor stopped pacing. "And the divine butcher? Unhorsed and surrounded? What saved him?"

I unsheathed the longsword. "This, sir."

Ambrosius hefted the blade. Minutely, he observed the length, wide hilt and precise balance. "Over three feet."

"Three and a quarter, sir. Long and heavy enough to give a horseman more reach than the *spatha*."

Ambrosius motioned me to his table. He spread out a sheep-skin palimpsest used and reused till it was smooth, thin and dark. There was a figure sketched on it: nothing like a boar spear or even a heavy pylum, the object flared gradually from the point through most of its length to a wide metal collar, narrowing in the haft or butt. It was a spear designed to be used from the saddle. The problems were obvious. The right wood would have to be selected, the proper length and balance would have to be found and standardized. But a charging wedge of these lances would be near invincible. Strange thoughts, fragment-scenes, fled through my mind. I felt suddenly light and unreal, staring at the picture, drawn into it as if it were a magic talisman.

"Last year a senator of Gaul, Ecdicius, won a battle over the Goths . . ."

The emperor's voice seemed to fade in my ears under the growing roar like tide against rocks or a thousand voices shouting as one. My eyes blurred. I heard Ambrosius as in a dream, a memory. He was the past, he was years dead and gone.

They say those men are blessed by God who fall down and foam and have visions. The Anchorites pray for such visitations, and I've heard that only persons in the highest grace attain them. How with me, then, to hear Merlin's voice, to see that incredible host of men, to *know* that man riding beside my grown self, even his name?

Being leagues from holiness, I must be plain mad. And yet I knew his name, and he was still young. Why then did I feel about him the familiarity of age in all things, in love and triumph and a sadness with the gray cast of autumn?

". . . Foot troops, of course, but a mounted force of only eighteen men. And these eighteen routed over a thousand Goths. Sidonius wrote me of it. They were led by a young man like yourself, a patrician. I forget his name."

The voice echoed in the dream valley. *See the men, how they ride.*

My mouth opened of itself. "His name . . ."

"Yes, Artorius?"

Such men come when kings dream them.

". . . is Ancellius."

"Yes, I remember now." Ambrosius looked quizzically at me. "You know him?"

And he rides with a doom on his shoulders.

"No, sir." I met him tomorrow, Merlin said.

The emperor shrugged in resignation. "Whoever; Sidonius said he developed this lance from watching Hunnish horsemen on the frontier. Short men, long stick. The man's a genius with cavalry. Or was."

The roaring had subsided now. "Was, my lord?"

"They say he's gone into a monastery." A short, dry laugh. "Three monks to every bushel of pears in Gaul, and *he* has to make one more, wouldn't you know it. Pity."

He unrolled a map in front of me. "Hadrian's Wall and its environs, the whole area claimed by the Parisi. The Sixth is more home guard than legion, been so for sixty years. They're loyal to Cador, but these squadrons will be led by young men like you who understand my thinking and must follow it." Ambrosius' head came up sharply. "Is that clear, Centurion?"

I tried to look positive. "Yes, sir."

"Your general position: just south of the Wall and in support of it. Your mission is twofold: to patrol and contain the Picts for Cador and to train your men as I advise you. Now look at this." His finger trailed southeast from the black line of the Wall past Eburacum to the coast and the wide mouth of the Humber. "Cador's trouble has always come from the Picts, so his entire defense is pointed north. But men like Cerdic in shallow keels could sail by night up the Humber into these tributary streams and Cador could wake up surrounded with his force unassembled. Not vital now, but Saxons are not stupid. I'd attack Cador this way; how long before the Saxons try it?"

He was right. Cador's back door swung wide, unguarded and inviting to sea raiders. "He must know he's wide open."

Ambrosius set the map aside. "Cador's allegiance has always been nominal. He's not one to heed imperial advice. As I said before, men are hard to change." He thought a moment. "But remember this. You're young, you're a new generation and so is this Cerdic. We call him a foreigner, but he was probably born here just as you were. This is his home, not Frisia or Jute-land. He's a young chief like yourself. He needs to grow and expand just as we need to contain him; he learns as you do. You could say he's your counterpart, Artorius; he's you with an ax in his belt." Ambrosius grinned at me. "Odd thought, isn't it?"

Ambrosius' new idea was sired by genius on desperation. A full cohort of cavalry to be attached to every legion, five squadrons, each under young Britons, *combrogi* like myself. No more mercenaries, there was no money to pay them. Almost every rider under me would be a Geraint, a landowner or the son of one with a vested interest in the country. When trained, these cohorts would be detached again to form a separate cavalry legion under a new rank and title created by Ambrosius: Count of Britain.

We couldn't know it all at once, but it was the end of one thing and the beginning of something else. That man called the Roman citizen hardly existed anymore, nor the elaborate system for protecting his rights or channeling his taxes to central government. More and more, Vortigern and Ambrosius after him had to rely on nobles like Kay, Caradoc and Cador to operate as separate powers, and the men levied for service rode for their own lord and spoke little or no Latin. Ambrosius picked men like myself to lead because we were connected by blood to power. The supply for my squadron would come from Kay or nowhere. These measures, out of hopelessness and isolation, had to be.

So when the minstrels sing of Arthur and his knights, when the Church praises our embodiment of *their* ideas, bear in mind that priests and bards have a common art. They know the soppy tune to lull the torpid mind. What we were was a patchwork shift stitched from the rag end of a shining mantle that once covered the whole of the civilized world, the Roman legion. Rag end, I say. Our whole eastern coast was Saxon now. Beyond them, in Gaul, the Goth was supreme and would be in Rome within a few years. There was no help for us but stitch and mend and make-do.

Bedivere was elated with our orders, bolting his supper and wanting to pack up at once, but Kay saw it from his own emotional view.

"It takes you even farther from home. We'll never see you."

"Of course you will, little goose. That's the idea. One day we'll be all over Britain, anywhere—"

"*Every*where!" Bedivere sang out.

My practical brother carefully finished dressing to meet Ambrosius, took the bronze coronet from Bedivere and set it on his head. "It's cold up there. Mother's women will make new clothes for both of you."

But I placed in his hands the longsword from Geraint. "Before clothes or anything else, tell Ambrosius you will send me a hundred of these."

The Earth Is a Woman

The physicians examine me with the eager gravity of ghouls, the priests remind me with delicate tact of final preparations—and Brother Coel wants to write about Guenevere. He adored her even in her exile. She was worthy of adoration, she inspired it though it was among the things she wanted least. *Patience, Coel, there's more than enough time.*

There isn't? How careful of you to remind me. Death will no doubt be as punctual; like an unpaid moneylender, I suspect.

Guenevere comes later. For now, write of her what everyone knows. The daughter of Cador, prince-magistrate of the Parisi, a Roman education to match my own, raised among princes and ministers, coming to her crown and my side with no uncertainty in her role, my queen, my wise regent, my lover. Not tall, but seeming so because of her bearing, her complexion very fair, the hair somewhere between red and brown. Those with short memories will recall us only in age and the troubles that drove us apart, but set this down: we were no mere alliance of tribes. We were a love match.

Surprised, Coel? Proportion is the key. The Greeks taught me that. We have ruled a long time, my queen and I, we've played the game for many years. You who gave yourself to God so young should have tasted the pungent world before renouncing it. People find different loves at different times for different reasons. We were meant for each other *then*, when it happened, Gwen and I.

But she was not the first or the deepest love.

Say the heart is a harp with music variable to the shaper's

39

hand. The first chords out of me—sweet, painful and dissonant—
were plucked by Morgana.

Brother Coel writes *Morgana* because British letters are hard
pressed to represent her ancient tongue. Her real name would
sound hard and harsh as the heather and rock that bred her. Said
loud and sharp it's like lightning slashed across thunder. She was
no Eleyne; we were not gentle. We came together like lance
against shield, battered and ground against each other. Possessed,
we tore from each other the elemental thing we fed on, and when
the combat ended, she cried like a she-wolf about the edges of
my soul for what I took away. No right or wrong or justice, only
need answered or left begging. She was the dark Faerie girl of
Merlin's dream. In the fire of our locked loins the Fate took its
life and grew, dark and angry and doomed as its mother, and she
called it Modred.

From Caerleon to Cair Legis was our first leg, four days' dull
ride. Rest for ourselves and the horses, then four more days
tagging after dispatch riders over bare hills and desolate moor.
The round bowl of the horizon was treeless and windswept, the
vastness muting the loudest shout to a bird's chirp. We saw more
wolves than men the whole time, but at dusk of the ninth day
clattered down the last stretch of paved road to the massive
portcullis and hailed the battlements of Eburacum. Our ranking
escort from the Twentieth Legion at Cair Legis was a quick-
tempered little Spaniard who had to call three times before a
head and shoulders leaned indolently from the guard tower with
a monumental lack of curiosity.

"Well, who are you?"

"*Nuncio,* Cair Legis, God damn! What you t'ink, we Picti
man come take 'ee stinking fort, eh?"

The gate rumbled up after some delay. We walked our horses
through the twilight into a silent and deserted marketplace, following the dispatch detail down a wide avenue where weeds
grew tall between broken paving stones. Few men in sight, none
in uniform. We glanced up at the sparsely manned walls.

"Slovenly lot on the watch," Bedivere muttered. "Old Trajanus
would have their skins for meeting officers like that."

I gazed about me at the lack of life and movement. "Is
someone in charge here or did it just grow with the weeds?"

We found Cador's palace in the center of the city, a low,
dilapidated building like a crossbred forum and church; it proba-

bly served as both at one time or another. Next to it was the officers' quarters. With some difficulty we located the bored duty tribune, who read our travel orders.

"Pendragon and—uh—Gryffyn, the new squadrons, right? One of my men will show you to the baths."

"Sir," I wanted to know, "when do I take up my command?"

The tribune was vague and plainly disinterested. "I couldn't tell you. You're the emperor's concern, not ours. The prince is seeing you tonight because his son fancies a command. Invest you all at the same time."

The baths were nearly empty, like everything else in Eburacum. One officer we found there told us it was usually like this. Only the Wall and its supporting camps were full manned all the time. Save in emergencies, only a skeleton force remained on duty in Eburacum. He had not been paid for months and wished he were home on his farm south of the city. Of course, if there was danger, the whole legion could assemble in a day and a half— aye, that quick they could.

I couldn't help thinking how it would cheer Cerdic to know he could be in Eburacum before its defenders.

Cador's palace seemed more home than headquarters. Crossing the casually guarded portico into the entrance hall, we saw as many priests as soldiers. The royal house of the Parisi had been Christian for many years. The bishops' fulsome praise of Cador as patron of the Church masked a reproach of secular Ambrosius who, so far from endowing chapels, had not even dropped incense on the old altars for longer than he could remember.

Bedivere and I were in full ceremonials, proper-hung and bright-shined, though to our growing disgust we saw no one else in harness. At the entrance to the crowded state chamber, we edged inside and waited to be noticed. This seemed unlikely; the chamber was full of long-robed officials in busy conversation everywhere one looked. Next to me I noticed the tribune who had met us earlier, speaking familiarly to a fat man whose flabby jowls shone with oil from the baths. At a stand near the raised state dais, a harried priest-scribe wrote rapidly as the prince spoke with this or that official. Cador himself appeared an agreeable, accessible man with an ingratiating manner, well advanced toward baldness, with a round face quick to smile, dressed in white with only the purple edging to his robe and the gold armlet to show his rank. But the young woman next to him—

"Jesu-Mithras, who is *that*?"

"The consort?" Bedivere guessed.

I couldn't take my eyes from her. "No, too young. Most likely his daughter."

"Let you hope so."

I still remember how she looked that day: in white like her father, hair in a single thick braid draped forward over her breast. Her name in the Parisi dialect means yellow-hair; it must have been lighter when she was small, but reddish now and bound by a single strand of gold wire. Not the coolness of her expression excited me, but the hint of warmth underneath betrayed by her easy laughter and the way she threw her head back as she shared some nonsense with the young priest beside her. A large bronze cross hung around her neck and moved with the gentle sway of her breasts under the soft kirtle. I remembered my words with Eleyne about faith. For a woman like this, I would be baptized in boiling oil. Slowly.

"What is there now?"

Cador's voice carried through the noisy chamber with unstrained authority. He was handed a roll and glanced at it briefly before speaking again. "We have the emperor's schedule of commanders for his newly formed *alae*. Let them stand forth as named. 'Ambrosius Aurelianus, *Imperator*, to Cador, et cetera. At our considered discretion, we attach to your own forces the five squadrons of horse elsewhere described, and appoint as commander of each the officers named below.' "

Cador passed the schedule to a hovering minister who barked out the first name: "Gawain, son of King Lot of Orkney."

The young man—the young mountain—lumbered to the dais and knelt. He was as large a man as I've ever seen, bristling in every point, black hair and thick beard, the dark fur on the backs of his ham hands. I am not small, but his cloak would have served me well as a tent. He remained kneeling, head bowed, until Cador addressed him.

"My princely cousin, most welcome."

"My honored lord."

Bedivere's lip curled. "*Ach-y-fi*, but aren't we courteous?"

"Lot's stupid elder son," the tribune chuckled to his fat friend. "Lead a squadron? He couldn't lead his mother to mass."

And yet as Gawain towered to his feet and full height, like a whale breaching from the sea, there was a power in his stance that made me glad he hadn't heard the tribune. Cador extended a small rolled parchment. "To you, Prince Gawain, the first-numbered squadron."

`Agrivaine, son of King Lot of Orkney."

I looked at Bedivere. "Keeping it in the family, too."

Agrivaine had his brother's coloring but not his bulk, and I noticed the slight limp he tried to conceal. He was born with it, I learned, and knowing them many years now in good times and bad, I say Agrivaine was never the half of his brother, though not for lack of courage. He could turn a good day's soldiering and grew worthy of some trust, but always marred by the spleen and envy that finally corroded his heart.

"To Agrivaine, the second squadron. We note that Orkney stands supply for both his sons."

Bedivere nudged me. "We're the only ones in harness. Do we kneel or salute?"

"Kneel nothing. Square it off sharp and the hell with 'em."

"Peredur of Eburacum!"

A sudden burst of applause. My first impression was of a very young man in white, slimly cut with long hair and an expression that reminded me somehow of a pictured saint. Not weakness, but detached and remote. What disturbed me was the way the beautiful young woman smiled on him as Cador handed down the commission.

"To my dear son, the third squadron."

Now Bedivere whispered in genuine concern: "*Artos-fach*, this is no legion but a clan!"

And so we must use them, Ambrosius said. Peredur was his nod to local politics. The son of Cador would be a link of goodwill, like a marriage between tribes. He had been on the verge of entering the priesthood when Ambrosius' letter caused him to hesitate and postpone the decision—*You have a lifetime to serve God, Prince Peredur. You would honor me with a few years* . . . Never say Ambrosius could not sway men to his side.

The young woman left her chair and skipped down to hug Peredur with a kiss on the mouth: "*Oh*, I am so proud of you!"

I felt a definite pang and prayed hopelessly she was his sister, but then she swung around to address the room with the ease of one born to it.

"Anscopius, holy bishop, fathers of our beloved Church. Never fear my brother will forget his calling—"

"He *is* her brother!" The stars shone again on my life.

"And you're back in the game."

Two priests shushed us with a cold stare of disapproval. We lowered our heads and tried to look official.

"—He only goes a short journey for his temporal lord. As

King Lot stands supply for his sons, so Guenevere does the like
for Peredur. My jewelry, all but that left by the queen my
mother, is casked and ready for sale. Peredur's men will want
for nothing."

A patter of polite applause, and Cador said, "Not even an
earloop? My daughter will feel positively nude."

"What need of gold?" said the girl who was gold herself.
"With such a family, am I not already adorned?"

When the hubbub of praise and congratulations subsided,
Cador's minister read again from the roll: "Lord Trystan of
Castle Dore."

Ah, I thought as he stepped out, here's a familiar face.
Familiar in its features. What it concealed took me years to
learn. A battlefield of a face, ravaged by the emotions that
warred behind it. A man obsessed, driven by furies he couldn't
control to a wasted, too-early end. And for what, Tryst? I ponder
that even now with yourself white bones in Gaul. For what? Ask
yourself, was she worth your soul? Better, ask a woman.

But that was Tryst later: for now there was only recognition, a
young man seen often at Caerleon as *nuncio* for Prince Marcus
of south Cornwall.

"To you, Trystan, the fourth squadron. Who pledges your
supply?"

Trystan tried to answer—somewhat *sotto voce*, it seemed—but
the minister, not to be robbed of his office, brayed to the court at
large: "Yseult, consort to Marcus Conomori."

Cador leaned over to his daughter. "Another lady gives battle
to our enemies with a silver sword."

"As is fitting." Guenevere nodded graciously to Trystan.
"You should call your men the Queen's Own."

"So he should," the tribune tittered to his fat friend. "I hear
she's supported *him* often enough."

I put the tribune down then and there as a loose-mouthed fool.
That wasn't the sort of gossip to be scattered carelessly about a
court, though there must have been reasons why Lord Trystan
left Castle Dore. Even the painfully just Eleyne referred to
Queen Yseult as "the shameful woman of Leinster." Years later
they said the same of Guenevere. Women's reverence seems
reserved for God and men; they can be wondrous uncharitable
toward each other.

"Centurion Artorius Pendragon."

I stepped forward. No genuflection from me; my movements
were snapped-to and squared off, left hand firmly on my sword

hilt. I marched to the dais, touched fist to breastplate and flung the stiff-armed salute.

"Ave, Legatus!"

On reflection, I can understand the momentary confusion that flickered across Cador's round face, and the subtle amusement of Guenevere. Against Gawain and Peredur and the rest, prince on prince like the back row of a chessboard, I must have seemed the mere tail of the dog. Cador frowned over the schedule, then comprehension dawned. "Pendragon . . . Pen—ah, *yes*. Prince Caius' brother, who stands your supply. We have met him in the Council, and your—er—father was also known to us."

Tactful Cador. I learned later it wasn't Uther he knew, but my real mother, Ygerna.

"The manner of your address somewhat disrupted my memory." Cador dropped his eyes again to the schedule. "But the emperor restores it." His eyebrows went up as he read. "Indeed. Indeed. Well. Who is Bedivere ap Gryffyn, is he present?"

Bedivere strode forward to my side, saluting so sharply his gear rattled: "Sir!"

None of this was lost on Cador or my fellow commanders who, by Jesu and Mithras, would know themselves in the presence of the regular army.

"You must understand, Lord Arthur. We have not been what you would call a real legion for some years. We commend your zeal." Cador raised his voice to the entire assembly. "And we read the emperor's amendment to your commission, as follows: 'To these two officers, for engagement of Saxon raiders against the heaviest numerical odds, the perpetual right to wear the gold laurel of valor.' " Cador handed me my roll. "To you, the fifth squadron and our warmest congratulations."

Bedivere and I could only stare at each other; in the regular army, life was cheap and bravery common. The gold laurel wreath went more often to grieving widows than living men. The very human Bedivere prayed, "God stop us from earning another," but I was less impressed by the miraculous honor than by the new respect in Guenevere's gaze, even let my eye linger when she looked my way. Aye, lady, we do such things in the south. Aye, there were a hundred of them, more or less. The distinction was more for what she thought of it.

Of course, Cador was too subtle a diplomat to let my honors crown the investment ceremony. He rose and signaled to the guards at the entrance. "My lords-commanders, let me now introduce you to your enemy—the Pict."

Commotion at the door, the sound of grated chains. The crowd parted as two guards led in a dwarfish, swarthy creature with matted, blue-black hair. The muscles of his broad back were crossed and recrossed with the festered ridges of a whip. Standing erect, he would barely top the shoulder of the smallest man present. He was naked save for a coarse wolf hide around his middle; the manacled arms were tattooed with strange designs. When the guards pulled him to his feet, I saw that his high cheekbones were each grooved with two straight scars into which blue woad had been worked to make them vivid and indelible.

I felt a wave of disgust and pity. They must have starved him besides the whippings. His black eyes held the agony in check behind stoic watchfulness. We learned later that Cador had only kept him alive to show us. The prince came down from the dais, holding a delicate cloth to his nose as he approached the prisoner.

"We caught this stealing food at Corstopitum. Silent and quick as a monkey, but not quick enough to save it. We see these so rarely, I caged it out of curiosity. You see, this is one of those wretched lumps our peasants call Faerie. We could not glean much even under the whip. They seem to feel less pain than humans. Calls itself Melga. Says its people are the Prydn, something like that. One of the three bucks of a female whose name it grunted out but which, for the soul of me, I can't pronounce."

Cador glanced around at us with an indulgent smirk. "Fascinating. The males do not take a single wife as Christian men, or even a number of wives. The bitches keep several bucks to litter with. It's said even Brude, King of the Picts, must choose a successor from the female line."

His nose took brief refuge in the perfumed cloth. "Unusual, is it not? As a doting father, I might not flinch to see Guenevere wed one of our deserving young prince-milites. But can you conceive what chaos to the natural order if she were to take all of them at once?"

Even the priests roared at that, Guenevere harder than anyone else. "Aye, father," she called over the cackling, "and what sleep for Guenevere?"

"A busy little animal," said Cador when the levity died down. "It raises sheep and cattle when it can't steal them, and breeds its own in a lair so foul no self-respecting dog would enter it, or else on the bare moor where the sickly-born are left to die under a rock. It knows no mercy. It builds nothing, owns nothing, but it can move with no more sound than the moon slipping behind cloud. Some say they have the power of a *boucca* to change their shapes. They can look like a goat, a hummock of turf, a rock, a hare—''

Then why didn't he change into a hare and escape, I thought?

''—One can't say. It's only known that their victims rarely see them.''

The filthy little lump didn't look very magical or smell very human, crouching in his dumb misery at the hind end of his life—more like the wolf whose skin covered his loins. But a wolf who knew it was going to die.

''So be wary, my lords.'' Cador dismissed the creature with a cursory gesture. ''Dispose of it quickly. No need to let it suffer more.''

When the guards had dragged the man through the door, two servants bustled about the chamber, dipping their hands in bowls of rose water and flicking the perfumed drops into the polluted air. Cador regained his chair of state and motioned us commanders to him.

''You are all commended for your valor.'' A glance at me. ''Nor do we pretend to school men who may wear the gold laurel. Nevertheless. You have seen your enemy, such as he is. You may have heard he paints himself blue. So he does, if he wishes to be seen. If he does not . . .''

Cador handed Gawain a short, frail arrow, flint-tipped, fletched with ragged feathers, the shaft not of solid hardwood but the straightened stem of some bush or perhaps bog weed. Agrivaine passed it to me with brief contempt: ''This thing couldn't kill a baby.''

''It doesn't have to.'' Cador made his point with silken efficiency. ''Though you're wrong; it could kill an ox. The head is poisoned with hemlock or worse. The slightest scratch is enough to put a man abed for days if not treated immediately. When you ride north of the Wall, let your eyes be everywhere. Otherwise this arrow may be your last sight of Picts or anything else.''

East from Solway to the mouth of the Tyne, across the neck of northern Britain, Hadrian built the Wall when Rome was still an empire. From sea to sea the stone spine runs over barren hills. Forts and roads have been built beyond it, but have never endured. Legionaries peering north from the lonely mile castles could truly say they stood at the end of their world, and mis-

spelled sentiments crudely daubed on its stones left no doubt
which end they considered it:

> BETTER TEN YEARS VP AN ELEPHANT'S ASS
> THAN ONE MORE YEAR ON THE WALL.
> C. FLAV. VI LEGIO

Some of them came from the south and the sun to shiver out
their service in the never-ceasing wind:

> HEP-SVT, IX LEGIO
> NILE BORN IN THE RA-SVN,
> MAY HE NOT DIE HERE IN
> THE CVRSED LAND OF SET.

Some men scratched the only grave markers of near-nameless
friends: HERE THE ARROW CAVGHT SILVIVS; THE SYRIAN NAMED . . .
DIED HERE. And others too faint to read, illegible names, illegible
men who faded and blew away with the dust to limbo.

We couldn't wait on the Wall, but patrolled far beyond it to
the ruined heath-villages and through the bare hills. We learned
expensive lessons like the mean harmony of an arrow keening
above the wind; that there must be armor to cover the arms and
legs as well as the chest, more flexible than the old stiffened ox
hide. That we must breed horses large enough to carry more
weight without losing speed. But we never learned fast enough.
The arrows flew, the men died or tossed in fever, but we never
saw where the missiles came from, and even those under me
with some education came to believe that the Picts were descended
from evil *boucca*-spirits. Time has no hour marks in such a
place. The wind blows, the rain falls, the snows come and melt,
the sun shines or hides in fog, the flies buzz, the wind blows . . .

We were miles north of the Wall that day, the patrol watering
at a ford half a mile back; a long way forward for two men
alone, but fatigue can dull judgment. This day's work should
have gone to the fourth squadron, whose area overlapped our
own, but Trystan was indisposed this week, black drunk in his
tent, and his Cornish riders wouldn't budge without him. My
own men, weary from one long ride, had to make another with
only a few hours' rest.

I slipped out of the saddle and looked around. To the west a burned-out village. To the north a long hill crowned with a ring of ancient stones. On a sober day, Trystan had reported pony tracks leading east. Peredur read others going west. This general area seemed where they might meet if meeting was their mind. Sheepherders we let pass, the occasional lone figure glimpsed at a distance, never close, but a larger group could mean a potential raid on the Brigantes who paid Cador for protection.

The exhaustion felt like grit under my eyelids. I rubbed at them and held out my hand to Bedivere. "Water bag."

He passed it to me, concerned. "The old sickness?"

"Haven't felt right since this morning." Since winter was more like it, but Bedivere was scraped thin too, windburn and worry lines cut into his face and etched with dust that never seemed to wash out, the sharp blue Belgae eyes reddened around the pupils and buried in crow's-feet from squinting into glare.

"You're worn to a ghost, Artos, tattered as your clothes. Will you rest when we get back to Cilurnum?"

I sagged down in the grass. "If there's half a chance."

"Na, na, no ifs, no half-chances. Promise me."

"All right, I'll rest."

"Cross your heart on it."

He hadn't asked that since we were boys, but he was serious now and dead right. Without a long rest, I wouldn't be fit to ride again. I drew the ritual X across my chest.

"*Cris croes tân poeth, Bedwyr-bach.* Who's got the maps?"

"Huw or one of his scouts."

"Bring them up. This is Trystan's area, but I'd swear we've been here before."

"Not here we haven't."

I pointed north. "You're daft. Don't you remember that hill?"

"Just from the map." Bedivere swung his mount into a trot down the valley. "The old village is called Camlann. That hill's *Cnoch-nan-ainneal.* I'll bring up the patrol. Be careful till then."

My eyelids drooped before the painful glare. I lay back in the grass with the buzzing like drowsy bees in my head. Good to be alone for one moment, good to be quiet.

Stay alert, don't close your eyes.

Tattered as my clothes, he said. Riding through a dusty summer, wet fall and freezing winter and into spring again, feeling every sweating, shivering day of it in my underfed bones. Our squadron proved the only one worth the name for a while. Gawain and his brother knew only tribal custom in their northern island home. Their camp near Solway was a brawling roil of

whores and men too drunk to ride or bleeding from arguments
too stupid to remember. Aloof and remote, Peredur showed
some competence, but a slowness of decision dangerous in command. He saw a thousand trees, never the forest, and spent much
of his time in Eburacum. I had no authority over any of them,
and they interpreted Ambrosius' orders as they lordly pleased.

Trystan was the flawed best of a sad lot, working well for
weeks at a time, drilling his men with sword and the new lances,
then one day he'd not come out of his tent; that day would
stretch to a second and third. No one could talk to him then.
Once, when the days became a week, I went privately to his tent
to shake him out of it. Trystan hunched over a table, red-eyed
and oblivious, glaring at me, through me, at a ship of the mind
and an Irish girl he brought home for a king but loved for
himself. I gave it to him without sweet.

"You're the emperor's centurion. Sober up and square off or
you'll have no command left."

Like so many of my generation, he affected to despise Latin.
"Centurion, no less. Aren't we the proper Roman. Have you
forgot your own tongue?"

"Have it your way, then. I don't need to see into a sack to
know it's bursting or into your heart to know it's full of pain."

"Ah, listen to the sage of Severn." Trystan glowered at me,
sodden. "You're not the man to speak of pain, never lost
anything. You're a list of rules, a machine. Trip its lever and it
rides. Pull the string, it gives commands."

"Ambrose-rix placed a trust in you, God knows why. Every
patrol you miss means one more for me."

"I'll ride when I see fit. Now, get out. Get out! Call your
little dog Bedivere and—"

"If you were the half of him," I said, "you'd be twice what
you are."

Trystan drained his cup and pushed it aside, heaving up from
the table. His smile was murderous. "Twice, is it? What a
lovely day to kill you, Arthur."

He was too drunk to be dangerous. One shove and he went
down heavily. Trystan sat up, befuddled, then clambered back
on his stool with the clumsy deliberateness of a mountebank's
bear. He shook the cloud from his head, peering at me as if I
were a stranger just arrived on unknown business. Then the
blank expression crumpled into agony and his head dropped onto
his arms. I heard a muffled sob. We're a mad and mournful race.
Our storms are dark and furious and quickly past.

"You're right," Trystan sobbed. "I'm a scant, weak man who can't get one small woman out of his soul."

"Not weak, Tryst. Just a mite single-minded."

"Well, now." He wiped his swollen face and looked reflectively at me. Incredibly, he seemed to have forgotten it all. "Will you have a drink, Arthur?"

I couldn't help laughing. "Haven't you had enough, you horrible man?"

Trystan poured a short drink, stoppered the flagon tight and shoved it aside. "Just one to bid it all good-bye. What is it now, four days, five?"

"Six."

"Only one, then. My health wouldn't bear the sudden leaving off." He raised the cup: "Lady, lady, what an angel you were. And what a bloody bitch." He tossed it down. "I'll ride tomorrow, Arthur."

When Ambrosius found no real cooperation in Cador's tribunes, he decided to appoint one from among us. More confusion: Gawain and Agrivaine left for Cador's court, each to argue for the office. Peredur placidly assumed it would go to him. Trystan was drunk again and couldn't care less. After considerable delay at Eburacum, Ambrosius' order arrived with frosty congratulations from Cador.

To the rank of tribune of *alae*, Centurion Artorius Pendragon.

Now all their weaknesses were mine to contend with. The Orkney brothers called it favoritism, subtly seconded by the gracious but distant Cador, who implied more than he said. I set about the business of building them into a cohort, overseeing their training and haphazard supply, fighting uphill against men who saw me as an inferior. No, Gawain, more important to have provender for the horses than a wagonload of wine. Agrivaine, where are the new cloaks your father promised? No, man, I never said King Lot was mean-spirited or even forgetful, but winter is coming. Prince Peredur, when you have quite heard mass and made confession, will you tell me why your men are so poorly fed with your own supply so close? (And tell me what you can find to confess and yourself not a drinker and nothing more female in your camp than a few goats.) Speak to your sister? Very well . . . "Lady Guenevere, the third squadron needs fresh food. What they have on hand is spoiling. They can't do their job half-starved."

"But surely the men hunt," she wondered. "Surely they can always find fresh meat."

"If they weren't worn out from riding and if the Wall weren't hunted bare these three hundred years."

"You care about them." Guenevere touched my hand in compassion. "You care so much, and so do I. But the jewelry brought less than I hoped. My money is almost gone."

"My lords have always been unhappy under our tax system," Cador allowed regretfully. "It's hard to enforce payment."

I took advantage of my new rank to contradict him. "That's hard to understand, my lord, since the system has always allowed them to weasel out of paying in any one of half a dozen ways. And pass the burden on to the *civitates*. Why, your own Church has preached against this for eighty years!"

"Certain radical priests," Cador ceded smoothly.

"Radical and right, sir. We should un-protect those fat sons of—"

"Lord Arthur." Guenevere gently elided my profanity. "It would please me if you stayed to dine."

Please her? God, the sight of her was food enough, but I was needed back, though she gave me a smile worth a banquet.

"You're a stubborn man, Arthur Pendragon. Were a woman your own wife and fair as truth, I don't think she could keep you from duty."

Damn it, I blushed—and damn her, she enjoyed it.

"But come again, Lord Arthur."

Letters to Kay on leather and harness, reports to Ambrosius that would unavoidably be read at Eburacum before passing on: My lords Gawain and Agrivaine have improved their men at sword and lance, but their patrol methods are wasteful of men and time. Lord Trystan (my poor, demon-driven Tryst) is not yet properly committed to his office. Prince Peredur needs more assurance in decision. Prince this and Lord that, always holding my temper in check. If I lost that, I lost them and Ambrosius' purpose.

Where did I learn kingship? In the dust and ice and wind that blew across the Wall. In learning why the Saxon deserves his half of Britain. With all his royal blood, Cerdic would never have seen a crown if he couldn't first command a raiding keel. Since the Druids, we Britons have been too respectful of rank alone, too jealous of independence and meaningless distinction to work together. We are idealists wanting a god for a king, then fighting to be free of him. It will kill us in the end.

Then that wretched patrol when Bedivere twisted in the saddle, grazed by an arrow from a bow we never saw. He lay in fever for weeks, burning all day and sweating all night while he whimpered and raved and his body fought desperately against the poison. Back on patrol, letters, reports, bad food and too little of it, ignoring the insults behind my back.

"Here's a morsel straight from Cador. He says Pendragon got the command because his mother was Ambrosius' favorite niece. Not Uther's wife, his real mother. Her that was married to Gorlawse. A much-traveled woman, if you take my meaning, and mad as they come. Why else did Caius take the coronet and Arthur with no more lordship than the bare name of it?"

Nursing Bedivere through late winter into spring thaw when the sun peered timidly from lowering clouds or disappeared in sudden fog, and I could write Kay at last:

> *We're scarecrows in torn leather and tatty breeches, nothing like a uniform in the half thousand of us. Don't send the new ceremonials, I've no place to wear them. It's like plowing with bulls to get the work done, and I feel I was born in that miserable saddle, but we are a cohort.*

Haven't we been here before? What place is this on the map? The village was called Camlann. That hill is *Cnoch-nan-ainneal*. Music. The low, throaty sound of a flute curling in and out of my dreams.

I woke with my back cold against the damp ground, wrapped in a blanket of fog where there had been clear sky. Fool, dozing off like that with no more thought to danger than a recruit. Where was Bedivere? My horse was gone, too. I whistled his call, but got no answering whinny.

"Bedivere?"

I dared not call again. Whoever else might be close could hear just as well. Time to move. With drawn sword I made a guess at the patrol's direction. Mist could rise quickly on the moor, men and horses could blunder into bog, but this was the heaviest I'd ever seen, a blindness laid on the earth by a malicious god, thick as sheep's wool beyond ten feet.

The flute still drowsed in my ears, teasing and familiar, then thrilled in an odd little run. Who'd be tooting in this fog? A shepherd lulling his flock, keeping them near? This can't be the right direction. This way. No, this. No, you're going uphill, that's not it. Bedivere, where are you?

"Back there, Arthur."

The voice was near and far at the same time. "Who's that? Who are you?"

Another run on the flute. "Forgetful man, didn't I say I'd meet you here?"

Frightened now, whirling about: "Damn you, where are you?"

"At the top of the hill, at the ring of stones. Come up, Arthur, to *Cnoch-nan-ainneal*."

The music rose and fell in its quavering song, and far away, I heard a woman calling someone, keening with a sob in her voice as if she knew the loved would never come back.

The great stones stood like ghosts in the fog as I passed into their circle. The music was very near, but now I knew who played it.

"Merlin, where are you?"

"Here, Tribune."

The tall figure leaned against a strangely carved stone, wrapped in a travel-stained cloak, as dull and worn now as he had been incandescent long ago, but a man grown like myself. I felt no wonder or friendliness. A boy has time for miracles and magic, but a man has other things to do.

"You again, Merlin."

He breathed one half-sour note of finality through the flute and put it away. "Merlin will do for a name. I'm called that and other things, a part of things. That midge that deals with the mite of Arthur. Welcome to the hill of the fires."

I could see a fire; the fog was damp and chill. I shivered and felt empty. "Let me wake, Merlin. This is no time for games. I fell asleep bone weary. I could be taken."

Merlin pointed. "You have been taken."

To the right, the left, all around me among the upright stones squatted small figures, dim in the fog. I swung about, sword at guard.

"You devil, am I out of time?"

"For a time."

"Let me wake, really wake. Why do you mock me with riddles and magic?"

Merlin's lean, fatigue-lined features registered a kind of sadness. "There is no mockery."

"No? Don't I know I'm mad, seeing tomorrows for yesterdays, sleeping with a hundred ghosts at my ear? I saw Bedivere full grown before he was. I knew Ancellius."

"And he will betray you, Arthur—"

"Stop!"

"—as the Christ-man's Peter."

My fear poured out in anger. "You *boucca*! You air-thing, playing on my sickness like your flute. I could put this blade through the nothing of you—"

Quick as I was, Merlin parried my swing with a subtle twist of his body that hurled me forward off balance to sprawl against the stone. My muscles bunched to move—and froze, unable. I could only stare up at his narrow, watchful face. Behind him the circle of watchers waited. They were not all men. The small woman-figure rested her head against the shoulder of a huge dog, still as herself. They could all have been smaller stones in the fog.

Merlin smiled a little. "And still you don't know me. No wonder, there's little you have learned for sure. Why me, why this place, why the vision you call madness? Have I not shown you the king you will be?"

I shivered against the cold stone. "That is mad."

"If it is, so are you."

The whispering laughter of the watchers, like a rustle of leaves.

"You will be king, Arthur. There will be victories at first and a kind of defeat in the end, but that won't last. You'll be remembered. They'll sing your name through long, dark nights and darker centuries. They'll conjure with it, make you a legend and a god and sacrifice you as all god-kings are sacrificed. *Ave, Imperator*."

Merlin's eyes softened with some of the long-ago warmth. "You've learned to read men's failings, but not the heart that churns them out. A little imperfection, Tribune, a little human weakness. A love, a loss, and then how will the world look when this fog lifts?"

"What love? Guenevere?"

"In time," said Merlin. "When you've learned to love. She's only an ambition now, a reflection of you."

Merlin laid his fingertips on my damp forehead. "The carpenter had a bard's flair for poetry: 'Thou art Peter, a rock.' You are Druith, a fool, and upon this fool, I will carve something like a heart."

He beckoned to the female figure in the fog. "Morgana."

The tiny woman glided closer to kneel beside me, skin the same coppery hue as Cador's prisoner, cheeks marked with the same ritual scars. Her sheepskin shawl covered only her shoulders, the short, fringed skirt very little at all. Her flat brown belly, veined with stretch marks, had borne child. She studied me with bold gray eyes, and I knew her from the last moments of dreams before waking, from the shadows beyond Cilurnum's watchfires, glimpsed as she slid around the corner of imagination, over the shoulders of other women whose faces were not half so well remembered even in my arms. A strong face that knew sorrow, joy and rage. But not beautiful.

"Very beautiful," Merlin answered the thought, "when you have eyes to see. And you, Morgana, what do you see?"

"One of the People," she said. "But it wears tallfolk clothes and smells of them."

"The fool needs you."

Morgana touched my cheek. "A's been too long from me. Only a child."

"Teach it, then."

She cupped my face in brown hands. "Many days did watch thee and want thee. Be thee so fair or far, do know our own. Hear of the Prydn, the First People. Your people. The beasts cut in these stones be elk and reindeer and others thee's never seen. When this land was half ice, the People were here, Earth's favored children who knew her secret names. Then tallfolk brought bronze to break our flint. Did learn the name of bronze and how to make it. Then more came, the redhairs and yellowhairs, with iron to break bronze."

Her voice compelled as the music of the flute. Most of her words I knew, a kind of British, but some were mere idea-sounds, as *flutter* describes the bird's beating wing.

"Iron took the land," said Morgana. "Iron hated our gods and called them devils, rubbed out our true name to steal our strength. Iron called us Faerie, made us part of the dark beyond their fires. When tallfolk are bigger, when they have iron-magic and all the good valley land, where can the People go but under the hill?"

Morgana raised her head to Merlin. "What does thee call it?"

"Druith," said Merlin softly. "A fool."

"And what must a see?"

"Too far and too much. A god-king who must burn for his people."

She flinched a little. "Cruel, even for tallfolk. Then know the way of things, Druith. All names go under the hill, stone before flint before bronze before iron, like waves on a shore."

Then Merlin asked, "What one thing can you teach it, one lesson to mark it a true man and your own forever?"

Her lips brushed across my cheek. "Poor Druith. New green

leaf in a dry old world. Do know my own and what I'll teach thee."

She kissed my mouth, a long kiss that pressed the magic and the memory into me. The scent of her was sweet in my nostrils, and there were tears in her eyes and on my cheek where hers pressed against it so that I couldn't tell were they her tears or mine, so mixed with the joy and sorrow of her magic. I felt my chest go suddenly hollow with a vast, soft ache, an empty space that had to be filled with Morgana. Then I was—

Free!

> Loosed, I
>> feel
>>> myself
>>>> *waking—*

unfettered, returning to *true* self inside Artos-tallfolk. My Prydn soul throws off its bonds like a frayed rope and thrusts Artos into the prison where he's kept me so long. Free, stretching out my arms to my brothers, who come out of the fog and lift me high on their shoulders like a prize to take me home under the hill.

Just the four of us. My *fhain*-brothers, Nectan and Cunedag. Morgana and me, Druith. Ears sharp for danger above. We stay in the crannog under the stone circle while the Briton-men search for the Artos I've locked inside me and bidden be still. Sometimes at dusk we peep above ground. Redhair is still about, sniffing like a dog on a cold scent. Finally he goes away, and it's time to go home to the *fhain*.

Nectan and Cunedag treat me well on our journey north. They tie me between the ponies only because the Artos in me is not yet to be trusted. Fettered, I have to run and stumble after them, but Morgana hovers close every step of the way, and anyway tallfolk feel less pain than humans or they wouldn't hurt others so carelessly. So the Prydn always thought, but it's not true. I suffered from the scrapes and dragging. My whole body was a lump of misery, and I know that, deep inside me, Artos bled and suffered too.

Now and then we have to hide, but that's not hard. Tallfolk are big but stupid. When we vanish on the open moor, tallfolk forget a man can *look* like the moor. They forget the old lesson of hunting, that game will only see you if you move. If you're still as a stone, tallfolk will take you for a stone. And this is a difference between the People and tallfolk. With their iron-magic and their fine looms to make rich cloth, they've forgotten that Earth is their mother. No longer are they brothers to wolf and marten. It happened long ago, and this is how we tell it to our children.

One day Earth went to her mate, Lugh Sky God, and said, "Man, our youngest child, is forgetting me. He's prideful and won't even speak to his brother animals. Do you go and give him a swift kick since he's grown too full of himself to listen to me."

So Lugh called all of his children, the men, the fish, the birds and the animals, to stand before him, and he said to Man: "Now listen to your mother Earth."

They tried, but had truly forgotten her language. Then Lugh said, "Speak to your brother animals." But all had forgotten how except a few of the smallest men, who were among Earth's favorites because she made them first. Only these were able to speak to their mother and brothers.

The other man-children grew jealous. "What's so good about speaking to wolf and cat and bird when we're bigger and better in every way? We don't even call them brothers anymore."

"Let it be so, then," Lugh decided.

And Earth said, "Let it be so. They're not your brothers since you are no longer my children. Go be what you will, but only these small ones who remember me will be called true men, my Prydn, the first ones, the only men worthy of the name."

The other children have been jealous ever since, maybe because they wish they'd kept the language of Earth, but Earth meant what she said. Tallfolk have a respect for the People, but they fear us, and it's hard to love what you fear.

We never forget our bond with Earth and Lugh. Each year at Lughnassad, the story is told to the new children so that they remember their real parents and their true name.

North, always north, with Morgana riding ahead now, looking for signs of our herd. We come on a small clan of the Taixali and approach with careful respect. They are friendly this time, though we can never count on it, and they leave shoes and harness for us to mend in exchange for the milk and meat we ask. I work all night for my swallow and mouthful. Still, it's good to be with the People again.

Now Morgana points out to me some of our old crannogs, the earth houses we use and leave as our cattle move on. Scattered as they are, the People know where each lies. From a disguised opening, the tunnel will lead for yards under the earth to the main chamber which has a smoke hole of its own. Warm and comfortable for us, though tallfolk would be cramped. The whole is lined with stones carefully fitted together, and there's another opening where the cattle can be driven in when winter comes.

The rath we carry with us, poles to be wedged into a base of loose stones around the crannog opening, wrapped with skins and the whole covered with turf so our house seems no more than a small hump on a bigger hill. The opening always faces away from the easiest paths. Whole tribes of tallfolk can wander through and never know they're in the middle of a *fhain* unless we show ourselves. And if they swear we appear and disappear by magic, that helps keep them wary of us.

Still, there are things that confuse me at first, words that seem strange. But Morgana, Cunedag and Nectan talk of the family— for Prydn, nothing exists beyond it—and slowly I know. More like remembering than learning, falling back rather than climbing, so easily do I become one of them.

Fhain is not owned land, as if a man could own the earth or even a piece of it. *Fhain* is family, the way of things. All is owned by all, and its shape is four generations of daughters, their husbands and children. There are only three generations in our rath now because of many deaths and fewer births. There is the head of the family, old *Gern-y-fhain* Cradda and her last husband, Uredd. Then there's Dorelei, first daughter with one child living, one lost, and another due this coming Samhain. She has two husbands, Nectan and Bredei.

Below Dorelei—and not near so peaceful—is second daughter Morgana, and her own husbands, Cunedag and Urgus. And me, Druith, who will be her happy third. Soon, let it be.

Most important is Dorelei's little son Drost. He's what we and the cattle and the year-round hunt for a living are all about. If Dorelei bears another boy and Morgana a living girl, the daughter will take both brothers for husbands. They are our meaning and our future.

A woman truly needs more than one husband. If one dies, there are more to give the *fhain* its next generation. With tallfolk, if a man has two or three wives, there's always dispute over property between the children—tallfolk say *mine* more than *ours*, *me* more than *us*—and each greedy wife wants her son preferred. If the man dies, his wife may go off to another man or place, so the family is weakened. With us, all children are the heirs of the woman, all blood is traced through her, and all share alike. Our days move slow and sure as the grazing cattle, the sun divides in four the year that measures out our lives. In the summer raths or nestled a-winter in the warm crannog, we are one, we are the People, living as Lugh and Earth decreed. Sometimes our children and cattle die, but there is no other way for us. We wouldn't live in silly hut circles that any fool could come and steal from or burn. Nor, when Earth has put the herds for us to follow, would we insult her by scratching for more gifts under her skin. How could we harvest crops and follow the herds all at once? We can't see any wisdom in the tallfolk way. It's lucky for them they breed so often. Else, with such a messy way of life, they wouldn't survive.

It's late afternoon when we climb the last hill and snake round the rocks that hide the rath entrance. Still cool, but you can smell the May-time coming. Then out to us pour all the *fhain*, Bredei and Urgus and sunny Dorelei hugging everyone, her son Drost chattering and climbing all over Nectan, peering shyly at me like another height to be conquered soon.

I wink at him. He grins and hides behind Dorelei.

We crowd into the rath in a fresh lather of kisses and greeting and the family smells are like braw flowers to me, hides and turf, dried gorse and cow-dung kindling, peat smoke, meat simmering in a broth of wild leeks and herbs.

We gather about the fire in proper order: Cradda and Uredd in the high places, Dorelei on their left because of the coming child, her husbands next to her, then restless Morgana and hers, myself last. Little Drost toddles about taking from everyone's bowl. Nectan is his father, or thinks so, but he's only named as Dorelei's son.

Well, now—in honor of our safe coming, a ewe has been butchered for the big pot. Not one of our own, but taken from the Venicone tribe. They owed it to us, anyway. Last summer, Cradda says, one of their women asked her to midwife her daughter of a boy-bairn. Cradda went to them, but the woman didn't trust her.

"Hovered about as if I'd eat the bairn or steal it, and gave cold porridge in payment," Cradda tells us. "And this Brigid-feast past, did a not come crying back to me, 'Oh Faerie Queen, the child of my child be feverish with bad color to a's muke. Do you make him well and take one ewe in payment.' "

Well, Cradda took the child's birth string, which she had preserved, and greased it with fat and herbs and laid it close to the hearth to break the fever, while she gave the child a draft of gentle lavender and a poultice of the same grease mixed with beech fungus. Then, the fever broken, Cradda asked for her ewe. "Alas," says that woman of the sly Venicones, "they be all going to drop young soon, and we promised no lamb with the ewe. Wait till then."

Well, the People are honest folk who take what's owed, nor more nor less—mostly. Cradda saw one ewe in the woman's fold no more ready to drop than a ram, and that night she freed it from slavery to such a dishonest mistress.

The old ones dip first into the pot, then Dorelei, then we all help ourselves. There's no great notice paid me, though it's known I am Morgana's. With deep respect to Dorelei, I'm glad. There's a beauty in Morgana, strength as well as the wild and mournful sorrow all Prydn have, as if they heard some last, half-forgotten song. She's eighteen and her brown body is marked with bearing children to keep us strong. The look and the smell of her puts me on edge like a stag at rutting time, robs the hunger from my stomach and kindles it between my silly long legs.

Little Drost likes me and takes from my bowl more than others. He squeals and wriggles and pretends to pull away when I wrestle and kiss him. I haven't spoken yet, it isn't time. But Morgana's eyes come to me again and again across the fire. The peat smoke curls up through the top opening. Summer is coming; the *fhain* is happy.

Cunedag begins the story of how they rescued me from the tallfolk. Many glances round the fire at Morgana, who pretends not to notice, but the edges of her mouth curl with a cool mischief.

"There lies the great Briton-man, dead asleep with poor Druith caught inside." Cunedag rises from the circle and plays out what he's saying. I watch with Drost settled down and quiet against my chest.

"Did wait till Redhair rode away, then sprinkled over a's nose the powder Morgana made. Then, oh so gentle, did li-i-ft." He staggered under the burden of Artos. "And carry the great lump of it under the hill of the fires."

Cunedag wipes away pretend-sweat. "Ah-*foo*! Did not know were so strong. If *Gern-y-fhain* needs whole barrows moved, let a put Cunedag and Nectan to it." Laughter around the circle. Suddenly, Cunedag stretches out on tiptoe to show himself taller, lengthening his stride up and down the rath floor.

"Then comes Redhair with a terrible fear: his chief is gone. A brings the Briton-men and the swords and horses, and the hill over us rumbles with their hoofs and anger. But did not care, because in the crannog, Druith wakes up to know us! Druith is free!"

"Yah!" cries the whole *fhain* in triumph with a great clapping of hands.

"Free but can't move, none of us. Did wait and wait and peep out only at dusk. Redhair be still there, the great long mile of him leaning on a stone, the iron sword swishing in his hand like the tail of a furied cat."

Cunedag turns serious. "But a's crying silent tears, and his men stand about with long faces. A day passes and a day after that, Redhair striding back and forth up hill and down, sniffing for tracks to follow. The others ask him to leave: the chief is dead, they must go home. Aye, but it's gently said to Redhair, as a looks like to kill someone. So, did ride off from the hill of the fires, Redhair last and always looking back."

Cunedag sits down and takes the bowl I filled again for him. He puts an arm over my shoulder. "Can see why Artos trusted him."

Strange, since our word for tallfolk and not-to-be-trusted are the same, but he says it with no doubt. The *fhain* thinks about this. Nectan agrees; he's considered this, too.

"True, have heard a can't feel pain or love, but . . ."

Cradda spits a piece of gristle into the fire to hiss and sizzle like the bitter truth she speaks: "A's tallfolk." And that ends it. We know what they are, we go on eating. The sky dims a little outside the smoke hole, Drost dozes in my arms, and we feel close.

There's barley beer to finish our feast. My tongue remembers it as mild stuff after the *uisge* Artos drowned me in. We pass the beer, sing a little, laugh much. Then Dorelei, in the middle of a story, starts to say a name. Just the first part of it, then she stops and in the sudden silence round the fire, she drops her eyes and whispers, "Forgive me, sister."

Just a moment, then all are talking again, but Morgana makes too much of poking up the peat fire. It hurts me to see pain in her. She has not Dorelei's peace, nor any child. Urgus speaks softly to her. She rises and leads him out of the rath.

Everyone is curious about my Briton clothes, and they make a game of peeling me to examine how they're made. Cradda and Dorelei admire the close weaving of the wool trousers and how such softness can be worked into a cowhide jerkin. The heavy cloak goes to old Uredd to keep the night cold from his bones, but the rest of the clothes are too big for anyone, and I roll them in a bundle for a pillow while Dorelei fetches me a good sheepskin and girdle. Nectan threw away the iron dagger long before we came home. It would be unlucky for the *fhain*. When Dorelei gives me the garments, I press my hands to her belly to show my love and respect, not only for her but the child-wealth she bears. She kisses me and laughs at the girdle that barely goes around me.

"Too little girdle and too much *thee*." Oh, there's dear fun in Dorelei, and when she has me giggling, she tickles my ribs and presses my face to her stomach. "Be *wasteful* to be so big, Druith."

In spring and summer, Lugh-sun never goes far under the rim of earth at night but glows there, lighting the duns and glens with a kind of magic twilight. To see it alone, to sit outside the rath and listen to our cattle settling for the night, brings peace to my soul, but to share it with someone would be better.

At last, Morgana comes up from the glen, hand in hand with Urgus. She kisses him; he goes into the rath. Morgana comes to sit by me, and the light is clear enough to see the shine of sweat on her skin and even the little bruises and bite marks Urgus left. She was away a long time, and Urgus missed her, but seeing his marks on her fills me with so much wanting, I want to cry.

"Did see thee many times on the Wall and riding with Redhair," Morgana says. "Dost remember his true name?"

I try hard to remember. Faces and happenings float to the surface without meaning, bits of sleeping Artos. "Was a long time ago."

She comes into my arms willingly enough, tiny, quivering with life, and I tell her how I hate being so big and ugly beside her.

"Not ugly, Druith. Saw thee ride often, and stand and shake thy yellow head full of worries." Morgana laughs quiet and deep in her throat. "Many days."

"And far from the rath. What did thee so close to Briton-men?"

Her hard little body presses against mine. She doesn't move, doesn't answer, but after a time she pulls away, eyes glistening in the twilight.

"Be good to have thee here. Thee will be my husband soon."

I try to pull her back down into the grass with me, but she won't. "Urgus needs me tonight. Have been away and do want him."

I take her hand and plant it on my own need, but it does no good.

"Be not—we can make no child-wealth, but Urgus loves me."

"Thee's crying."

"No."

"What is it, Morgana?"

"Be not!" She tears her hand from mine. "Urgus is waiting."

She lay all night with Urgus. He's a gentle husband and twice wakes her from troubled dreams when she cries in her sleep and calls a name.

Three days to Bel-tein fire, the spring festival. Life stirs and wakes, the lambs and calves are born, there's green in the world again. Urgus and I go miles to the sparse forest east of our grazing where the old birch trees stand and climb them all to pluck from their tops the agaric, the *tein-eigin* that grows close to the sky. From this we will kindle the Bel-tein fire. It will be a special time for me. Bredei has come by on his way from the scrap pit where we save our broken tools. Melted and recast, they'll make a new bronze knife to mark my cheeks with the *fhain*-sign. That done, the knife is mine to keep.

I haven't bedded with Morgana yet since Cunedag and Urgus have older rights, but should be soon ere I start chasing ewes.

Cradda and Uredd sit outside the rath now that the sun has real warmth in it, close together and silent, needing no words for love and understanding. Dorelei passes, walking a little heavier, her face high-flushed with the wealth of her body. Drost tugs away from her, wanting to play near me. It's a game we've made up with no words but strict rules. I pretend not to notice him, and Drost becomes very busy, and if he catches me looking, he's the winner.

Today he really seems to forget me, lost in some world of his own. Something on the ground, a stone or ant, who knows, has caught his eye, some small miracle grown large with wonder.

Still, still as a cat before pouncing. What could it be? I lean in to see—

To *see*! It's clear as sudden sunlight, something looked at so often and never seen: a child playing. But more than play. Meaning. Drost moves to a sure music I've forgotten in growing up—dances to it, floats, celebrates and delights in it. Drost is three, and in this magic, discovering summer, *sees* the world fresh without hanging names and signs on it, reaches for and touches it before knowing it forever apart from his prisoned self. The small feet stamp and mountains tremble before his challenge, the arms sweep up in the growth of flowers, and I know why men lose sight of the face of God: because it is so close. Then—

"Yah!"—and he's won again, caught me watching and loving him, and as he runs to be hugged, I learn a lesson deep in my heart. I'm a fool and named one, but never so blind as Artostallfolk, who could ride all his life, carving his way with the great sword toward the crown mad Merlin promised, could bed the pale Parisi bitch, hunt a silly cup for a dull Cornish girl with nothing more important in her life, conquer, rule, make laws—and never, in all that royal wasteland, find a greater treasure or truth than this small, shining life in Druith's arms that is the sum of the world to this moment. I lift him in triumph to Lugh-sun.

"Mother! Lugh! Look at thy children, me and Drost!"

One of the secret names is mine to keep.

Small wisdom beside what's yet to learn. Morgana, now: there's a coil of a woman. Cunedag's been with her two years, Urgus one, living, eating and bedding with her, and both feel married to the wind, lovers to the mist. Like a pot before boiling, the surface moves just a little to hint of what's heaving and surging below. The others give in to her headstrong ways; only Druith-fool is reaching to understand the woman and yet a little apart from her, returning her curses with the same. It's because we haven't loved yet, and I'm drawn tight with it. She's been gone since morning, who knows where.

When her pony plunges over the hilltop, lathered and straining, we puzzle what there is to run about on a day like this in the good warm sun, but Morgana jumps off the poor spent beast just short of the rath and stalks inside without a word. Uredd wonders what ails her. *Gern-y-fhain* just shakes her head.

"Has always been between two fires. A loves more what's lost or never can be."

I put Drost down. "What's that?"

"There be more fools than you in the rath," she says. "Go in and comfort her."

But just then Nectan hoots from the glen where two new calves have wandered away from their mothers on perilous legs and stuck in a patch of bog. It takes a good while to pull them out and drive the herd to high pasture, and Morgana's not in the rath when I get back. Uredd prepares me with a knowing look.

"A's below in the crannog."

"About what?"

"About a pot of beer and sad songs and cursing the stone walls. Do you go down, be ready to fight."

Well, that would be thought about. Climbing down into the tunnel, I wonder *why me*? Cunedag and Urgus always walk clear of Morgana when she's brewing a storm, but I don't and won't. Maybe it gives her something she needs then, something to batter against. I won't be soft or pitying; will get softness when she gives it. She cannot caress without drawing blood, it's the way of her, and perhaps me, too. We want each other, that's the only easy part of it all. For some there might be the plain reaching out, but for Morgana and I, there's always an anger in it, a darker need to tear at love before accepting it. Oh, must be lovely to be a sheep or a cow with such a simple future.

She's there in the crannog with a fat lamp for light and the beer beside her. Her face is twisted tight with the things that eat at her, but I think never have I seen her more beautiful, a sum of things all wrong adding to right, eyes too big, nose too long and thin, mouth too wide and curled in a snarl now as I sit down across the light from her.

"Thee's a sad lump, Druith. Be not man enough in thee to give thy hair true color."

"Says most-fair, looking and smelling like the hind end of a sick horse."

"Did come just to flatter?"

"*Gern-y-fhain* sent to find what ails thee."

Another long drink. "Nothing."

"Only nothing?" Silence. "Will speak of this nothing or let it feed on thy heart?"

Morgana drains the pot. I watch her, looking for the right words with my own fire rising, knowing it will not be any word that calms her. "Thee's a marvel of weakness, Morgana. Aye, thee's lost a husband and none may speak a's name, so that the silence of him crowds us out. Thee's lost a child and what else, and fed on the *fhain*'s love and pity like a horse let loose in a grainery, till thee's swollen fat with—"

Then duck—just fast enough for the main part of the beer pot to miss my head, though the base catches me a nasty rap as it sails past to shatter against the crannog wall. We face each other, boiling, across the lamplight.

"Morgana, wife—"

"May not call me that yet!"

"Was not brought here to pick flowers."

Seething: "Speak so to second daughter?"

I uncoil across the space between us and pin the squirming mite of her under me, holding her wrists. "Be still, now, be *still*. Thee's a treasure among women—"

"Let go!"

"—and heavy with loss and sadness—*ow*!"

"Will cut thy heart out—"

"But if ever dost strike for no reason again, may count thy remaining teeth on one thumb, dost hear?"

Morgana makes one great effort to push me off, earth itself heaving to reject what fetters it. Then the fight sobs out of her and she lies still.

"It just—"

"Let me touch you, wife."

"Just . . ."

"Let me touch you."

Her hands cover her face, her small head snaps back as the agony tears out of her and batters at my chest. Not at me, but what holds and wounds her. I'm not what she strikes at, nor do the blows hurt. She tires, slows, and I hang on to her. Then her arms go tight around me, holding on to keep from slipping away and drowning, her mouth clasps and tears at mine, pulling me over her.

"Druith, *help* me."

"Do love you, Morgana."

It is painful and delicious between us, a starved need beyond hunger, and somewhere in it is the thought: I have never said *love* before. And though there's a memory of beds and faces gone or yet to come, the echo of the same words deeply meant and even better understood, this first time a piece of self arcs out like a fierce comet, burning with a never-again brightness and falling, always remembered, down the lonely space of life.

Brief and blurred and too soon over. We have cried and clasped and fought to the brink, hovered and plunged. Sight returns, time returns. The tight knot in Morgana loosens, shudders and trembles to quiet. Her breathing evens, the little face peers up at me, eyes intent as a fascinated bird's. I hold her a long time, stroking her hair and back, caressing away if I can the misery that holds her.

"Will talk to a husband now?"

"Of what?"

I raise on one elbow over her. She's not looking at me but into the darkness for something lost beyond the lamplight. "What, indeed. With riding off and near killing ponies and sour looks and hurling of beer pots at husbands. Such a what that thee must—"

"Fight something!"

"Fight or love or cry, and thee's done all. Why—why is there so much pain, Morgana?"

Still and quiet at last, she tells it.

"Because there's no wealth in me. Because thee plays so well with Dorelei's Drost, and cannot look at that without remembering. Because this empty body mocks me with a's bearing marks. This morning . . ."

I listen to her on this discovering day, sadder, happier, richer than any man who ever breathed. Did the Artos ever hold a woman like this, lover and hurt child at once, shield her, comfort her, open to her pain? Never; in all its beds, did only snap up leavings and call them plenty.

This morning Morgana passed a village of the Venicones. She was thirsty, though none was in sight but a young woman rocking a cradle by her house. Others peeped out, women and old men only. They saw Morgana was Prydn and fetched their charms, rowan sticks and woodbine, and one old man made much of laying an iron bar across the hut entrance.

Morgana spits, "Do beg our magic with one hand and warn us off with the other."

"Lucky the fathers didn't come out to beat thee."

"There be no young men left in the village." And when she asked why, the woman said they were all gone to the meeting on the coast, Pict-men and Saxons from south and oversea. No matter, the woman went to draw the water. Her baby seemed safe enough under the eyes of her village.

"But the slattern'd not changed a's swaddling. Could smell it and see the poor bairn chafing. Did want to comfort it, as if—only wanted to—"

Without thinking she picked up the child to soothe it. "Was

like my own that died, my own before the sores covered it, and Melga—''

Holding the child she remembered her own lost wealth and husband, for a moment not empty but filled again. But they came shrieking at her with switches, and the woman tore the baby from her: *drive the witch out, a would curse my bairn*. And they flayed her with the rowan switches till she leaped to her pony and escaped to scream her rage at them from the hilltop. It is out now, told, but Morgana is trembling again.

"Curse them? Yes! Curse their bairn, their blood, their plenty while Prydn go without, their cradles where we've left our own so they, at least, might not starve. Nor ever come near again for fear of heartbreak. Curse them with all do have in me, with the strength of Melga lost because did only try to feed us. Curse them with *ghort a bhaile*, famine in their farm, famine to their loins and may their children come withered and dead from their fat, fed bodies."

Her hard little fists shake in mine.

"Melga and I were south looking for better graze since that here was poor. There was nothing. Our oats ran out, we ate roots. Melga went over the Wall to get food for me. A never came back, though did wait and cry for him and mourn alone under the hill of the fires till Cunedag and Nectan came after to fetch me home. Be happy with what thee has, a said."

Morgana gazes a long time over my shoulder. "Be happy? Not yet. Do know what will have, what the People will have again. Melga was more than husband. Did teach me and bring hard truth to my eyes. We lose, we lose every day because we are small and weak and fewer each Samhain-time. Because we be not bound together like tallfolk, but a poor *fhain* here, a poorer there. Because we *let* the gods forget us. Be you truly of the People now, Druith?"

"No other."

She pulls me to her again, the anger not dead, but banked, glowing behind purpose.

"Tallfolk took my husband, will take one from them in kind. And such a one, Druith. When I saw thee walk. Oh, when I saw thee. Love me again. Now." Her mouth seeks for mine, undeniable. "Nay, thee's rested, love me again. And from the king and queen of summer will come Belrix, lord of fire. The People will rise again, Druith. Iron-magic will go down, and Earth will remember her first children."

*   *   *

My knife is finished and hammered over wood to a fine edge.
I lie on a blanket in the rath with the *fhain* gathered about, and
Cradda uses the new blade to cut two straight lines over each
cheekbone. She is deft and draws little blood, Morgana staunching
it and working woad into the cuts with a needle. There will be a
new name for me; till then, I am no longer Druith, but simply
Dru, which means oak tree and is much more respectable.

Bel-tein comes. At sundown all other fires are put out and the
charred wood from last year's fire is brought from its drying-
place. With the *tein-eigin* we gathered, this will kindle the new
spring fire.

The fires are laid and lighted. With the first flame that comes
forth, *Gern-y-fhain* lights a torch and passes it to Cunedag, who
runs his pony along the hilltops and ridges, torch held high for a
signal to the valley tallfolk that on this night they are welcome to
festival with us.

The Venicones come with the customary oatmeal cakes, some
to be eaten, some rolled for luck through the flames. They settle
in a ring about the two blazing pyres of logs laid three on three,
and as the barley beer passes round, I listen to their gossip.
Morgana was right: there are only a few young men. All the rest
are gone to the sea.

"North to Cathanesia," an elder tells me.

"So far?"

"So far as Skirsa." He doesn't know why, nor do I care. The
fires blaze up. We drive the cattle and sheep between them for
the blessing of Earth's new spring. Dorelei follows with Nectan
and Bredei. The sky darkens, but from far hills all about the
bowl-rim of Earth, other fires reach to honor our father and
mother.

Cakes are eaten, beer drunk. Little Drost gets his share of
both, pinching from mine and trying to out-burp me. Morgana
nestles between me and Urgus, arm linked with mine. We are
wed now and happy, though we fight more than the *fhain* thinks
respectable, and though he's my brother-husband, Urgus seems a
little jealous. He tries to hide it; the *fhain* would call him foolish.
When the fires are highest, all who care to leap across the flame
for added blessing from Lugh. Again and again we race, jump
into the air, feel the heat on our skin as we pass through it,
others catching us on the other side, beating out the sparks from
our clothes.

At Bel-tein and Samhain, someone is always given to the fire. Long before bronze broke flint, the gift was very real, a tallfolk prisoner or one of their babies. So the story they still frighten bad children with: "Mind or the Faerie'll come for thee." But now it's only fun. Someone is caught up and hustled toward the flame with everyone yelling for Lugh to come and claim his well-cooked gift, whose wife or husband implores the god to take something else. We never know who it's going to be. One large cake has been cut into equal shares around the fire. One portion will have some small token in it, a stone or the like, and when it's discovered, the finder must show it to all. This year it's me.

"The carline!"

"Carline!" roars the whole circle. All four young husbands of the *fhain* leap on me, one to each limb, and drag me between the fires, and the cry goes up: "Come, Lugh, and take thy gift."

Morgana runs about the fire, imploring, "Nay, a's a poor gift and stringy!"

Dorelei prays, "Would take my sister's last husband? Would find no pleasure in it."

"Come, Lugh, and take thy gift!"

"Oh, Lugh, can see a's crippled."

"And dull-witted."

"Does barely answer to a's name!"

"Be patient, be still," Morgana promises the heavens, "till can bring thee better."

Then a grass-doll or oatcake must be thrown to Lugh instead of me—and am all in favor of it since my drunken brothers are holding me too close to the fire. There are sparks smoldering in my sheepskin, and I'm smoking away like mutton a-curing. Morgana still runs about the fire with the doll, bargaining frantically with Lugh. My brothers heave me back and forth and one and two and *three*—

Morgana hurls the doll into the fire, but Urgus and Bredei stumble and fall. Urgus' leg goes into the flame, along with most of me.

"Mind out!"

"Drag him free!"

Morgana's pleading and praying and cursing in earnest now as they haul me out and roll me on the ground with my sheepskin a Bel-tein fire of its own. All I can see is feet and flame, being tumbled about, ground, sky, ground, sky, and then the fire's out with cheers of relief. Little harm done, but Bredei is tongue-lashed by Dorelei, and Urgus—ah, God, do pity the poor man, drunk as he is and feeling foolish and sorry for it all, covering his head from the blows Morgana rains on him.

"Foolfoolfool! Drunken, dirty horse!"

It's funny because Urgus is worse burned than me. The oil in the new sheepskin makes it burn hard, but it's thick and I'm not hurt. I tear it off and jump between the two of them, but Morgana flails out at me, too. The tallfolk men wonder why we take these humiliating blows without striking back. They beat their own wives regularly, but that would be deepest insult to a *fhain* woman. Besides, few Prydn daughters are mad as Morgana. But when she draws her knife on Urgus, it's too much. I turn her over my knee and spank her skinny bottom till Cunedag stays me, laughing, and Urgus pulls Morgana away, panting mournfully:

"Thee would not kill me."

She seethes, "Dost think not?"

"When I'm so painful burned and do love thee so?"

"Ha!" hisses devil-wife. "Give back my knife and ask again."

"Nay," Urgus trusts. "Would not."

"Would!"

Urgus stops her mouth with a kiss.

"Would . . ."

Again, pulling her to him.

"Would." She relents, suddenly, completely. "But, oh, would much regret it, Urgus."

She kisses him hard, then points to me. "A sign!" she cries to Prydn and tallfolk alike. "Was a burned by fire? Was a hurt at all? My husband be oak no more, but Belrix."

She rises to face the tallfolk, smiling, though her eyes dance with a cold elation in the firelight.

"And from this lord of fire will come another. Hear me, Lugh! Hear and remember the name of Prydn. Mother, wake and remember your own."

The night spins out, the fires burn down. The east, light for hours, becomes early morning, and the Venicones go home. Crops and cattle have been blessed, good fortune sought for one more year. We've eaten and drunk together, but the brief feast that made us one is over. We are separate again. They go home tired and happy and drunk, shaking their empty heads over the ways of the Faerie who steal and brawl and love in a single breath, who have no sense of fitness or dignity.

"Like children," they say. "Give them beer and oatcakes, they're happy enough. What can you expect from people who live dirty as their miserable herds, won't put a seed in the ground, won't own any more land than the wind? Children.''

But they can't read Morgana's face or the set of her jaw. Something stalks behind it, livid and raging. Even I will never know where it was born; perhaps one curse, one rowan switch, one broken bargain, one insult too many.

"Belrix," she whispers against my throat as we lie together. "Belrix, firelord." And it is not me she names.

Spring deepens into summer, a good year with plentiful rain. We follow the herds as they graze east toward the sea, moving carefully with cattle and sheep under close watch. This coast land is claimed by the Votadini. We're not sure of our welcome, though Cradda says they've never troubled us before. They are valley dwellers, we stay on the ridges. When we do meet them, they are much like the other tribes, a little distrustful and wary of us. Priests have been among them; some Votadini wear the cross, but the old fear of Prydn is deep in them. A pale around the village marks how close we may come unasked. We enter to trade under a dozen hard looks: fresh milk for eggs and vegetables, half of a butchered calf for our women to use a loom. There is no hut without iron or rowan charms.

And yet, where Artos-sleeper learned of soldiers and princes, I learn of men. They respect our magic, we show the same for their space. The men I meet feel a need to look down on us, even though I can see the fear that prompts it. I understand and humble myself under the scorn. We Prydn tread a narrow line between their contempt and reverence, and address each man or woman with a huge respect we ape and laugh at in the rath, but we play the game no matter how false. They cannot show their fear; we can't let them see how few and helpless we are.

One man is decent to me. While I draw water at his well, he talks easily of crop signs and chasing wolves and how hard it is to find good provender for horses. He is concerned for the same things we are, and as I look into his eyes, I see there is little difference between us. He must understand; he looks away, then says, "Not for myself that you have to stay outside the pale, but for the women and children. They—they're afraid."

So I learn. Behind a man's actions, the things he must do, is the fear for his own little space or that generosity may cost too much. Mercy, kindness, these step back while someone or something says "This must be." So men at the end of a life may wonder, Why? That's not what I meant at all. But it's done anyway.

"Few young men about," Uredd muses over his broth by the rath fire. "A said be all gone north like the Venicone youths."

"And a great cutting of trees," Bredei ponders, "and dragging them down to ships, did hear."

"Be sailing somewhere," Cunedag guesses. "Maybe Skirsa."

"Fine," says Morgana. "Does leave more room for us."

And no more said on that; tallfolk are not much to talk of, and tonight all the *fhain* is most interested in me, you'd think I was about to shatter did they not watch close. How dost feel? Dost rest well a-nights? Belrix must keep up his strength this week. Much giggling and elbows in ribs and nods to Morgana. There's some secret joke on me. I leave with Cunedag to take our watch over the herds and to settle them for the night, but when I come back to the rath, there's a sheaf of green leaves on my blanket and a sprig of vervain blossom.

The *fhain* has chosen me for summer lord.

Morgana shouts from the glen: "Summer king, summer king, come to me!"

I jolt forward down the steep hillside, balancing only by wide leaps and digging in my heels. Our bodies are tight-wrapped in leaves and vine, and I look like a drunken tree staggering uphill and down in the dance with Morgana, Bru-dog running after and woofing his joy in the game. We dance the summer in along the ridges and fire-gleaming hills, circle the herds and leap over the *fhain* fire as day fades to twilight and the moon, risen for hours, grows from pale to bright in the sky. There will be no real dark, only a softening of light. Tomorrow Lugh sits on his highest throne before beginning the long descent to winter. All through the night in this Votadini land, summer lords and queens will dance on the hills and run through the forests till exhausted, but spent or not, they will couple before the night is out. In some places they will roll downhill locked in each other's arms, or take each other in the furrows of the sown fields. For Prydn cattle-folk, it is dancing on the hills, circling the fires and the herds, and coming to rest gasping on the cool hillside grass.

From far away I know my body is tired, but I don't feel it. My skin shines with the ointment Cradda rubbed into it, mutton grease mixed with nightshade and foxglove, stinging a little from the small cuts she made to let the magic work in. To drink it would be sure death, but taken beneath the skin it makes me drunk without dizziness, lets me fly weightless over the hills after Morgana, stabs beauty into my eyes. The moon is a fountain of light, earth a shimmering pool to catch it and Morgana the center of the world in sheen and shadow, reaching to pull me close.

"Now," she whispers. "Now, Belrix."

She strokes my loins to excite me as if that were needed. I try to free us of the vines, impatient, then furious, give up, no longer able to wait, and Morgana wraps around me, half flesh and half green, so that each movement rustles and whispers as dark whispers to coming day. We love each other through most of the night while the magic of the ointment works out of our bodies; till, able to fly no more, we flutter down to stillness. Silver becomes gray, night becomes morning. A moor bird sings. Nearby Bru snorts in a dog dream, and Morgana sleeps in my arms.

The white-hot furnace of her energy, the dark drive of Morgana, are hard to imagine when she sleeps. The restless god has moved off for the time, leaving a tiny girl less than five feet tall, soft and vulnerable in a mass of black hair, leaves and vine. Watching her sleep, I frame the silly words *I love you*, but they're beggars. Words put space between will and being, between people. There's no room for them in us. What I feel is a kind of wonder and fear, for where once I was whole—dim, hard to remember—now I'm only half. Morgana is half, and if something tore us apart, the halves would die. I can no longer see her complete or apart any more than myself. It's like the moment when I lifted Drost to heaven and cried aloud for happiness, so close is meaning and the smile of God.

She stirs a little and nestles closer, her mouth warm against my throat. The morning breeze ripples the hillside. Bru's nose twitches. He wakes, sniffs. I catch the scent myself, breathing deep to know it better. Now Bru's up, circling nervously, trotting back to growl at me. He doesn't know what it is, but his nose says *wrong*.

Morgana wakes and sits up, lashing the hair back from her narrow face. Without a word to me, her nose lifts into the air, separating the right traces from the wrong. We both know the smell of dead cattle. The morning wind blows from the east over the Votadini pastures where one and perhaps more of their animals is bloating untouched by any scavengers but flies. It is sickness, blight.

We must move our herds quickly before they're tainted with it, before the Votadini accuse us of witching their stock. Blight in Prydn cattle is our misfortune; in theirs, our malicious fault. Right or wrong, before the sun climbs high the rath skins are folded, ponies loaded and even little Drost helps with the hasty milking. Morgana and I see to the readying of Cradda and Uredd. Bredei helps Dorelei to horse. Nectan, Cunedag and I move ahead with arrows hemlocked and ready. With a line of hills between ourselves and the Votadini, we move on eastward toward new pasture.

With a month between ourselves and the blight, we reach the sea and turn north along the cliffs and lowland downs. Now Dorelei is too heavy with child to ride a Prydn pony, and it's in Nectan's head to trade for a bigger breed. Moving ahead of the *fhain*, we raise a lone farmstead with a large herd of horses. Nectan judges the mares in the stock enclosure, and one young gray catches his fancy.

"That one there," he points. "Two good milk cows for her."

The trader is a thick-bodied man with light coloring and possibly more Saxon blood than would be considered respectable among Votadini. Eyes the color of winter sea, a shrewd, measuring man. He sees how Nectan wants this horse.

"Three cows," he says. "Two to calve."

Nectan laughs in his friendly fashion, as if the man were having him on. "Now, now, sir. Do bargain for thy horse, not thy house."

"Three."

"Two. One to calve next Bel-tein."

"Faerie lad, you want this horse or you don't. Which is it?"

Well, it is, then it isn't. They haggle on while I look over the man's stock. He must want the trade as much as Nectan, since he has horses a-plenty but only a few cows and those not the most thriving. And such horses for a simple farmer, long-legged, high-shouldered beasts, all with saddle marks. Not foaled among the Pictish tribes, not these. More likely night-borrowed from south of the Wall. But I study Nectan's choice and some knowledge from who knows where tells me this mare has more trouble in her than Morgana, that she's fast but not quite broken to steadiness.

"Choose another, Nectan. Can do better than this."

The owner turns on me as if to say, "Who in hell are you?" But he doesn't, because I'm big as he is and that puzzles him. He looks me up and down.

"You must have been cradle-took. The likes of you wasn't Faerie-born."

Very humble, I know my place: "Don't know, sir, and have never asked." I run my hand slowly over the saddle marks on the mare's back. "And who could tell where this mare was foaled?"

We understand each other, but Nectan wants the mare. "Will run like the wind, Belrix."

"Na, brother, but thy wife be in no race." Ah, it does no good to argue, nothing will say him nay. I wander away from them to stand by the storage croft. There are two near-full sacks on the ground near the door, and there's been a thought growing in my head through the summer. When the trader's not looking, I take a pinch from each.

The bargain is sealed at three cows, two to calve next Beltein, Nectan to have the use of a bull to stud. So we go home with his prize. Dorelei is so big now only I can lift her to the mare's back. Thrilled with her gift, she perches there happy and proud of Nectan, shrewd bargainer and the handsomest of men, while I hold the nervous mare's bridle and whisper black threats in her twitching ear.

"Woman, did know from far off thy name's Trouble. But mark me. One bit of temper, it will be Regret."

And yet my hands stroke with an odd familiarity along the fine head and neck, and for a moment I seem to remember . . . no. Nothing.

But there's discontent around the rath fire, and not ill-founded. Dorelei might be first daughter and bearer of child-wealth, but *three* cows?

"Will have the bull to stud," Nectan defends his choice.

"And what till then?" Cradda challenges. "Can not milk a mare. Can not stay here long and the grass this poor."

Old Uredd broods over his pease porridge. "The seasons be not as good as a were. Must go back to better grass. The People must go back." And he does, into his memories.

Morgana has something on her dark mind. Her eyes gleam coldly. "Better grass, I'll tell thee where it is. In the glens of the tallfolk. In the valleys where a keep us out. Go back, father? Go back where? To what-was, to old times? Will be no better grass beause we own nothing. Because be no hill, not one foot where we can say 'Stay out, this be Prydn land.' "

"What's this *own*?" says *Gern-y-fhain*, curious. "As if thee was no more than greedy Venicone."

Morgana lashes back: "Our herds be not smaller than at Bel-tein last year?"

"Aye, but—"

"And that year smaller than the one before? And before and *before*—"

"Peace, wife." Cunedag tries to stroke her cheek, but she shakes him off.

"Peace, hell!"

Urgus sputters through a mouthful. "List to Lady Tallfolk, doth curse like Christen now."

The wrangling annoys me. I hardly listen with the other thoughts in me that will have to be shared soon, perhaps this night. Already my wife has spoken the first of it. "Morgana, can it not wait?"

A she-wolf turning on me. "And thee! Off all day with sister's man, trading good cattle-wealth for that useless *naig,* and fondling and talking to it while thy wife goes without greeting."

"Is that what angers thee?"

"Oh, do not ask the whole of what angers me."

"Ah, God, thee's got a mouth like forever. What's the silly horse to do with owning of the land?"

"There's child in me, Belrix."

Sudden silence in the rath, an *oh* of breath. It is a great moment when a *fhain* daughter tells of coming child, but Morgana wants no honor now, her mind is set on one thing and we must listen.

"That's why would own grass, mother. Would own a place. Melga said it before me. Did scorn like thee once, but that was before my child was barrowed on a hill where we may be welcome next year or not if the signs be bad, if a's mood be bad, if do but frown at one of them. And Prydn will move on. And on."

Cradda is patient with her daughter. "Be no owning of earth, no more than child owns pieces of a's mother. Does the wind live in a house?"

Morgana gets up and comes round the fire to stand by me. I press my hands to her stomach in respect.

"The wealth is from me, Morgana?"

"From thee. From Belrix comes another lord of fire who will not live without home to call a's own or shrivel in one more hungry winter, or be buried in borrowed ground. What says my husband?"

Well, husband says nothing right away. It's much to swallow

in one gulp while I'm still trying my first taste of fatherhood.
And there are the other thoughts that have been with me since
Midsummer morning when we woke to smell the dead cattle. I
think of all these things and take Morgana's hand. We face the
fhain together.

"*Gern-y-fhain*, Uredd, Morgana is right. Would never go
against the People's ways. Have never spoken foolishly nor
much at all in the rath, only listened and learned. But must speak
now for the sake of the child, for all of us. Prydn wealth grows
smaller and cannot last forever. Must trade wisely to build our
herds again. Build them to what they were, must think of
nothing else."

Uninterested, Cradda licks the porridge off her fingers. "This
is new wisdom? Have not tried?"

"And when the herds are strong, must trade for land."

Urgus almost drops his bowl. "Wha-at?"

I kneel before Cradda, bringing out what I stole from the
horse trader. "Here, see. The best wealth of all, seed. Why do
tallfolk prosper? Be this. Why do Saxon-men whose fathers were
sea pirates now call half Britain their own? Be this. Wherever a
stays long enough to plant, crops are sown. And the women and
the houses come after, so their roots go deep in the ground. So a
has something worth staying for."

"Yah!" says Morgana, proud of me. "Thee remembers so?"

The question should not sadden me, though it does. "Sometimes at night . . . I dream."

Cunedag tries to speak. All this is beyond him. "But Earth
and Lugh—"

"Will not *help* us!" Morgana hisses. "Land. Must trade for it
or take it."

"Take it?" they wonder.

"Others take, so can we."

But Cradda's heard enough. "Daughter, sit. And thee, Belrix."

But Morgana's defiant: "Remember what Melga said, day on
day, Belrix says no more than that."

"Belrix! First name was fool, and Melga no wiser." Cradda
puts an end to it. "Be still now."

It is out, said. The *fhain* is silent. They look at the seeds on
the earthen floor and no one speaks for a long time. Then old
Uredds nods slowly.

"Must range further next year."

"Perhaps north," says Bredei. "The Attecotti pastures. Have

not tried there for three Samhains. And have heard the northern grass is coming back.''

Cunedag agrees quickly. ''Be Prydn there already and many good crannogs.''

Cradda muses over her porridge. ''A good thought. Perhaps will try north next year.''

My wife looks at me. We are alone in our plain truth. It's as if we had said nothing at all and the seeds on the earth were dead pebbles, and we must listen respectfully as the *fhain* plans not a future but an end.

The trader's bull has stood with at least seven of our cows, thanks to his own ardor and a little help from Cradda's magic in his feed. The owner may wonder why boyo-bull sleeps so much for a few days, but he's a wee spent, bless him.

The grass is not the best here by the sea. Our few sheep can manage, but the cattle need better before autumn sets in. Yet we linger; the weather is still blue and gold, the east wind has no bite. We fish the beach shallows, salting away as much as we eat. Morgana and I run on the downs or lie together with great Bru's shaggy flank for a pillow, making dream shapes out of clouds. Every day she makes me look to see if she's grown. Our child-wealth is still mouse-sized, and I have to stretch a bit to say yes. Morgana wants it so much, it's not a very big lie.

We speak no more in the rath about land, but often between us. We have passed other Prydn folk during the spring and summer and hailed them as family, but we are a straggling few beside the tallfolk. *Fhains*, we decide, should band and travel together for strength. A dozen *fhains* as one, a hundred folk! Morgana finds it hard to picture. She's never seen a hundred folk at once or owned a hundred of anything, but she labors at it.

''What be hundred like, Belrix?''

''Ten times ten.''

''But what dost *look* like?''

''Well, do have ten—ten times.''

No, that won't do. She'll have it laid before her, so I must find a bare patch of earth, draw ten strokes and nine more rows of ten under them. But once she sees it, she's triumphant as Drost and the mountains themselves are not too tall for her to step on.

''A hundred folk,'' she dreams. ''And a hundred after that,

and still a hundred. Cattle and sheep like waves on the shore, crannogs loud with children, tens and tens of braw horses—*yah!*''

I grab and wrestle her down beside me, biting her ear, her breasts and the laughing mouth. "And *Gern-y-fhain* Morgana over it all."

"Stop, fool, stop. Not till Dorelei."

"Ah, sister could not rule such a thing."

Though Dorelei is first daughter, I can't imagine her leading such a great, bustling *fhain* full of comings and goings and things to be done. Gentle Dorelei is as much child as wife and mother, lazy and playful, uncursed with Morgana's will or restless discontent. Her love is the giving kind. I've seen her wait at the pale of a tallfolk village while her husbands traded. Just waiting, no more. Sure and soon there's a clutch of shy, curious children drawn close around her, just watching or bashfully asking who she is. Is she in truth queen of the little folk? Can she do magic for them? Their suspicious parents always snatch them away. Dorelei does nothing the whole time, but children and dogs are a good measure of grown folk. They can't pretend to see a love, they feel it there or they don't.

In the slanted morning sun we wait on the downs for Dorelei and Nectan, who are to help with the milking today. It's a game to Dorelei, who only wants an excuse to ride her new mare. And here they come slowly across the meadow, queen and groom, Nectan leading the horse, Dorelei brave in her new blue wool gown, and we wave back to their greeting.

"Hail Queen Dorelei, hail Prydn queen!"

It happens even as we stand watching, so suddenly there's no time to cry out or even feel the horror of it. The flushed bird drumming into the air, the startled mare rearing high with a scream, Nectan snatching at the loose rein, Dorelei's arms flailing to catch at anything, and we're running hard even as she falls. When we get there, Nectan is kneeling beside Dorelei as she writhes on the ground, trying to curl into a ball against the agony. When he looks up at us, we see the whole thing in his face, see it wash out replaced with red slaughter. With a scream, he leaps at the horse, but I head him off.

"Nectan, no."

"Will kill it."

"No, fool."

"Get out of my way!"

"Put up thy knife."

He puts it up in a vicious blind slash at me that goes wide.

Small as he is, I pick up and slam him down hard on his back, the wind out of him.

"Enough, brother."

"Kill it, kill it, *kill* it!" Tears of helpless rage and guilt rolling down his cheeks. "Was me brought the beast to do its evil. Should be whipped from the *fhain*. Did thee not tell me—?"

"Enough, be still. Be strong. Look to Dorelei, who needs thy hand more than the blood of a stupid horse. Leave that to me."

When the murder's out of Nectan, I let him up and turn to Trouble-woman, who waits, skittish, ears laid back.

"Now, you misborn daughter of a dog."

I grab the dangling rein, get a grip on her bridle. She rears away, but I hold on and pay her a cruel rap across her tender nose. The pain stops her long enough to get hold of one tender ear and twist. When the mare finds she can't move without pain, she stands still. I let go the ear a little, soothing her. "There, now. Be still. Were only frighted by a silly bird. There, now."

Morgana runs to me, urgent. "Nectan must ride home for Cradda."

"Dorelei?"

"Not hurt, but a's waters broke. The child comes."

It's too much for a man to grasp. Here, now? "Be not time yet."

"Tell the child that. It *comes*."

"Will go myself."

But she stops me. "Nectan will only hinder. Need thee, Belrix."

True. Hovering Nectan is helpless with love and desperation. Morgana coaxes him away to me, and I try to embrace him with one arm and hold Trouble with the other.

"Ride, Nectan. Morgana's with her. Will be well."

He climbs up, eyes still blind to all but agony, a man hollowed out as he kicks the mare's flank to run away across the down.

Dorelei lies on her back, brown fists clenching as she fights to keep from hindering her sister. Dangerous to move her at all; Morgana slits the gown up the front, freeing the distended belly. I strip off my sheepskin to make a pillow, feeling sick inside. This is no place for a man, but Morgana was right. Better me than Nectan. If it were she lying there, I'd be no use at all. I smooth the hair away from Dorelei's face with a shaking hand, frightened in the presence of things beyond me.

"How is it, sister?"

"Give—give me something to hold."

"Thy wrists," Morgana tells me.

Dorelei's small hands close so tight on my wrists, I couldn't tear them loose. Morgana can no longer count between pains, they're so close, and now the first great wave comes.

"Now, sister."

The cry tears out of Dorelei as out of rended Earth herself, pain and the impossible strength to bear it. Her fingers dig into my wrists and I feel my will, my self pouring through the joined flesh. My whole body tenses and strains with her, we sweat as one; not she but *we* bear this child. In the bright morning sun, we lurch together through a darkness.

Morgana straightens her back a moment. "Good, sister. Do see a's head. Again."

And again that dawn-cry of creation. Dorelei grips till there's no more feeling in my big, useless hands. Still I try to pour strength into her. Another wave—

"More, Dorelei. More!"

She pushes again, but it's not enough. She goes limp, breath rasped with exhaustion. She lies still, lets the pain take her while she gathers herself to go on. I'm glad Morgana pays me no mind, because I'm praying so hard it comes out in tears. Because I see too much at once, that the fall hurt Dorelei more than we knew, that the little body can't do of itself what it must, and the desperation hits me like a fist. Mother and Lugh, Mother and Lugh, give us this child alive. Take cattle, sheep, this is all that matters. Give it to us and we will spend our lives in service to you.

But our parents only watch with the cruel, unblinking eye of their sun.

Morgana pushes the hair out of her eyes. She's sweating, too. "Wipe a's face."

Dorelei's pale, but still better off than me. "Need not fret so, Belrix. Be not the first time or the last for me."

I get behind her head again so she can't see how I'm crying, how much I care. That's an answer of a kind. It's not mere life our parents gave to make us human. No, we're human because we care, and where have I wandered and wasted that I shouldn't learn this till now?

One small truth to hang onto, the only profit we will see. For all our struggle and caring and Dorelei's pain, the bairn comes just as Nectan and Cradda appear across the down. Too small, too early come, the child not due till Samhain. A girl born dead.

Nothing left but to let Cradda read it in my eyes, to face
Nectan with the plain fact, let his numb, naked grief stab into me
as I hold him a moment before he stumbles to Dorelei to
say—what? What does life say in the face of Not?

Cradda wraps the child in the swaddling she brought. It must
be buried, but Nectan can't be torn from Dorelei, won't even
look at the tiny dead.

"Go away. Take it away."

So it's mine to do. I mount Trouble. Morgana passes the small
bundle up to me. Her gray eyes are dark as slate with the
helpless anger pressing behind them.

"Dost see now, Belrix? Dost feel it? Our own must live. If we
tear Earth apart for it, Prydn must *live*!"

I stand alone on the cliff. Overhead the noon sun sparkles on
the sea beyond. There's a cleft in the cliff face that draws down
to the beach, and here I dig the small barrow, line it with stone.
Carefully clay over the infant eyes that never opened. Cover the
barrow with dirt and turf.

Finished now. Done.

Trembling.

Trouble-horse grazes. Still part of life, she eats. But for me,
after the love and the hope and the desperate caring, there's only
rage and a spear of *why* to hurl at Lugh. I can't, I won't accept
such waste and loss without a reason. Like Morgana, I'd tear at
creation for this, rip the earth, throw the pain back in God's
face.

Deep in me, Artos stirs.

Stay away, I tell him. Go back to sleep.

But Artos wakes.

I scream at him. "Go! I don't need you."

But Artos opens his eyes inside me. "It's time," he says.

Time for what?

"I know what Merlin wanted to teach me," whispers Artos in
my soul. "To be a king over men. To know what they are, and
the price of knowledge."

And then Artos with his tallfolk words tells me what he's
learned, how we tumble out of darkness into brief light, and
because we know there's so little time, we breathe our moment
full of magic. We reach for something we have named beauty,
touch each other in a need called love. We plan and hope,
endure and dare for these flickering wonders, then go back into

darkness not finished, still caring, still asking why or not even given the chance, like Dorelei's child. And the mourning and the loss ball our souls into fists to strike, not at God, but at that pregnant silence where we think He hides.

"And that's the joke," says Artos in me. "Some ancient fool saw in a dream the true face of Man and, having no name for such a beauty, called it God.

"And this is what Merlin would teach me. To love, to care, to be small as well as great, gentle as well as strong. And a burden. To walk filled with the knowledge of that silence while still singing the name of God. To be a king, to wear a crown, is to know how apart and lonely we are and still exist and *dare* to love in the face of that void. To crown your brow with knowledge sharp as thorns, bright and hard as gold."

"I don't want to be king!"

"Neither do I," says Artos sadly. "I don't want to leave Morgana. But I've slept long enough. Let me out."

"No. Morgana needs me."

"She needs *me*, fool. A man, not a mother-reaching child. Let go!"

Artos heaves in me, straining at the bonds of will. I try to hold him down, but he's much stronger now. Nothing will stop him, though even now he's gentle.

"Don't be afraid, fool. You'll always be with me. I've grown to need you, too."

And

    I

        was

            free.

               Come back.

Lonely, huddling there on the cliff, crying for Dorelei and stubborn Morgana, for all of them I loved and couldn't bear to lose now. Crying for the end of summer in me as well as the world. When I raised my head, I wasn't surprised to see him looming over me, nor even wondered how long he'd been there. Always, I guess.

"Merlin."

He was still dressed in the worn cloak and cavalry leather, looking intently out to sea. The same face I remembered, but subtly changed. Less superior. No longer remote. "Hail, Tribune."

"You brought me to this. Why?"

"Time to go, Arthur."

"Damn you, why?"

"You needed it. Part of you wanted to be born." Merlin kept his narrowed eyes on the water. "I only see what is. You learned."

My soul was sobbed out, not a tear left. "I'm not going back."

Merlin didn't move.

"You hear me? For all the—the—"

"Loss, waste?"

"For all that, there's too much to leave."

Silence like that Belrix raged against.

"There's a wife, a child coming, people who love me, a place where I fit in. I *belong* to something, can you understand that?"

Merlin sighed. "I try, Arthur. I do the best I can."

"Morgana worked weeks on that magic and never knew the real power of it was my own hunger for someone like her. I was born when she put that silly dust on my eyes. Before that, even with you to infect me with visions, did I once know who I was? I've smelled of nothing but sweat and horse and iron since I was fourteen. One friend, one Bedivere lonely as myself, and the rest nothing but roads, barracks and duty. Until she came, I never slept with a woman whose name I could remember. In a year on the Wall, I could count on one hand the decent meals or good nights' sleep. Ready to collapse when I saw you on that hill. How much magic did it take to lure me away from *that* to a moment of warmth? You think I'll leave it? The hell with the army, they think I'm dead anyway."

Still looking out to sea, Merlin said, "Life is a long good-bye made out of smaller ones. Will a king stumble over the first of many?"

Why did I feel so frightened and desperate now? "Will you bugger off with your bloody king! I won't go."

"It will be, Arthur. No gift without a price."

"You can't make me."

And then he turned to me. "You still don't know who I am. *I* never made you do anything. Because you've found one answer, you think life will let you write the questions too? They're being written even as you stand here denying them."

Far across the down, I saw Morgana coming for me. "There's my answer, Merlin. The other part of me. What can you match against her?"

He swung his long arm toward the sea. "That."

I looked out over the water. My brain responded out of habit and training: Jesu-Mithras, they've done it. They're coming. Bedivere—no, get away. You're not part of me.

"All summer at Skirsa," Merlin murmured at my side. "All the young men, all the trees felled to build ships. It was only a matter of time."

I stopped my ears against him. "I don't care."

"And you know where they're going."

"It's no—part—of—*me*."

"Look at them, Arthur."

Over the lead ship, Cerdic's serpent banner ruffled in the wind as I had seen it from the parapet at Neth Dun More. Behind, the long formation of keels moved inexorably south like a school of deadly swans.

Merlin had no pity now. "They've already come a long way from Skirsa. Wherever else, the Humber is too necessary to miss. Supplies, fresh water, loot. And Eburacum through the back door. Your cohort could stop them cold."

"Get away, Merlin. For the love of God, leave me alone."

"But they'll never know in time, will they?"

I twisted away from the gently relentless voice. Drowning, I sought one thing to hold on to. "Morgana!"

Still far away, she flung up both arms in greeting and broke into a run. The morning had been cruel; she would need me now.

"Will they?"

"You bastard, do you see her? Do you see what you're asking me to leave?"

"Will they, Arthur?"

I felt like dying again. "No."

Merlin looked away to the little figure coming fast across the down. Gently, he said, "Then do what you must. I'll be waiting."

I turned back to the sea and the moving ships, already weighing speed against time. Already gone from her. What was left to say came out in one quick breath to keep my voice steady. "Yes, you'll wait. You'll always wait, because now I know who you are."

The tall figure strode away to the south. I whispered to his back, "I know your secret name, Merlin."

Morgana called, running to me. "Belrix."

Her voice pierced me with cowardice. I couldn't face it. Once started, I mustn't stop or touch her, God knows I mustn't meet her eyes. One look and there'd be no leaving. I'd lock her in my arms and stay forever. The fading ghost of Belrix cried, "Do it, fool! Let me live with her, she's all there is."

I forked the mare and lashed it into a dead run toward Morgana. She thought I was coming to carry her home, stopped and threw up both arms in her childlike greeting. Coward, I pulled up to a halt at a distance, not able to look straight at her.

"Belrix, take me home."

"I can't go with you, Morgana."

"Nay, be tired. Take me up behind thee." She stared for me again, still not knowing. I jerked the horse around and retreated even farther before I could face her again.

"Husband?" she called.

This is how it ended between us, speaking over this cruel distance because I was afraid. "Stay. Please. Don't come to me."

"Why, Belrix?"

"I have to go back."

Back had no meaning for her, nothing beyond us, *fhain*. "Go? Where?"

"To what I was when you found me."

Morgana took a step nearer. "But be nothing there, Belrix."

"No."

"Be here in me, in our child-wealth." No, she smiled and knew I was fooling, even called me by my first name. "Druith, hast been a suffering day, should not joke with me. Did wash Dorelei and comfort her, the while thinking of thee. Come, take me up behind."

And the ships moved further south while I sat there murdering her because she could never understand. She started for me again.

"For God's sake, stay *away*."

The harshness halted her like a blow. "Belrix?"

"I love you. I love our child. Take care of it."

She began to know then with a dawning fear, and the slow words came thick and incomprehensible to her tongue. "Thee's gone from me. Thee's—him."

"I'll come back. I'll find the *fhain* wherever it is."

"Thee's gone from me!"

"Damn you!" Why did I wait, why not turn and run? "Do you see those ships? I have to stop them. I have to go back."

"*No!*"

Morgana sprinted forward, arms reaching for me. In a flicker, one more heartbeat, I'd break, let her touch me, never leave. I wheeled the mare and kicked it into a hard run, screaming loud to drown out Morgana's cry. "God damn damn damn all!"

I never looked back, but I could still hear her.

Merlin waited several hills beyond. I reined up, shading my eyes toward the sea. Only part of my mind was still on deaths and burials. The rest moved on, measuring and planning.

"The wind's against Cerdic," I decided. "There's still time."

Merlin stood with hands on hips, "Well, Tribune, it's a fine, clear day. You can see fate in all directions. Where first?"

"To Corstopitum to gather the cohort. When Cerdic lands, all he'll see is horse and iron. Bastard."

The old humor flickered in Merlin's eye. "Cerdic or me, Tribune?"

"If the shoe fits, Merlin."

"It fits." He stood smiling up at me, more of a king than ever I'd make. Yes, I knew him, should have known him from the first, but his is the face men recognize last and least in this world.

"We'll meet again, Arthur."

"That we will."

His eye sparkled with satisfaction. "Well now, what can a little magic not do for a fool? Show him a child, he sees the face of God. Let him love a woman, and what do we have? Not only a humor but a heart, so well I worked." Merlin glanced one last time across the hills to the north. "All men dream of a place called Midsummer, green days and silver nights; you had it. All men search for Morgana somewhere; you found her." Merlin threw his arms wide and high like Morgana's joyous greeting. "*O Arglywydd,* do you know me at last, King of Britain?"

"Better than all else."

"Then say my name."

I gathered the reins tight to bring up Trouble's head. She must run faster than the wind, faster than fate itself. "Arthur Pendragon."

The mare leaped forward over the crest and down the hill.

Behind me I heard Merlin's great shout of victory as Trouble ate up the downward slope and flew onward over the level moor, stretching with ease into the run she was born for. I didn't look back; he wouldn't be there. Swift as we were, Merlin would be ahead of us, dashing toward tomorrow.

Guenevere

I picked up one of the two imperial roads leading south, gave Trouble her head and let her fly.

Fifty miles to the Wall. The best mount in Britain couldn't get me there fast enough, but there was never such a horse as Trouble. She ran through the last of the pale sun, ran through the night, burning her heart out. Twice I stopped to walk her briefly, then could give her no more respite. Mounting for the last time I whispered, "Now, Trouble. Forgive me."

And we flew on. Numb with fatigue, I heard nothing but the wind in my face and the tortured shriek of the mare's laboring breath. The road stretched white in the late sun, gray in the moonlight, a dim ghost-line unraveling forever before me. Giddy pictures flashed in my mind, repeated senselessly over and over: Dorelei clutching my wrists, Morgana running for me in that last moment. I raved at them, light-headed and hoarse, while Morgana's words molded inanely to the drumming of Trouble's hoofs. Never go *back* never go *back* there's *noth*ing there *noth*ing there thee's *gone* from me thee's *gone* from me.

Trouble ran, Trouble soared, mere horse no longer but goddess of all flight, mother of all speed, until the road topped a low hill and I saw in the first morning light the long, straight line of the Wall.

I tried to shout "We did it!" but only a raw croak came out. Trouble bolted forward, obedient to the rein, took two great bounds and fell under me. There was no need to dispatch her, dead when she fell. She had atoned for Dorelei. Only a moment I lingered over her, then began to run.

A bowshot from the mile castle, I cried hoarsely at the two

sentinels who leaned on their pylums and stared at the ragged apparition pounding toward them across the moor. When I stumbled to a gasping halt at the access ramp, they put their spears up to the ready. The older one called down to me.

"Where d'you think you're going?"

"I'm Tri— Tribune Pendragon." I waited for more breath to go on. "Sixth *alae*. Got to get to Corstopitum. Need a horse."

The grizzled sentry only scoffed. "Go on, Picti-lad. It's a quiet day, no need for trouble. Get away from the ramp."

His companion marveled at me. "The cheek of him. Pendragon six months dead and this one thinking we wouldn't know it."

"I was a year on the Wall and never saw you either." I glared up at him. "I was captured."

"Na, killed. They said so. Peredur's head of the *alae* now."

The sweat poured down me, and the breath whistled in my lungs. "Do I *look* dead, Goddamnit?"

The older guard raised his spear again. "The look of you's a different matter entire. You didn't get those cheek scars in the cavalry. Be off."

Precious minutes wasting, bleeding away while these two dolts held me here. I flailed my arm to the east, exasperated. "Listen. Out there at sea are half the Picts and Saxons ever born, sailing half the ships ever built toward Humber mouth. Cador's got to know and Bedivere and Peredur, and if I have to stand here any longer, I promise you sons of bitches will carry slops and dig latrines from now till hell holds mass. Now snap to, square off and *get me a horse.*"

The gray-headed guard regarded me with a thoughtful expression. "Well," he allowed finally, "looks is one thing, but if that's a Pict, so am I."

Convinced, they allowed me up the ramp to gulp leek-and-turnip soup while one of them unharnessed a wagon horse. They stared at me while I knotted a rope bridle and hauled myself up, a weird scarecrow in greasy rags. They believed me: tattered or not, I was a soldier of the emperor, and they pitied my plight. Ah, Jesus, caught and tortured by the rotten Picts, was there any fate worse? Give thanks for my escape, and what godless savage scarred me so?

"Faeries." I slapped the reins and left them gaping after me in the morning sun.

The east-west roads ran the length of the Wall and joined at Corstopitum, base supply camp for my cavalry stations. I dashed into the fort an hour later with a fragmentary explanation to the bewildered centurion in charge who recognized me without parlay. Someone ran to draw me fresh duty leather and trousers while I scrubbed several layers of Pictland off me and fired rapid instructions at the centurion. Three of the fastest mounts and best riders to depart instantly for the Solway, Cilurnum and east to the third squadron. If patrols were out, leave them. All available men were to join me here, fully armed, with extra horse and equipment for me. Another courier for Eburacum to alert Cador. Not in half an hour, Centurion, not five minutes, but now!

The orders given, I sank down onto the offered bed and dropped through it into soft, black, dreamless sleep—to be dragged up out of it two hours later with the news that the first of them had been sighted on the east road. Red-eyed and wool-brained, I doused my head with cold water and lurched out to meet them.

One of my precious days was already spent as the third squadron clattered down the Via Praetoria and wheeled onto the drill ground where I awaited them. As they drew up, some of the men recognized me.

"Suffering Christ, it *is* the trib."

They were led by a short, barrel-bodied little centurion named Gareth, once Peredur's second-in-command. An Irishman, Gareth had a long torso and short legs, one of those men who managed to look like Mars on a horse and a monkey on foot.

"God and the squadrons welcome you home, sir," he greeted me in his Leinster lilt. "And was it a pleasant journey?"

"Not really. I understand Prince Peredur commanded in my absence. Where is he?"

Gareth was slightly embarrassed. "Well, sir—when not needed, he's usually in Eburacum."

I glanced up at the squadron; the men crackled with readiness and spirit, every one with a lance and longsword. Perhaps Peredur had done a good job with them, or maybe it was Gareth. No time to ponder.

"The need would seem to be now, wouldn't you say?"

"Aye, sir."

"Unsaddle, let them rest."

If the men were astonished by my reappearance, no one, least of all Gareth, questioned my authority. Any complaints from Peredur or the royal house of the Parisi would be heard when time permitted. While his men unsaddled and trooped toward the kitchens, Gareth and I went over the maps of Eburacum and the imperial roads south of Corstopitum. Furthest away, Gawain and

Agrivaine must follow as they could. When Bedivere and Trystan came up, we'd move with the three squadrons. If the Orkney brothers raised Eburacum in time, so much the better. If not, we could still hurl almost three hundred lances at Cerdic in a new kind of warfare he'd never forget.

Ambrosius and I had long since worked out the problems and possibilities of a raid up the Humber. If I were Cerdic and planned merely to harry the undefended villages on the coast, I could go in any time. But if I wanted to take Eburacum, I'd lay offshore just over the horizon from Humber mouth until dark and then go in. Five hours of steady rowing would see me well into Ouse River, turning north into the Use. Another three would put me in sight of the city's watchfires. I'd rest and go ashore at first light against an unprepared skeleton force.

With the wind against him, Cerdic needed at least thirty-six hours to raise the Humber from where I sighted him. That meant tonight at twelve. If he chose to lay out and come in under cover of the next night, that gave me eighteen extra hours. He should do that; once into Humber, he ran against time.

But what if he didn't wait?

What if he assumed he'd be sighted and made it part of his plans? He couldn't afford delay then, but must sail straight in and pull hard to make Eburacum by dawn with exhausted men. Would he gamble that against Cador's force?

The coast must be written off. We couldn't defend it, they wouldn't stop for it. Like all combined raids, this was an investment. It had to show a profit. A Pict might sell his mother, but only if the price was right. No one could gather them into such a force just to raid a few villages. If they came in at all, it must be for the city.

Did Cerdic know of the cohort?

In my mind, Ambrosius chuckled drily: Wouldn't you?

Yes. He'd know from a hundred sources, spy or buy the information before planning the venture. Very likely Cerdic knew where we were, how many, how long it would take us to gather and move. The answer was simple arithmetic. Even if we were already on the move, even if we got there first, he'd be rested, we'd be spent.

Please let him think that, let him wait.

I kept asking, what hour now? Near four, sir. Repeated calls to the sentries on the west rampart. Do you see them? Even dust? Not yet, sir.

Gareth sat on the ground, carving apples and sharing them

with his horse. His squadron lounged about us as the sun sank lower, some singing, others setting a fresh edge to their swords, the *zang-zang* of the whetstones counterpointing their music.

Mellow and wistful with the melody, Gareth murmured, "My wife was just gone to chapel down the road when your message came. I sent a man to tell her, but it's a poor farewell."

"There's worse." I thought of my own parting on a lost green meadow a million miles and a thousand years gone since yesterday. Gareth spat out a seed and offered another tidbit to his stallion. "Is it in your mind we can stop them, Tribune?"

"If we're in time."

"That's not a thing to ponder," he admonished gently. "We're in God's hands to win or lose. After this, will they not call you Arthur of the Hundred Battles?"

I rubbed my gritty eyes. "The Irish say that about anyone who's run off three head of cattle."

"Not a whit, my good lord." Gareth laughed and slapped the saddle he rested against. "We only take plain truth and give it a bit of style."

My glance happened to follow his hand; but for that, I wouldn't have noticed his saddle. From each side of it dangled an extra strap ending in a wide leather loop.

"Gareth-fach, what are those?"

"What's what?"

"Those straps."

"A gift from the heathen, you might say, added since you were captured. Makes it easier to mount. Braces the feet with a lance. Ten times harder to unseat you. Comes from the Huns in eastern Gaul. Stirrup, he called it."

I inspected the leather loop. "Who's that?"

"A new lad of mine, a weird one but clever. He's about somewhere. I'll call him."

But just then a sentinel hallooed from the west rampart. "Column, Tribune!"

"Gareth." I rose. "Saddle and form your men."

He threw his saddle over the stallion's back and roared at the lounging men. "All right, my lovelies, they're coming in! Let's show them something like a squadron."

I paced out to the center of the drill ground and stood with feet apart, hearing the rumble grow on the west road beyond the rampart. As Gareth's squadron drew up in four ranks behind me, I turned to survey them—and thought of old Vortigern on that night long ago. They didn't look quite like Roman soldiers, and they never would. Like Geraint, it was impossible for two of them to dress alike. But these were no ragtag mercenaries to snoop about and run errands, no rabble from the edges of the empire. These were Britons, *combrogi*, landowners, sons of tribal chiefs, descended from the charioteers who drove Caesar into the sea, horsemen to follow me the eighty miles to Eburacum and fight at the end of it.

I faced them with pride. On Gareth's command, they dipped their lances. I returned the salute and turned to see—Jesu, my heart leaped at the sight of him!—Bedivere riding through the gate with the fifth behind him, harness jingling, lance tips gleaming in the sun. He saw me and gave the command without breaking out of formation.

"Right wheel, form behind me."

Raising a wall of dust, the fifth whirled into parade formation facing Gareth's squadron with myself in the middle.

"Dress it, dress it!" Bedivere bawled. "Front rank, you look like a herd of monks. Square off."

Not till his men were paraded smartly as Gareth's did Bedivere turn to face me. He saluted and the fifth dipped their lances. I tried to keep my voice steady as I gave the command.

"Centurion, rest your men."

"In place—rest!"

A great shout went up from my squadron. *"Hail Arthur!"* Bedivere leaped from the saddle and in three or four bounding strides engulfed me in long arms. I felt him shaking under his leather, choked, angry and tender all at once.

"Damn you, Arthur. Damn you . . ."

Now the fourth squadron clattered through the gate, headed by Trystan. With no order but the *Hail Arthur!* that rose again and again from the other squadrons, Trystan formed his riders into a third side of the square. Under the roar, Bedivere and I were a little giddy.

"Catch me leaving you alone like that again," he fumed. "Sick as you were. You're rutting Goddamned impossible, you are! I said you were sick. I told you to be careful. Didn't I say that, the last words out of me? I suppose you just dozed off—"

"Ah, Bedivere, you're a lovely sight."

"—as if you were home in a comfy bed. That's just like you. Other men die, not *you*, not Arthur bloody Pendragon. You're immortal. No thought for me or the men, how we'd have to get on without you. Well, we got on fine. I didn't waste time looking for you, I can tell you that. Brought the men straight back and on about our business."

"You were right, Bedivere. One man's not worth a squadron."

"Teach you to be careless, it will." He ducked his head, trembling, trying to control something. "You're unsafe as a child, a blind child. And if we weren't ringed round with men who expect us to behave like captains—by God, Artos, I'd hammer you flat, and I can do it. Where the hell have you been?"

I tried to answer, but the hails went on rocking the drill ground.

"Hail Arthur!"

Someone tapped me on the shoulder, and I heard a Cornish drawl. "That damned Dobunni's been screaming at the top of his voice for six months. Now you're back, pray he subsides."

"Trystan! Well met."

"Welcome home, Arthur."

I put an arm around each of them. "Give your men a few minutes to eat. It's the last hot meal before Eburacum."

"Na, you don't get off that easily," the dogged Bedivere persisted. "I think I deserve to know how you let yourself be taken with not so much as a plaintive whisper for help. That's what I'm waiting to hear, no more and no less."

"Hail Arthur!"

Trystan glanced back at his men, annoyed. "A bit much with that noise, aren't they?"

I put my hand on Bedivere's shoulder. "If I were to tell you I was taken under the hill by Faeries, that they made me lord of fire and lord of summer, gave me a Faerie princess for a wife; that I met a prophet much like myself who promised I'd be king—would you believe me?"

His look was my answer.

Trystan sighed. "Ask a silly question . . ."

Bedivere exploded. "Damn! Will you *listen* to the man? Caught napping by the Picts and too ashamed to own up, that's the whole of it. Not half brazen, is he?"

"I confess, you've seen through me. They caught me sleeping like a babe. Come eat."

"Hail Arthur!"

Bedivere swallowed hard. "They never knew what they had till you were lost, that's why they cheer. Don't go to sleep again."

"Hail Arthur!"

Trystan winced in genuine misery, and I noticed that his cheery grin seemed fragile and tinged with a familiar green. "I wish they'd just wave at you," he moaned. "My head is splitting."

We couldn't afford one crippled or wind-broken horse. Lose a mount, lose a man. We didn't strain them, but kept them at a steady pace with regular rests every hour until just before dawn, when all needed food and sleep. Two hours, graze and water for the horses, a quick bite for the men.

Cerdic could have made Humber mouth at midnight. Where was he now? I found it hard to sit still, but had to conserve energy. I pulled my cloak close against the chill in the morning wind, fretting to Bedivere, "If he didn't wait, he could be in Eburacum now."

Bedivere took one more bite of his bread and offered it to me. "Would you go dead tired against a walled town?"

"No." I bit into the bread savagely. "No, he's got to rest."

"Well, then."

"He's got to!"

"Eat," Bedivere soothed.

"Move in five minutes. Tell the men."

We raced on. The sun climbed high, bunched our hurtling shadows under us, then slanted them further and further east. I began to search the horizon for telltale smoke. Nothing yet. In the hazy late afternoon, the road crossed a hill from which we could see the far walls of Eburacum. My captains drew up beside me, peering for any sign of trouble. The whole column fell silent, straining for any sight or sound.

Faint and distorted with distance, the rapid clanging of an alarm bell.

"No smoke," Bedivere decided at length. "And there's still someone there to ring the bell."

My whole body sagged with relief. "There's time. Our courier had four hours' start. They're already preparing. We'll swing south of the city and enter only if there's no sign of Cerdic on the river. There won't be enough grooms to go around, so no man rests till his mount is walked, grained and watered, is that clear?"

"They'll love that," Gareth chortled. "Some of my penny-princes think it's beneath them."

"So is the horse," I snapped, "and if it falls on the field, so do they. Those are my orders."

We streaked across the last few miles in a flat run as the iron screaming of the bell beat louder and closer. Ranging beside me, Bedivere shouted: "Listen!"

Faint under the bell, we heard cheering from the walls, saw now the tiny figures hopping up and down, waving their arms at us. The toy noise grew into a mighty roar as we swept by the west wall around to the south, gaining a view of the Use River—smooth, serene and Saxon-less.

Gareth gasped, "Praise God, we did it."

The first heat was ours. We had taken the initiative away from our enemy, but again I asked myself the question that whispered in my mind a thousand times over the years until that last cold day at Badon. Where are you now, Cerdic? What are you thinking?

My men followed me toward the gate already opening to admit us amid the clamor from the walls.

We rode lathered horses down the narrow street into the central square outside Cador's palace. The bell still clanged with monotonous urgency; soldiers ran back and forth along the square on various errands. The people of Eburacum hurried about, locking up shops, packing in wares laid out for sale. I stopped one soldier.

"Where's Prince Cador and his staff?"

"Forming the companies that live close in, sir. He'll be back soon."

"And Peredur?"

"At church, I think."

"Logical," Bedivere muttered as the soldier hurried away. "What will you do with him?"

"What can I do? I've just relieved a Parisi noble of his own command on his own ground. Very like Cador will never love me so much for coming back as he did for getting lost. Touchy, but till Cerdic's dealt with, Peredur must be second-in-command."

Bedivere only shrugged. "I was never ambitious." Then, on reflection, "And neither is Peredur. He wasn't the worst trib I've ever seen. Just that his heart's not in it."

"Bedivere, you're an observant man for all you scold me."

"Well, even God had the prophets to nag Him."

"Or so it's said." I reined out of the column. "Take them to the stables. Make sure the horses are looked to before anyone puts a bite of meat in his own mouth, clear?"

"Did I join the army yesterday?" he snorted. "Where will you be?"

"Demoting Peredur."

I found Cador's son emerging from the church adjacent to the palace. Peredur was draped in scale armor, buckling on his sword. His stint as cohort commander seemed at least to have put some determination into his bearing.

"Greetings, Peredur. I hear you were tribune in my place."

With his usual detachment: "You seemed to be absent, my lord. With the emperor's approval, I took command."

"That was farsighted of you. However, I've just brought in the command from which you seemed inconveniently absent, though as ranking tribune, I'd be honored to have you as second-in-command." I saw him stiffen slightly and said less formally, "Peredur, the cohort has accepted me home. Though I see they've lost no edge under you, this is no time for vanity in either of us."

"Well, then." He relaxed a little. "What matter, anyway?" he said, and his slim hand indicated the church. "It was only courtesy to Ambrosius that I took up arms. There is my home."

Tactfully: "Amen. Tribune, please inform your father we'll take up position outside the city awaiting his orders. Where are the Lady Guenevere and her women?"

"Father told them to keep close within the palace." Peredur's composure bent a little in something like a real smile. "Gwen doesn't like it at all. Spitting nails."

I thought of fierce little Morgana. "And why not? I know one woman who'd take on Cerdic with a bronze knife and probably win. And Guenevere? A woman who paupers herself to support her men is not going to twiddle her thumbs while those men fight. Find me with the cohort."

The palace chamber of state swirled and eddied with agitation. No soldiers about, but a throng of court women—daughters and wives of officials—and a few priests. Guenevere stood alone on the throne dais, trying to restore some sort of order in the gaggle of them, and a little exasperated. I edged through the women—excuse me, pardon me, by your leave—and knelt before Cador's daughter. "Lady Guenevere."

She seemed extraordinarily glad to greet me. "Lord Arthur, welcome home. You—"

Guenevere broke off. Her expression changed as she studied me. For a moment, the cool reserve that characterized her family faded. "Wherever you have been, you seem to bear the marks of experience."

"I've come to ask your help and that of your ladies," I told her. "May I address them?"

"By all means." She took my hand and drew me up onto the dais. The last of my energy deserted me then; I must have reeled a little. Quickly, Guenevere said, "Or perhaps you would care to sit. Be still now!" she commanded the others sharply. "Gather round and Lord Arthur will have answers to your silly questions."

With royal disregard for protocol, she seated herself on the edge of the dais and invited me down beside her. "Come round us." She might have been instructing children. It was the right move at the right moment. Seeing her so calm, the women quieted, curious to hear us. "Lord Arthur says he has need of us. Listen to him."

They hushed expectantly, moving in closer to the dais. I spoke very casually. "You've been told to stay out of the way, and no doubt that rankles."

"So it does," one elderly woman grumbled. "The women of Eburacum are not cowards."

"We've just ridden in," I went on. "Who here will give support to my men?"

A buzzing among the women and priests. They looked to Guenevere to speak first. Without hesitation, she asked, "What can we do?"

"When we're in position, it would cheer the men if you all went out to greet them."

Guenevere considered. "That makes sense." Then, in a low voice meant only for me: "They've never been in battle, most of them, and never as a cohort. They'll be uncertain. And we'll feel better busy than just sitting and stewing."

"And your father?" I asked.

"Will disapprove," she laughed. It surprised me how intuitively she grasped the situation, but this was a woman full of surprises. She raised her voice again. "I will go! Who is with me?"

"Me!"

"And me!"

"I, too." A young priest thrust up his hand. "I was not always tonsured."

"And I!"

Guenevere spread her arms to all of them. "We'll all go together."

"Thank you." I bowed my head to them. "Thank you all. If our spirit is half of yours, how can we lose? Go among the men, talk to them, sing to them, let them see they matter to you. After the battle, there will be men who can't be moved but must be treated where they lie. Every lady here, every priest could help by bringing the infirmary supplies to the field then. Will you do it?"

"My lord." A very young woman, very pale, plucked at my sleeve. "Could the Saxons get through to the city?"

"Not at all." I hoped it sounded more convincing than it felt. "They've never faced massed *alae* before, and one man on horse is worth five on foot."

"Of course." Guenevere jumped in staunchly. "Didn't Lord Arthur himself and two others stand against a hundred in Cornwall?"

"We'll go out to the men!" The young priest shouldered his way through the press to confront me, grinning. "I'll carry the great cross from the church and the Host to say mass with."

"I'll bring my harp," one woman volunteered.

"And I my lute," trilled another.

"We'll give them such a welcome!"

"I've got to change."

"I *won't* go out in this kirtle, it's old as I am."

"That old? I thought it quite your best. Is my hair all right?"

"Out to the darling Sixth *alae*!"

Patriotism is catching as plague. The room seethed with their excitement as the women chattered with preparations, happy to have some direction and purpose. Forgotten for the moment, a small island of calm in a sea of fervor, Guenevere sat quietly on the dais. She offered me a gold cup of fruit wine. I toasted the women.

"Live a hundred years, none of them will ever be as beautiful as they are this day."

Guenevere looked closely at me. "By God's holy eyes, are you crying, Arthur?"

"Just—these people pull at my heart. They make a lot of things worthwhile."

"An improvement," she said. "I wondered if you had a heart outside of duty. I thought they wound you up each morning, something like a catapult."

I took a drink. "That was before."

"Before what, Arthur?"

"Before. Was I all that pompous?"

"Oh, at times."

"It was only eighty men in Cornwall."

She pretended surprise. "So few? The Cornish already have it at a hundred."

"Stay a while. Next year it'll be doubled."

Guenevere laughed. "Good to know you while you're still mortal," she countered with mock gravity. "Gods aren't very interesting." She was teasing me again in that cool way of hers, a subtle and tender challenge I wouldn't have fully understood less than a year ago. "Arthur, won't you offer me a drink?"

"From this cup?"

"Why not?" She took it from me and drank. "We're in the same battle. The rest of the set was sold for Peredur. Cerdic doesn't know what beggars he comes to rob."

I realized and said with conviction, "Lady Guenevere, if you set your mind to it, you could be formidable."

She hid her smile behind the wine cup. "For whom, Arthur?"

"Tribune!" Stubby little Gareth hurried through the crowd, knelt clumsily to Guenevere and saluted me. "Messenger, sir."

"From where?"

"The coast near Humber. He's ridden all day." Gareth paused for breath; he'd evidently run the length of the long hall. Like many superb horsemen, he didn't manage his own legs all that well. "This morning at dawn, it was. Some fishermen were working their nets off Humber mouth when they spied longships. They ran inshore straight to report."

"Did they say how many ships, Gareth?"

"They were far out but the messenger said fifteen, probably more. They were almost over the horizon, he said."

"Moving?"

Gareth shook his head. "The sails were reefed."

I felt a weary satisfaction. Cerdic was waiting, doing what I expected of him. *It's worth the leaving, Morgana. It has to be. We'll be ready.*

Ready or not, he still surprised me.

I should say something about this man Cerdic who haunted the outskirts of my life, as I his, for so many years. Church scribes are a biased lot with their own cutlery to grind, and you never know who's going to rummage your life with a goose quill and a viewpoint. Tacitus used the relative monogamy of the Germans to scold Rome for its vice, and I hear that young Gildas is writing of my early reign as if it were a lost golden age. Suffice to say, we were not always inspired or the weather that good.

On their side, the Saxons have embroidered Cerdic with the usual gods and heroes for ancestors, claiming that his familiar spirit appeared to herald his birth as a king. Some have sworn that, to this end, Cerdic was born with a sword in his hand. Symbolic of course, but awkward for his mother. God help a king without a sense of humor. He may stand close to his legend, but he should never lean on it.

His father Ossa came to Britain with grim old Hengist, one of the first mercenaries hired against the Picts. When Vortigern gave them Wight, Ossa settled down to farm and, as no Saxon women came with the first ships, he took a British wife. Cerdic could boast as much Belgae blood as Bedivere. They are an energetic, aggressive tribe. As much of Cerdic's ambition came from his mother as from Ossa.

He grew up in two languages, British and Jute, read and wrote passable Latin. He founded the West Saxon kingdom and well deserved the crown, possessing several indispensable qualities for kingship: a quick grasp of complex situations and the ability to make decision and act one fluid sequence. Probably not cruel by nature, he could nevertheless use cruelty as a tool, a necessary example, repugnant though it might be. So have I. And he did have a wonderful way with words, a trick of charging them with immediacy and fate, something that should be graven on Sinai. He could stir men. I heard him exhort them that day at Badon.

Personally, he was charming, handsome and vital and a splendid guest. He gave grave attention to men with minds shallow as a birdbath and made them feel profound. The same approach worked to ravishing success with women, I hear. Guenevere was not unimpressed—the ultimate accolade—but was wise enough to see the hard glint of calculation beneath.

Weaknesses? The usual for a comely man keenly aware of his endowments. He was vain of his narrow-waisted figure and affected a British style of dress, tight tunic and trousers of the closest-fitting material. His brownish hair and beard, naturally leonine, were put through several styles, Roman and British, before returning to the simple Saxon braid. With advancing age, his barber and tailor were urged to greater lengths of misdirection. And taste, one might add. He tended to overdress at first, though always to startling effect. Like Geraint, Roman austerity passed him by.

We first met (without weapons) at my coronation. Cerdic asked to be presented in peace. Bedivere called it downright crust, but I was delighted and gave Cerdic safe conduct, wanting to meet him as much as he wanted to come. I remember him at the banquet in clashing green and blue with a ceremonial gold-headed ax in his enameled belt. We talked of Eburacum with careful generosity toward each other's skill, when suddenly Cerdic broke off in the middle of a sentence and narrowed his eyes at me.

"It *is* you!"

"My lord?"

"The village at Neth," Cerdic said. "You and two others burned my ships and charged the clout of us."

I couldn't resist a coy smile. "I was wondering if you remembered."

"Remember?" Cerdic hooted with delight. "You'd have finished me off if you weren't half dead yourself. When I stopped running, I said to myself, there's one man not afraid to take long odds on the dice."

"You must meet Geraint sometime."

"Oh, but that's the way to do it, Arthur." Cerdic's admiration was unfeigned. "The only way."

I signaled for our cups to be refilled. "Then why did you wait at Eburacum?"

The question seemed to embarrass Cerdic. He frowned at his cup, then off at the jugglers gyrating before our table, silent so long I thought I'd offended him.

"A man would think you were elf-charmed," he allowed finally. "You have the damnedest luck. The plan was to come straight in, no waiting. But when we reached Humber, the Pict princes held out for a bigger share of the spoils. Most of the ships were theirs; they had me over a barrel and haggled away all the advantage of time. Otherwise, we'd have been in, out and gone when you got there."

I could only gape at the colossal absurdity of it.

"Damned Picts," Cerdic finished ruefully. "All greed, no discipline. Amateurs."

We were young then, still learning, and Eburacum taught us both. We measured the ground, made decisions and committed our strength. Then, because of a few avaricious fools, the whole thing turned over and a city survived when it might have been gutted. Gareth would say God was at our side, but then God was notably absent other times when it mattered just as much. Where the one thought humbles a realist, the other helps his skepticism to its feet with a reassuring pat on the back.

Cerdic had one other quality that hardly needs mention: audacity. He still caught me by surprise at Eburacum and, damn his genius, he almost won.

By sundown my squadrons were in position on a crescent line facing the river, with the southwest corner of the city wall as its axis. Cador returned with a scraped-up cohort, barely three hundred men. He was dutifully cordial about my safe return but not too pleased over my disposition of Peredur, whom I kept rather busy as link between myself and my centurions. Cador was in the full ceremonials of a legate, ornamental bull's-hide breastplate and gold-plumed helmet, the lot. I must say he cut an imposing figure beside the rest of us who looked—and always would look—like partly mobilized tribesmen. A time was set for the commanders to meet for final preparations, then I returned to my men.

Sundown in overcast. Cerdic should be setting his sails for the Humber now, watching the light fade. We wouldn't have much moonlight to help us. I passed the order through Peredur: at midnight all fires would be doused, all talk held to a murmur. A watch would post on the riverbank southeast of our line, listening for the creak of an oar, straining to see dark hulls against deeper darkness.

Dusk. With the lighting of our fires, the city gate opened and out to us came Guenevere with the ladies of the court, a train of servants and priests. They were singing as they came, and they moved among the men, cheering them, bringing blankets and small gifts. They made music by the fires, the gallant, wistful, always heart-stirring music of our people. I could hear Bedivere's voice raised, saw Trystan plying his harp beside Guenevere, who was in green that evening, gold-belted and -bordered under a scarlet cloak, her hair unbound and flying as she led the men in song. It was as good a way as any to face a coming battle. At least three marriages came out of that songfest, young people who might not otherwise have met at all. However we mangle it, life has a way of getting on with the things that matter.

A mass held in the center of our line was very well attended. Priests heard numerous confessions. Bedivere went, and Peredur and Gareth. Trystan was not a Christian and never became one—"My sins are yet too lovely to forego"—and preferred, like me, to sleep while he could. Leaving word with Peredur to

wake me at midnight, I rolled in my blankets and drifted to sleep
on a warm, rapid tide.

Peredor was faithful to his charge. He gently shook me awake
in chilly darkness. "Time, Arthur. Father's waiting for us."

I peered at the white blur of his face in the gloom. "Gone
twelve yet?"

"A little before."

"Condition?"

"All fires out," Peredur reported efficiently. "The river watch
is set. Gawain and Agrivaine got in two hours ago. I saw to their
meal and the quartering of their horses."

"Good work, Peredur." I rose a little stiffly and fastened my
cloak. A great quiet enveloped the dark around me where men
slept before battle. Only a few stirred about, their voices muted.
The loudest noise by far came from Peredur's cumbersome scale
armor.

"Leave it off till the boats are sighted," I advised him. "You
sound like a busy kitchen. Here, I'll help. Have you slept?"

"There was a deal to do," the young prince allowed. "Setting
the watches, inspecting the line. Then the Orkney brothers roared
in just as I was settling down. Irksome lot."

I pulled the heavy mail over his head. His arms seemed
uncommonly stiff. "Relax, boy, you're tight as a drumhead. Get
some sleep after the meeting. You need it."

Without the armor, his dim form seemed slight, hovering and
tentative. Peredur said tightly, "I . . . can't sleep."

"Is something wrong, Prince?"

He seemed about to speak, then changed his mind. "No,
nothing."

"Thinking about tomorrow?"

"Of course not."

That brittle young pride of his. My second-in-command and I
barely knew him. A different tack was in order. "Well, I
certainly am. As Tryst said, there's a hundred things I'd rather
be doing. Fine poet, Trystan. Have you heard his songs? Hardly
for mixed company, lovely as they are. They're about a woman.
All women, I guess."

"He's a bawdy sot." The force of the words betrayed the
emotion under them. Peredur was in agony.

"Oh, at times, but—"

"Arthur."

"Yes, Prince?"

"It's so real now!" The words burst through the dam of pride, painful but honest. "Tomorrow, I mean. They'll try to get ashore, and I'll have to ride straight into them as if life didn't matter at all. I've told myself all day that I only grudged this soldiering because it puts aside God's work, but that's a lie."

Peredur shifted restlessly. The armor rustled metallically in his hand. "I babbled venial nonsense at confession, wasted the priest's time when, God knows, there were braver men waiting. I think he sensed what I was afraid of. He said, 'Is there anything else?' That's usual, but he seemed to know there was—that." A long silence. "It's well you're back. I can drill them, but I'm not fit for this work."

We stood close together in the middle of the night with a damp wind blowing off the river. "It will help to say it, Peredur. You feel afraid to die."

Grated, full of self-loathing: "Yes."

"So am I. Is that all?"

"All?"

"Peredur, any man with the sense to love life is afraid to die. Who says else is either a liar or a fool."

I had opened the door for him; the rest came in a rush. "Oh, you should hear Agrivaine raging around: no prisoners, first into the fray. Not only him. I've heard the same cant from the men all day in their boasts, even their prayers, how they'll gladly die for this or die for that. Dear God, it makes me want to retch."

His disgust was honest as his pain. I suppressed a tender amusement, though there was nothing funny. "Let's hope they're liars. I don't relish leading fools." I looked off toward the dark river. "A year ago I might have faced tomorrow with less fear, or perhaps simply less appetite for living. But now life has some meaning for me beyond horses and iron. I've seen the price paid for it, how it fights to be born and sometimes fails. It has great value for me now, and great sweetness, so that it's not death I fear so much as leaving something so beautiful as life. We're told there's better to come, but our flesh only knows how dearly we paid to get here and how good it is to breathe. That may be sinful to a Christian, but—"

"No!" Peredur broke in fevently. "No, it may be thought a sin, may even be one, but it's the truth. Perhaps there's a truth for flesh apart from the soul."

"Then render unto Caesar." I took him by both arms and shook him gently. "Just a little now and then. Who the hell are we to be perfect?"

I could hear the expelled tension in his tremulous laugh. "Who, indeed?"

"Feel better?"

"I feel naked, Arthur."

We should have set out for Cador's meeting, but this moment seemed peculiarly rich, one of those rare times when a man's heart lay open for me to study. I never saw Peredur so clearly as that night, like watching a marble statue wake to warm life.

"Did you know, Peredur," I said, "all my life I've had a ridiculous fear of the dark."

"No!" Peredur laughed in spite of himself. "Do you tell me so?"

"At the damnedest times, the small hours when courage wears very thin. I seem to remember a time—I guess it was before Uther took me from the castle where I was born—when there was nothing but dark around my cradle. It's my earliest memory, being alone and frightened for so long. I kept hoping someone would pick me up and hold me, but no one ever came."

The wind lapped around us. Close by, someone stumbled in the dark and cursed softly. "Seems a night for confession." I threw the cloak across my chest. "Time to collect the centurions."

Peredur hefted his armor. "I'll see to it, Tribune."

"No need." I put an arm through his. "Let's go together."

And that was Peredur who became Prince of the Parisi and the Brigantes. His rein was firm and his lance steady next day, but he lacked the health and stamina for steady soldiering, much too wispy. He took a wound that day, a cracked rib that never set right. There must have been a splinter of bone left protruding, because he coughed blood at times throughout his life. We began as strangers, became loyal brothers-in-law and finally royal enemies, for he had to oppose me when Gwen was banished.

Eleyne of Astolat thought him a saint, but then she would. He had all the ingredients, sufficiently pious to be revered, ill enough to fret over. But he did find her Grail.

Percival? No, Coel, spell his name as he wore it: Peredur, good and British. Only the Saxons call him Percival, and they can't even agree on the calendar. Will you believe your king or someone who barely knows what day it is? Indeed.

*   *   *

Brother Coel wonders why I detail an unheroic exchange with
Peredur and wish to skim over a fateful meeting of British
warlords; I suppose because more of significance was uttered at
the former. The conference was a squabbling shambles, but on
reflection someone should preserve it as a monument to British
density. As such, stone would be more than fitting.

"Why should I hate Britons," Cerdic once remarked, "when
they're so good at hating each other. Half the time I just picked
up the pieces."

When I suggested that Cador's small force be placed in
support of my *alae*, his officers of foot bridled that they should
stand second to mere cavalry, that the hand did not serve the
elbow. Bedivere observed laconically that the elbow was whole
while the hand lacked most of its fingers; that Cerdic would
rather face a legion of foot than a cohort of horse. Cador knew
the logic was too clear to argue.

"I've not always agreed with our emperor's theories," he
confessed in an understatement bland as it was Olympian. "But
the cavalry is in strength while we are a handful. We must
support their salient."

More serious trouble erupted when I tried to lay out the attack
order for my own force. Gareth's squadron, the only one equipped
with the new stirrups, must be the center of the first line,
Bedivere and Trystan on his flanks. This wide leading element
would attack Cerdic's men as they floundered in the river shallows, never giving them a chance to organize. The supporting
line, under Peredur, would be Gawain and Agrivaine, to deliver
a second blow while the first line reformed. Agrivaine balked
immediately.

"No, Orkney will never take second place against Picts.
There's too much to pay them back for. And more than that,"—he
acknowledged Bedivere and Gareth with insufferable tolerance—
"no slight to good soldiers, but there are some disproportions
that cannot be allowed."

"Disproportion?" I wondered.

Agrivaine seemed puzzled that I didn't understand. "Gareth
mac Diurmuid is only man-at-arms. Bedivere ap Gryffyn is the
son of a groom. Able both, but a prince cannot be expected to
hang back while commoners comprise the first line."

"Isn't that large of him," Gareth retorted, stung, "when I
could ride any one of his Orkney whoremongers into the ground."

"And *I* intend no slight," Trystan added in a tone bristling
with it, "but the Cornish will stand down for no one."

I had to explain for them the basis of the disposition. Gareth's men were best mounted of the entire cohort. Trystan and Bedivere's squadrons rode Arabians for the most part, bigger and faster than anything in the Solway camp. "And therefore, centurions—"

Gawain shouldered his brother aside like a bull brushing past a puppy. "Centurion hell! We're tired of that meaningless title, tired of pretending to be Roman officers. Do we get Roman pay? There are Picts with Cerdic who've raided Orkney for a thousand years. I don't care if Gareth rides Pegasus, we know how to deal with them, and we will be first."

"Peace." Cador rose at the head of the table. "Peace, all of you very young men. This is no time for dissension."

But Gawain blundered on, passionate. "We've always been farthest away at Solway. Farthest from news, from supplies, from advancement." A significant frown at me. "We've had to stand aside for royal pets. Not good enough to wait for or council when battle comes, we must run like demons just to arrive late on the field."

"At the order of a tribune who appears very healthy for a Pict captive," Agrivaine insinuated. "I believe those marks on Lord Arthur's face are family-signs, their way of showing affection."

"Prince," I told him in a level voice, "you waste this council's time."

His tone was a sneer. "We have not heard where our tribune will be during the attack."

Before I could answer, Trystan cut in, his voice gentle but with a cutting edge. "Agrivaine, one could call you vicious were you not so wondrous thick."

Agrivaine would have leaped clear over the table at him, but Peredur caught his arm. "Enough, you foolish man. You'd lose a city for the sake of pride. Lord Arthur will be forward of the first line. Need he say as much?"

"*Lord* Arthur, yes. And *Lord* Trystan." Agrivaine's fury was leashed but unabated. "You see what Rome did to us when we give titles to bastards."

"I said peace!" Cador's sword slammed on the table. "A pack of boys, is that what the *alae* is? Boys who rattle their swords to hide their fear? Agrivaine, school your temper that it hinders us no more. Trystan, you the same. I charge you both."

"Easy, lad," Gawain muttered, draping a great paw over his brother's shoulder. "You're right, but easy on. Later."

"Aye, soothe him." Trystan's eyes were murderous over the studiedly negligent grin. "Give comfort to the royal afterthought."

With a snarl of frustration, Agrivaine slammed his gauntlet down before Trystan, who reached for it, but I dove, swept it up in my fist and brandished it.

"Stop, both of you. And all of you listen! It makes me sick to see this. Don't you realize that while we bicker like children, Cerdic is moving? And if he wins tomorrow because we can't agree tonight, what matters who we are? If we can't plan as equals, we'll die that way. It won't matter to Cerdic or the flies."

Trystan only said, "You hold a challenge thrown to me."

"Shut up, Tryst. And you, Orkneyman. Ambrosius burned out his health and his fortune to build a weapon out of nothing. And succeeded. Not in six hundred years has there been a force like ours, but make no mistake as our fathers did who lost the east while they argued and mistrusted. If we fail today, the north, the south, the west and even far little Orkney will not be worth a whistle in the windstorm that follows."

Unmoved, Agrivaine said, "You hold my glove, Dobunni."

"So I do." I tapped it against the other hand. "You leave no alternative, Agrivaine. You and your brother will form the second line of attack under Prince Peredur. If you refuse—in the presence of your legate with battle imminent—he has no recourse but to have you executed for mutiny."

"Mutiny?" The implication so stunned Gawain that he could only stare. Agrivaine, almost as speechless, turned to Cador. "Good *God*, must we stomach this?"

A polished ruler, Cador did not indulge his feelings openly, but I saw the way he measured each of us, especially me, with a slight shaking of his head. I'd nailed him to a cross; as legate he must uphold my authority or admit in the face of an enemy that we had none.

"When time permits," he clipped off the words, "I should chastise every officer in the *alae*. For the nonce, I must uphold Lord Arthur, roughshod and careless of tradition as he is. His disposition will stand. As for insults, if we must air personal grievances, let us do it now and be done. Prince Agrivaine, you maintain your right in arms?"

"I do."

Again Trystan reached for the gauntlet. "The challenge was to me. Nice distinctions of birth are strange in one who worships a god born in a stable, though it helps to have a deity for a da. My parents were mortal but married. The glove, Lord Arthur."

But Cador wasn't through manipulating. "I believe the circumstances touch the tribune himself."

Until then, I hadn't realized the two-edged diplomacy of which Cador was a master. He would mollify Orkney and teach me a lesson. On the other hand he judged me cooler than Trystan, who was a competent swordsman but not an instinctive killer-ferret like Agrivaine.

"Tribune?" he urged delicately.

Let it be then, but let it happen in a way that made Agrivaine think hard on its worth. "If I accept, Agrivaine, will you abide my choice of place and weapons?"

"Name them." He seemed just as glad to be at my throat as Trystan's. "The time?"

"If we survive, day after tomorrow, ten of the morning. The city market square."

"Impossible." Cador dismissed the notion impatiently. "If we have a city at all then it will be full of people going about their business. No room for horse or lance."

"No horse, no lance, no sword." I held Agrivaine's eyes with my own. "We'll need only a circle ten feet across. We'll be stripped to the waist and barefoot. One dagger each."

"Dagger?" Gawain echoed. "You expect my brother to brawl like a peasant?"

"Since your brother knows so much of Picts, I'll fight him as one."

Agrivaine understood now. A knife is brutal and quick, and I intended to take full advantage of the defective leg he hid from the world. Even if the fight were not mortal, he would be shamed in a way intolerable to him.

"You may send me your acceptance later, Agrivaine." Meanwhile he could sweat over it.

Then and later I saw how Gawain cared for his brother. He whispered quickly to Agrivaine, who straightened away from him furiously.

". . . withdraw *nothing*, damn you." Then to me: "I accept now."

"So be it." I dropped his gauntlet in front of him and turned to the rest of the table as if nothing had happened. "Now, to repeat the order of battle . . ."

Sword-rattling, time wasted. It all came to nothing anyway. While we argued, a picked force of Cerdic's men beached miles downstream, skirted wide around the city and moved in from the north. Well before light, while we sat confidently watching the riverbank, the cry went up from the city behind us.

Fire! Fire!

Cerdic's scaling ladders hit the north wall in pitch darkness and almost complete silence. Before the sentinels knew what was happening, the first berserkers were over the parapets quick as mousing cats. The first wave carried only sword and throwing ax, those behind were laden with sacks of oil. By the time the clamor reached us, fires roared lustily in Eburacum and the few guards on the wall were fighting grimly with little hope of relief.

Our frantic preparation had for light only the flames from Eburacum. Cador strode, armed, into the fumbling knot of us, hurried and urgent, to embrace Peredur.

"My men are no good here. I've got to get them back inside the gates. Good fortune, my son."

"And to you, father. Farewell, if that's God's will."

"Lord Arthur, I assume you'll move when formed. Good fortune." Cador moved away into the dark, shouting commands. Peredur finished buckling his armor.

"What orders, Tribune?"

What indeed till we organized? The darkness around us was a roil of shouting, confused men, rattle of iron, frightened horses.

"Light a torch, Peredur, and let every centurion take one from yours and stand by it so their men can find them."

He ran to execute the command. One by one the torches flared in the dark, a line of fireflies as the flames from Eburacum rose higher to redden the black sky. Cador's men were inside the gates now; with the ruddiness swelled the ugly human sound of war. Tightening my saddle cinch, I heard Bedivere's clear voice:

"Fifth squadron, form on me."

Then Trystan. "Fourth squadron here, hurry. Form on me."

"Third squadron here!" Little Gareth, exuberant and furious. "Jesus God, don't amble! Move, *move*, you sad little men! Form on me."

Agrivaine then. "Second squadron, Orkneymen, here to me."

And finally the great, primal roar of Gawain, whirling his torch in great circles overhead. "First! First, here I am, here! Damn you, first, here!"

My mind raced ahead to the next move, working on unsteady ground, nothing from experience to fall back on. The north wall had to be cleared first. Till that was done, nothing else mattered. I hauled up into the saddle and set my lance in its socket, hearing Peredur's command, tense but sure.

"Centurions, report your order."

"Fifth formed."

"Third formed."

Bedivere had chosen my own equipment well. The sword was from Kay's own forges, beautifully balanced and responsive. My mount was crossbred Arabian and native stock, heavy in the chest, intelligent and obedient. Not a fabulous Trouble-horse— no, never such again—but a sturdy mate for battle. I patted his shoulder.

"Now, friend. To work."

"*First* squadron formed."

"Second squadron formed and waiting."

A bishop of my acquaintance once noted how religious conversions rose sharply just before a battle. Understandable; a man going to war wants all the help he can get. I kissed the hilt of my sword, asked Jesu to bless it—then, not at all parochial, pattered the habitual litany to Uther's household deities, including Mars and Mithras, while the old fear and anticipation tightened my stomach.

Peredur again, sharp and impatient as a terrier. "Fourth, what are you doing? Let me hear you!"

"Fourth squadron formed."

They were ready. I whispered my last, most fervent prayer. "Mother and Lugh, protect me today and my wife and the wealth she carries."

Peredur's light guided me to him. There was a pale smudge of pink in the east as I grasped his taper and waved it high.

"Commanders to me!"

They trotted in close to ring me with light. The noise from the city was louder. Cador would be engaged by now. My hasty plan called for splitting the cohort into two elements, but inexperienced Peredur must be given the most disciplined squadrons to lead.

"We've got to clear those scaling ladders, put ourselves between Cerdic and his men in the city. Cador's a match for them now, but not if they all get over the wall. First, second and third will follow me around the west wall, fourth and fifth with Peredur to the east. Whatever opposition, those ladders must come down."

"It's perishing dark," Gawain rumbled. "Can't see who we're fighting."

"Tribune." Gareth urged his mount forward a pace or two. "My man here has a darling idea for light."

Until Gareth spoke out of the half gloom under his torch, I

hadn't noticed the rider beside him, features down-shadowed but the torch gleamed dully on his shirt of ring-mail. Such armor was rare in Britain.

"Well, what? There's no time for talk."

"Just below the north wall in the stables," the stranger said, "there's a shed full of old wicker cages once used for dove sacrifice. Dozens of them, Lord, and dry as dust. Fill them with anything that will burn, soak them in oil, throw them over the wall and Cerdic will no longer have the advantage of dark."

Audacious, but certainly worth a try. What struck me most was his educated Latin, spoken in an accent I couldn't place. "That north parapet's a busy spot. How many men will you need?"

"But five, my lord, already chosen and willing. Give us leave and you shall have light."

"Better than tumbling about in the dark," Gareth urged.

"All right, get to it."

The rider wheeled his mount away toward the third squadron. Gareth watched him, musing. "He's one to mark, Tribune. It's himself fashioned our stirrups."

"What's his name?"

"The men call him Lancelot."

"If he's still with us later, I want to talk to him. Peredur!"

"Here, Tribune."

"Take your squadrons, and remember: the ladders are most important. Once they're down, no matter how you're obstructed, push through to join me."

As Lancelot's small detachment trotted out toward the city gate, I gripped Bedivere's hand in a wordless blessing and took my place in front of my element. The faint streak of light in the east had not widened. False dawn and far too long till morning.

"Forward!"

Under the din from the city we rounded the northwest corner of the walls and saw the dim monkey shapes scrambling up the nearest ladders, others scurrying behind. So many of them, like rats in a dark cellar. We would crush more underfoot than our lances took.

"Bring down those ladders!"

We charged into the darkness beneath the north wall, the base of our line streaming around the scaling ladders, some levering them down with lances, some broadsiding their horses to push them over. The ladders swerved and fell and with them came the bellowing men caught climbing up. On foot in the dark with no kind of formation, they went down like wheat under the mill-stone of our force. Many tried to retreat; others doomed them-selves by closing back to back as Bedivere and I at Neth, fighting with sword and shield. These were the fabled berserk-ers, the warrior-caste who formed the hard core of a Saxon attack force. They owned nothing, saved nothing and lived only for battle and the glory of their chief. Even in the gloom I could see they were huge men, disdaining helmets, pale hair tossing with their exertions.

One of them swung his ax at me, and I covered myself. The first blow splintered my shield, the second left it dangling shat-tered and useless from my arm, but before the ax landed, the lance was out of my hand, the sword in it. The berserker cursed and lunged at me again. My blade sank deep into the haft of his ax, blocking it, jerked free, slashed at him. He went down, but in the split second of the blade's movement it gleamed with a ruddy new light. Near me, someone shouted hoarsely:

"Look, it's Lancelot. He's done it!"

On the parapet above, amid iron clamor like the forges of a million mad smiths, the men were dropping five, ten, two dozen burning wicker cages. The dark became flickering twilight, brighter each moment, and in the glow I saw Peredur surging toward me, cutting his way through a desperate knot of Picts, Bedivere and Trystan barely behind him and the whole element flying after. Any man in their way had no chance, simply disappeared under the sheer impetus of that hurtling wall. Those that survived retreated out of the deadly light into the darkness beyond as Peredur clattered up beside me, crumpled forward oddly, holding his side. A dark rivulet of blood trailed from his mouth.

"The ladders are down, sir." Peredur coughed with a sicken-ing wet sound. The rivulet became a spray, and he fell forward over his mount's neck. Even as I reached to steady him—"Gareth, help me here"—the cry went up from a hundred throats.

Lancelot! Lancelot!

Giving Peredur over to men of the third, I yelled with the last of my breath: "Cohort order, form!"

The riders broke away on all sides of me to execute the command, but still the cry went up: *Lancelot!*

For there he stood on the wall, hurling down the last of the cages that turned night into day, serene as a bishop in that hurricane of battle, crossing the longsword to his left hand, hilt upward, offering it like a cross to the men below.

"Not Lancelot but God's Will!" he cried.

"Lancelot! God and Lancelot!"

In a lull in the cheering, I hallooed up to him. "How does Cador?"

"We go to join him now," Lancelot replied in his formal manner. "God with you, my lord." And he disappeared behind the parapet as Agrivaine reined in at my knee, helmet gone, black hair hanging loose around his dark face, broken shield flapping in two pieces, visibly shaking with rage and excitement.

"I've fought this kind before, Arthur. It doesn't feel right. Na, call me mad, there's no love 'twixt you and me, but something's wrong."

I put out a hand to steady him, but he shrugged away. "What? I've prayed to every god with a name tonight. If madness will help, I'll use that."

"I think we've been had," Agrivaine said bluntly. "This is not their whole force. If there was more light, you'd see it's not. Picts rely on archers; hardly one shaft's been flown at us. They're gone, done what they had to, pulled us away from the river."

I looked into his streaked, fire-glinted face. "A diversion?"

"That for a fact," Agrivaine rasped. "If I'm wrong, call me old woman, but we may have given his main force time to land."

"Thank the gods for one suspicious man. We'll take up our original line."

He gathered his reins, glowering. "There's still a quarrel between us, brutish as you've made it."

"Meanwhile, Peredur's wounded. Will you take the second line on the river?"

Agrivaine blinked. "You mean command?"

"I mean lead. Not a vengeful mob but a line, Agrivaine. Can you do it?"

"Can I—?" For the first time in his life, Agrivaine gave me something like a salute. "Done. And until we meet, you're *still* a bastard!"

As the sky brightened from ink to a dingy gray, we squandered a few precious minutes in gathering up dropped lances, borrowing unbroken shields from the wounded left behind. Then, as the cohort wheeled in formation to follow me, a rider galloped toward us around the northeast corner of the wall and came to a halt beside me.

"Ten longships," he blurted. "All in line, all hard against the shore. Christ, they can't draw more than three feet of water. The pigs are pouring off like wine from a stove-in butt."

Bless dour Agrivaine and his canny northern instinct. He deserved a commendation.

"To Cador in the city," I directed the messenger. "His archers are no good in there. I need them to support me at the river, clear? Go on."

Pounding out onto the river plain before the city, it was just light enough now to see how right Agrivaine was: the fog-wisped river and the line of ships, the men plunging over the sides into the shallows, clambering up onto the beach, the first wave with scaling ladders. When they saw us move between them and the gates, they wavered and halted, hastily trying to set up a line of spears.

"Can't let them form!" I yelled. "Centurions to me."

The cohort wheeled into two broadside lines of attack twenty paces apart as my commanders ranged about me. They seemed to quiver; the light in their eyes might have been madness but it thrilled me. They were for this, needing no spur. I couldn't have held them back.

"Keep to the plan, two lines, Agrivaine in front of the second. Hit, reform, attack again. And again and again as long as we have a line. He's lost the dark and we've got him. See where the sun comes up."

"On our day for once," Bedivere exulted.

"To your squadrons."

Our day at last, our turn. Old Vortigern, gritty bargainer with one unsullied dream, where are you now?

Cerdic's first men had stopped, others running to join them. They were cut off from their prize by two solid lines of lance. There was no noise from their line, as if they suddenly knew what faced them. I gave the order.

"Couch—lances!"

My command echoed from the centurions. "Lances . . . lances . . . lances."

The iron tips dipped to the ready in a rippling wave. Now, for one moment, we were not mere tribes but something called Britain. I scooped my shield arm in a wide arc.

"For*ward*—charge!"

And Britain followed me.

A few more minutes and Cerdic might have won, reached the south gate with ladders and battering rams, archers massed to repel my cavalry. But we broke him with speed. Arrows flew, but no concentrated storm. Most of the archers never got ashore. And then Cador's own bowmen were in place and peppering the boats.

We shattered them as a line, battering into the first spearmen, taking them on our lances, trampling them down, wheeling to reform and attack again. We broke them at a cost as men were dragged from or went down over the heads of spitted horses, but always the line reformed, whirled and came again, a great scythe in the early light, until I sent a messenger racing out of the battle to the waiting archers behind us, and the first flight of arrows exploded into the morning air—up, over and down on the ships and men like a swarm of angry wasps.

Each attack pressed them further back toward the river until our forward movement bogged down in the sheer mass of bodies. We cut and kicked clear, reformed and came again. They tried to lure us into scattered fights to break the line, but our discipline held. For all his perversity, Agrivaine served me well. No sooner was the first rank disengaged than it maneuvered aside to let the Orkneymen through. That done, the first wheeled to reform again. Foot by foot, the yellow-haired berserkers and tattooed Picts retreated toward the river shallows. Faces flashed by me in the red smear of battle, blurred as the light-streak on a falling ax before my shield blocked or sword parried. The balanced blade seemed alive in my hand as it caught the new sun's rays, knowing of itself where to strike.

Gradually the retreat became a hapless rout to regain the ships. On the last charge, we won clear to the water's edge. It was then that I caught sight of Cerdic standing up to his hips in the frothing water with only a sword in his hand, urging the men past him to the ships. An arrow grazed his arm as I watched, just deep enough to protrude fore and aft from his flesh. With more impatience than anger, as if to say, "I haven't got time for this," he snapped the shaft and hurled the fragments away. I pushed toward him, but just then, another horseman plunged across my path. In that moment Cerdic turned, floundered to the nearest ship, snaked nimbly over the side and disappeared as the boat heaved away toward the middle of the stream.

"Cohort fall back," I grated to Bedivere with a voice raw from yelling. "Archers forward. Shoot as long as the boats are in range."

Bedivere looked demented, helmet awry, nose and cheeks grime-streaked. "Are you hurt, Arthur?"

"Don't think so." It hurt to talk. I could barely whisper. "You?"

"No, but Trystan's down."

"Oh no, not Tryst!"

"Think it was him." Bedivere nodded dazedly. "Think it was him."

"We did it," I croaked. "God of all luck in battle, we did it! Pull them back. I've no voice left."

There are truths remembered long after tactical details are forgotten, pictures bristling vividly from the unchanging face of war that historians like Caesar seem to overlook. Men in battle are much the same. They rage and fear and try to stay alive. Men after battle are more eloquent. The violence leaves them exhausted. They slump in the saddle, jolting limply with the movement of stumbling horses, or limp on foot, leading the wretched beast behind in an aimless, dream-like progress. Some cry softly with the release of tension, some curse like praying or pray like profanity, shuddering down from the violent height they have scaled. Fumbling and gentle, they help a wounded friend, encouraging, scolding as they coax him along. "Come on, damn you, hold onto me. Na, I know it hurts, you great fool. Come on, not far."

They gather together, staring back at the place they have come out of. That gaze is unseeing and all-knowing, and they will have little to say of what happened. They were in a battle and survived, that's all. These things never change.

Among the last of them hobbled Trystan, leading his mount, apparently unhurt except for a peculiar limp. Gratefully, I went to him.

"Down, Tryst. Sit and rest."

His eyes were fever-wild, but the sardonic smile was immutable. "Thank you, I'll stand."

He grabbed his saddle horn with both hands, shoulders heaving, head sunk unto his arms, and from those depths I heard building laughter.

"Absurdity, Arthur! Tragic, were it not so funny. Lord Trystan of Castle Dore, heart with a thousand songs, harp that knows woman like a hand on her breast. Sing it, O Britons!"

He paused while the helpless mirth shook him. "Nay, was my sword not magic? Was I not so thick-rounded with Saxons I seemed to wear them like a coat, and yet come from it unscathed as from a field of flowers?" He raised his head, the tears of a terrible glee rolling down his cheeks. "And then this horse—"

Whatever the joke, it was too much for Trystan; he fell gasping on my neck. "This insensitive, unpoetic beast, when I am off his lathered back and leaning for rest on my sword, this traitorous *ox*, does he not kick me in the arse and knock me flat before all my men and such of the Saxons who cared to watch?"

His laughter rose to a high-pitched splintering giggle as he collapsed on the ground in a ball, holding his stomach. The spasm passed; Trystan rolled over on his unwounded front, wiping the tears away. "And then by way of comment, he just stands there and makes casual water. Oh, Arthur, I'll write love songs alone. I'm not for epic. I seem cursed with futility."

He started to sputter again, but with a different sound, as if a new emotion sprang up to choke what held it in check. Suddenly his face was a slate wiped clean of all but horror and exhaustion. "Did . . . did you see the water in the shallows? It was pure red."

And then my garrulous Tryst had no more to say, just stared at nothing and shook.

The legion officers reported Cador unharmed, but no one knew his present whereabouts, certainly nowhere about the deserted palace. Some of the raiders had won this far. The halls were littered with broken statuary, looted chests, a few beams blackened by fire. Only a few servants crept about, straightening up. I passed one woman crouched on the stone steps leading to the upper gallery, and asked for Cador.

"Don't know," she mumbled.

"Guenevere?"

She wagged her head vaguely toward a chamber on the gallery. "One of them got her."

A trail of blood led from the door along the gallery. Too weary to deal with any more than the dull fact, I followed the spatters until they ended in an alcove. Not Guenevere, but the body of a young Pict. The knife wound was centered just under his heart. He wore the tattoo marks of a Venicone. I turned and plodded back to the door and pushed it in.

The chamber was a shambles, chairs and sconces overturned, the bedclothes half dragged to the floor. Guenevere huddled on the edge of the bed, ashen, knuckles white around the hilt of the smeared dagger. She might have been there for hours, unmoving but for the trembling of her rigid body.

I sank down heavily beside her. "Give you good morning. I found your visitor."

Guenevere didn't move or look up, just shook. I saw her clear then. Men praised her beauty even in age and never realized it was only her reaction to them, a vital charisma with which she invested her life. Drained of it, she looked vulnerable and almost pathetic. Druith-Belrix gazed with me now and saw her with a wiser heart, no longer a mere prize but a woman apart, a human being who must win or fail on her own strength.

"Did he die?" she spat suddenly. "Did he die? Did he die?"

"Thoroughly."

"Good."

With some difficulty, I coaxed the knife from her tensed fingers and held her tight to stop the trembling. She vibrated against me.

"Father?" she asked finally.

"All right, I think."

"And Peredur?"

"He took a wound, but he'll recover."

"I should go to him." But she didn't move, just dropped her head on my shoulder. "Is it going to be like this always? Are we going to live our lives at bay, waiting for those animals to come again?"

I was too tired to lie, and a woman self-possessed enough to dispatch a man with one knife thrust deserved better. "Probably."

Another long silence. "Well, I shall just have to get used to it, then. Was it bad at the river?"

"Oh, Trystan said it best. Hordes of strangers, no one you'd really want to meet."

Guenevere ventured a hint of smile. "The fool, that does sound like him. Was he hurt?"

"Not mortally," I said, trying to keep her spirits up. "His horse kicked him. Somewhere between the epic and the ode. Now if I may impose on your hospitality—"

The Venicone hadn't laid hands on her wine. There was a full beaker on the hearth. I filled a bowl and made Guenevere sip it carefully, sharing with her myself. Some of the color crept back into her sallow cheeks. Her fear was a palpable thing. It must have been a nightmare hearing the harsh voices, the footsteps running across the hall below, mounting the steps, flinging her door wide. Even now, with our faces close together, I could see the echo of that fear as she touched my cheek.

"He had marks like this," she wondered. "But who gave them to you?"

"An old and very honorable woman."

"Pict?"

"Not really. Prydn. You call them Faerie. She is called *Gern-y-fhain*. That means head of the family or Purest One or even queen if you want. Picts call such women Faerie queens when they might not rule more than fifteen of their folk. Most of the year they have no home but where the cattle end at sundown, and they—"

Over Guenevere's shoulder, Dorelei laughed and little Drost threw up his tiny and imperial arms, summoning the powers of obedient creation to his whim.

"—they live hard lives, perhaps, but they taught me the names of things hard to say in words and all the gentleness I've ever known."

Still her fingertips trailed over my cheek. "That must be it, Arthur. What was missing before. They were wise teachers, I think."

Footsteps came along the gallery, then a stocky, powerful-looking cavalryman in ring-mail filled the doorway.

"Lord Arthur, I have the centurions' tally of lost and wounded."

"Let me have it."

He passed me the vellum roll. At second glance, I recognized the man they called Lancelot. Close up and in daylight the hero of the third squadron was a sober and ordinary young man of less than average height, with a square, unsmiling countenance. Going down the ranks, you wouldn't look at him twice.

The casualty list was glaringly disproportionate. Bedivere and Trystan suffered heavy losses, but Gareth a mere handful. The implication seemed clear: we would not go into battle again until every man could set his feet in those stirrups. The roll made no mention of the first or second squadrons, however.

"I could not find the Princes of Orkney for an accounting," Lancelot explained in his queerly accented Latin. "They were given the Pict captives."

Guenevere said with cold venom, "That's fitting."

Lancelot approached her with a huge deference. "Lady, there are wounded men on the field. Did you not say you would go out to them?"

"Yes, of a certainty." She tried to rise, still spent from her ordeal. Each of us reached to help her. She wiped the blood from her hand on a piece of linen. "What is your name, friend?"

"Lancelot, Lady."

From his deference and avoidance of her direct gaze, I judged him unused to the company of women. "He may have saved your city," I put in. "Ask your father what service he did today."

"Indeed?" As always in the company of men, Guenevere scraped up enough vivacity to charm. "Well, Lancelot, we must remember you. Meanwhile, I'll take what women I can find and go to the field. God be with you, my lords."

I inclined my head and stepped aside for her. Lancelot bowed deeply—a little too deeply. She was a woman, after all, not a vestal virgin. As he gazed after Guenevere, I had another chance to observe this puzzling, capable man. Some of my cohort were simple men-at-arms like Gareth and Bedivere, but none more self-effacing than Lancelot. Still, common soldiers didn't speak Latin better than a bishop; he was obviously raised in the language. And something else: this chilly morning the cloak was thrown across his body and draped over his left shoulder. Unconsciously, he held it in place with his left hand. Very un-British, but quite natural for one accustomed to Roman dress.

"Lancelot, have we met before?"

"I think not, Tribune. You'd been captured when I came to this service."

"From where?"

"Gaul, sir."

Yes, where else? With a soft shock, I knew those plain, sad features as well as Morgana's, had known them since Merlin's first vision. "Your name isn't Lancelot."

He shrugged thick shoulders. "It's what the men call me, the best they can do with Latin."

"You are Ancellius."

"Why, yes," he admitted. "Ancellius Falco. My father was lord of Clermont-Ferrand."

"You fought the Goths with Ecdicius."

"Yes again." He seemed mildly confused. "But how did you—?"

"How do I know?" The laughter sounded harsh. "Because I'm bewitched or a genius or mad. All three, very like. Ambrosius said you'd taken vows."

From his sudden reticence, the subject was clearly distasteful to him. "I lacked the grace to serve God."

Oh, don't you see? Being here, being real, he made my dreams augury and Merlin a prophet. "Why have you come?"

His answer wasn't meant to be ironic. There was no irony in this man. "Why not? There's no more Gaul, no more world really but here. It seemed the thing to do."

That was a long day. An endless mass and requiem for the dead, avoiding the field where Gawain and Agrivaine herded the Pict captives, trying not to hear them. Moving from bed to bed in the infirmary or blanket to blanket by the river among men too shattered to be moved, pausing a minute by Peredur as Guenevere tried to coax soup into him.

"I got through it," he kept saying in a broken, reedy voice. "I got through it. Mark me, Gwen. This Arthur, he's immortal. He has God in the saddle with him."

There were others to kneel beside, men who contended with the vast bafflement of death. They had faith, they prayed, yet this dark thing waiting was of no religion, simply was. Gradually as they drifted away from this shore toward another, bewilderment gave way to serenity. They left life like a room no longer needed, blew out the candle and were gone.

I had led them to this and would lead more to it again, and who in the bleeding world gave me the right? Not humility I felt but a great, leveling reality. I was only a piece on the board myself, riding the mare of fortune and toiling under it as well. Move by move it happened, shaped as Merlin foretold: Morgana, Guenevere, Ancellius. Yet the emerging pattern still made no sense. King of Britain? I, with no ambition beyond going home under the hill?

Liar, Merlin prompted.

Shut up, madman.

No, he persisted. *You see how they need a god. This name, that name, what matter? The Nazarene was only a builder with a genius for men, but their need for a Messiah made him a god.*

And they crucified him.

They needed that, too.

What wonder I got drunk that night?

For want of a better word, you could call my mood self-pity, the natural need of a man who's worked a long, hard time and wants to be petted for it or at least to have his feelings acknowledged. What better friend than Trystan for such a moment? In the palace chamber given to me, with a warming blaze from the firepit, Tryst and I shared a beaker of wine while he plucked soft melodies from his harp, sober and reminiscent, closer to his thoughts than the drink this night. He let me finish most of the beaker.

In his way, Trystan was as much a friend to me as Bedivere. Not as close; you weren't allowed that near to Tryst. He kept you at arm's length with a laugh or a self-deprecating joke that irritated blunter men and drove women to distraction. Self-immolation seems to carry its own glamour, the heightened perfume of a dying flower. Mature women may avoid it, but none are totally impervious. It appeals to the maternal or annoys their sense of order. They saw Trystan going to hell in a peal of hard, bright laughter and longed to save him. He sang them songs, allowed them to feel both saintly and sensual for a night or two before they found how truly unapproachable he was. Most were uncharitable in recalling him, but did so with flattering frequency and detail. If the grapes were sour, they were still plentiful.

His lyrics were not the heroic lies that make giants out of ordinary men. He sang of waking beside Yseult, of her breasts brushing against him in love making, the combat of passion, the satiate quiet afterward; of loving in the wrong place at the wrong time but loving nonetheless. Of lying on her, in her, their motion part of the rolling ship that carried them back to Marcus.

So many versions of their story have been mangled by minstrels, let me briefly state the bare facts. The King of Leinster in Ireland raided south Cornwall and was thoroughly trounced by Marcus Conomori to the tune of disaster and a ruinous ransom. It would have meant years of tribute. Leinster, however, noted that Marcus was a widower and offered a compromise: a portion of the tribute, some of it in cattle, and a perpetual peace to be sealed with Leinster's jewel of a daughter in marriage. Even allowing for his possessive pride as a father, Leinster felt honorbound to admit more men fell in love with Yseult at first sight than did not. And of *course* the tribute would continue to be paid. To put it baldly, Marcus bit. Letters sent, tokens of faith exchanged: done.

With Trystan as emissary, Leinster sailed home. He was minus a few good warriors—among them his nephew Morhalt, who'd been slain in the chance of battle by Trystan himself. Leinster saw no reason to announce the fact, but word got out anyway. Yseult flatly refused to meet the Cornishman who killed her cousin, but the court of Leinster is small. They had to meet, there was time before their voyage while her wedding clothes were made, and Yseult began to find that loyalty had its limits.

Trystan was handsome and kind, certainly well-mannered, he sang beautifully and glittered with the romance of a civilized court that dealt with far, fabulous Rome. Trystan couldn't have been more than twenty at the time, Yseult about sixteen.

I met her myself a few years later. Her father didn't misrepresent. She was heartwrenchingly beautiful, with that whiteness of skin that makes any color in the cheeks seem sudden and hectic, black hair and eyes almost that dark. Loving, too, in a very dependent sort of way, a kind of lost-waif quality that made men yearn to protect her. Yseult gave the impression she couldn't get through dinner without the help of God and the nearest male. She never really lost her looks, though with age they ran to a bovine fleshiness and an expression of placid content that never quite resolved to enthusiasm, the look of a cow not particularly fond of its stall but unable to think of a better place to survive. So much for smug hindsight. At sixteen, she was exquisite, and the alchemy ran through Trystan like plague through a city.

He talked softly now as he plucked reflectively at the harp strings. Trystan didn't speak often of the past; gossips were ample for that. I let him ramble on, lulled by the music and wine, the fire's warmth and my own thoughts.

"The love potion?" Trystan caressed a chord from the strings. "There was one, but we didn't need it. We were in love when the boat sailed."

The Irish believe very strongly in magic, Trystan told me. Not surprising in a people who, until Caesar's time, slaughtered their kings when they showed signs of age. The king was the incarnation of their tribal fortune, a god who must mate with a tribal goddess before crowning, usually a symbolic animal like a white horse. I'd always thought they left it symbolic, but Trystan assured me the ceremony was dramatically literal.

"Rather like a lapdog assaulting a wolfhound, if you can picture it," Trystan said. "The hapless lout must rise to the occasion, but if he can't, there's a potion ready that would make him randy for his own grandmother. As with the horse, so with his queen. If the wedding night's a failure, that augurs poorly for crops and cattle. In Ireland kingship is uphill most of the way."

Yseult's mother knew that Marcus was well beyond the first shout of lusty youth. Trusting the brute power of the wedding potion, she sent along a phial of it.

"The boat was our world for the precious few days we had," Trystan remembered. "We talked as much as we made love, or rather I talked and she listened. Until she came, I didn't know how much sharing was locked up in me. I nattered her blue, but she loved sitting at my knee, drinking in the life I laid before her. It must have seemed very impressive to a girl never more than a day's ride from home.''

Trystan grinned ruefully. "I told her of my father's castle, that impoverished little hill-fort with its stockade and hall. In times of trouble, every cowherd and his kine had to squeeze in with us. But it sounded very grand to Yseult. She listened by the hour while I talked of everything but tomorrow. We had a few days, then Marcus met the boat and . . . took her.''

Trystan drew a brief, sweet phrase from the harp. "But I'd touched someone and, because of it, I was changed for all time. It's not our innocence we lose in loving, only our ignorance.''

The wine worked swiftly on my empty stomach, but I welcomed and surrendered to it. This was needed, this exchange with another human being. And on this night more than one ghost hovered in the shadows beyond the firepit.

There's child in me, Belrix.

Go away, I'm tired. I don't want the pain of you now.

Still, being part of reality, how could she go away? She walked the world as I did, grew big with the reality, riding the hills after the *fhain* herds. The wealth would form in her through this autumn, poise to leap into life through long nights by the crannog fire and be born near Brigid-feast early in February, in the dark months when *fhain* and cattle alike nestled under the hill.

Ghosts walked my mind, ghost-senses mixed with the smoke from the fire, brown skin wrapped in green leaves on Midsummer night.

Thee's gone from me.

All of it was coming true: move by move. Merlin placed them on the board. Morgana, Guenevere, now Lancelot. Pawn, queen, knight and—king? The thought was sudden and cold as it was honest. I'd never go back to Morgana. Plan, dream, promise, delude myself, what difference? Merlin's bit was in my mouth, Merlin who was no more than myself, spurring me toward tomorrow. Twist as I might to look back, I could only run on.

No, you promised her.

Trystan lit one candle from another. "Gloomy in here. ' 'Tis better to light one candle than curse the dark.' ''

My tolerance for truism was thin as his. "Who mined *that* gem?''

"I'd rather not know," Trystan decided archly. "Someone

with a razor gift for platitude. What is it about homilies makes you want to retch? I mean, I'll light their silly candle, but someone's damn well going to hear about the dark.''

He was in good form, worthy of my bleary toast. "Well said, bard.''

"Arthur, I believe you're drunk.''

"A little. Aren't you?''

"Not tonight,'' Trystan answered quietly, taking up his harp. "I'm a perishing bore drunk. No company at all, no wit, just curse, drink and cry. No, tonight I want to talk. I need it. Many more days like this, I may not get the chance.''

He looked away into the fire and struck an eerie, dissonant chord.

"So we came home to Castle Dore. Uncle Marcus was not required to wrestle with a mare, but there was the royal consummation with a picked group of nobles on watch outside the wedding chamber. I never drank much before that night, but thank the gods we were allowed it. Marcus came out from time to time, flushed, sweaty, calling for wine and sometimes food. He'd drunk the potion and, on his faith, Yseult's mother was Cupid's own sorceress. Nay, he felt twenty again. Bring on all the maidens in Cornwall, he'd stomach for the lot.

"There were the usual jokes. I pretended to laugh, but all I could see was Yseult in that big bed, the royal pawn in Leinster's shabby gambit: lose a war, win it back with a wedding. Then Marcus would sigh with a vast regret as if to say 'duty calls,' pretend to gird up his loins, and swagger back into the wedding chamber.''

A little foggy myself now, I could still see how the truth of Trystan shone through his brittle, supercilious mask. He looked very vulnerable in the firelight.

"There was an hourglass on the table before me while we watched. Getting very drunk, it seemed not sand but my insides were running down the glass. My face hurt from smiling when I wanted to shriek at all of them *shut up*, wanted to break down that filthy door and—''

Trystan reached for his cup but took only a small sip. "No, I'm not going to get drunk tonight. She put up with it better than I. Women can do that, they're—what are they that we're not?''

I hiccuped. "Realists?''

His turn to salute me with raised cup. "Well put. She endured. We met when we could, but it was painful to see her leave my bed for his. To come to mine from his. To see her torn apart like those captives today, because Marcus really cared for her, too. Sometimes I wondered who suffered most: he learning later all at once or me knowing all the time, or Yseult in the middle. We began to quarrel, began to learn how far across a bed it can be. A battlefield. I hated myself and her and Marcus, drank to dull the hatred and hated all the more. And she paid. I gutted her because I couldn't live with it, because she was someone I could make suffer for my suffering.''

His voice broke suddenly: "I mean, she's not that strong. She can't stand alone. She needs a place to be safe.''

Trystan came to sit by me, refilling my cup. "Marcus caught us together. Perhaps I wanted him to. You see the ax poised and long for it to make an end. I couldn't stay at Castle Dore. Ambrosius was my savior, recruiting court idlers for his new *alae*. That's how I came to your friendship, you cleansing comet of a man.''

I was rather befogged now, more than the wine could warrant, ears ringing queerly. "Firelord . . .''

"My men say you have a destiny. Perhaps I'm part of it. I feel that ax hasn't fallen yet for either of us.''

Shivering suddenly. "Cold, Tryst. I'm cold.''

"Come by the fire.'' He took my arm to help me up. "I believe my comet has had enough.''

A figure loomed out of the darkness beyond the fire. I squinted at it. "Who's 'at?''

"Prince Gawain,'' said the mountainous shadow. "I must speak with you.''

"Not now,'' I slurred. "Let it wait.''

"Cannot wait.'' The great bulk of Gawain came into the light, strangely tentative. "Please.''

That was an odd word from Gawain. "Well?''

"It's about tomorrow.''

"He means your duel,'' Trystan prompted cordially. "The one you pinched from me.''

Gawain's presence sickened me for his granite arrogance, his treatment of captives, but none of this could account for the mindless, murderous anger his nearness inflamed. He and his brother were of one cloth, and only the Prydn word could name it. Tallfolk.

"Well, Prince? Has your brother sent you with an apology?''

As well ask if he'd grown wings since breakfast. "Apologize, hell! I came because he will not, cannot apologize, and—''

Gawain labored under the vast burden of humility for the sake of love. "He can't fight your way."

The strange anger still mounted in me. "The Pict way? Why not, the son of a bitch called me one."

Gawain couldn't afford to heat now; something else was too important. "Tribune, you may have noticed his leg. You don't know how he hates it, how it makes him feel less than a man. Let it be lance or sword, anything else, but don't shame my brother like this. He won't go barefoot. He'll die first."

"Unless you persuade him to withdraw. I think you've already tried."

"I have," Gawain admitted, not without difficulty. "Done everything I could. I know Agrivaine's not easy. His temper's a laid tinder fire, all it needs is a spark. He's always been that way."

"Got to learn, then."

The fog thickened around my senses, making me an island of rage in a mist. I could tell Gawain would rather have his teeth pulled one by one than ask anything of me. What I was doing was not the way, but I couldn't stop.

"Lord Arthur, I'm not a man to be asking, much less begging. But I beg you. He's not afraid, but leave him his dignity. His pride as a prince of Orkney."

Aye, tallfolk. Like the woman who had Morgana driven from the village with sticks when she only wanted to comfort a child. Like the one who tried to cheat Cradda of her ewe, or the Votadini farmer at the well who was a decent man, a humane man so long as certain lies were perpetuated, certain lines left uncrossed. They must be left their pride, someone to feel better than.

"You and your brother are not men to talk of dignity, Gawain. Life I'll leave him, but that *stiff back will bend*."

Was that whipcrack my own voice, full of demonic energy, barely human?

"You call that leaving him life?" Gawain asked. "Making him show his weakness to the world? Is he not a fine soldier? Was't not himself saw Cerdic's plan in time to stop it? You are cruel."

"Well, that's news." I controlled my thickening tongue with an effort, dimly aware of the buzzing in my ears. "This afternoon while a priest warbled a hymn of gratitude, you personally cut the heart out of a man as an offering to Christ—and you talk of leaving dignity? Tied men between horses and pulled them apart,

and call me cruel? Sent the rest home without tongues or their
eyes burned out, and *I am cruel?* If I were half that, I'd deal
with you like the Rome you sneer at, line the road from here to
the Wall with crosses and hang an Orkney lord from every one
as a lesson to your petty arrogance. *Damn you both, there isn't
time for that anymore. It doesn't happen that way!*"

Someone tried to steady my drunken career around the fire,
someone who looked like Tryst, but dim, washed out by the
mad, white glare in my brain. "Easy, Arthur."

But the anger was a terrible engine. "Be cruel, a says. Dost
think Melga felt no pain? Any one of my brothers be better men
than thee. Nectan, Urgus, Cunedag—better!" I staggered and
wove. "Good God! To be king over such as you."

I lunged for Gawain, but Trystan held me back. "King, is it?
What the hell are you—?"

"Get away from me!"

But Tryst gripped tighter. "For the love of reason, man.
What's the matter with you? They're only a buggering lot of
Picts."

For what happened then, magic or madness, I have no explanation. With a roar, I struck blindly at Gawain. The thrust of the
blow didn't end but went on and out, dragging me after it
through the white glare to come crashing down on my knees.

In sudden silence the glare receded to definable colors. The
room, Trystan and Gawain were gone.

I crouched at the summit of a bare hill near a heap of heavy
stones from which protruded the heavy hilt of a longsword. A
chain ran from the depths of the stone pile to coil about my
waist, locking me to it.

Below me on the plain, a vast multitude waited, expectant.
While I looked, they raised their arms in salute. The hails from a
million throats racketed between ground and sky.

A-ve! A-ve!

"Merlin, are you there? Help me."

But there was no Merlin, only myself and the waiting throng.
Then Morgana sprinted out of the press, running up the hill
toward me.

"Belrix, come home."

I tore at the chain, lunged this way and that with furious
strength, but it held tight.

Morgana called: "Take thy sword and free us!"

No strength of my own would drag the chain from its moor-
ing. Desperate, I clutched the sword hilt—

A-ve!

—raised it and brought it down on the links. They parted like butter, and I ran toward Morgana's outstretched arms, caught her up, swept her high off the ground.

"See? Have found thee again!" I laughed with joy. "And will never leave now."

"Forever," she whispered against my cheek. "Would see thy child-wealth, thy son?"

"Yes, show him to me, Morgana."

She held me tight, impossibly tight. "A waits for thee," Morgana whispered in a harsher, deeper voice.

Then I felt the cold shock as the knife went into me and, falling away from the arms that held me hard, saw they were not Morgana's at all. A stranger poised over me, knife ready to strike again. Stranger, yet not so alien I couldn't recognize the set of the eyes. We made this killing machine, she and I. He was us.

"Morgana!"

The light failed and the shadows crowded back, and I was dying from the knife he raised again. "Why, boy? You're all we ever wanted."

"You're all I ever wanted," he said. "Come hold your wealth."

Hard to see him now, the light fled so fast. "We made you together. Why do you kill me?"

"Because you killed us."

He hurled himself on me, and the last of the light gleamed on the bronze knife before he drove it home, on the rings of her fingers as she framed my face in them.

"Arthur."

"You're all I ever wanted . . ."

"*Arthur.*"

"Why do you kill me?"

"Arthur, look at me."

I was on my couch. Guenevere knelt over me in her nightrobe as the world rushed back to imprison me again. I blinked stupidly up at her, feeling her cool hands on my face and neck. My jaw throbbed. Someone had hit me very hard.

". . . Where's Tryst?"

Guenevere laughed softly. "Gone to bed. He said you were mad drunk and raving. Gawain had to bless you with his good right hand."

"That he did. And you came?"

"I wanted to come all day. This morning when I was so pitiful and frightened—and ugly, God knows—you were so gentle, as if you'd come from church and not a battle.'' Guenevere brushed her cheek against mine. ''You deserve to go a little mad. But when you talked of the Faerie and what they taught you—there was a woman, yes?''

''All I ever wanted . . .''

Guenevere put a finger over my lips. ''All *I* ever wanted. Perhaps. Today I'm not sure of anything, whether I want you or just not to sleep alone in the bed where I almost died.'' Her mouth against mine was what I imagined it would be: searching, cool, not everything given yet, as if she were honestly thinking about it.

My body still burned with phantom pain where the dream knife had stabbed, still tensed for the coming death stroke, part child again, wary against the dark that held nothing but fear and strangers. I reached for Morgana and Guenevere all in one hope, life reaching for life on a death-ridden day. Reached for Gwen to join with her and live. She came to me in perhaps the same simple need. I unlaced the front of her nightrobe and freed her breasts, heard her slight shudder-breath as I ran my lips and tongue over the curve and the nipple.

Who loved, joined with, surrendered to whom? Clasped together, mirror to mirror, we sent reflections into infinity, though the faces blurred and changed. One was Morgana's, and there must have been others for Guenevere over my shoulder. Part of what we are is whom we've loved, and we go to each new wedding bed with all our lovers in our eyes.

Agrivaine withdrew his challenge, choking on that less than a revelation of his infirmity. Blind with shame, he was close to pulling his squadron off the Wall and going home. Since he wouldn't speak to me at all, I was grateful when Guenevere offered a solution.

''Arthur, didn't you say he deserved praise for guessing Cerdic's plan? Give it to him, heap it on him. One of those gold laurels would be very nice.''

Dear Gwen, she thought of the laurel as casually as a wedding gift. No use pointing out how rare they were or that Bedivere and I had not even received our own.

''And besides,'' I argued, ''only Ambrosius can give the laurel.''

Mere detail to Guenevere. ''Well, he's coming, and you're his darling, and you could recommend it. Then one could give out to

Agrivaine that you *especially* wanted him commended for valor. Frankly the idea does you credit, Arthur.''

Light began to break. She wasn't Cador's child for nothing. And just who would carry the news to seething Agrivaine?

"Why, myself, silly! We'll award it with all the pomp and God knows what—how can it fail? If Agrivaine receives the laurel from my own hand, who dares slur his courage? Thus, you keep a hundred men at your side.''

She looked very much like her father then, adding lightly, "I was going to make a laurel for you, but you'd never wear it.''

"Of course I would.''

"Oh, you would not.'' She wrinkled her nose against mine. "You're such an old scruffy. You've gone quite tatty since you came from the south to disorder my life. Dear God, how you glittered the day I first saw you, shined and proper and standing so stiff you actually teetered. Now,'' arms coiling about me, a gentle serpent offering her apple, "what about Agrivaine?''

The scheme worked. At least it kept Agrivaine from going home in a huff. He never forgave me, but wore his gold laurel on every possible occasion thereafter.

"A shrewd woman,'' Bedivere commented, "but I have the feeling you've been somewhat managed, Artos.''

Perhaps, but it was this quality that earned Guenevere her title when we wore the crowns of Britain. Some kings have queens, others mere wives. Mark's Yseult looked decorative on a royal progress, but she knew nothing of Britons and cared less. Outside of cattle tribute, the intricacies of royal finance eluded her. Diplomacy, to Yseult, was the bedroom and the ax.

Guenevere was raised on Latin. Its precision ordered her thoughts. She had her father's undeniable gift for government, which Cador once defined as the gentle art of getting as much as you can for as little as you can pay and escaping without violence.

"Anyone can steal,'' he maintained. "But to be loved for it takes art.''

Guenevere possessed the art. When I built a seat of power, she was the silken cord that bound the vital north to me. She knew command because she knew males. Princes might chafe under my yoke, but they were always salved by Guenevere's frank appreciation and graceful praise. Not surprising that she quite often sensed better than myself which men could be trusted and which not.

Of our troubles later, some wise heads have wondered if we

ever really loved each other. People like to think in those terms. Blacks and whites are simple, but we were never simple people.

A star rises and burns bright, and perhaps two stars, drawn close, will spin about each other and give light as one so that you forget they're separate. Perhaps for a time the stars forget, too . . .

The hell with it: say *love* if you wish. We wouldn't argue.

In love then, Cador acceding to what he considered his daughter's passing fancy. A princess was privileged after all, though the question of marriage was beyond the pale. Good *God*, not Arthur Pendragon. His brother Caius, perhaps: crowned, close to the emperor. Or Gawain or even Geraint. The one might be crude and the other colorfully unbalanced, but they would both be kings someday, potential allies by marriage. But a mere soldier, emperor's pet or no, a landless lord-by-courtesy? Thank you, but no.

As usual, no one reckoned on high-vaulting Ambrosius, or that he would lose his last battle in the south that winter, or how little time our weary master had to live.

Or how wisely and well he built his house to last.

When princes struggle for power, it doesn't matter at all to the peasant, to the Morganas and Nectans and Craddas whose lives don't change a whit. But when Ambrosius unleashed my men to range to the four winds in Britain's defense, we became a symbol to the farmers of the isolated villages, who knew very little of princes or powers beyond the next hill. Speed put us everywhere, made us known to everyone. Already the army couriers, the bards of the west, the travelers from north to south were spreading the tale of Cerdic's defeat at Eburacum—"Hundreds of horsemen with lances and longswords, and at their head a man called Arthur"—through the far corners of Britain. The common folk of the Catuvellauni, the Coritani, the Silures might not know a prince from a partridge outside of their own, but they remembered the faces and names of men who could dash across the width of Britain to protect them.

They remembered Bedivere and Lancelot, Gareth, Gawain, Trystan and the rather busy young man who led them. Who cared where we came from? We were there, a bright new candle against the dark.

And they began to say, "Send us Arthur."

To Wear the Crown

Ambrosius' terse dispatches told us his visit to Eburacum that winter would be one of grave importance. His messenger also brought letters from Kay and my stepmother.

> *The emperor's train is short these days. The Council turn from him and call for a new king, one who can win for us.*

In some vault of memory, the dust of Vortigern stirred and cackled.

> *The situation is bad here, choked with refugees from Verulamium and the midlands. My chiefs complain daily . . . Mother is fine and asks of you whenever couriers stop. It's been so long . . .*

Flavia's letter hummed and fluttered with the busy trivia of our home on the Severn: it was necessary to manumit some of the older slaves. Replacements, when they could be found at all, were layabouts and slatterns who refused to speak Latin. Such used to know their place, she didn't know what the world was coming to. Please tell Bedivere a certain female relation wondered when her fair cousin would come home.

> *and yourself as well, though you have never gone from our hearts. Kay said your wounds at Neth were slight, and that relieved me much. Still, you have the*

*breadth and height for campaigning, though it defeats
me where you got them. Uther was hardly tall and your
mother Ygerna never larger than a child . . .*

Odd. This was the first time anyone had ever described Ygerna
to me beyond her name. Flavia never mentioned knowing her
before, and only through gossip had I learned she was Ambrosius'
niece.

"Ask him when he comes," Bedivere advised. "Now read
again that dear bit about my cousin Myfanwy."

Suddenly we both realized how long ago it was that two very
young men rode away from Severn.

Bedivere said with a dying fall, "When will we go home,
Artos?"

He married his cousin Myfanwy, but home for me was a
harder place to find.

The streets of Eburacum were already lined with soldiers and
citizens when the emperor's *bucinas* sounded beyond the gates.
Watching from the ramparts, Bedivere and I saw that our lord
rode in a litter.

"Then it was a bad wound he took," Bedivere murmured.
"You'd nigh have to kill Ambrosius to put him on a cart like
that."

Ahead of the procession rode the royal ensigns with their
leopard headdresses and the imperial eagles flaring on their
standards over the bronze-graven SPQR. Men have called
Ambrosius the last of the Romans. Certainly that was the last
time I ever saw the eagles carried in state.

When Ambrosius entered the city, I waited in the cold with
Cador, Guenevere and the other officers of high rank. Fur-cloaked
Gwen held a welcoming cup of hot wine for our emperor, and all
around the marketplace the people of Eburacum strained to see
him from behind the guard of honor. On two sides of the square,
my third and fifth squadrons dipped their lances on command.
The rest of the cohort was long departed for the Wall. This small
force had stayed behind, slated for the coastal defense Cador
needed.

We had no idea that Ambrosius came to change it all and my
life as well.

When his slaves set down the litter, we wondered why no one

helped him out, not knowing that proud man forbade it. I ran down the palace steps to kneel before Ambrosius.

My breath caught at sight of him.

Before me lay an aging, sick remnant, the vitality gone out of him like juice squeezed from a pear, the face gray paste, eyes sunken into puffy pouches of flesh. Always spare, he was now frail. Between the folds of his heavy cloak, the gold-bordered purple of his garment was stained where his wound bled through its bandages.

My eyes stung with tears. My lord was dying.

"Ave, Imperator."

"We hear what service you did Eburacum. Our thanks." His voice was dry and lacking the old resonance. "Damned young scamp, you look like a peddler. Where's your ceremonials?"

"I'm afraid—" Painful to look at him. "I'm afraid I have none, sir."

"Oh, I see. And pity we have no more to send you. Just a moment while I climb down—no, don't help me, damn it, I'm not crippled."

Still I offered my arm. "Will my lord not honor me?"

"Go to hell, Artorius. I'm not going to be lifted out of this thing like a bride." Then in a lower voice: "Cador's been waiting for me to cash in like all the rest of 'em. I think he's going to have his wish."

Ambrosius gathered his strength for the exertion, chuckling maliciously. "But not today."

He alighted unhelped, but I saw the cost in the clenched jaw and trembling, wasted limbs. He stood emaciated but erect, drawing the cloak over his stained garment, hand raised in imperial invitation.

"Come down, Prince. And bring your lovely daughter with her welcome cup."

The emperor's slave-taster approached to intercept the cup. Ambrosius revived this ancient office when one of the (late) Coritani chiefs tried to assassinate him at dinner. Now, as the prince approached with gracious smile of state and open arms, Ambrosius mused softly to me: "Cador doesn't need poison. That oily bastard could charm you to death."

Guenevere's scheme worked. Agrivaine considered it quite his own hour when, before the high blood of the north, his commendation was read out by Cador's minister and sealed by Ambrosius. When Agrivaine knelt to receive the honor, Guenevere came forward with the new-made laurel—"The last gold leaf I could find. Dear mother, forgive me"—and held it high for all to see before setting it on Agrivaine's dark head as the cheer went up.

"Hail Agrivaine!"

I caught his vindictive eye and bowed formally to show my complete approval.

Bedivere nudged me. "Are my eyes going, or did Guenevere wink at you?"

"Wink? Oh, no."

Smoothly done, Gwen.

"Let all give ear!"

Cador's portly little minister rapped his staff on the dais. "Princes and magistrates of the Parisi and Brigantes, lords, ladies. Give ear to Ambrosius Aurelianus, Emperor of Britain."

The hall grew quiet, yet even the smothered rustle of garments and breath made it hard to hear the ailing, feeble voice.

He spoke of his defeat in the south and the inadequacy of fixed legions to counter a seaborne enemy like the Saxon. Beyond that he reminded us that spring would see them pushing west again toward Severn. The resistance so well begun and so brilliantly developed must move even further, must carry the war home to the enemy. Only a mobile force could do that. Therefore, with allowance for sufficient horse to maintain the Wall of Hadrian, and with the concurrence of Prince Cador—

Ambrosius held up the cohort's *notitia*, our roll of muster. Before our eyes he tore the parchment in two. Bedivere and I exchanged a dumbfounded look. What in the name of—?

"We detach from Eburacum the *alae* heretofore known as the Sixth and declare it henceforth a voluntary fealty of man to his lord by the hereditary custom of Britain. Call Artorius Pendragon."

The minister whacked down hard with his staff. "Artorius Pendragon, stand forth!"

I shouldered through the crowd to stand before my king, not knowing at all what would come next. As of now, we weren't a cohort or anything at all but a disparate mob bound by no law or oath. Any one of us could pack up and go home.

Ambrosius held out his hands. "Give me your sword, Artorius."

I laid the longsword across his callused palms.

"We declare your legionary rank and that of your former centurions null and of no force, and further declare that no monies may be claimed by virtue of *notitia*."

A Roman precaution for you. We never received so much as a gold *solidus* on the Wall. Our own princes supported us.

"Nor any suit of legion law pressed against you under those same voided articles. Artorius," my emperor said, "will you swear by the custom of your fathers to be my man?"

His cheeks glistened with perspiration, cold as it was in the great hall. Just speaking cost him strength.

"Imperator, I will."

The custom of my fathers eluded me for an embarrassed moment, then I remembered the old Dobunni chiefs renewing their allegiance to Uther, and the simple words by which they bound themselves to him. A plain oath for illiterate men, but deeply sworn with life as forfeit in the breach. I knelt, touching the top of my head and the sole of my shoe.

"I swear on life and the gods of my fathers that, head and foot and all between, I am your man, to call you lord, live by your laws and look only to you for increase."

"So do I swear," Ambrosius gave the response, "to be your faithful lord before this company and by the gods"—he caught himself and went on—"before God and His Holy Church. And by this oath, I create you *Comes Brittaniarum*."

I gaped up at him, forgetting to breathe.

He held out my sword. When I received it, Ambrosius took a simple bronze circlet from the couch beside him. While I knelt, still numb, Ambrosius placed the circlet on my head.

"Rise, Arthur, Count of Britain."

The cheer began with Bedivere and Trystan, but swelled with the voices of all my *alae*:

"*Hail Arthur, Count of Britain!*"

Quick impressions in my confusion: Cador's unreadable face as he applauded politely. Bedivere pounding me on the back, the knot of my men around me, and Guenevere leaving her chair to kneel and kiss my hand. I raised her up.

"My God, Gwen," I stammered foolishly. "Look what they've gone and done."

Coming from the baths, I looked for one of my men to carry a message and spied Lancelot, usually somewhere near the palace these days. Unlike some of my men who took advantage of leisure to primp, Lancelot wore his old brown robe and black cloak like a homeless monk.

"Lancelot, please take a message to the palace."

He was more than willing. "Of course, my lord."

In some haste I jumbled the instructions. "Ambrosius sent for me and I'm already late, won't be able to dine till later."

His brow furrowed. "This to Cador, sir?"

"No, sorry I'm in such a rush. To Guenevere, we're dining alone."

Lancelot just blinked at me. "The lady, you say?"

"Yes. Now head off, I'm late."

Without a word of good-bye, this normally courteous man turned and plodded through the dirty snow toward the palace. Closed in as Trystan, but without Tryst's laughter.

Cador had prepared an opulent house for Ambrosius, though I doubt the emperor even noticed the luxury. A stool, a table, cot and dry roof would content this man who slept most of his life in a tent.

Passed in by Ursus Strabo, tribune of the imperial staff, I found Ambrosius at work as usual. By now one was used to the ever-present blood spot where it soaked daily through his bandages. The wound would not close and the infection gained. Ambrosius chose to ignore it; like the other ordinaries of daily life, it made way for work or did not exist. Amid a profusion of papers on his table, the remains of a frugal meal grew cold.

"Artorius, come in. Sit here by me. You look a little fresher than the day I came. Such a robe, too! From Caius?"

"From Lady Guenevere, sir. A gift."

"Ah yes," Ambrosius remarked. "An ingratiating family."

"I'm very glad to see you better, sir. Have you talked to Lancelot? I mean Ancellius?"

"Yes, he came yesterday. A modest man, I must say, but he knows cavalry. That ring-mail's a beauty. Will you adopt it?"

"If Kay can make it, yes."

"As for my health," Ambrosius made a sour face, "I seem to have mislaid it. Damn nuisance, up one day, down the next."

"Your physicians?"

"Will not lie to me. I wish they would now and then." He drew toward us a vellum map of the southwest and middle provinces of Britain. "Now let's to work. You're going to clear the midlands this summer. Since you're more than an officer now, I wanted to acquaint you with the policy."

All very well, he said, for *alae* to dash here and there heading off piecemeal raids. But each spring more fortified Saxon farms dotted the midland downs, and the Catuvellauni refugees were becoming a problem for western princes like Kay.

Ambrosius nibbled absently at a scrap from his supper. "This Saxon peasant is quite different from your own. When he says *mine,* he means it. He carves out a holding, the reeves reckon his worth to the penny, and it's his by law. If you were his lord, you couldn't enter his house without permission."

Ambrosius' fingers slid over the map, familiar with every feature and strategic ramification. "But the midlands are the key to Britain, Artorius. Specifically here on Mount Badon." His stylus pricked the map. "A cavalry force on this hill controls the midlands and the west, the whole game in fact. You agree?"

By the map, no other logic held. On Badon I could defend the west and be within three days of any point in the midlands. A Saxon on that hill could corner the southwest and the heart of the rich Severn lands. My own home. Kay and Flavia.

Ambrosius poured fruit wine for both of us. He drank in silence for a few moments, regarding me thoughtfully.

"You'll win, of course. There won't be any organized resistance, certainly no cavalry. By midsummer, the Catuvellauni will be able to go home. And they'll go with every hope of staying this time."

I caught his emphasis on *will.* "Yes, sir. I'll clear as much as I can, pack the women and children back east—"

"You'll pack nothing," Ambrosius corrected deliberately. "You'll leave them where they lie."

Surely I misunderstood him. "Women and children?"

Ambrosius looked away. "Some things have to be, Artorius. Just do it and don't dwell on it."

He made himself clear. There was nothing to say.

"The Catuvellauni are our buffer in the midlands like Cador here. But not if they're hiding in Caerleon. They'll go home this summer over a highway of bones. Big ones and little ones to tell those thick-skulled Saxon princes that their land-grabbing days are over. You'll root them out, burn them out, fight when you can and slaughter when you have to, but at the end you'll empty the midlands. Do you understand?"

Only too well. A dirty, dishonorable job with no songs or flags flying, and none of us would sleep very well at the end.

"Sir, I . . ."

The cup paused halfway to Ambrosius' colorless lips. "Eh?"

"I don't know if I can. It's not a question of disobedience, but—"

"But you're not Herod to slaughter the innocents?"

"No, Imperator."

"Oh, lad." Ambrosius rested his head on his hands. "You have the instinct to be noble and the ambition to be great. You won't be both together, not bloody likely."

His head came up suddenly. "Bedivere's more than your captain, he's your friend. Trystan, Gareth, you care for these men, don't you?"

"Yes sir."

"Then remember this summer that every curly little head you spare now will be back to fight them later or breeding more for their sons to fight. More agony. Ultimately, how many Britons will you kill with your misplaced mercy? You've read logic, Aristotle. Can you refute me?"

"No, my lord, but—"

"Artorius. There are no buts." The emperor spread another map before me, showing all Britain. He leaned over the chart, visibly tiring, his breathing more difficult. "And if these reasons aren't enough, here's another. You know how my very loyal princes are wondering who'll succeed me. And who is there?"

Who indeed among the parochial princes of Britain? As for Merlin, he was my own problem.

"Not that we lack hopefuls," Ambrosius went on acerbically. "We're crawling with royalty. But which of them can see beyond his own province?"

He looped circles in the air over the map with his stylus. "Marcus Conomori? Interested in the south coast and sea trade, doesn't give a damn about anything else. Caradoc of Dyfneint? If not for his son Geraint, he wouldn't know there was a Britain beyond his beaches and cliffs. Just keep the raiders off his coast, thank you. The west, the Silures and Ordovici? I'm not even sure who rules them now. They don't pay taxes unless I go in after them."

Another loop over Eburacum. "Our gracious Cador, watchdog of the north, smartest of the lot. Has Church support, and he knows how much we need him. He's the bung in the barrel; pull him out, there's nothing to stop the Picts. But he puts too much trust in his ability to make two and two come out five. He's not happy losing his *alae*. If that old fox turns north for an alliance, Britain's that much weaker."

He rooted among the papers and handed me a rough-draft note in his own hand. "But we are reminded there's at least one homeless count with no particular tribal loyalty. Out of Cornwall by Severn, with perhaps a few other strains thrown in. You *are* Britain right now, Artorius: schooled in my thinking, at the head of the fastest, most powerful force from Orkney to Castle Dore. Whoever reaches for the crown will ask: does Pendragon back me? Your name will be among those considered. These articles declare you as my own choice for the crown."

So there it was, the last move on Merlin's board. Pawn to the eighth square. Miracle accomplished not through dream or magic but simple step by step. Whatever we make of life, it happens that way.

Ambrosius put his hand to his side, breathing heavily. "Give me your arm, boy."

I helped him down onto his couch.

"Damn bother," he fretted. "Feel good for an hour, then— hell, it couldn't be quick. That's asking too much. One more cup and we'll say good night."

I filled our cups, trying to think clearly. My nomination was no real surprise, but the sudden nearness and *reality* of it crowded the doubts and questions over me. "Sir, do you think . . ."

Ambrosius cocked his head at me. "Well?"

"Choosing me over royal princes. They'll say you want to found a dynasty."

Ambrosius snorted in disgust. "Dynasty hell! If I wanted that, I could recall my son from Rome. Fat chance, he wouldn't have this foggy barnyard as a gift." Ambrosius coughed, grimacing with the pain it caused him. "Dynasty, my—I'm about as royal as the cook's cat. When I was chosen to replace Vortigern, you know what I thought? Why me? Simple. Power is its own argument, Artorius."

"Wasn't my mother your niece?"

Ambrosius took his time answering, sipped at his wine, the cords on his wasted neck moving as he swallowed. Unusual; he was always so direct.

"I suppose she was."

"Suppose?"

"My sister Julia lost three children before Ygerna. Couldn't carry them past the third month. Didn't Uther tell you all this?"

"Nothing beyond her name."

"Gorlawse wouldn't acknowledge Vortigern's power, so Uther went into Cornwall to enforce it. He also met Gorlawse's wife. When the smoke cleared, Gorlawse was a dead rebel and Ygerna was pregnant. She died bearing you. Uther took you home."

"I see."

"I hope you do, Artorius. It was a long time ago. Flavia's a loving woman, but what's hers is hers. It happens."

The unusual gentleness in his tone prompted me to ask, "What was she like?"

"Ygerna? Oh, tiny, quick, full of wild whims and humors. And temper! Took a knife to a servant once. Had to be thrashed like a boy. I'd say there's a great deal of Ygerna in you." Ambrosius studied me closely. "There's a saying that they always know . . ."

"Who, sir?"

Ambrosius sighed and sank back on the couch. "Oh hell, just old wives' tales. And tenacious as women are, they'll never give a straight version of anything. There's letters of Julia's packed away. I'll send them on sometime. But I'm spun out now, got to rest. Leave me for now."

He lay back and closed his eyes. I rose quietly and went to the door, but before I could open it, Ambrosius called me again.

"Count?"

"My lord?"

His eyes were still closed. "Just one word on the things a king must do. When I saved the Demetae from Irish raiders, they called me Caesar, offered me undying loyalty and a few of their daughters. When I hanged their leaders for rebellion, they called me butcher and anti-Christ."

He paused, breathing hard.

"Don't ever expect them to love you."

Guenevere had no supper laid for me in her chamber. She was in her nightrobe, hair loose about her shoulders, agitated and short.

"You can't stay with me tonight," she said. "There'll be a guard on my door any moment."

"A guard? Why?"

"To keep you out, Arthur." She hugged herself, shivering. "I'm cold. Put another log on the fire."

I drew Guenevere down to the hearth's warmth. "What's happened?"

She took the hot wine I offered and drank deep. The cup trembled in her hand. "No more than we might expect. God alone knows who'll wear the crown when Ambrosius dies. And since he's graciously presented your *alae* to Britain at large, we need a stronger alliance with the north. Orkney *and* the Picts. Ambassadors have already left.''

Then the guards on her door meant only one thing. It was comic; Cador was so devious, he was predictable. I couldn't help laughing.

Guenevere failed to see the humor. "You're amused?''

"A marriage with Brude?''

Her smile was thin and hard. ''That's not how it's done. The hint of a marriage, the possibility, at least until the issue of the crown is settled.''

"Brude! Good Jesus, that doddering, unsanitary old man.''

"Who no doubt loves his horses more than me, but that's rather beside the point.'' Guenevere's head slumped on my shoulder. Every line of her body sagged with exhaustion. ''Cador didn't give a royal damn about you and me before. I can have any man I want. But now I'm required, and I can't fault father's thinking. Brude is a simple man. We give him a simple picture. Our ambassadors will sing my virtues and, above all, my virginity.''

To laugh or curse? It would be funny if it weren't so damned calculated and obvious. ''A hundred years of war and suddenly an olive branch? Brude's not an imbecile.''

"That's part of the game,'' Guenevere said as if to a child. ''If the marriage is profitable to him, he'll be forgetful.''

"So now I'm an inconvenience.''

"Never that.'' Guenevere nuzzled her lips into the hollow of my throat. ''My feelings are private, but my virtue's gone public. Oh, Arthur, I'm so *damned* tired. I just want to sleep.''

"Gwen, listen to me.''

She twisted weakly in my arms. ''I've listened so much tonight. Father, his ministers, then father again. Good God, let me go to bed.''

"Listen to me. You care.''

"About you? Too much.''

"About people.'' I held her close with my mouth against her hair. ''You're too good to be thrown away while Cador plays games for the crown. You know how to rule because you know why. You care.''

"Oh, I care.'' Her voice husked with fatigue. ''Still, at mass today when Anscopius spoke of Christ in the temple, I felt like one of the moneylenders.''

"Kiss me, Gwen.''

"I want to sleep.''

"Damn it, I said—" I kissed her hard. She held on to me, desperate.

"Father's right, we need this. It's be friendly or helpless. But I feel so shabby."

"Gwen, what if I were king?"

She laughed soundlessly against my chest. "You imagine I haven't thought of that? You're the only clean thing I know, you and your men. Like Lancelot when he brought your message tonight, standing there like God's conscience with his own bare need in his eyes. He's your man, find him a wife. Soon. Wretched, honorable man."

"What if I were king?"

She sighed. "It would be so simple then. I'd open our gates and come out to you with flowers in my hair and the white veil of virginity that we could at least pretend was valid. We'd make a strong marriage, strong children and, God damn them all, a strong country." She tilted her head back to regard me with sleep-sensuous eyes. "I'd even ask now and then if Arthur Pendragon loved me."

"Now and then."

Guenevere kissed me with her old, cool enjoyment of the act for itself. "And I love you. Most of the time. Do you think we could do it, Arthur? Could we take all this mess and make something clean?"

Agrivaine flatly refused to serve under me and sued instead to remain as commander of Cador's *alae* on the Wall. My trouble with him taught a valuable lesson. We were no cohort now, only lord and men, unable to afford petty differences of rank. Every man under me, whatever his birthright, must serve as simple lord-comite among equals, as *fhain*-husbands considered each other brothers to love, trust and protect.

On the oath-taking day, I requested the services of Bishop Anscopius and an ancient stone altar disused for more than a hundred years. Anscopius' reliquary rested on a little stand and contained (by repute) the toe bone of St. Paul. To the other side stood the small altar, its concave top filled with hot coals, a dish of incense to one side. Beside me flared my brave new banner, the gift of Guenevere and her women: a red dragon's head on a field of white.

Despite fires on the hearths, the great hall remained late-winter clammy and cold, nor was it warmed at all by Anscopius' disapproval of the pagan altar. With his piercing blue eyes over an aquiline nose, he peered at me like a stern old hawk.

"Count Arthur, this is sacrilege."

"But some of the men are not Christian, your grace. If they're asked to swear on life, it must be by something they hold sacred."

Anscopius shook his mitered head. "Men like Trystan who believe in nothing."

"He has the greatest admiration for the Church, your grace."

Anscopius was not to be buttered. "I daresay; like a work of art in someone else's house. And you, Count? I have not noted fervent piety among your attributes. By which of these will you swear?"

"By Holy Church," I said, adding with a straight face, "Surely I am as devout as your own prince." And that was that. The razor rather than the ax.

My men arrived in twos and threes. Freed from military custom, they dressed to personal and often arresting taste. Trystan was in scarlet, Gareth in blue and brown under the remnants of his legion gear. Lancelot looked as usual like a monk, somber dun robe under the black cloak. Gawain rumbled through to a place in front, resplendent in fox-trimmed green. Plain Bedivere wore his legion leather and old cloak, and I thought, I must make him a gift of something for occasions like this. Behind my captains the dozens stretched away to the doors, a sea of clashing color, furs, here and there a battered legion helmet with its discouraged horsehair crest.

When I rose to speak, the stamping, shuffling hall grew quiet. Someone harked from the back: "Trib—I mean Count Arthur, is't true we're free to go home?"

"As if you had one," someone jibed.

"You're all free to go," I called. "But hear me at least. You know I'm a plain-spoken man. Some say a little too plain."

A mutter of wry laughter.

"I want you—every man of you—to stay with me. We've built a force such as Britain's never seen, and all of us had a part in it. The emperor says, and these are his words, that *we are Britain*. So I ask you now, who will be Arthur's man to come with him to the midlands?"

"That's Saxon country now, most of it," Gawain puzzled. "Who's raiding?"

"We are!" I let the words ring through the hall. "For the first time since they came here, we raid *them*. The emperor has promised Prince Maelgwyn and his Catuvellauni their ancient home this summer.''

Young Lord Pwyll stepped forward, an arrogant Dobunni, one of my own countrymen. ''I hold no friendship with Catuvellauni, and themselves the worst cattle thieves God ever created. They're your enemies too, Artos.''

''Pwyll, I serve my king. I have no tribe. That will be understood before any man swears today. I go to the midlands for Ambrosius. It won't be the battle you knew here. No flags, no glory, not very dangerous, not very clean.'' I ran my eyes over the crowd of them to measure their reaction. ''Because we will take no prisoners of any age or sex. Understand that now. None.''

No one moved, but a few glanced at each other, appalled.

''So if there's any man too tenderhearted for that, he can leave now. He's not sworn. The door's still open.''

A sibilant murmur as the men shifted about, weighing the meaning. Fire eaters, most of them, they were being offered something meaner than fire.

''And mark me further about your oath. The man who offers his sword to me takes it back as simple lord-comite. Whatever title he bears at home stays at home. While he rides with me, he's *combrogus*, companion, equal with all his brother lords.''

Pwyll spoke again. ''You expect us to put aside our right of birth to become common knights like the Saxons. Why should we? It's stupid.''

''Not too stupid,'' said Bedivere. ''They're winning.''

Only Trystan found that amusing, but then Tryst was known to giggle over the Book of Revelations.

''We need to learn every lesson we can while there's time. When Saxons serve a chief on a particular boat or raid, all personal quarrels are put aside on forfeit of life. As we swear today, I promise by that oath that any man who draws a sword against his brother while serving with me will suffer death or banishment.''

Now the heads really wagged and the tongues buzzed busily. I brought it home to them in a simpler way. ''When you go home, you can carve each other to your hearts' content. But do it in my camp and it's your lot. Nothing's plainer than that.''

The hotter heads found this wanting; others, like my captains, knew the simple necessity behind it. A brother must be a brother. We had no other intrinsic strength. At my signal, the old bishop came forward.

"Anscopius will now give benediction and instruct us in the gravity of our oath."

Leaning on his heavy crozier, Anscopius signed the Cross. "In the name of the Father, the Son and the Holy Ghost. The blessing of God and Holy Church upon this endeavor. My young men, there is no more solemn compact in Christendom than the oath binding lord and man. You take it with no reservation or you perjure, there is no middle course. Your oath clasps you to the very Hand of God. Consider not only the gravity but the particulars of this oath. You are of different peoples with different laws. This oath, sworn on the most holy relics, supersedes all and binds you personally to Count Arthur. No tribal law or loyalty may come before your bond to him. Weigh carefully, then. Not only are you sworn in this world, but in the next as well."

"Now," I sang out, "who'll be the first to join me?"

Two stepped forward together, Gareth and Bedivere. Each hesitated politely for the other, then Gareth moved aside.

Bedivere stood before me. "We being oldest friends, he let me go first. Need you and I swear, Artos?"

"We more than others, Bedivere, and rest bound to it. Give me your sword."

When I held the blade across my open palms, Anscopius asked, "Bedwyr ap Gryffyn, how will you swear?"

"By God and Holy Church."

Bedivere knelt while I stated the questions of the oath. Then he rested his hand on the reliquary, repeating the quaint words of the Dobunni.

"I, Bedivere, the son of Gryffyn, swear that, head and foot and all in between I am your man, to obey your laws and look to no other lord for increase. That I will be brother to my brother lords and hold faith with none but you saving only God. I swear by God and Holy Church."

I placed the sword in his uplifted hands. "I create you lord-comite in my service. Rise, Lord Bedivere."

He was the first who was the oldest and most faithful friend. To hear himself named lord momentarily robbed Bedivere of his decorum. "Well, damn all," he mumbled.

"And accept one more task as well." I lifted the banner from its iron socket, held it out to him. "Carry this for me."

So much all at once was too much for my open-hearted friend. "Your standard, Artos?"

"Haven't you always carried it, one way or another?"

All this murmured between us, no one else heard. A good thing because Bedivere's feelings were too much for him. He blinked and looked down at the stone floor, then grasped the standard firmly. "Well. Well, now. My da won't be half proud, will he?"

"Stop sniffling, idiot, and stand on my left. We've men to swear."

And all through the day they were sworn: Gareth mac Diurmuid, Trystan of Castle Dore, Ancellius of Clermont-Ferrand—even Pwyll, despite his earlier cavils. One by one they rendered their sword, swore on their deities. Their hand brushed the reliquary or dropped the pinch of incense. Two hundred odd in all, grooms' sons like Bedivere and men born far above me gave up their past for a future and became simple knights with only the blazon of their shields to tell them apart.

Not all of them liked or held with me personally, an illegitimate upstart from Severn, but they trusted my law and my heart. For these Gawain said it best as he knelt to swear.

"Na, hear me, Pendragon. You're a deavin', sly little swick of a Dobunni, and I do swear naught beyond the letter of my word."

I lost my hand in his huge bear paw. "But you came, Gawain meqq Lot."

"Aye." He whisked the longsword from its scabbard light as a butter knife. "Because, damn you, you're right."

In the summer of that year, Arthur who was yet only count or dux bellorum, went into the lands east of Severn and harried the Saxons and everywhere his arms prevailed. The people of Britain came forth in gratitude for their deliverance, for they had seen in all their days no fairer company than Arthur and his knights.

Now Arthur was by nature merciful and wished to spare the heathen despite the king's stern order. But they were hardened and unrepentant and fleered at his grace. Then Arthur, being much wearied by war, lost patience and delivered them all to be killed.

Anon came a young and comely woman of the heathen with a child at her breast, and said, "Most noble lord, if there be no mercy from you, I fear me there be none in the world. I do beseech you spare my child and me, for certes such as we can do thee no harm."

Then spake Sir Lancelot thus, "As to the king's command, natheless we are Christian men, and if ladies cannot look to such as us for grace, where then shall they seek in all Britain. As boon, I beg you let her go."

And the woman wept pitiably so that even Sir Trystan the paynim was moved to sue for her release. And so did the faithful Sir Bedivere and mild Sir Gareth as well, so that, enrounded by his fairest men all pleading mercy for the woman and child, Arthur then

No more of that.

Brother Coel said he's discouraged recording so bald and secular a history, so I let him try his own hand. Gladly. There's little I can remember about the midlands without my insides turning over. He got so far before I stopped him. We were going to throw the page away, but on second thought I let him leave it with the others. Not much for style, but a comment of sorts.

He still thought I glossed too lightly over a significant British victory and asked for one symbolic picture or event to illuminate the shadowy scene.

I said half a baby in a ditch.

Sensitive little fellow, he's excused himself for a while. He should come back soon. I don't think there's all that much time left.

None of us spoke much afterward of that summer; I don't propose to elaborate now. We left it a burning garbage heap that stank from Badon to Verulamium. The Saxons had nothing to put against my cavalry but spears, shields and a few bows, but they stood firm when we charged, their big, ruddy-faced women shouting encouragement and holding up newborn children to give the men heart. The few battles were a gulp of fresh air before the inevitable end. When the nightmare was accomplished, my report to Ambrosius began:

> The midlands are cleared. The Catuvellauni are coming home.

—and somehow never went any further.

The first refugees poured in after us with their wagons, oxen and plows. They called us saviors (Ambrosius, did you hear?), met us with gifts and songs and garlands of flowers, wondering why the lords of Count Arthur smelled so of greasy smoke. Such grim young men who never sang and who had forgotten how to smile.

One day is enough to tell of, the last. Lancelot and myself. The woman and her child. A significant scene for Coel.

I sat in my tent pondering the dispatches for Ambrosius, hoping he was still alive to read them. Lancelot had volunteered to make the long trip back to Eburacum with a small party. The papers were sealed and ready to go, all but one. Mundane lists on supply, the condition of the men, casualties, the good, practical observations of a Roman soldier. However, the report of accomplished mission still consisted of two bare sentences. I read them a hundred times; they mocked me, now pitifully bald, now more than enough.

The midlands are cleared. The Catuvellauni are coming home.

From outside came the clop-clop of two horses nearing at a walk. Then Lancelot, sharp and peremptory:

"I don't care, hold them here!"

A fly buzzed my ear. I batted it away, feeling hot and gritty, looked once more at the laconic report and tossed it with the others to go.

Ave, and the hell with it.

Lancelot thrust himself into the tent and stood at the entrance like a man bidden to come against his will. Normally fastidious, he hadn't shaved for several days. Under the cheekbones that stood out more sharply now, his thinned face was shadowed with brownish stubble. He wore only breeches and a linen shirt grimy as my own. All our garments smelled of the thick smoke that hung over the midlands in memory of a hundred burned byres, immolated cattle and fowl. Lancelot was just back from firing one of the last.

"Done?" I asked.

"Yes."

"All burned?"

"All."

Still he didn't move, increasing my own irritation. They all had that look lately, a bafflement as of being in an alien place where nothing was familiar but the sour taste of disgust.

"Don't just stand there. Come in."

Lancelot sank down on a stool by the table, jerking his head at the dispatches. "They're ready to go?"

"You can see they are."

"So am I."

The fly buzzed between us. Lancelot swung at it with the fury of a frustrated cat.

"Get some food and rest," I said. "You can leave in the morning."

"Who can eat?" he grated. "Every mouthful tastes of that filthy smoke."

"I eat it, too."

His red-rimmed eyes bored into me. The scrutiny rubbed me the wrong way. I knew why he volunteered to return to Eburacum besides escaping this charnel house, and for that reason never mentioned Guenevere in his presence. Whether he loved or was merely fascinated by her, who can say? He was not a Trystan; where Tryst needed an object for passion, Lancelot needed one to worship. He idolized Gwen but never knew her, not even in bed.

"What's wrong, Lancelot?"

"The same thing wrong with all of us. We stink."

Christ, they all sounded like that nowadays. "None of us like what we have to do."

"So?"

"So don't come in here like a bleeding saint with your arse-paining principles and tell me what you're sick of. A sensible man would ignore it."

"And that thing outside in the ditch that you won't even cover with an inch of dirt. Do you ignore that?"

"Completely." Controlling my irritation took effort. It pressed down on me with the weight of loathing behind it. "You know why it's there. No one is going to forget the midlands."

"I don't think we will," Lancelot agreed thinly. "I've tried to remember the reason all summer. All this morning."

Something in his tone made me ask. "What about this morning?"

"All this morning," he echoed. "I thought about the need for it. There was nothing different about today except when I woke up I knew it was over for me."

He sounded so earnest, searching for the words. "Just one more day, one more fire and then out of here to Eburacum. But whatever kept me going didn't quite reach. I burned the place, yes. There was only one animal alive, a ridiculous, sway-backed horse. Stolen, I suppose. These people never have horses, not the peasants. Somehow I couldn't kill it.''

He seemed so pathetically dogged in his desire to explain, I tried to ease him. "Well, one horse. The Catuvellauni can use it.''

Lancelot stared down at the table. "There's more. When I fired the byre, there was a woman inside hiding under some straw. The smoke drove her out. A big cow of a woman with dirty hair and not many teeth and a child squalling in her arms. So we stood there, I with my sword, she with that child that never stopped screaming. And we just stared at each other.''

"Well, you only did—''

"What I had to? Count Arthur, do you know how often this summer I've done what I had to? Eighty-six times. Thirty-six women and fifty children.''

"For Christ's sake, you *count* them?''

"Why not? God will.''

"What are you, an Anchorite?" I lunged off the stool, raging around the tent like a fire set by his words. "Pain and suffering will make you noble, hugging them to your breast? Not bad enough when it's faceless, you have to bloody count them. Our private conscience. Does it help to count two more? Does it?''

He shook his head listlessly. "Not today. I told you it didn't reach.''

"What?''

"I couldn't.''

I understood then. We faced each other across the tent, sweating, aware of the buzzing of that stupid fly. "You let them go?''

"No, my lord.'' Lancelot's bulky shoulders heaved forward as he rose from the stool. He moved heavily to the entrance. "I am your man to obey your laws. I brought them here. They're outside. But if you need them on the heap with the others today, you may have to do it yourself.''

It carried no taste of insubordination, only helpless finality. Lancelot had not ignored the order, only postponed it, put execution back in my hands.

"I see. All right.''

He followed me out of the tent. A few yards away, by the fly-bitten horse, the woman squatted on her haunches in dirty homespun, wisps of straw in her braided yellow hair. A husky farm woman past the first bloom, she held the child close, darting fearful glances up at the men around her. My captains hovered near, aloof and yet oddly protective: Bedivere, Gareth,

Trystan and Gawain. They seemed vastly relieved when I came to handle it.

"No one seems to understand orders today," I said.

They avoided my glance. Bedivere twisted a short length of halter around his palm. Gareth jabbed sullenly at the earth with his sword. Big Gawain glowered off into limbo. Perhaps the most sensitive of the lot, Trystan could not disguise the troubled self-disgust in his eyes.

Still I mouthed the words that no longer carried any conviction. "Ambrosius said just do it. Don't think about it."

Bedivere spoke now. "Have you tried that?"

"Yes, damn it!"

My old friend dropped the halter and spat eloquently on the ground.

Trystan murmured, "Lancelot's not the only one who counts."

Then I understood completely that baffled expression. Not refusal, not inability to sup at horrors, only surfeit. They were stuffed with it. They couldn't swallow any more, and the song of their misery was the mean hum of flies over the small carcass in the ditch. Suddenly that was too much for me, too.

"Someone get a spade. Cover that thing. Now."

"Aye." Relieved, Gareth moved quickly to obey.

"So everyone's had enough."

"Damned right," Gawain mumbled.

"Even my terrible Gawain who divided men with horses?"

"Those were men, Arthur!"

"Oh yes, those were men. That's a difference. And I called you a butcher, didn't I?" I went back to the woman and leaned on my sword. "My lords, who in hell do you think you are? You think I haven't pondered the reason for this insanity?"

"If there is one," Trystan wondered fervently, "I'd dearly love to know it."

Starting to reply, I realized how futile any answer to them would be. They were warriors, a means somehow deluded into seeing themselves as an end. They never worked for food, they fought or waited in a hall to fight while someone pulled their food out of the ground, someone cooked it and someone else served it to them. Not one ever worried over sick cattle or drove them miles to grass that wasn't there or went hungry so gaunt children could eat. Not one ever bent their stiff backs one inch because someone stronger enjoyed a right that was denied them.

None of them except me.

It always added up the same. Lords were not of themselves

terribly important when you came down to it. If we vanished from the earth, the Morganas and Cunedags, this woman and her child would prosper, make new children, draw new food from the earth. Just keep the lords off their backs, they'll do fine, thanks.

But take them away from us, and we have no purpose, mere violent children scuffling over a pointless game. And because it's pointless we puff it out with self-importance, gild it with tinsel like honor, courtesy, pride of descent and blood. Our function is to keep the land clear for the vast majority who work it, to clear away the carnal debris like carrion birds. The Catuvellauni coming home to plant, that's our reason and our only meaning. The rest is the rarefied delusion our vanity puts between us and the horror.

A Guenevere, a Trystan, an Arthur may be the flowers of the earth, but its fruit is a Morgana. Still, try telling that to the flower.

I hauled the woman erect. She cringed away from me, clutching the dirty child.

"My lords, this woman would kill you without a second thought and use you sensibly for manure. But then she's closer to reality than you lot. Ambrosius knows this, that's why he's king. Learn it now and never forget."

Faint cries of welcome filtered down the line of our tents, and under them the sound of a galloping horse. The yelling swelled louder as the horse hove into sight. The rider wore plain leather, but a Roman helmet crested with the imperial gold.

Hungry for news, for anything that smelled of elsewhere, a crowd of my men collected around the burly, aging man as he walked the horse down the row of tents to meet me: Ursus Strabo, aide to the emperor. He dismounted and gripped my hand.

"Hail, Count."

"Ursus Strabo, greetings. How does the king?"

"That's why I've come. Late, I admit." He said it loud enough for all to hear. "Ambrosius is dead."

Bedivere crossed himself. "God rest his soul then."

There was a mutter of *amens*.

"Bless the old man," I said. "He was so damned tired."

From his dispatch case, Ursus handed me a wax tablet with the imperial seal. "This testament's gone to every prince in Britain. Ambrosius names you as his choice for the crown."

"By God, he's earned it." Bedivere clapped me on the shoulder. "Not a worthier lord in Britain, mad though he is."

Ursus's nose wrinkled at the unpleasant air. "What's that stink?"

"The world," said Trystan. "Just ignore it."

"And the Council," I pressed Ursus. "The princes, what of them?"

"They meet near Humber to choose a new king as soon as all can assemble." Ursus lowered his voice. "Artorius, there's a private message for you. May we speak alone?"

"Of course. Bedivere, it seems—" I looked around at the dung heap that had sickened us all for so many weeks. "Strike my flag. Let's get out of here."

In my tent, Ursus loosened his leather jerkin and gratefully accepted a mug of barley beer. "You all look like the tail end of piss-time," was his blunt assessment. "Filthy business, wasn't it?"

"All of that. What's the message?"

He rooted in his pouch. "It's bad in Eburacum since the old man went. We staff weren't too popular, watched all the time. Cador held me there long after the funeral. Right, here it is."

A small scrap of vellum sealed in plain wax, evidently written in haste. "She slipped it to me at the south gate."

> *Arthur—*
> *Father will bid for the crown. He's put Agrivaine between you and Humber, alae and legion. Go round him and come home. I feel like a traitor, still God bless you. G.*

"Bad news, Artorius? Not that any of it's good."

"Nor this. Ursus, what's my situation?"

He drained his beer and belched. "Dangerous."

"Who's on my side?"

"All and none, boy. Every prince wants you to back his grab for the crown. And every one of them would be just as happy if you never reached Humber alive."

"Cador for one. He's even willing to bet on it, set Agrivaine to stop me."

That didn't surprise veteran Ursus. "Agrivaine's grown pretty important up there. Good soldier, but . . ."

I wanted to know about Guenevere and Cador's alliance with Brude. Ursus only snorted in contempt.

"That was a joke from the beginning, you know that. That just kept Brude off his back. The offer and the princess have been withdrawn. Agrivaine's looking in that direction now."

"To Guenevere?"

"Why not?" Ursus grinned. "Politics aside, she's a piece for any man. She knows what she wants, too. Must have taken some fortitude to risk that letter."

Guenevere never lacked courage, nor Cador when it came to that, though he was probably encouraging Agrivaine subtly in his suit because he still needed the earnest Orkneyman. He'd play both ends against the middle as long as possible. Well, if a battle came, my men were spoiling for it.

"Ursus, how many men do you command?"

"Are you serious? Me, and lucky to be here."

"Will you stay for me? Will you be my man?"

"No, Artorius." He rubbed his bristly gray beard. "I'm old and used up and I want to go home. There's a house and a wife in Brittany. My pension land, the only decent thing I ever got out of this rutting army. Damn it, I only stayed for Ambrosius. This was my last mission."

"Then finish it." I grabbed for my maps, chose one and spread it on the table. "You'll ship from Severn anyway. Have you a good horse?"

"The best," Ursus chortled. "Stole him from Agrivaine."

"You larcenous old crow." I poured his cup full again. "You'll have years to get bored in Brittany. Will you give me just five days? For Ambrosius?"

Ursus took a long pull at his beer, considering. Then he slammed it down on the table. "Hell, I owe him that much. Orders?"

"You're a friend and a Roman." I gripped his hand gratefully, then grabbed for stylus and vellum, scribbling as fast as I could. "Map, Ursus. That one there."

Men were what I needed, not to fight but to raise their voices, as many as would come from reserves which must now be drained shamelessly. Kay from Severn. Maelgwyn, Prince of the Catuvellauni, who owed me his restored power. Beautiful, mad Geraint whose debt at Neth could now be called. I appealed to Kay's political sense, Maelgwyn's gratitude and Geraint's honor. Each for his reason, they must come. Ursus watched with enjoyment as I scratched away, my tongue stuck out in concentration.

"You're the old man's own for sure." He chuckled. "You're going to try, aren't you?"

"Try?" I went on writing with sure, rapid strokes. "Ambrosius taught me one thing. How to be the best, and that's by Jesu what I am. Try, hell. I'm going to win!"

I strode down the line of tents as the men struck them to load on the packhorses. We traveled light and fast; no grooms or servants. The packhorses were the only part of us one couldn't use as an attack weapon. The sun sat on the western horizon. Only a little light left, but we'd traveled by night before. In the morning, we'd be a long way north.

In the middle of this leave-taking flurry, calm Lancelot still had in his charge the woman and her child and the sad horse.

"I'll take her, Lancelot. Get ready to leave and see I'm saddled, there's a good lad."

"Yes, Count." He patted the child on the head. "I told her it would be all right."

A weight was gone from all of us. Even the smell wasn't so oppressive now. "You were that sure of me?"

Lancelot squinted away toward the sunset. Was he smiling? "You can call it that. God be with you, sir."

He touched the child once more, lingeringly, it seemed. Then Ancellius Falco, God's own millstone, actually *sauntered* away.

No longer frightened, the woman still didn't trust me as she fed a morsel of pear to her child, shifting the infant to her far side. Besides pear mush, the baby sported a milk moustache. Someone had fitted the discouraged horse with a cast-off saddle and a fat sack of provisions. Whatever my judgment, the men clearly indicated their own.

"You understand Brit, woman?"

She didn't look up, but the dirty braids wagged. "Some."

"Get up. Go home."

"Home?"

"On the horse, damn it. Here, I'll hold the bairn."

"No." She flinched away, wrapping herself around the child. "I won't hurt him. Up, go home."

Barely convinced, she relinquished the smelly child just long enough to mount. A boy, wouldn't you know it. One more to come back later. Mounted, the woman snatched him back. I handed her the reins.

"You know me, woman?"

"*Ja.*" The cold forest eyes had an unforgiving set. "Ar-tur."

"Then tell your thanes what Arthur says. This is British land. *Briton* land. You hear?"

She gathered the reins in one red hand, settling the child in front of her. She spoke in halting gutturals.

"Saxon land. We made the corn come. Land was nothing, just grass. We made corn, Welshman."

"Get out of here." I gave the horse a vicious smack on the rump. *"Go."*

Startled, the ancient animal stumbled forward a few steps, then lapsed into a shambling walk, rolling and swaying like a foundered ship. The woman never looked back.

Caesar's roads were my friends again. Next day toward noon we raised the monastery at Cair Luit Coyt, which the Saxons now call Lichfield. The monks were a healing order and suffered comparatively little from heathen raids. Somewhat dismayed at our numbers, the abbot nevertheless made us welcome. While the weather turned wet, we settled down to wait for allies. That we slept on benches and tables mattered not at all. The rain cleansed, the plain food was free of taint. We rested, scrubbed the smell of death from our skins and breathed clean air.

Prince Maelgwyn came next day, a rotund, easy-tempered man leading a dozen Catuvellaun chiefs and their sons—all he could scrape up, having just come from exile. More rain, two unrelenting days of it while my men looked to the south and asked *will they come?*

Kay and Geraint? Ask that of any other man in Britain, I told them, but not those two.

On the fourth day, the rain let up. Slogging through the last of it came my blessed brother and a hundred Dobunni, bedraggled young coxcombs with plumed helmets and garish cloaks. Some from the remote hills of Kay's domain even painted themselves stylishly with old-fashioned woad.

And dear little Kay with his now luxuriant beard, whooping and grappling me to the ground in rough affection and a tumble of breathless greeting punctuated with punches.

"By the gods! My own brother to be king! My big! useless! vagrant! horse's *butt* of a brother!"

"How long's it been, Kay?"

"Caerleon, a thousand years gone," he said.

Bedivere caught Kay's arms and locked them tight with the homely greeting, *"Sut mae'r mab, Cai?"*

"The Gryffyn, is it?" Kay twisted free, collared Bedivere and wrestled him off his feet. "Na, who's this *Lord* Bedivere we hear of, who has not—"

"Get off me, you fat ox!"

"—sent one stinking word to his cousin Myfanwy these two long years?"

Bedivere writhed, never able to take a rib-tickling. "Ow, stop. Stop, you rotten little bugger, you know I can't write."

"Ach-y-fi," Kay let up on him. "Ignorance is a pale excuse."

Another day passed and then another while the rain began again. We took damp solace that it mired the other princes as well. Bedivere wondered, but I knew Geraint would come. His very failings as a leader would bring him: his sense of personal honor over everything else and his demonic lack of caution.

The rain ceased again. On a day of fresh-washed blue and gold, Geraint came leading the men of Dyfneint. I recognized him at a great distance easily; only Geraint could dress so dashingly in a mixture of red, brown and attempted purple. Behind him the burnished helmets, jaunty with flowers, flashed in the bright sun. We turned out beyond the monastery gate to welcome them. Bedivere shaded his eyes, peering at the far column.

"His sister's with him."

"You're daft," I said.

"Look for yourself."

I did. She was. Now, why in hell—?

What would we do with her? We planned to move as soon as they rested, a hard ride with perhaps battle at the end of it. Eleyne would have to be kept safely in the rear in case of ambush. If anything happened to her, it meant a rift between Dyfneint and myself, ill affordable now.

More immediately it demanded one of my own lords as escort, and as Geraint drew nearer, the problem grew larger. Touchy lot, the Dumnonii. Geraint would want a prince as escort. I had three, but how suitable? Kay would talk horses and pick his nose. Gawain's arrogant condescension would stand out like a rash. Fatherly Maelgwyn would imply Eleyne was a child to be kept at someone's knee rather than an eligible princess.

Bedivere? Out of mercy, no. A man's man, blue of speech now and then, and he couldn't stand Eleyne. Not Pwyll, too crude for a sensitive girl. Of course Eleyne's sensitivity protruded like a sharp horn. Who, damn it, who?

Gareth? Yes, perfect. Warm and kind, personable, devoutly

Christian, implacably married—and half a day north nosing for signs of Agrivaine.

Trystan? Good God, no. Geraint would froth at the mouth. That lecherous, cuckolding whoremonger to escort his sister?

Standing near me, Trystan perhaps read my thought. "I'll withdraw a little, Arthur. One's heard of whores, but yonder comes the only woman in the world to make a profession out of virtue."

Smiling officially as they drew near, I raged inwardly. Why did he have to cart her along? Even without danger she'd have a miserable trip.

Then they reined up amid shouts of greeting all around, the rainbowed Geraint leaping from the saddle to surround me, a one-man siege of affection and a breath-defying monologue begun before his boots hit the ground.

". . . And well met, by God's grace. Would I wait one minute after the hearing of your message, even with Marcus breathing down my back? Ha! said I to him, you've had our support for years and ourselves of older blood, if the truth be told. But when it comes to the Mother of God crown of Britain, look you, Dyfneint will choose for itself. What's to eat, Arthur? And would the good abbot mind a suggestion as to supper? In faith, I can't abide lentils or turnips. *Well,* said I to Marcus, when it comes to a voice in the crowning of a king, will not mine go up for the man who stood with me at Neth against a hundred or more? Nothing for it then but to mount and ride, and here I am, and no more but to ask the name of this misguided fool waiting at Humber in the vain hope of stopping men like us."

Geraint looked around quizzically in the nonplussed silence that followed his torrent of energy, and found himself gazing up at the Olympus of Orkney.

"My brother," said Gawain.

Geraint's answer was too full of compassion to hold an ounce of insult. "Ah well, sir. For your sake, then, I'll not let him suffer. And now, Arthur, will you not greet my dear sister and herself come so far to see you crowned?"

I bowed to Eleyne. Perched on her mare, she gave me her sweet but self-possessed smile. Most men who knew the lady remember her as frail and clinging. Only a few noted the set of her mouth: unmalleable iron and God-given Right.

"Now that you are truly lord of men," she condescended, "it

is hoped you are to mass more regularly. Give you good day, Count Arthur."

My men pressed around her, eager, pawing awkwardly at their overgrown hair to smooth it back. She was something they had not seen in some time, a woman of their own kind. Eleyne actually glowed with the male attention, though she returned Trystan's gallant obeisance with a bare, frigid nod. Two years had defined her face more clearly. Not pretty but ripening. Caradoc would be hunting a husband soon if not already.

"And which of your higher lords will attend her?" Geraint asked, serenely sure I had an archangel on hand.

"Yes. Well—"

Bedivere became absorbed with the buckle of his sword belt. I looked about in desperation—and felt the hand of fate on my elbow.

It was Lancelot. "I've just seen the abbot, sir. Since we're so many, he'll hold mass presently in the courtyard."

I gripped his shoulder, battened on it. "Of course. Prince, allow me to present Lord Ancellius, whom I hope it will please you to attend Lady Eleyne."

Lancelot bowed formally to Geraint, who sized him up and said, "Is't not yourself men call the Lancelot?"

"I have been called that, sir."

Eleyne surveyed him haughtily. I suppressed a giggle. Damn her little crust, she was being regal. Chin high, hand at her breast, she inspected Lancelot like a dish at table she might or might not sample, depending on the ingredients.

"Of what holding?" she condescended to ask.

Lancelot moved to her knee and swept down in a low bow. "Of none now, Lady. Here we serve God and Arthur alone."

Only Lancelot could have managed such convincing humility, because he meant it. He stretched out his arms to help her alight. She seemed to weigh nothing in his grip. "Lady, will you hear mass with us?"

By the time she touched ground, Eleyne was not quite so self-possessed, even fluttered a little. "My lord, I—I will."

"Saved," whispered Bedivere.

Heroes are born, not made.

By pure accident I offered Eleyne the very mold from which her dreams were cast. You may remember they were married later. Eleyne wanted it most. She loved Lancelot with all the concentration of her constricted soul, cleaving to him with the grim fidelity of a barnacle. She even undertook to instruct him in Scripture. That he'd forgotten more of it than she'd ever read gave Eleyne not a passing qualm. I've mentioned the set of her mouth; she will no doubt correct God's grammar on Judgment Day.

As her escort Lancelot was an inspired choice. They were both serious and fervent, and a warmth must have passed between them to form the initial bond. They rode in contentment behind my column, too far behind, and because of this Lancelot and I nearly died at the Caldor.

Freed of the helmet, Gareth's sandy hair sprang up in all directions from his scalp. He rubbed it vigorously as he traced a stubby finger along the highway between Cair Daun and Kaelcacaestir on the map. Gareth couldn't read but he knew the spider web of Roman roads on the chart.

"Right here, sir, that's where I saw them."

Correctly, Agrivaine guessed I'd choose the most direct route to Kaelcacaestir and deployed his forces across it in a wide net. Cool Gareth took his time and counted well: an entire cohort of Cador's foot plus over a hundred cavalry. They must have drained the Wall forts, men from my old first and second squadrons. Men I knew, some of them friends.

"It's God's will you should be king," Gareth sighed. "But so many good men will die because Cador can't see it."

His words haunted me as we drew closer to the trap. My objective was the crown, not a battle. The thought would not leave me alone.

At our next rest halt, I sent for Gawain.

He trotted up, shirtless in the day's heat, beard and black body hair matted with sweat. Shaving would have helped, but he'd have none of my effete Roman ways. While the men walked their horses about us, wiping lather from flanks and harness, I gave Gawain the picture as Gareth reported it: if we kept on going, battle with Agrivaine was imminent.

"Would you fight your brother, Gawain?"

He wasn't a man to speak hastily. He ruminated on the question, the great, sweaty continent of him, chewing on a stalk of grass.

"He'd have Cador for king," Gawain owned finally. "And while the same is a fine prince, well—not that *you're* always right, mind." He glowered at me from under bushy brows. "But I'll say this: devious and sly and over-given to thought as you are, did never see a lord more straightly do what he must. And did I not swear an oath?"

I passed him my water bag. "And I'll give you this. You're not an easy man, Gawain meqq Lot. Nor an easy flatterer." I showed him the map, our position and Agrivaine's. "His horse are almost all Orkneymen. Now, are we thinking the same thing?"

"I do think we are, Count."

"Why fight good men we may need later?"

Gawain said, "I've worried on that since I learned he was waiting."

"Then go to your brother. Say that I want him with me. With the future, not the past."

Gawain's frown vanished; he understood me now. "Not to fight?"

"Would you if you could avoid it?"

Silly to ask. Gawain would fight the ocean if it crowded him, but his own blood? "You know my brother and how he thinks."

"Nevertheless, find him," I said. "Ask him to join us. If you leave now, you can be back by tomorrow noon or before."

Gawain heaved himself up. "You'll be here?"

"Until you return. Tell him that, too, as earnest of my peace. And that I hope he returns with you."

"Not likely." Gawain took a deep breath and wheeled his thick arms wide, slapping them down hard on his smoke-grimed breeches. "It's a fool's errand and all for naught. He'd rather fight you than be king himself. But do not fancy killing my own lads."

I gave him leave to take a small party of his own choosing, Orkneymen like himself to insure welcome.

Gawain mounted. "When he says no, what then?"

I tried to look regretful. "Then tell him he's in for a fight, embrace him like a brother and get the hell back here."

My big captain nodded grimly. "I fear that's the shape of it. But rest you here, I'll be gone in the half hour."

And so he was, and I watched him out of sight on his mission. Some twenty minutes later, the rest of us mounted, left the road and struck northwest at a hard pace across the rolling foothills.

Shameful lying to Gawain like that, but the feint was necessary. I'd used Cador's own well-named tactic: constructive dishonesty. By the time Agrivaine heard my offer and had a roaring good time strutting and refusing for the benefit of his patient brother, I'd be around him and running for the crown.

We rode across the hills through a moonlit night and forded River Caldor at dawn, resting briefly on the north bank. We were now only an hour south of the road between Cair Legion and Eburacum, which Bedivere and I had traveled before. Once on it, we would raise tiny Kaelcacaestir by late afternoon.

Sitting with Trystan, washing my feet in the shallows, I felt rather proud of my ruse. We'd get there without a sword drawn or a man lost.

"And only Gawain to face," said Trystan thoughtfully.

"*Ach-y-fi,* don't remind me. I'll probably receive a challenge, despite his oath."

"At least one," Trystan said.

"But he has to catch us first."

Trystan squinted off down the river shore. "Here comes Geraint. And out of sorts, I'd say."

I wiped my feet and put on my boots while Geraint trudged up leading his horse. He was definitely uneasy. He greeted me shortly and ignored Trystan like a stone.

"I took a notion to see to my sister's doings, not doubting for a moment she's tenfold safe with the Lancelot, but I can't seem to find them since we crossed Caldor."

Neither had I. Geraint would be hanged before he asked Trystan, but that courteous man told him anyway.

"The lady's horse picked up a stone in its hoof a few miles back. Lancelot stopped to remove it. Perhaps they rested there."

Geraint bristled. "Rested there? Stopped to sleep there and the two of them wrapped in the same cloak and—"

"Geraint," I soothed, "you said yourself Eleyne's tenfold safe. Still we ought to bring them up. Shall we ride together?"

"Aye." Geraint mounted and swung his horse away. "There's more than Agrivaine's men loose this day. This is the route Marcus must take north, and it strikes me I'm not his favorite subject."

Trystan reached for his sword belt and stood up. "Shall I come, Arthur?"

"You are not needed," Geraint snapped. He stared at Trystan as if daring him to reply. I interceded.

"Geraint, as a friend, do not insult a battle-seasoned lord who is forbidden by oath to answer you now. Tryst, get what rest you can. Tell Bedivere we'll be back in an hour or come look for us."

"Sir," Trystan acknowledged, then bowed with sardonic grace to Geraint. "My respects till a more suitable time, Prince. And to your sister."

"Such as you do not address her," said Geraint. "Forbidden indeed. Come, Arthur."

The current at the shallows was no swifter than Geraint's free-flowing condemnation. A *shame* I was so desperate for men I need swear into service a wastrel the like of Trystan. The sin of adultery aside, Geraint had no use for perfumed poets who warbled their way into women's favors. Men who, for a night's sport, would make a queen out of a whore, for certainly had he not made a whore out of a queen? Did not the charitable Eleyne avoid Yseult at Castle Dore before the house of Dyfneint fell from Marcus' favor? And furthermore and thus and so and on and on.

I maintained politic silence while Geraint judged and damned his way through Trystan's questionable pedigree and half the noble blood of Cornwall, giving him minimal attention, the rest alert for Lancelot. But finally he got on my nerves.

"Geraint, have you ever loved a woman?"

"No, in truth, not yet, and myself only one and twenty and what with one duty and the other."

"Well, why don't you wait until you know how a man feels before you judge him?"

"What mean you?" Geraint said. "How he feels, indeed. Should I then top the queen myself?"

Oh, the man could weary you. "No, Prince, only—"

"Truly, Arthur, it confounds me that so fine a man as you should attain high rank so misinformed. Did not my own sister say as much? Arthur Pendragon is a *good* man, she said, but sadly lacking in the gentler graces of refined blood, and what is more—"

"Geraint, will you belt up!"

He drew away from me, bruised. "Well now. Well, of course, to be sure. If you're going to sulk, then go your ways."

We rode in blessed silence over a rocky stretch of hillside, eyes open for our two stragglers. My horse snorted, tossing his head. When he did it again, I pulled up and dismounted.

"What's afoot?" Geraint asked.

"Hush." I flattened out against a slab of rock, ear pressed

against it. Not even breathing, I listened and felt what the rock had to tell me. A footfall or a dozen hoofs clattering tallfolk-careless over hard ground.

Several horses coming at a trot.

"Riders," I told Geraint, mounting again. "Not too far off."

"Sister and Lancelot?"

"Maybe." But *fhain*-shrewd, I wouldn't bet on it. This country was patched with thick woods, well suited to hiding an ambush.

"Let's hurry, Geraint."

We found our charges by ear a few minutes later—the sound of a harp and Eleyne's singing—in a grove of trees lining a trickle of brook. The sun was still not far up, and since Lancelot knew my own halting place, he considered it safe to let the lady rest after the wearying night ride.

They seemed quite at ease by the little brook, Eleyne with her harp, Lancelot stretched out at her feet, rapt in her voice, absently dismembering wildflowers and throwing them into the stream. Seeing us, Eleyne ended the song she was assaulting with a dramatic if inaccurate chord and sprang up to greet Geraint, who was fussing at her before we dismounted and somewhat put out with Lancelot.

"Lord Ancellius, I do not question your intentions—"

"They are honorable," Eleyne vouched with perhaps something less than satisfaction.

"But your wisdom in remaining so far behind us, since Arthur's already heard strange horse nearby. We must hurry back across the river."

Eleyne shushed him with a kiss, animated by an excitement that made her almost attractive. "Oh, but it's been such a lovely morning! We rested and sang, and this last hour I've told Lancelot of our family and the searching for the Holy Grail."

And Lancelot himself was lit with the same enthusiasm. More than that, the light of fervor. "The Grail, my lord! In their very family and lost in their own land. When there's time, when you're king, God's love, let me seek it with them."

His passion reached out at me, almost clutched at my shirt. "God knows I'm not worthy even to see it—"

"But you are!" Eleyne took his hand. "And Arthur promised me such a man as you. You did, Arthur."

"Did what?"

"Oh, do you not remember your words as you lay wounded at

Neth, your *very* words which I took as oath and promise? 'If I find a man of sufficient grace, I will send him to you.' ''

Geraint was duly impressed. "You feel this to be true, sister?"

She nodded firmly. "Was I not spared the fever death because of my trust in God? I know it is true."

Geraint nailed it home. "My sister has always lived in the hand of Christ and knows her spiritual kindred. I do beseech you, Arthur, let him seek the Grail for her."

Well, they were all a bit much for a quiet morning. Lancelot dropped to one knee before me, face uplifted and shining, more beautiful than ever I'd seen him. Lancelot, the sad, deep man, more homeless than any of us, who most hated himself for what was done in the midlands. God damn him, God love him, this was *his* passion, strong as Trystan's, the thrust of soul that must reach for purity ever beyond its grasp. Not the finding but the quest.

"Arthur, you are my lord and my king-to-be on earth, a fulfilled man who knows nothing of emptiness. I've sought God in empty places, prayed in empty churches, walked unhurt through empty battles, not worth killing. But this is something that can *use* me, *must* use me. When there's time, when you're crowned, can I—I mean—"

"Yes, quite. But now we've got to—"

Ask the broken dam to hold back the flood. "All my life I've heard of the Grail, how it was lost somewhere in the west, in the mist—"

"Well, when there's time—"

"—In the sins of weak Mankind. That I find it is too much to ask—"

"Ancellius, will you—?"

"—I'm not worthy of that, but to be allowed the chance to seek it, perhaps point the way—"

"—Will you get up off your silly knees?" I hauled him up, his eyes still glazed with holy intoxication. "Yes, you Gallic monster. *Yes,* you can find their Grail and build a church to house it, but now we have to go!"

I released him and sank down by the water to drink and wash my face. Geraint gathered his sister and Lancelot into his arms, beaming.

"That's well," he said. "A sovereign must think of God as well as his throne, and you will be known as the king in whose reign the Grail was found."

"Hurrah," I spluttered, slurping water. "Now let's ride."

Eleyne was radiant; her happiness encompassed Lancelot, her impossible Grail dream and myself, never knowing her man of sufficient grace would always love another woman simply because she was unobtainable. We play very dangerous games with life and no one knows our rules.

"Bless you," she whispered.

"Oh, hell." I swabbed water about my face and neck, rolling over to grin up at them. "You're all demented, you know that? Nattering on about Grails when there's—"

That was the picture of us when it happened, Geraint with his arms about Lancelot and Eleyne, myself on the ground, a bird singing somewhere. I saw the sudden flash of sunlight on armor through the trees. Not far across the meadow, not far enough to give us any time.

"Look out!"

Geraint and Lancelot lost a precious second shoving Eleyne behind a tree. I ran for the untethered horses, grabbed the two closest and swung them broadside to impede the four riders plunging down on us with swords raised.

It worked partially, gave the others time. Three of the riders veered left and right, but the damned stupid horses just walked out of the way of the fourth man, who came straight on at me. My heel caught on a half-buried root. I went over backward, already seeing myself dead as the horse and rider grew larger, the biggest, loudest things in the world coming to mash me flat.

But even as I unfroze and tried to move, a form leaped between me and the coming death, a form with a sword in its hand. Lancelot—oh, beautiful to see him in that split second. With a mere two yards between us and the horse, he thrust forward both arms full extended with the sword. The horse took it square in its chest to the hilt. The animal made an indescribable sound, reared perpendicular and sent the unbalanced rider flying over its rump.

No time at all to think. I freed my sword, seeing Eleyne streak toward Lancelot—Christ, what's she doing?—as a second rider plunged at him. The two swords clanged together, Lancelot's parry a streak of light before it flashed home. Wounded, the rider reared his horse, the hoofs lashing out like weapons. Lancelot went down, the full, falling weight of the horse slamming against his chest, and then I had to guard myself against another of them.

I caught the flash of helmet, a swinging sword and the mad

eyes of the horse before dodging clear, parrying and slashing viciously to hamstring the mount as it passed.

Geraint's howl of battle joy rose over the sunlit carnage. Another horse passed me, the rider comically stiff and sedate in the saddle, the headless neck a red geyser. My own adversary wheeled, the horse clumsy with its leg wound, unable to respond. The man slid quickly from the saddle, tall with blond hair wisping out around his cone helmet.

"Now, Pendragon!"

He was quick and long-armed, wielding the sword two-handed in a slanting overhand attack, the hardest to block. I met him hilt to hilt and kicked him hard in the groin.

His eyes went dull with shock before he fell and I pinned him to the ground. Then, too late, I saw the swift shadow moving in behind me, wheeled and brought up the blade too late before the world stopped—

—And jerked into horrible life again with the taste of blood in my mouth and jagged points of light needling my eyes. I blinked up at the faces that circled over me, made out Bedivere, Gareth and Kay. Geraint was at my shoulder, helping me sit up. My whole face felt stiff. A mirror would have showed a badger mask of blood dried on both sides of my nose from the long shallow gash across my scalp.

"I thought you were gone." Geraint fussed tenderly over me. "But never did I see a hand so quick. Coming to take the pig off your back and knowing I'd never reach him in time, and his blade that close to cleaving your skull. And you stopped him."

He looked up at the other men as if they would argue with him. "Did I not see it myself? Parried so close his sword was flat against his own head. But just enough, thank all angels. The next trice I sent the back-stabber to heaven or hell, whichever fancies him."

I croaked at him, "Are you all right?"

"In the hand of Christ like my sister, and she's fresh as brook water. But the Lancelot's hurt."

I spat bits of dried blood. "Who were they?"

Bedivere surveyed the four bodies laid neatly in a row. "Marcus' men by the look of it. Damn it, Artos, when will you learn? Every time you leave me behind, you get hurt. I was always the better sword, you said that yourself. You need me with you."

"The sight of you's enough to make a man weep," said Kay. "But there's not much time. Can you ride, brother?"

"Come to get *me*, they did," Geraint muttered savagely.

"Oh, Marcus, you devil. Damn if we should not gut this land one end to the other to show who has the right of it."

"Let me up," I croaked.

Geraint tried to restrain me. "Lie back, rest."

"Let me *up*."

I pushed him away, scrabbling up awkward as a doll, head throbbing from the wound in my scalp. The matted hair lay thick and stiff over my caked forehead. Lancelot lay with his head in Eleyne's lap. When I came near she bent over him, protective and fierce.

"I will tend him." She was trembling. "No one but me."

"How bad? Where's he hurt?"

She stroked his hair. "Where not, and himself crushed in the saving of your life. He will not rise this month, look you, and only I will tend him." Her eyes blazed with cold murder. "We killed that dog before he fell. Lancelot and I, myself clawing at the villain's eyes and wishing they were Mark's."

"You must take him home with you, Eleyne. Back to Astolat."

Lancelot's eyes fluttered open, unfocused and expressionless. "Arthur . . ."

"Don't talk." I bent close to him. "We're all safe."

He tried to smile. "You don't look it."

"Thanks to you."

"I think I can ride, but it must be slowly."

"You dear, damned fool, the only thing you're going to ride is a bed. Go home with Eleyne, Ancellius. Find her Grail."

Find peace, I meant. Something you can have and not just yearn for, something clean that doesn't smell of blood and the dirty little games princes play. You are not for that.

"That might be best," he admitted. "It's hard to move."

"The gods bless you, Ancellius."

"I'll come back," he promised.

"Only when you're well."

I took Eleyne's hand. "Lady, please. I . . . Please take care of him."

"I must," she said softly. "For such men come once only in the world."

The sun shone on the meadow. Birds sang, the horses shied and snuffled. My men stood waiting on me—always on me: the choice of Merlin or ambition or fate, who knows.

And who cared?

The men would wait on me while flies buzzed over Britain. Dead men, dead children, all to make a country and secure a crown, and I thought: I'm twenty-three and I feel old. But I'm going to be king.

How long ago that first sight of Ambrosius' cohort seen from a Severn hill with Kay and Bedivere, the boy-wish and the vision of Merlin. We'd come a way since then, all of us. The battles fought, the women loved, the honors and the prides and the banners. And the learning that this was how it was done, not with honor but betrayal, not flags but flies.

Let it be. For a time I'd questioned fate, wanted this, wanted that. But let it be. No more questions. Right, wrong, I accepted the burden, took it up on my shoulder to make a world as Ambrosius did.

The realization built and throbbed with the wound in my head. There would be no choosing of a king. I would take the sword because I was the best. Me, not Marcus who turned aside viciously to crush one small rebel. Not Cador with his balances of power and clever games. Not the myriad littler men in their narrow pride. Britain was one great body that breathed and felt and suffered, one hand needing only another to hold and lead it.

Bedivere winced as I lurched up, a gargoyle of matted hair and blood like a ravaged peasant. No better symbol for this ravaged land. I would go to Kaelcacaestir—blood, pain and all—to finish the job for Ambrosius.

And nobody would stop me.

I raised my sword over the bodies of Marcus' men. One was headless already. I worked with demon ferocity until four heads lay at my feet.

"Kay! Bedivere! Gareth! Geraint! Each of you will ride behind me with one of these heads on your lance. We don't ask for the crown, we don't wait to be chosen. We *take* it. Do you understand?"

Bedivere hauled the lance from his saddle straps and speared a head on it. "Give the order, Artos-bach."

"We ride to Kaelcacaestir, and nothing stops us. Whatever's in the way, whoever raises sword against us, we ride through or over them. We stop for nothing today. Not today, do you hear me? Nothing!"

Geraint thrust his lance into the gored base of another head, lifting it high. "For God and Arthur!"

"God and Arthur!" my men echoed as I faced them, shaking with the passion of determination. My voice was harsh as a vengeful crow's.

"We take the crown, we take the imperial sword. And good or bad's for later to decide, God damn it, but we will *rule!*"

"God and Arthur!"

"Geraint, leave some men with your sister. The rest of you, let's go."

Eleyne waved in farewell as we moved out. "My thanks go with you. Let me be first to salute my royal lord."

"And I second," Kay shouted, ranging in at my knee. "You've taught them all to stand straight again. *Ave,* Artorius."

"God and Arthur!"

I led them on toward the crown.

We picked up the road in an hour, pushing the horses hard. Our men rode in close formation, no straggling now. Bedivere relinquished his lance to Trystan, claiming his right to bear the dragon standard at my side. So it was the two of us in the lead, the red dragon overhead. Then Gareth, Kay, Trystan and Geraint with the piked heads, and behind them the massed hundreds of the heart of west Britain.

My head burned and throbbed as we rode, bleeding afresh now and then. I rode with no helmet or armor, in ragged linen shirt and filthy trousers spotted with blood and blackened with smoke. That was how the people of Britain, for whom all the horrors were done, would accept me. They would see the reality of what they wished for. Their king, their executioner, their chosen sacrifice.

As we rode, we kept alert for danger. There were only a few farmers on the road with their carts, hurrying aside as we thundered past. Sixteen miles to Kaelcacaestir. Thirteen. Nine.

Now across the open moor we sighted the low regular line of the old Roman fort walls and the dust cloud rising from the plain beyond. Four miles. We began to spy larger groups of people, nobles and peasants, all moving toward the gathering on the plain. The nobles swung away from the road, the oxen lumbered the wagons out of our way. All saw the red dragon flying and knew who had come to be crowned.

Two miles. The dust cloud loomed nearer and larger, the multitudes seething in their color and flash, distorted with distance but growing into individual shapes on the plain. Great masses of men and women and horses and flags and steel. The wagons of the peasants, the pennanted litters of the great, crosses of the monks, the bishops with their gold and silver croziers catching the sunlight.

One mile. Now we turned off the road toward the meeting plain, passing by the small thatch-and-wattle village where timid kerns peered out to see who rode so bloody and begrimed with severed heads on their lances to the place of choosing.

"A dragon. A dragon. It is Arthur!"

And Merlin whispered, *Ave, Imperator*.

"All very well to take the crown," Trystan worried beside me, gesturing ahead at the throng. "But what makes you think they'll take you?"

My head ached savagely. I shook it to clear my sight. "Because I'm all they've got."

Trystan grinned. "It's your humility one loves."

Geraint cried suddenly, "Arthur, look sharp!"

Out from the milling crowd, directly in our path rode a column of armed horsemen led by a gray-bearded man who wore a gold circlet about his helmet.

"Mark," Geraint hissed. "God rot his guts, riding straight and proud as if his murdering hands were clean."

"Don't slow down," I said. "We stop for nothing."

King Marcus gave an order we couldn't hear. The column opened left and right in a flank line directly across our path, some with drawn swords.

I called to the gray king. "Marcus, you know who I am. Don't try to stop me."

He answered smoothly, "It is nothing, Count Arthur. Just that you come straight through the ranks of the people. Turn aside and take your place with the other princes. We have waited for you."

"And in the strangest places," Geraint jeered. "Do you not see some friends on our lance heads?"

Marcus was too distant for me to read his expression, but it seemed he froze a moment.

Ave. Somewhere deep in the crowd the cry began. *Ave* for someone.

The distance narrowed between Marcus and myself. One hundred yards. Fifty. "Marcus, get out of my way or I'll run you into the ground."

"Boy," he threw back at me, "you threaten a king?"

"There's only one king here today, and it's me. Move aside, old man." I twisted in the saddle, feeling the dried blood crack around my mouth as I shouted the order. "Forward—charge!"

Ave, said Merlin again.

I dropped my lance point and ran straight at Marcus. The king held his ground for a moment, as if he couldn't believe I'd charge, then felt the force of that human arrow-shaft of purpose, my men, streaking for him. With a quick hand signal, he swung aside. His men crowded back to let us through. Not a sword was raised against us.

Now we surged through the massed crowd. My men pulled ahead in two long files to sheathe with iron my path to the imperial sword.

Ave!

Princes on all sides, and behind them the armed men that propped up their jealousies, their prides and their fatal indecision. And behind those, the common people, gathered from as far as men could walk or ride. Dumnonii who remembered me at Neth, the armorers from Severn who forged our swords under Kay and remembered why they were made. Men from the Catuvellauni whose homes were their own again and who knew the reason for the smoke over the midlands. Further on, the people of the north, Parisi and Brigantes who were alive today because I could ride eighty miles overnight to beat an enemy from their riverbanks. And over all the people and the dust rose the great, rocking, resounding echo of that cry begun on a hill near the Severn long ago.

Ave!

There was Cador at the head of his Parisi tribunes and ministers. I reined in abreast of him for a moment, searching for Guenevere. Cador flinched visibly from the stench of us.

"Where is Guenevere, Prince?"

"Behind the walls of Eburacum," Cador said. "With the gates locked."

"She'll open them for me," I told him.

"I believe Agrivaine gave orders to the contrary."

"Oh yes, the busy Agrivaine. If you're wondering where he is now," I laughed, "he's half a day south stoutly refusing to join me. Can you manage a smile for that, Cador?"

We moved on up the path the common people cleared before us. They were cheering, but the faces close by showed their horror at the sight of me.

"Has he painted himself, then?"

"That's blood. The man's half dead."

"Where's he been?"

"They can't kill Arthur. They can't kill the Pendragon!"

"Pendragon! Pendragon!"

Ave!

At the top of a low rise the mound of stones stood as in my death-dream, the great sword jutting hilt up from the top. I dismounted and gave the order: "Fan out. Cover the hill."

It seemed the top of my head was about to come off. I reeled with pain and exhaustion and would have fallen but for the arm that gripped me.

"Come, Artos," said Bedivere in my ear. "Just a bit farther."

We went up the rise together, Gareth, Kay, Trystan and Geraint coming after with their lances. Old Anscopius stood near the sword, gripping his crozier amid a gaggle of priests and monks.

"I've come to take what's mine, Anscopius."

The wrinkled, hawk-fierce visage did not draw back from the bloody apparition of me. "This sword is not for taking, Count, but for choosing."

Ave! Ave! Pendragon!

"Do you hear them?" I choked in the dust and heat. "If ever there was a choosing, they've done it already. Did Christ choose?"

Anscopius stood his ground. "What are you doing, blasphemer? You wear no thorns. There is no cross here, no sacrifice."

"Is there not?" I turned to face the multitudes below as the cry went up again and again like the baying of hounds on a scent. "What do you think they're cheering for, Anscopius? For the blood. For the heads on my lances. For the man who can wallow in this filth to give them what they want for as long as they want. The Irish killed their kings when they lost their virility. We only betray them and leave them to die alone like Ambrosius."

I reached out a dirty hand to grab a handful of his vestment. "So you cry *Ave* for me like the rest of them, old man. Say it! Because *you* made us, you and the rest of those princes that deserted Vortigern and wouldn't support Ambrosius. You made us necessary. And now we no longer serve. We take. Because there's no one else strong enough to do the job or stop us. Say it!"

Anscopius looked at me, then at the sweaty, intractable faces of Kay and my captains, and saw the truth of it. We were made fit for what we must do by what we had done.

"*Ave,*" he mouthed ironically. In submission, in pity, in compassion, in a wise old man's understanding of too much.

"We both know the mob, Arthur. But now they cheer you. Hail, Emperor of Britain."

And still there was a choosing of a kind. As I moved to the mound of stones, the *Ave* that had never ceased since I came on the field grew to a roar that was no syllable or word, but only an unending wave of assent from a single throat called Britain. And as I grasped the sword hilt, they knelt; first a few in front, then more, then all, going down on their knees in a rippling wave of acceptance.

You are the god-king now, Merlin whispered. *Do you love them?*

Yes, I—no. I don't know.

It doesn't matter, hostage that you are. See how they kneel. See where your men ring you round. How can any doubt you are the chosen? And does it impress you, Druith-fool? Does it make you drunk?

No, Merlin. Look at the bloody mess of me. Look at the faces of my men, at Bedivere who left his youth on the Wall and in the midlands. Look at the heads on the lances, smell the death in my clothes. I know the price. A king is only a sacrifice. Another sacrifice will come after me. Flint before bronze before iron. Waves on a shore, shaping it a grain at a time. You taught me that and I accept it.

Then take the sword from the stone. Ave, Imperator.

I lifted the imperial blade and held it high for the people to see. *Ave*—Merlin's voice faded but the roar went on shaking the earth and sky.

"Damn it, 'torius, wait!"

Kay's shorter legs labored to match my stride as we hurried toward Gareth waiting with our horses, past the holiday-fair crowd of merchants, jugglers, wine sellers, thieves and religious reformers who mushroomed on the plain in the wake of king-choosing.

"You're the rutting emperor now," Kay panted. "At least wait till you've washed your face."

"The ground's full of kings who waited. I've work to do."

I mounted and waved to Bedivere to bring the standard. All across the dusty plain, my men rose and moved to horse.

"Gareth, tell the princes: I'll count those men friends who come in friendship tomorrow."

He grinned up at me. "King of a hundred battles, it will be a sinful pleasure to carry the news."

"And Cador?" asked wary Kay.

"Halfway to Eburacum now," I judged. "And thinking on Guenevere. If he can't have the crown, he can sleep with it. And he'll love me with his whole ambition."

A new young king going to claim his queen! There's a ring to the notion. One can see the ranks of proud knights behind him, hear the blare of polished trumpets and cheers of the people as he dismounts to take his dewy-eyed virgin, royal consolation for the royal sacrifice. Actually it was a little taut at first: Cador's archers eyeing us from the walls of Eburacum, my weary men in wide ranks behind me, just out of bowshot. And very still.

"Let them try something," Geraint seethed. "One arrow, look you. One."

The gates opened. Cador rode out in full ceremonials, Peredur at his side in armor, the polished shield with its blazon of a British circled cross catching the late afternoon sun.

"Come, Bedivere." We paced the two horses over the flat ground, one eye on the walls. At ten yards' interval, Cador and his son halted. Cador saluted formally.

"Ave, Imperator."

But Peredur's greeting was warmer. "Greetings to my most royal lord."

"Peredur, *sut mae'r mab*! Good to see you well again . . . Bedivere, stay up."

Dismounting, I walked to the lords of Eburacum. "There are archers on your walls, Cador. You didn't greet Ambrosius so."

He spread his hands with a deprecating gesture. "A mere precaution such as you yourself would have ordered. We wondered if you truly came in peace . . . inasmuch."

"Only for my queen, Cador. Is she ready?"

"This last hour," Peredur affirmed. "And never have so many women toiled so fast." He scanned my waiting men. "But where's Lancelot?"

"Wounded saving me." I threw a significant look at Cador. "I've sent him to Astolat with Geraint's sister."

"He was kind when I was ill," Peredur remembered. "I'll go to him when I can."

"Well, Arthur." An exquisite nuance to Cador's brow. "You have the crown and the power and a queen fit for Solomon waiting. It's a new game on a new board. So with a kiss we bury the past."

We exchanged the kiss of peace—Cador daintily, grimy as I was. Over his shoulder, I saw Guenevere coming alone on foot through the gate. Cador glanced back at her with his slight, ambiguous smile.

"I would say we are all waiting, dearest son-in-law."

Like my first sight of her, she was in white, a simple linen *tunica* cut sleeveless in the Roman fashion, head bare except for a working of pimpernels twined through her hair where summer sun brought more red to the auburn. We met alone between the crowded walls and my watching men. Guenevere knelt gracefully. Only she and Cador could do it and make you feel like the supplicant.

"Hail to my royal lord."

For an asinine moment I had an urge to say something imperial for the ages, but nothing came.

"They've made me king, Gwen."

"That was clever of them," she said in a voice that caught on something. "You're all over blood."

"It was your letter saved us. We'd never have known about Agrivaine."

She touched my lacerated scalp. "What—?"

"You said you'd have flowers in your hair."

"Just pimpernels, all they could find in a hurry. Oh, Arthur." Her arms went around me, sudden and fierce and needing. My hands moved on her back as if to feed from it.

"Where's your white veil?"

"Conscience denied that. I didn't think you'd mind."

"Will you like being queen?"

Her head moved against my stained shirt. "I've always fancied it."

"Then where's a priest?" I held her away from me; she was crying. "Not Anscopius, we'll save him for Sunday best, but I want a priest now."

"Idiot, what in the world for?"

"Damn it, we're going to be solemnized six times over before we're crowned and done. I want to do it this first time just for us."

Her eyes widened in excitement. "Now? Here?"

"Right here and the hell with all of 'em."

"What fun!" She laughed as she did the first time I fell in love with her, head thrown back and the sound lilting up and out in an arc of pleasure. "And it's such a lovely day for it. Father! Someone up there on the wall. Find us a priest!"

Guenevere kissed me hard, strangling in the middle of it with her mouth still against mine.

"What's so damned funny?"

"I must do something about your clothes." She surveyed my bedraggled shreds with vast pity. "You have absolutely no sense of style."

We were married on the spot by a nervous young priest, to the cheers and weepy good wishes of my men, as well as the lords and ladies, merchants, fishwives and scullions of Eburacum. Of course it had to be done again at our coronation, but that would need time. All the nobles of free west Britain must assemble to see us solemnized and to swear their allegiance, always doubtful in a folk whose loyalties are first to blood and second to tribe. For the time, the old fort at Kaelcacaestir was my crude but watchful court.

Agrivaine raged in Eburacum. Once again I'd cheated him of a fight and taken Guenevere in the bargain. No doubt Cador salved that to some degree. ". . . Entirely out of my hands . . . by the way, have you met Lady Blodwen? Dazzling child, her father's my tributary . . . dining tonight, you must come."

Marcus Conomori grumbled about my method of succession, but made his peace and returned home. Not, however, without some tension. Geraint wanted to challenge him as a sneaking dastard and almost burst into flame when I forbade it.

"Mother of God, the scant snake's a blot on royalty and manhood!"

But he would obey out of loyalty. Guenevere made the task easier by nudging it into the sphere of gallantry.

"For manhood, Geraint, there's none in Britain who wears it more gracefully than yourself. Marcus is a slave, but having thrown it in his teeth, is it not manly to forgive?"

"Well, now . . ."

"Especially when your queen asks?"

"Well, I—" Fuming but confused, his lance blunted by the dove.

And Guenevere leaning forward to stroke his anger-darkened cheek, close enough for Geraint to breathe the subtle perfume of her body.

"For me, Gerry-fach?"

Peace in Cornwall.

But Gawain was a different matter, thundering into camp and

planting himself before us, livid. We were alone with Bedivere, who tried to interpose himself, but Gawain pushed him aside like a child.

"Damn your bloody, cheating eyes, Pendragon! Using me against my own brother who trusted me before God, but no longer. Damn you, why?"

"It was necessary, Gawain."

"You admit it, then?"

Bedivere would have drawn on him, but I signaled no. "To save lives, yes. I knew he'd refuse peace and needed that time."

Gawain trembled with the shame of it. "I'm dishonored among men, proud men who must someday support me as king. Men who have kept much grief from falling on Britain. My brother turns his back on me. On me who helped him take the first steps on his poor, unequal legs."

Guenevere tried to gentle him. "Gawain, there was so much at stake. Would you have Marcus king? Or even my father, God save him? If Arthur is Britain, he is all Britain and can no longer play foolish games of honor."

"Honor is not foolish! It is all a man has." Gawain turned away with a breaking voice. "I swore to Arthur, but he to me as well. We are done."

"I regret that." I left my chair and faced him. "But when you swore, you said it was because I was right. And right is bigger than men; if not, the next assassin who doesn't miss deserves that chair as well as me."

"Listen to him, sly with words as he is."

"As a king, I apologize for what had to be done. As a friend—"

"Friend! Oh, Jesus!"

"—I'd give anything to have you back."

"I trusted you." The vast, eloquent back to me. "Like no other lord. Did think you a man."

I took off Kay's borrowed coronet and tossed it to Bedivere. "As a man, I'll make what answer your honor demands."

Gawain fingered his gauntlet as if he might strip it off and throw it down, head lowered and mouth tight. The silence was heavy, the soft voice that broke it not threatening, but every syllable from Bedivere's heart.

"Wronged you were, Gawain. But if you hurt Artos, there's no place in God's world so far but I'll be waiting. On my salvation, think twice."

Not prudence but something else stayed Gawain, ravaged him.

His love and respect were not easily won; he had given me both. He had a friend and a brother. One made him fool and pawn against the other and now both were gone, leaving only a stubborn habit of honor. He dropped his hands.

"Good-bye, my lord."

My guts felt heavy as lead. "Good-bye, Gawain. If you can ever forgive me, please come back. God hold you in His hand."

Kingship has its squalid side, but it allows little time for regrets. While summer waned, with Kay as my *pro tem* minister, plans went ahead for the crowning. Monies must be collected, the reins of the whole tax structure put in my hands, a hundred messengers dispatched with orders, questions, invitations.

The old fort was little more than a bank-and-ditch enclosed square to which a few buildings and a stockade had been added, then left to decay. Space within and without the palisade was crowded with tents for my men and Kay's, the constant visitors, chiefs or their ambassadors, cooks, butchers, forge fires, the clang of hammers, the bustle of armorers, the sound and smell of horses, the throaty, jigging wood flutes and jingling tambourines of the players that sensed a paying audience like sharks and flocked to us.

In the afternoons we heard mass, then back for whatever conferences we needed with Kay, who knew more about taxes than either of us. The late evenings Guenevere and I kept for ourselves, but even by the rude bed where we slept and played and fitted to the hollows of each other, there were piles of tax tables, maps and dispatches, writing materials. Young and new as we were, we remembered the tragic failures of Vortigern and the lonely battles of Ambrosius. For the time, we rode the first glow of our people's hope and trust, but if we did not draw Britain together, someone else would kill us and do it themselves. No doubt some would be glad to, but never enough at the same time: for once, that first nervous summer, the tragedy of Britain worked in our favor.

The weight never left us, even in bed. Even wrapped around each other and moving to our climax, Guenevere's expression would change—

"Of course I love you, goose."

"Then what?"

"You *really* trust the Coritani?"

"Oh God, Gwen, not *now*!"

Or writhing under the caress of her wise mouth that set the center of me on fire, I'd explode gloriously, wrenching and panting down to sanity again. Quiet then, spent, with my heart slowing and Gwen's long hair flung cool and soft across my thighs, she would ask in the contented silence, "What are you thinking?"

"Nothing."

"Finger's twitching."

"Those damned Demetae taxes. Kay said—"

"Oh, really!"

Long bare legs sliding over the edge of the bed to snatch her nightrobe from a chair. "God in heaven, even when I'm—don't you ever leave it, Arthur?"

"Do you?"

The robe drops back on the chair. "No."

And she'd slip back into bed, nestling with one smooth leg between mine. "We do need so much money."

"Well, go to sleep."

"Mmm . . . cover me."

"Rest you gentle, Gwen."

"Sleep you sound."

That fall the last ineffectual Roman emperor abdicated in favor of a capable barbarian named Odoacer, who sent me greetings and styled himself King of Italy. Funny to think that Rome ended when we began. We were her children; she gave Gwen and me the language we thought in, but I was always more of a Roman at heart than Guenevere. And this must be remembered when you judge her.

Guenevere grew up in the north and enemy to her meant Pict. It was a thing deep in her vitals that the tribes north of the Wall were vicious dirt. As for Faerie, they were less than human. She heard at her nurse's knee how little folk were the reincarnated souls of the pagan dead, and where her educated mind later scorned, her Parisi soul still put the iron over the doorsill. And she could hate—not entirely without reason. It was a Venicone who tried to rape and murder her. The prejudice lived deep and implacable in my queen.

There were other things later, things that work on a woman. Although she was an astute ruler, some girl-part of Guenevere was yanked too soon into womanhood. She had never suffered injury or loss that could not be righted by a word to a hundred obedient hands. When our own child miscarried, she was helpless. No one could put it right. Is it any wonder she hated Morgana's son, who had the insolence to be beautiful as well as bold?

Guenevere was asleep, but I worked by fat lamp with a good blaze in the firepit against the wet autumn night. Bedivere knocked and entered, followed by a bedraggled little monk who dripped and shivered as he knelt to me.

"God's b-blessing and long life to the Emperor of Britain."

Brother Lewin he was, and he bore a letter for me.

"And that's all he bears." Bedivere had made sure. "We searched him like a beggar looking for lice."

"Sit by the fire, monk. What letter?"

Brother Lewin had a nervous stammer and the haggard look of a fat man gone thin too fast. His habit hung on him in sodden folds, but his eyes were honest and unshifting.

"Forgive me, Lord. I could not write her name, only what it sounded like. So m-many of her words were not words at all. I did my b-best."

"Bedwyr, some *uisge* for Brother Lewin."

The worn scrap of parchment was thin and brown with use. I read the letter through, read it again, feeling hot and cold.

"That's all, Bedivere. Get you to bed."

He glanced doubtfully at the monk. "And him?"

"He's done me a kindness. He'll sleep by my fire tonight."

The *uisge* warmed Lewin, half fire itself. He'd come a long journey from the far pastures of the Attecotti with nothing more than water to drink. And water was his downfall, that and the inhumanly dirty food of the otherwise blameless Attecotti to whom he preached the Word. If their dark gods were not invincible, their filth was. The water fevered his blood and a dish of boiled sheep's stomach opened up his bowels for a month.

My mouth watered. "It's a delicacy. They were offering their best, but it does tend to spoil."

Brother Lewin shuddered. "Yes."

The sickness was no laughing matter. The Attecotti nursed him, but his condition worsened until he couldn't eat or even sit up. Fearing for his life, the villagers decided that only Faerie magic could save him.

"By that time, Lord, I was so far gone with fever I knew not real from dream, and those dreams were of women. My old weakness. Satan much tempted me before I donned habit. So I thought the woman was a succubus sent to test me.''

Lewin's expression was more man than monk just then. ''The dark jewel of her, tiny but near perfect and nigh all of it showing as proof. And when she uncovered the rest and got in bed with me, I thought my soul was lost. But it was not for that. The warmth of her broke my fever, that and the magic drink she gave me.''

She cured him where none else could, coming each day to tend him while the wary village women hovered outside with iron and rowan against any evil she might take it in mind to work. And the dark woman demanded no payment of the Attecotti for curing their priest.

''Only of me,'' Lewin said. ''When I could sit up, she put her knife to my throat, my cowering self catching one word of her every four, and said the fever she banished she could bring again or cut my p-poor throat on the instant did I not pay her in service.''

Brother Lewin gulped at the *uisge*. ''Och, she was determined, my lord. Never have I seen a face so hard and set. But desperate as well. I think she would have begged if that had served.''

''And she asked you to write this?''

Lewin shifted uncertainly. ''Forgive all, m-my gracious lord. I do not know if this is impertinence, coming to you with this thing, if indeed this woman is what she says.''

''She was.''

''And forgive my Latin, but her language—God love me!—she has n-no notion of pronoun. You and she and he and us and ours, it's all the same, just said a little differently. It took me so long just to understand the gist. With your permission.''

Lewin approached and pointed to the bottom of the page. ''This word near the end, it's not a word at all. I could only scratch out what it sounds like and the sound is like nothing in this world.''

Mangled as it was, I recognized the Prydn word. It translates inadequately in British. It could be a whisper, a cry of joy or despair, carrying all the taste of the emotion, meaning *you* or *my knowing of you*. Wanting or fulfillment. So complete and all-embracing that Adam must have said it just so.

''It just means love, Brother Lewin.''

Lewin's letter as written made little sense, but I translated Morgana's heart with my own.

*Belrix third husband, lord of Briton-*fhain,
You said you would come home but did not.

*Venicone rode north with tale-speaking that Artostall-
folk is now first husband to Briton but I knew that was
Belrix.*

And I heard of adaltrach [*second wife*] *called Gwynhwyfar. I will not beat her when I see her, though I
have first wife right, she being pale and ugly as they
say and much older than me.*

Belrix has given fhain *son-wealth. He wracked me
being born, but I bit on the cloth and Dorelei held me
and I thought on the hills at Bel-tein and my lord of
summer.*

*Wealth is called Modred for Cradda's sire, but
Earth-name is Belrix.*

*Your wealth will come to you and you will know him
lord of fire. He is born of Mother and Lugh and
greatest beauty of all Prydn.*

I am filled and not filled with [love] *you.*

Morgana second daughter

Oh yes, Brother Lewin saw her child. It seemed impossibly
small like all Faerie children, but the woman told him it was
born at Brigid-feast six months past.

"And indeed beautiful, my lord. Nut-brown skin, black hair,
eyes slanted like his mother's. Oh, and angry, bless him! As if
she'd forgot to feed him and he wasn't going to stand for it."

Wheel of Shadow, Wheel of Sun

Ambrosius never built a seat of power, but Guenevere and I knew we must gather the reins in one place and keep them there, the hinge pin of Britain. In the midlands campaign I freed a number of slaves, some of them Iceni masons and carpenters from the eastern city of Camulodunum. Their homeland overrun, they attached to Maelgwyn. Learning of my desire for a royal seat, he sent them to me.

Severn river and valley is the heart of free west Britain, the home of Dobunni and Silure. On the west bank of the river, the Iceni built us an imperial villa not unlike Uther's, but much larger and better-defended with log and earthwork ramparts vitrified by fire. It was Roman in all but the subtleties: we needed firepits and outside latrines, since the builders knew nothing of Roman heating and sewage anymore.

A community more than a dwelling, there were houses within the walls for my *combrogi* and the entourages of tributary princes constantly coming and going. We named it Nova Camulodunum to honor the Iceni, but my people never called it anything but Camelot.

Within its precincts, there was no tribe or tribal interest, only the peace of Britain. Couriers came from Rome and even Byzantium; merchants brought us the riches of the east. Arabian stallions clattered down our quays, side by side with fine steel ingots from Damascus and Frankish armorers to wrap my *combrogi* with new ring-mail. And outward with our wool and tin and lead went our greater wealth, the singers of songs, the missionaries of Christ with their peculiar British taint, preaching social reform along with the Word—bright, diligent worms boring through the fat apple of the rich; the artisans in gold and enamel whose work was the glory of the Church.

My *combrogi* settled and married, bore children and flocked back to court on my command in surges of strength and color. The whole west and north felt a stirring of hope, of new beginnings fashioned from old dreams. In the ruins of Gaul, even in Rome, they began to hear the reviving heartbeat of their old province, and to returning envoys they said, "Tell us of Arthur and Guenevere."

When I want to remember without sadness or pain, those first years are best. Gwen and I walking by the river, watching twilight turn the water to purple and ink against the wheat-colored far bank. Listening rapt when someone near started a song, taken up by three or four or a dozen others—music the Saxon will never know. O Lord, give to Thy servant a voice. And He did. To the birds, He gave the lark. To man, the Briton. In such a place as Camelot the years can pass quickly, and they did.

Wheel of sunlight and shadow turning, and with its revolution, the face of the world changed. In the lost east of Britain, moss and weeds grew over Roman villas while the eastern land took new names like Bearruc Scir and East Seaxe. Yesterday's chief became today's king. The West Saxons crowned Cerdic.

"And thus they dignify themselves," fumed Guenevere whose royalty descended from Boudicca in the days of Nero. "That miserable thief a king!"

"He's royal as I am, Gwen."

"Rot!"

"And he gets the job done, that's what counts to Saxons."

She hacked aggressively at her breakfast pears. "He's a jumped-up barbarian who killed my people and sacked my home. Should I call him equal because he's learned to eat at a civilized table without embarrassing his host? Oh, he has a veneer of charm, and I know you like him—eat your eggs before they get cold—but that shouldn't keep you from pushing him into the sea. Arthur, are you listening to me?"

"Sorry."

"What are you reading?"

"Letters from Rome. Have you seen them?"

Letters from Odoacer, love letters to Britain that made the older princes remember imperial times, dress nostalgically in the last of their faded senatorial stripes and balk me in council just

long enough to lose our initiative with the Saxons. Masterly
letters with just enough promise and veiled hint of power to see
how the wind blew over Britain. To test our strength or the
lack of it.

"And that's just what he's doing, make no mistake!" I strode
around the council table, pleading with each man—Cador, Marcus, Caradoc, Maelgwyn—as I caught his eye. "The time to
move east is now while the people are full of hope, but I can't do
it with cavalry along. Whatever we take we have to occupy."

"All the more reason to wait for Roman reinforcements."
Marcus rose from his chair, tall and gaunt, watchful eyes shadowed by beetling brows. "These letters are not only from Odoacer,
but from Lucullus, the son of Ambrosius. How can we doubt
their sincerity?"

I stopped pacing. "Lucullus hasn't spoken Brit since he was
ten years old. He lives in Laurentium with both his lovers, a
sweet young girl and a cherubic boy. And if that's not sufficient
indication of his ability to change directions rapidly, reflect that
Lucullus was envoy for the last emperor of Rome before sidling
up to Odoacer. A biddable man who'll do what his master tells
him. So much for the native son."

I stood behind Marcus' chair. "Prince, no one stands to gain
more than you by stronger ties to Rome, which means Roman
galleys to protect your shipping. I'll listen to an agreement for
protection of trade, but I won't put a knife in their hands and
bare my neck."

Maelgwyn agreed with Marcus, though for vaguer reasons.
"I'd like to see them come back. Not only the legions but the
culture, the permanence. Our children grow up ignorant now."
He shifted his corpulent bulk in the chair. "Let Odoacer's legions
sail up Severn, then we'll talk about the east."

"Odoacer's legions!" I slouched into my own chair at the
head of the table. "Do you think we're unique? That what
happens here happens nowhere else? If there's a whole legion
anywhere, could they ship to Britain any faster than Cador or
Trajanus could budge their farmers from home? Fat chance,
boyo! The world is changing, my lords. Be so good as to glance
out of doors at it now and then."

Guenevere caught my glance—with me to the hilt, but warning: a little less rhetoric, a little more reason.

Kay toyed with his stylus, running stubby fingers through his beard. "They've made no firm promise of help, and I doubt Odoacer could mount an effective force right now." He touched his fingertips together, thinking aloud. "But say he could. Are we foolish enough to think he does it for nothing? Here's your east coast back, call again when you need me?"

"That's occurred to me," Cador mused. "But meanwhile, a policy of open but watchful friendliness costs us nothing. We should wait and see. As for the east,"— he shrugged—"I can do nothing now."

"It'll be harder the longer we wait," I countered wearily. "As for Rome, their only profit here is a tributary province, and that we are not. They might have left us the tools, but we built the house."

Marcus wouldn't swallow that. "He wouldn't dare ask for tribute!"

I shot back, "The Saxons didn't dare with Vortigern till they had a knife at his throat!"

They didn't see the knife in the Roman ploy. Not conquest but control. A legion in Britain meant a hand on our rein. They might retake the east, but for whom? And under what conditions?

Still, Maelgwyn was wistful. "My grandfather used to tell me of the old days. The law, the peace, the security. Finest schools in the empire. Seventy years ago we were begging them to come back. Arthur, at least listen to their offer."

"Eagerly—from behind a tall fence."

"On a high hill," added Kay.

And on and on through the afternoon. Deep in their hearts, they knew the Rome they remembered or had heard about was gone. But they could still conjure with the magic of that name. They saw the villas restored, peacocks strutting through manicured gardens, the sculpted fountains and ponds: Cupid peeing to the replenishment of languid goldfish. The last remnant of old empire still intact, ready to become a center of the new. Luxury, riches, power. A dream like the Grail, and dreams die hard.

I listened, thinking desperately: What would Ambrosius do? Rome was like a parent that turned her child out to fend for itself. Then, old and feeble, she begged our love once more. No, the sun rises on tomorrow, not yesterday. We couldn't go back.

"Is there not a full legion in Gaul?" old Caradoc wondered, rousing himself from reverie. He knew and cared very little about Rome, but felt he ought to say something as oldest prince of the Council. Long ago some scrap of information must have found its way to rustic Astolat. "That of—what was his name—Tiberius, yes, that's it. Perhaps he could help against the Saxons."

"My good lord," I said, "Lucius Tiberius is up to his patrician arse in Franks. In a year or two, he'll call Clovis king."

Cador observed, "Our young emperor is admirably informed."

"A part of your taxes go to keep him so, father."

Guenevere knitted serenely a little apart from our group on a chair specially cushioned to ease her pregnant weight, but missing nothing. "This business of Rome is like the seducer who couldn't bed the girl without a solemn promise of marriage, and we all know that sad ending. If we take Odoacer to bed on a promise, we'll find ourselves had and left. For Cerdic, the man is Arthur, the choice is yours, and the time is now."

Her father demurred. "I can't. My own taxes are barely dribbling in."

"Shame, father. You collected in full last month."

His composure fled for a second. "And how does my queenly daughter know that?"

"We pay to know. As you taught me." Guenevere inspected the uneven stitchwork plied by her needles and rose cautiously. "You must all excuse me now. The doctors say I must rest, and it's far past nap time."

As with Ambrosius, the issue was a draw between myself and the Council. I kept Rome at a wary distance, but the princes refused my war until it was too little and too late. You wonder why our music is so haunted with sadness. We are perverse. We love lost causes. We love losing.

Little Gareth panted up to where I stood alone on the ramparts and thrust the dispatch at me.

"From Prince Peredur, sir. The courier said it should come straight to you."

I leaned against a crennel, not interested but skimming over Peredur's precise Latin. It seemed barely more than routine. Someone was raiding Votadini villages and peculiar circumstances showed in each case. Suggest I send an observer, et cetera.

There were more important problems. Guenevere's pregnancy was vexed with complications. The doctors cautioned her not to rise at all. Beyond that, Trystan had disappeared on the Saxon borders, long overdue. Maelgwyn held out scant hope for his survival. Between wife and lost friend, my heart wasn't with the northern news. Brude's savages butchered each other every day; what in hell could I do about it?

Still, if Peredur thought it warranted a single observer—

"Gareth, send me Bedivere. Have him meet me here."

He squinted in puzzlement. "Sir?"

"Are you deaf? Get Bedivere. Now."

"In a trice, good lord, had my horse wings. He's gone home this last week."

My mind was still on Guenevere; she had looked drawn that morning. "What?"

"You gave him leave to go, sir. His little lass is down with colic."

And myself so used to the man called the right hand of Arthur, I reached with it before realizing it was gone.

I've talked very little about that man so close to me our shadows merged as one. At my side from boyhood, sweating with me to learn sword from Uther's men, the same roads, the same battles, cold meals shared out of the same clay dish, the same fortunes from the beginning. And finally slipped away to a life of his own in a moment so full of cares, the busy emperor didn't notice his shadow was gone.

Marriage cultivated Bedivere like rain on thirsty soil. The long, too-taut body relaxed and filled out, the eyes and mouth lost the hard vigilance learned on the Wall. When he brought his bride to Camelot, I barely remembered her from childhood, a shy young woman in worn best linen kirtle who lisped "G'bless our king" in a Dobunni accent as she knelt, stiff with propriety. And there she remained until Bedivere took her arm.

"Myfanwy, love, get up. It's Artos from home."

He came and went now, with me when needed but always preferring home to Camelot. I cherished his visits, but now there was a daughter teething and they'd be up all night with her chafing. And then Bedivere would be off teaching Myfanwy to hunt with hawk or hallooing old friends to show off tiny Rhonda with insufferable pride.

"And already talking." Bedivere jiggled the damp infant in his arms. "Just one word. Da. Say da, love. Who do you love best?"

"Ging," burbled the child.

"There, will you listen to her!"

Or he'd be showing wide-eyed Myfanwy the almost-Roman splendor of Camelot, the view from the walls and this and that, and seeing them together, close and turned in to each other, I realized that friend I might be still but no longer first. And no right to ask it beyond duty. Bedivere had something of his own for once. Let be. Still, I missed him.

Myfanwy turned him out well. Bedivere no longer went about
with holes in his seat. She did more, opened the locked places in
Bedivere so that my old friend's scolding mellowed to tolerant
wisdom. The moment came when I needed that wisdom, and it
was there.

Guenevere lost the child. She wouldn't stay in bed but insisted
on sitting through the councils with me, whose government,
especially of the north, was her charge as well as mine.

Yes, I was useless as Nectan. *Fhain*-custom, I wanted to be
with her, but the midwives blushed and never heard of such a
thing and the emperor should not even speak of it. I lunged about
the anteroom with Bedivere sprawled in a chair trying to make
me light somewhere.

"There's something I can do, Bedwyr. Let her hold my wrists
or—"

"It's not a man's place; you'd be in their hair. And they don't
preserve birth-strings anymore except up in the hills. Peace now,
sit down and tell me the news. What of Lancelot? Has that
horrible woman permitted him to bed her yet?"

Their last letter reported a child on the way, but Eleyne was
not too well, suffering from "retention."

"What in hell's that?" Bedivere asked.

"A euphemism out of his gallant nature. She's constipated."

"Hah!" Bedivere threw back his head and roared with rich,
easy laughter. "Oh, that's Eleyne to her granite maidenhead.
She can't let go of anything."

He made me laugh, he eased the time. After an eternity, the
women came out to say that Guenevere would be fine in a week
or two. They never showed me the poor thing taken from her.
And I was not to go in just yet.

"What do you mean? Get out of my way!"

Frightened of my anger, the women still held their ground.
"Please, my lord, the queen said—she begged that you not—"

"Move aside, damn you!"

A midwife I might cow, but not that iron Mars suddenly
blocking the door.

"Get away, Bedivere. I'll knock you flat."

"You never could and you know it. She doesn't want you yet.
Isn't she proud as you and thinking she's failed? Let her get the
handle of that before she has to deal with you."

He never left my side, though the long hours dragged. When
Guenevere did call for me, Bedivere followed me to her door,
staying me a moment before I groped for the latch.

"It doesn't matter now what *you* feel. Not a word of it, you hear? Give her all the giving you've got. Be a father, a husband, be a bloody fool if that's what she needs. But give."

"I can't. I feel so empty."

"I know," Bedivere answered gently. "A woman loses it out of her body, but we do, too. It was a gift that came so close."

"Yes. And I—" Crumpling against his shoulder. "And I—God damn it—"

My friend held me. "Na, you never touched it, never felt it move in your belly. But you did walk with it in your heart. And when it flies, the women wonder why we're crying, we never carried it. But we did. Go on."

When I bent over Guenevere, I was steeled to be a stone saint, but not for what met me. She lay on the pillow like something left by a storm, white as the linen. Behind the exhaustion there was a bafflement and something else I couldn't name. Her fingers were cold and limp in mine.

"It was a girl," she managed in a weak little mew. "It tore me."

A priest hovered by, and a gaggle of solicitous Parisi women with broth to strengthen her. I took the cup and waved them out. No one would tend her but me. With one arm around her shoulder, I fed her the broth in sips, thinking, Frailty and sickness don't go with this woman. She's too strong. She's awkward at needing anything. Where do the strong go when they need to be weak?

"There was never anything taken from me I couldn't have back or better," Guenevere trailed on in that faraway voice. "Never lost anything, never got hurt. Even that Pict who tried to take me, I could kill him." Desperate, trying to understand in a language she knew. "But where do I stab now, Arthur?"

"Rest now. I'll be here, won't budge even when you sleep. I'll take care of you."

"Was that a priest here? Who thought I was going to die?"

I settled her back and pulled the covers up. "He just wondered if you wanted to pray. That's his job."

"Pray?" I saw the thing behind her bafflement. It was red and it could kill. Guenevere turned her head away. "I'll pray to God when I've forgiven Him."

In the end Gareth went to observe what Peredur reported. No better scout existed than the little Leinsterman, who could be trusted to take no chances and bring back a clear picture of what he saw. He did.

The Votadini were slaughtered in their beds, horses and cattle run off. No trouble at the Wall yet, but Agrivaine was doubling the strength of patrols and mile castles.

"Then what's peculiar?" I pressed Gareth. "They kill each other every day up there."

"*Daone sidhe,*" he muttered in his own language. "Not Picts, my lord. Picts steal food, but not extra mouths to feed. There's only one kind that steals newborn from the cradle. *Daone sidhe.* Faerie."

That he tracked them was a measure of his courage. The Irish have a fearful respect for Faerie greater than our own. Gareth's language is rife with tales of folk caught spying on a Faerie gathering. He found their tracks near a crannog and settled down to watch, praying to God and a full company of saints.

"And a few others a priest would not hear of kindly," Gareth confessed. "But magic's driven out by magic, and the moment of trial's not the moment to doubt."

They rode across the moor to the crannog and disappeared under the hill while the moon swam through swift-moving clouds and Gareth shivered with an ancient fear.

Still it didn't seem right to me. "Gareth, are you sure of this? Prydn don't have the numbers for that kind of raid. They're peaceful folk."

My comite drew himself up, pride touched. "Did I not count Agrivaine's strength for you down to the last stone-slinger? When did I say one thing when it was else? I saw no few but a horde. A hundred."

Easily a hundred, Peredur's next report confirmed.

> And led by a woman who rides with a small boy. We can't get much sense out of the tribes, you know how they fear these creatures. When this woman rides, the Picts get out of her way. She leaves nothing alive in the villages. Most curious, there were empty cradles and no dead infants. So the old tale may be true. Children are taken to be raised by these demons and become like them. They call them changelings . . .

Morgana meant what she said. The enduring was done, the paying back begun. Prydn would live if she had to tear the world to bear her dream alive.

*   *   *

Shadow and sunlight, the wheel turning, days becoming weeks becoming months. April again.

Spring comes early in the islands off the tip of Cornwall, with a burst of flowers the rest of our country rarely sees. The grounds of Camelot at her disposal, Guenevere took up gardening with a vengeance. She sent to the islands for cuttings and bulbs and labored to make them thrive in Severn valley. Dressed all her life for the public, I think she enjoyed mucking about on dirty knees with homespun skirts tucked up in an apron, and she handled the bulbs like children, placing them reverently in the fine-troweled earth and watering with the care of a benediction. This is where I found her when news came to please her. Since the loss of our child I hunted for things to make her happy, perhaps to convince myself *I* was.

"Gwen! Up here on the rampart!"

She squinted up at me. "What is it?"

"Trystan's alive! He's coming home!"

The floppy peasant hat sailed high in the air. "H'rah! Hurry, come down and tell me."

My lost lamb returning to the fold. He was inspecting Maelgwyn's eastern border for signs of new Saxon encroachment when he sent asking leave to go home on completion of his task. That was the last word or sight of him. He disappeared, presumed dead after a reasonable time. Marcus sent lachrymose condolences and must have been vastly disappointed to find them premature.

"There were two sides to Trystan," Maelgwyn said after my comite disappeared. "One a good soldier and a bard to silence the angels for shame. Is it any less than truth, Arthur?"

The old Catuvellaun prince sighed over his drink. "But there was a sickness to the man. I'll say it out. Self-pity that wrapped him round like a snake and, once bitten, he stayed drunk. Just staggered about muttering to himself and playing the harp till he fell dead asleep over it. If playing's the word. Have you ever heard a harp scream?"

Aye, Trystan could draw beauty from strings, but there were times when a disease crept through them to produce eerie chords stained with subtle dissonance. These wordless songs were usually rhythmed by an odd, three-note figure that dominated all and seemed to obsess Trystan himself.

Guenevere's women withdrew to a respectful distance, but

close enough to hear: Trystan was always news. Gwen leaped at
me, hugging and swinging off her feet to hang on my shoulders.

"Now, what's this? Where is he? Is he all right?"

"Your favorite harper's coming home."

"Wonderful, wonderful! I knew he wasn't dead. That scamp,
would he die without an audience of tearful women and a bard to
catch his last, singing words? Never! Where is he?"

"The messenger said he took the word at Wight. His ship
stopped there."

"Wight?" Gwen's brows knitted in bewilderment. "That's
Saxon."

And it was virtually a Saxon who entered our private chambers some days later. Trystan in a thick beard, wide-skirted blue
tunic, gartered wool leggings with a seaxe knife and a purse full
of Saxon silver hung on his belt. And a gift for us we couldn't
buy: a knowledge of the Saxon mind.

"The truth is, I get bored," he told us over a private supper.
"Nothing seems to be enough. Once it's there, I need something
new to keep me thinking. Or from thinking. The world's a
ghastly, ghostly place, but at least when I'm drunk the phantoms
are my own."

Gwen said tenderly, "You fool, why don't you marry?"

"And be court musician to my queen? There's a life. Who
played for you when I was gone?"

Gwen made a face. "Lord Pwyll, and he keeps missing
notes."

"His mind's on women." I dipped a morsel of fish in liquamen.
"That man's four wives now and still hunting."

"Stuff." Guenevere would have none of that. "The truth is,
he hates women and keeps wiping off the last with the next.
Though it would be easy and a pleasure to arrange a match for
Tryst. I believe you grow handsomer each year."

"You flatter me, and I don't believe a word."

"Of course you do." Gwen patted his wrist. "You're the
vainest peacock in Arthur's brood. The beard and the lines help.
You look traveled and interesting."

Oh, it was good to sit and watch them both. "Take him back
out of the grave, Gwen. He's not yet thirty."

"And where's my growling, scowling Bedivere?" Trystan
asked.

"Home with wife and bairn," said Guenevere.

"And happy?"

"Disgustingly," she trilled. "The way he lugs poor little Rhonda about, you'd think he bore her alone."

Trystan grinned wickedly. "I hear Myfanwy bore her nine months to the day after nuptials."

"Six," purred Guenevere. "We counted. The doctors considered it a wonder of anatomy."

I threw a shrimp at her. "You nasty little gossip. As if a queen didn't have better things to think on."

"Oh, sweet, we were *delighted*, all of us. To think somebody got the Gryffyn off a horse for five minutes. I used to think he grew out of it."

Good to see her laugh so freely again. When the servants withdrew, Trystan spoke of his time among the barbarians. Maelgwyn, it seemed, kept a Saxon *scald*, a harper like Tryst, and from this man Trystan learned to appreciate the language he once likened to the sound of a dying crow.

"But it beats like a drum, it strides! And by my gods, you can hear that drum like a messenger riding ahead of fate, riding toward Asgard and the final war with evil. They're fatalistic, they see all going into darkness anyway. The struggle is what counts."

The language fascinated him. When his mission for me was done, he had clothes made in the Saxon style and began to sing for his supper among the pagan tuns of the east. He represented himself as a Belgae with a Saxon father, raised in the Brit language by his mother. No matter, a harper is welcome anywhere. He sang for thanes and farmers alike, learned their language and how they thought.

"Forget the warriors, they're only a few around the chiefs. The man to understand is the farmer. Each man has his own. He doesn't huddle close to his kin, but spreads out and settles where he pleases. If there's a lord at all, he owes him certain duties and no more. He's frugal. And no wonder, you should see what they live on waiting for a crop. May I never taste another turnip again. And he farms with a passion I'd reserve for bed or music."

There was another vital difference in them which eluded Trystan entirely until he stopped thinking like a British lord. Power was based on property more than blood. Land gave a man power and a certain amount of it could give him rank.

"Would we do that?" Trystan challenged. "Perhaps here and there a Bedivere or Gareth. But Saxons are born knowing they might be landowners for a little effort. If Cerdic doesn't lead this ambitious man west, mark me, he'll come by himself.''

Guenevere found that outlandish. "By themselves? Peasants?''

"Lady, your notion of peasant doesn't exist in Saxon. They have their slaves, but anyone else can own land. And if all the east is claimed by others, where to go but west?''

It cast a new light on our old problem. We could make a treaty border with Cerdic. That might stop expansion for a time, but it would be interpreted as legally recognizing Saxon right over the east. No British king has done that, or will.

We could launch a massive campaign to take back the east a piece at a time. This would require years and ample foot legions, and these my princes would not part with.

Conclusion: we must skirmish continually with what we had, two hundred *combrogi*. A half measure, like skimming the tops off weeds and leaving the roots untouched. But that's the story of Britain. Maelgwyn had promised a bit of help at least. We would commence in early summer to push the new settlers back.

For services already rendered, I would have left Trystan at Camelot as lord-milite under Guenevere but he turned it down.

"You'll want an interpreter." He poured his cup too full of Falernian wine. "And the truth is, as I said, one gets bored.''

Those words and that act were the story of his life. Trystan did not have long to serve me.

A few days after he returned, we received an envoy from Marcus Conomori. The prince would attend my planned meeting of the Council. Queen Yseult would accompany him to pay her respects to Guenevere. They'd met only once or twice, but Gwen defended Yseult where others turned up their noses.

"A simple soul and fragile as an egg. *And,* when it comes to that, no more a slut than a dozen I could summon without raising my voice.''

But there were problems. "Arthur, can we keep Trystan sober or out of sight? Or both?''

On a sultry, sunless day, Marcus stepped off his ship onto our quay followed by the most beautiful woman in Britain.

Guenevere and I waited, flanked by Gareth and Kay in their formal best. My own queen was radiant, the flawless product of her women's maximum efforts. An affection for Yseult did not include being outshone by her, but they embraced like sisters.

"Two such women together," Gareth eulogized. "Is it wonder the poor sun hides for jealousy?"

He was to be Yseult's escort of honor. After the formal greetings, I presented him to Marcus and then Gareth knelt, saluting Yseult in her own dialect.

"*Cead mille failté*. A thousand welcomes and yet a thousand waiting for the Lady of Cornwall."

No woman ever brightened faster. "You *must* be from home with such a tongue. Of Leinster, Lord?"

Married and faithful Gareth was, but not deceased. His chest swelled visibly under the dazzle of her. "Of nowhere else, Lady."

"Then no other will wait on me." And yet her dark eyes swept quickly up the quay and through the knot of my people for someone else, and in them I read a mixture of disappointment and relief.

Suddenly, Yseult clapped her hands. "Gwinny, sweet, can you even guess what it is I've brought?"

"You're too generous, whatever it is."

"Not a whit, not a bit. Grapes!" Yseult gestured with a flourish toward the gangplank where several of her entourage were carefully unloading sack-covered vines. "Snippets, cuttings all the way from Rome, no less of a place."

She could bring nothing to endear her more to my wife. "Oh, you angel! Yes, they look good and healthy. Come along now, tell me how they fared and how did you cut. Did you keep them from the sea air?"

"Like sick children."

"It's so bad for them, you know."

Arm in arm, they chattered up the steps to the palace.

"Marcus." I took his arm. "Most welcome."

"My duty to my king. Prince Caius, greeting." Yseult's husband seemed to search the quay as she did. "I hear my nephew's safe. You don't know how glad that makes me. Why isn't he here to greet his loving uncle?"

Because I damned well made sure he wasn't. "On an errand of state just now. I'm afraid we keep him quite busy. The Silures—most important. Do hope you'll forgive it."

"Of course, of course." Marcus was expansive. "Come, I'm anxious for dinner and talk of the Council. Now, these hill forts you want me to restore. Is the need really so great, Artorius? Not to mention the expense . . ."

"Yseult is a dear," Gwen decided that night before bed. "She tended those vines herself the whole voyage from Dore. Such a country girl, really. Before she married she had two kirtles to her name and a tatty old shift to sleep in. And credulous as a babe: she still wonders why priests don't do magic. To her, they're just druids in different clothes."

She went on nimbly plaiting her hair as she talked. "But how these damned women go on about her. She's this, she's that when the plain truth is, she's just beautiful and they hate her for it." Guenevere frowned critically at the mirror, patting her chin. "But she is putting on weight."

There are days when even an emperor can't make a penny. I'd sent Trystan on some trumped-up errand to keep him clear of Yseult, but Cador arrived tardily. The Council and Yseult were still in residence when Trystan returned. Sooner or later he'd find a way to her. It was my questionable fortune to see it.

I happened to glance out of a casement that commanded a view of Guenevere's garden hidden by an angle in the wall from most other views. I saw Yseult strolling alone and at ease through the straight avenues of spring flowers. The attitude of her whole being was peace and repose, as if this moment alone were a delightful treat. Ready to call a greeting, I just watched rather than intrude. She made me think then of little Drost spying out some new wonder to study.

Her head turned sharply toward something I couldn't see. Her mouth opened in a soft cry too distant to hear. Her arms went out and Trystan came into them. They locked together, rocking back and forth, Trystan's face buried in her hair and neck as her head fell back to drink in the pleasure of him.

I turned away from the casement.

Dinner that evening was held in the large hall since Caradoc, Maelgwyn and Kay and all their high officers were present. Trystan appeared in a bardic blue robe, harp polished and fine-tuned. Never did he sparkle more, never was the dark of him so vanquished by the light. He greeted his uncle with convincing affection and was courteous beyond reproach to Yseult, tactfully leaving her service to Gareth whose office it was. That Gareth was more than adequate to his charge inspired his wife Rhian to grumble, "Were he not my husband, I'd say the Irish were too light of tongue and loose of eye."

"Surely," I protested, "not Lord Gareth."

"Surely not," Rhian affirmed grimly. "He sees through the like of her, but too kind to show it."

"So it's said of your husband. There's not a kinder man in Britain."

Our tables were formed in a horseshoe, servers tending from the center and Trystan among them, singing like a lark, turning aside to joke with this or that man as the fancy took him. Now he caught the arm of an old carver.

"Llewellyn-fach, can you swim?"

The gnarled Llewellyn denied it. "No, my good lord, that I cannot."

"Why then you'll live forever."

Kay called, "And how could he do that?"

"Life's an island surrounded by sleep, and if you can't swim on the dark, I fear you're stuck on this shore."

Llewellyn considered that seriously. "I wouldn't mind."

Trystan took up his harp. "Only so long as the shore is beautiful. No fear, man. Stay high, stay dry. I'll go for us both."

He swept an arresting chord across the strings. "Emperor of Britain! Princes, lords! Ladies to shame the light of day and make the moon think twice before shining! One last song—and what shall it be?"

"A love song," Guenevere bade him. "The one you sang for me."

"A love song by command of my queen." Tryst bowed to her and Yseult by her side. The dark Irishwoman dropped her eyes. I thought she looked troubled and sad.

"Now, this is truly a British love song," Trystan prologued. "A shepherd finds his love, loses her and, after much travail and sorcery, finds her again and never lets her go. As he shouldn't have done in the first place. This lay was not popular among the Saxons: they're for a different tune. The farmer finds a woman, the woman bears child, the land gets plowed by both of them. All of which demonstrates that the heart of Saxon can usually be found with his turnips."

Laughter around the table, a rattling of cups on the board.

"No more, then." Trystan rippled a chord over the strings. "A love song."

He played—the simplest, loveliest music I ever heard from him. But I remember when it ended, his fingers wove against the clear melody a hint of that weird three-note figure oddly unconnected to the rest.

*   *   *

"Arthur, are you asleep?"

"Yes."

Gwen pulled my face around to her. "None of that, you great child. We must talk. I'm worried."

I turned over with a sigh. "Just drifting off. Thought they'd all never go to bed."

One lamp burned near the bed. In its light her face was heavy and serious. "We've a problem."

"Just one?"

"Listen to me. It's Trystan."

"Now, was he ever better than tonight? He didn't touch a drop."

She bounced up on one elbow. "And do you know why? He thinks she's going away with him."

That opened both eyes. "When was this?"

"She told me before dinner tonight. He found her in the garden and—"

"Yes, I saw them. Pray no one else did."

"Well, she was glad to see him, thinking him dead for so long. And she said things she didn't mean to say. She made promises."

Guenevere sat up beside me, arms crossed under her breasts. I wrapped the coverlet around her.

"Does she still love him, Gwen?"

"It's not that simple."

"Well, he goes away again tomorrow, by God."

"She doesn't want to hurt him, but she can't do what he wants."

"Not now," I agreed. "It's too damned expensive."

"She wants you to do something."

More than a love affair was at stake. With Cerdic building his forces and probing my coasts like a surgeon deciding where to cut, I needed Marcus to re-arm every possible hill fort on his south shore. He saw no need for the expense and might use this insult to refuse, possibly break with me and ally on his own with Rome or even Cerdic.

"God damn it, Gwen! Would she were born a pig or not at all! She's comely, men are *going* to be at her, why can't she handle it? I wish she had your sense."

"Me?" Gwen said wistfully. "I was never that beautiful. A skinny little girl clever at Latin and sums, but I knew my worth. She never did."

She hugged the coverlet to her. "Everything hurts her. Dear

God, how she prattled at me over the planting of those vines. She's starved for a woman friend, just someone to be close with. And you know how the women down there treat her. That bitch from Astolat. Poor Yseult, she'd be so happy loving someone simple, without a brain or a nerve in his body."

Guenevere sighed. "But it was Tryst, and he's too complicated. They'd never be happy anywhere. He loves the wanting, not the having. Dull as she is, Yseult knows that."

She burrowed under the covers again. "You must do something. Think on it?"

"I'd rather have my teeth pulled."

"So would I. But you're the only one Tryst'll listen to." She kissed my cheek. "Good night, love. Rest you gentle."

"Sleep you sound."

Nothing for it but to see the two in private, have it out and done. The matter took some light of hand, but Gwen and I managed it. We arranged an elegant hunt for the princes of the Council and their chief men, a jaunt that would take them hours from Camelot through lovely country, with wine and musicians to attend them, everything done but the bending of their bows.

Then I sent for Yseult and Trystan.

The chamber selected was reserved for private audiences, with no furniture but two state chairs raised on a small dais. I planted myself on one of them and waited, hating virulently what had to be done.

A freshet of flower-scented breeze came through the open casement, a bird sang in a pear tree, the warm spring sun bathed all Severn in its glow. A day to fall in love, not end it. My fingers drummed on the arm of the chair. Footsteps. My fingers paused.

Yseult slipped into the chamber. She would have knelt, but I stopped her.

"No ceremony, love. Come sit down."

I deposited her in the other chair. She was in green with the dark hair curled tight and prim about her neck. Over the green kirtle was a loose *supertunica* of the same shade, well cut to conceal the slight tendency to flesh. We are a people vain of our figures; our clothes are close-fitting when we have something to show off. No doubt Yseult ate sparingly, but wile served where will could not.

"I don't want to hurt him," she said. "He thinks I'll go away with him. When I saw him, I forgot all my common sense and the promises to myself and I said what he wanted to hear."

She stirred restlessly in the chair. "It's almost ten years, and I'm not his—not what I was. Just tired, and Trystan will never see that."

"But you know it has to end."

"It is ended. Long ago, and it can't be anymore."

I sat down next to her. "Then you can't help hurting him. Cut deep and quick and be done with it."

Those helpless, wounded eyes turned on me again. "Then truly we'll both have nothing. For myself, it's being numb, no more than I have been all these years. But what's there for him, Arthur?"

"Damned if I know," I confessed. "I'm wondering what to say when he comes that won't sound righteous or bloody stupid. I've seen him before a charge, the two of us so sure of death we were white with it, dry in the mouth and wet in the pants, and then he'd follow me right down its throat and come back with a joke to hide his trembling. I've covered him up when he drank himself to sleep. I've cursed him awake, trusted my life to him, and all I've ever known of his heart was that he wanted one thing. Now, *I* have to say he can't have it. And if you think being king of the whole Christly lot makes it any easier, you're wrong. There, he's coming."

His rapid, light footsteps came down the passageway, then Trystan swung into the room. "Now, sweet king! What's—Yseult."

"Come in," I ordered. "Close the door, sit or stand, but listen."

Listen? He barely knew I was present, taking Yseult's hands and kissing them. She avoided his eyes, but the empathy of them was like another person in the room.

"Hear Arthur," she told him in a small voice. "Heed the High King of Britain."

"Arthur, what is this?"

"It's a good-bye, lad. Yours." I took a breath. "I'm sending you away, but I want your oath you'll never see or send word to Yseult again."

I might have chattered in an unknown language. "What did you say?"

"You heard me."

He gave me his quick smile. "Ask my blood, I'll pour for you. My life? On the block with yours any day. But not this."

Yseult was miserable. "Trystan, please listen to him."

"I've listened to him for years. And I love him, but he's no part of this. What's he want of you, what's he said?"

It was going to be worse than hard because he wouldn't believe it. "Lord Trystan, I'm not speaking as an old friend now. This touches more than the two of you. Mark is a tributary prince and I owe him loyalty."

He laughed, high and strained. "Don't come the moralist with me, I helped you to the crown. You need him."

"All right, I need him. Now more than ever."

He said it with contempt. "My uncle would cut your heart out."

Yseult slammed her hand down on the arm of the chair. "Peace! I can't listen to this, I'm Mark's wife."

"You were mine first!"

"When?" I catapulted out of the chair and down to him. "When was she ever your wife? And you called Agrivaine thick? Look at her, do you think she finds this a pleasure? Whatever she said, whatever you planned, forget it. You'll not see her again. I can't have it!"

He knew I meant it now. A tinge of fear crept into his eyes. "You use everyone, don't you?"

"I want your oath."

"No."

I pointed to his scabbard. "On your sword or leave my service."

"So it comes to that." He hesitated only a moment, then reached for the belt.

"No," Yseult whispered. "Not your oath-sword."

He laid the sheathed sword at my feet. "With regrets, my lord."

"No, Tryst!" she cried. "That's your life and honor!"

"That's nothing," he shushed her gently. "Don't speak of what you don't know. What I've done for Arthur or where I've gone for Arthur or the insults I've swallowed because of the oath I swore to Arthur on that stinking piece of iron. Live for him, die for him, and none more willingly, not even Bedivere. But there's a rag end of me you don't get, Arthur. Send me away, I'll find her. Hide her in the earth, I'll find her still or she'll find me. She'll come because she loves me. Because she needs me and we've lost too many years."

Neither of them felt worse than I did. The point of the knife wasn't enough for Trystan; he'd take the whole blade and have it twisted in him. "You think I asked for this meeting, Trystan?"

"What?"

"Tell him, Yseult."

It was hard and it hurt, but she did it without flinching. "We have to forget yesterday, forget it all. It's over, Tryst."

The room was suddenly quiet. The color drained out of his face. "You don't mean that."

She nodded, hands limp in her lap. "I haven't loved you that way for a long time."

"He made you say that."

She looked up at him, firm. "No. Myself made me say it. Finally."

But he still wouldn't believe. He clutched at her shoulders, pulling her out of the chair. "Oh, he did. I know him, he's good at words, better than me. 'Seult, listen. I'm older, I'm changed. When I was singing for Saxon farmers, I thought of you and how life—how it boils down to very simple things. Men and wives and children. And I knew I wanted these things more than anything else. The sword's too heavy and the music's gone sour. Just you and a quiet place and a little rest."

"Yes," she said. "Rest."

"And we can have it, you and I. You said you'd go with me." She tried to pull away. "Oh, good God, leave me be."

"You love me, 'Seult."

"No, I—"

"You love me. It's all we've got. Yesterday—"

"I saw you living when I thought you dead." She touched his hair, pitying. "And for a moment I could not help remembering, but that's all."

"You love me!"

"No. *No!* Will you for sweet Christ's sake *leave me be?*" Yseult wrenched away from him and retreated to the casement. "You, Arthur, Mark, *all of you. Leave me be!*"

The force of it stopped him from following her. She hunched over the casement sill, rigid and shaking. "May I sometime hear the last of that honey-sweet poison of a word. Love? Love who? When? Where? I was sixteen. We had a few weeks, we had the boat, and then it was Mark. And, oh, the things my mother carefully taught me to say to him. How to touch him and make him feel like a man, and what did I know of men but you? And then it was him and then you and him and you, and what was I but a torn scrap of meat between your jealousy and his fumbling?

"And who would it be this night? You or him, and what must I say? If Mark, I can't call him Tryst. Or if it's Tryst, I must seem dying-eager for his touch when my eyes are closing for the want of sleep. Oh, and always, always the begging question in his eyes and yours alike: Am I better than him? Do you like it better with me than him? Till I prayed the next thing between my legs be a knife to cut out what you want and throw it at the both of you."

Her fists slammed down on the sill. "Fight over it, tear it, *swallow it whole, but leave-me-alone*."

After a moment, she turned to Trystan, spent but dry-eyed. "Don't say love to me, lad. All I've had of it is a drunken dreamer and a tired old man. Don't look for what was. I'm twenty-six, not sixteen. There's gray in my head; I can still hide it, but it's there. Mark is kind to me. We're friends, we've learned to get along. He wants me still, but I can manage that. It's you I can't manage anymore. Don't talk of love, because that takes more time than we ever had. Don't throw your life at me, because I won't catch it. I have what *I* want now, and little enough. I'm safe. I have some peace. And I can sleep alone."

Trystan slumped on the edge of the dais, stunned. He believed it now, he had to—his dream ended by the dream itself. He barely moved when Yseult bent to kiss his mouth.

"Good-bye, Tryst."

Naked hurt, the tears running down his cheeks. He wiped them away, groping for the sword, drawing it from the scabbard.

"On this sword by which I swore to be your man, I will never see or send word to Queen Yseult again."

"So be it," she whispered.

"So be it," I said. "Put it on, Tryst. I still need you, that doesn't change."

I led Yseult out of the chamber to the hall. She looked ravaged as Trystan. "I'm sorry. He made you butcher him, but you were strong."

"There are just no tears left. We come to that." Yseult bowed to me and moved down the corridor. Her shoulders were straight.

In the audience chamber, Trystan stood frozen with the sword in his hand. Beyond the casement, that idiotic bird still bellowed in his silly pear tree.

"Tryst, there was a time when I had to make the same choice. A woman I loved or something else. And someone said, there's fate in all directions."

"You cold bastard."

"That's what I called him, but he knew the shape of time. This could be a beginning for you. Your life's your own again and no post you can't fill for me. Stay here with Gwen when I go east. Be her lord-milite.''

"Is that all, Imperator?" Trystan rose deliberately and buckled on the sword. "May I go?"

I dropped into my chair, vastly tired. "Don't throw it away, Tryst."

"May I go?"

"Yes . . . go."

I stayed alone in the chamber, feeling very much what Yseult had confessed: the cosmos could go to hell for an hour or so, or cut out that part of me that ticked like a king and fight over it somewhere else. Just leave me alone one minute.

They came to fetch me far too soon. Something important, I can't remember what. I went and tended to it.

Jolted awake. Heavy rain falling, and through its dull hiss the cries and shouts and the pounding at our door. Gwen made to get up with me, but I stayed her.

"Don't. I'll go."

I threw on the first loose robe to hand, a premonition already squeezing my stomach, barely hearing the guards as they hurried down the corridor in my wake.

"Demon-drunk, sir, a madman . . . got him ringed, but it's too late. The body's hacked like a roast."

I lurched out into the rain, the sour taste of apprehension in my mouth. Two knots of people illuminated by torches that flared and sputtered over the garish scene. The circle of archers with bent bows, and the tense, warning commands of the centurion: "Steady . . . steady. Don't shoot unless he makes you."

The courtyard was a sea of mud. I slogged to the men and women kneeling over the mutilated body, pulled away the sobbing woman who covered the body with her own. She came away in my arms, hoarse with grief and fury.

"Murder! It was murder. Pwyll was unarmed."

One of the guards had seen it. "True, sir. Only his belt knife against a sword, and that not even drawn."

The woman sobbed, "I want that dog's life. Give me justice, King of Britain."

I looked down at what used to be Lord Pwyll, its blood already mingling with the rain and mud, then rose and strode toward the circle of archers. The centurion stepped aside for me.

"Do we shoot, sir?"

"Easy on." I stepped into the circle. In its center, his blue robe sodden and muddy, the murderer reared like a bear at bay, swaying over his planted sword.

"Trystan."

The haggard bear raised its head to see what called it, grinning vacuously. "Arthur?"

"Drop your sword."

"It *is* you. My comet, maker and breaker of destinies." He managed to straighten up, raising the sword. "I should have killed you ages ago."

The centurion hissed, "My lord, let us shoot."

"No."

Trystan started for me. "I'll do it now."

"Get out of the way!"

The command came out of the darkness beyond our circle. A rider broke through the ring, running his horse straight at Trystan from behind. Little Gareth, leaping feet first from the saddle to pin Trystan to the ground.

"Bring me some irons!" he snapped.

Murder plain and simple, without a ghost of defense. A brother comite murdered on royal ground and my own person threatened. Death or banishment. Even with his personal admiration for Trystan, Kay could ask no less than his death for Pwyll's Dobunni wives and kinsmen.

I questioned Trystan in his cell, squeezed him for one ounce of extenuation, but he only hunched on his pallet, stared at his manacled hands and said nothing. Pale and shaking, but not from fear. I'd seen him after too many drunks and battles. Drink and passion burned his body like tinder. He was paying their price.

"Trystan, the guard who saw it said Pwyll didn't even draw his knife. And Pwyll always spoke you fair. They said he just walked up to you and then he was dead. For nothing."

"Let it go, Arthur."

"Fool! Kay loves you, and even he has to vote for death. The Dobunni consider it an insult to their whole tribe. If there's anything you can say—did he insult you, anything—say it now."

Trystan leaned back against the rough stone wall. The aftermath of drink made his face look battered. "Arthur?"

"Will you talk to me now?"

"I've been thinking on my soul."

"Oh, Jesus."

"And on him, too. If he walked in with a drink, he'd have a convert."

I sent a guard for a jug, not *uisge* but thick barley beer and better for his stomach. Not that he had that much time left.

I pressed him. "Now, what of Pwyll?"

"Simpleminded, single-minded. Good Lord Pwyll with all his pride in his crotch."

"Are you going to talk to me or not? I don't have much time. Did he do anything to provoke you?"

Silence.

"Tryst, give me something to help you with. Please."

He drank some more beer, staring at the wall. "You have it already. I wanted to kill something, even you. He got in my way. I had no argument with him, that uncomplex engine of procreation. He was just there."

I gave up with a sigh. "Do you want to die?"

"No, strangely enough." He rubbed bleary eyes. "But a little sleep wouldn't hurt. You might leave the beer, my lord."

He said no more then or later at his trial before Guenevere and myself, the vengeful Dobunni and my assembled lords-comite, but stood silent in his chains while voice after voice condemned him—Pwyll's widows, his kinsmen, the guards who saw it happen.

One small humanity lit the miserable scene. Bedivere came specially from home to be Trystan's guard, Gareth another. They would hear of no others to stand by him in the court, pleading for his life and banishment. Others echoed them, men of Trystan's old fourth squadron who knew the man as well as the demon.

There was no question of guilt, only sentence. In the final judgment, the voices for death far outweighed those for mercy. Marcus and Yseult absented themselves entirely from the trial. Marcus, of course, sent a courteous and reasonable plea for mercy couched in language that wouldn't dissuade a child from stealing pastries. At last he was rid of Trystan.

The moment of sentencing came, and all in my hands. The Dobunni were always my strongest support in the west. Much as I hated the verdict, I couldn't overturn it without ponderous reason.

All through the trial, Guenevere and I had sat on our dais apart from the crowd. Now I took her hand with a funereal sigh. "Might as well get it over with."

She held onto my fingers, leaning close. "Now that there's a moment, you should know that Yseult sent her vote for clemency."

"She has no voice in this, no more than Mark."

"A very loud voice," Guenevere corrected calmly. "Those hill forts, for instance, that you want Mark to build."

I kept my face a mask of state gravity. "A bargain?"

"Strictly."

"I'm listening. Can she do it?"

Gwen patted my hand. "Darling Arthur. You're not a goat like Pwyll or a fool like Trystan, but if such a woman invited you to bed, what would you refuse her?"

Dawning light. Perhaps not the radiance by which kings get to heaven, but how they safeguard kingdoms. "Does Mark love her that much?"

"But not that frequently."

I had to pass a hand over my mouth to hide the glow of relief. "Tell Yseult she has my gratitude and respect. And if she doesn't deliver, we'll take it out of her hide."

"With a blunt knife," said Guenevere. "She knows. Go banish poor Tryst and let's be done with this."

"The Dobunni will disown me, but shake your head if I look too pleased out there."

I rose and stepped to the edge of the dais. "Lord Trystan, you stand condemned and dishonored. Will you speak before we pronounce sentence?"

Barely audible: "Nothing, my lord."

A murmur rippled through the hall as I stepped down to the anvil with Trystan's sword laid across its face.

"Then hear the judgment of the crown. We declare, for the death of Lord Pwyll ap Evan, first that your lands and goods *in toto* be forfeit to his heirs. For the oath you dishonored, we break you from our service and the fellowship of *combrogi* and the rank of lord-comite forever, even as we break this blade."

I slammed the flat of the sword over the anvil's edge. It shattered with a dull sound, the point half clanging to the floor at Trystan's feet. He didn't look at it. With the broken hilt in my hand, I finished the sentence.

"And we further rule that within two days you quit Camelot—"

"No." The dissent began to flare like grass fire among the Dobunni. "No, death to the murderer."

"Cornish pig!"

"Death!"

"Kill him!"

"—And within five days you quit our lands altogether, never within your life to return on pain of death."

"No."

"*No!*"

"The sentence has been given!" I faced them all with the broken sword in my hand. Bedivere and Gareth led Trystan away, his head bowed; he might have been weeping. With one glance at Guenevere, I stood at bay before the seething Dobunni, saw my brother's unbelieving expression before he turned his back on me, and it was not Merlin's voice in my mind then, but that of old Anscopius: *We both know the mob, Arthur. Ave.*

"Dangerous, Artorius," Kay raged later in private. "Suicidal. *I* didn't want his death, but there was no choice and certainly no question of his guilt. Our own people, and what justice can they expect from now on when you overturn a clear, just verdict for personal friendship?"

Maddening, but until Yseult copulated us into some forts I couldn't confide my reasons. "Kay, the emperor's mercy is above the will of the tribes."

"But not his welfare," my brother shot back.

I didn't know what he meant. "Is that a threat, Kay?"

"I'm a cautious man, Artorius. I don't threaten. It's a warning."

Marcus fortified the southern coast. Neither he nor the Dobunni knew I traded their revenge for their safety. Probably they wouldn't care.

The galley wallowed back and forth against the quay in early morning fog, the squeak of hoisting sail and the rusty-hinge *scree* of sea gulls muffled and eerie.

A dreary little train clumped down the path from the palace and onto the ship. Two servants, one carrying a small chest. Two horses, one pack-saddled. Trystan's accumulated life to be stowed on the ship bound for every port between Severn and Antioch. In one of them, Trystan would lose himself.

He came down the path alone in an old sea robe like a monk's habit. In the mist he didn't recognize me until we were close.

"You needn't have come, Arthur."

"There's something I want to ask."

Trystan looked back up the path. "Thanks for my life. I was terribly frightened. Can't think why I should want to live, but I do."

"Will you answer one question?"

He kept glancing over his shoulder. "A dozen now."

"You never said a word, just that Pwyll got in your way. Was that all? Was it that meaningless?"

"You're not going to be sentimental?" The hard smile accented the deepening lines around his mouth. "I won't have that from a comet."

"Was it, Tryst? Because I don't believe it."

He looked back along the path again. She wasn't there, would never be there. "Oh, you know Lord Pwyll. He'd a drink or two himself, and he said—with the delicacy that endears him—that he liked Irish dishes and would be tasting of her himself now I was done. Poor man. And paradise so celibate, by report."

I sighed, looking away at the dim form of the ship. "I almost knew it. Why didn't you tell me?"

"Good-bye, Arthur."

"Why didn't you speak? God damn you! Always the gesture, the graceful irony. You think I'm going to feel sorry for you? Well, I'm not. Go to hell. Go away and stay away and mutilate yourself where I don't have to watch."

For a moment the ironic smile vanished. "Arthur, I know my uncle and what you need from him. If I claimed Pwyll insulted me, I'd have to declare how on oath."

We understood each other. One word of Yseult at the trial and I could whistle for her husband's loyalty.

"Arthur, was there—?" He hated to ask but had to. "There was no message?"

Only that she loved him enough to save his life, and I couldn't even tell him that because he'd wrap his heart around that one fact and keep it alive forever.

"No."

"Well, then." Trystan struck his hands together, rubbing them briskly. "Time to go."

This time I had to ask. "Where?"

"I've a notion to see Rome," he said. "Do they still perform Plautus there?"

Damned fool, talking of Plautus in the middle of a fog. "No. I don't know. I don't think so."

"Pity," said Trystan. "I'd be good at comedy. Farewell, and mind out for Cerdic and his lot. They'll be coming. Kiss Gwen for me."

We stood awkwardly for a moment, then Trystan knelt quickly— "Long life to my King"—and hurried up the gangplank.

End of the story, or at least my part in it; not the end for Trystan. Our singers have a way of turning plain history into

plumed legend. He ended in Brittany, married to another girl
named Yseult and holding a castle for her father. The immigrant
Britons there were at war with Clovis every other week. Trystan
rode out his years on the borders as soldier, husband and—I
hope—musician now and then.

He took his mortal wound in some two-penny skirmish, and
they say Yseult crossed the sea to be with him at the end. If so,
she went with Marcus' approval. They were older then and some
things mattered much less. I like to think she went. It makes a
good end to the song.

You see, it's a piece of music that ends the tale for me. Years
later, barging up Severn to see Kay, I heard an old harper of the
ship's company playing something familiar and asked him what
it was.

"A song without words, my king." The bard went on playing.
"I learned it from Trystan of Castle Dore."

The music pressed out of the strings. Standing in the prow, I
heard again that strange three-note figure that dominated all of
Trystan's later songs: two notes rising, a hesitation, a fall on the
third. And again and again. And I knew at last what it was.

The motion of a ship rolling.

Neither Bedivere nor Gareth was really cut out for the post of
lord-milite and neither wanted it. My next logical choice was
Ancellius.

> *I know this is not a post you would choose, Lancelot,*
> *nevertheless I must overbear your modesty. Bring Eleyne*
> *and Galahalt if they are up to the voyage.*

The journey up Severn wouldn't be dangerous, but any other
would. Cerdic darted in and out along our coasts in rapid feints
to search out our weaknesses. Daily couriers brought Marcus'
concern about the raiders cruising offshore, turgidly majestic
letters that never relaxed to a personal pronoun. Marcus wrote
for the ages, he did.

> *We do sorrow for Caradoc, our loyal tributary of*
> *Dyfneint, who passed to heaven in peaceful sleep.*

No doubt Marcus sorrowed more for the result. As heir to
Astolat, Geraint was thorn enough. Crowned he was chaos, but

his sheer thrusting energy made him an inspiration and rallying point for every young warrior in Cornwall and a nightmare for his harried ministers. If they wished to consult, they did it riding or running to stay abreast of his loping stride as he caromed from one place to another, bridle in one hand, breakfast in the other, a volcano of changing mood, innocent wonder, ignorant ire.

But his affection was lavish as his wrath. We had some happy days at Camelot that summer before I left. Guenevere and I had never felt so ringed with loyalty. Peredur was visiting. Lancelot came to take up his new post with Eleyne and their small son, Galahalt, in tow. And to wrap the gift, Geraint erupted from the ship with his sister to swear his new-crowned allegiance to me.

"Just that and farewell, though I'd give my heart to stay. But I must be south again to set things right. Look you, Mark trembles at every sight of a fishing boat off his banks, and there's a whisper Cerdic will try Llongborth next. Ah, it'll come to naught all—Mother of God, will you look at that! A rent in my breeches that were new not a fortnight gone. Now what good is it, Arthur, what *good* to be a king and not even able to get my poor breeches mended? Na, sister, I know: I should marry, and I *will*—Devil if I don't—the first moment God and Mark give me to breathe."

By the fire in our private chambers, Peredur thoroughly charmed the house of Astolat, especially Eleyne. He had his father's easy grace without the underlying craft. Cador stoutly refusing to die, Peredur had grown into an idle and vaguely unsatisfied man, now absorbed in the defense of the north, now ready to return to the Church.

He'd been a month on the Wall before coming to us. The dust aggravated his bad lung, and he coughed a good deal of blood. Thin and tired, he must have embodied Eleyne's conception of a saint, deep-set eyes burning in a narrow, ascetic face, devout and sensuous at the same time. He was someone to bully with her mothering as he sprawled in his chair and listened to her prattle.

For all Eleyne's attention to Peredur, you always knew who she was married to. Lancelot wasn't long out of her sight or off her tongue. He grew squarer and thicker and quieter through the years, and I wondered now if anything since had struck the chord of joy I heard from him the day Eleyne told him of the Grail. He spent a great deal of time searching for it, but was no nearer discovery than that day. Now and then as we talked about the fire, his eyes would go to Guenevere—a moment only—and something would peer through that was no part of God or Grails.

His son seemed to have little of Lancelot in him, purely his mother's child, solemn as a tomb and already millstoned with a heavy bronze cross around his fat baby neck. I searched in vain for some of Drost's darting mischief. Galahalt's wide, complacent stare looked from birth on a fixed cosmos where God sat ringed about with the house of Astolat, the archangels somewhere below the salt.

Eleyne chattered on to Peredur's gallant if passive attention, but one subject did fascinate him: the Holy Grail. Her rendering of the tale was as sepulchral now as when I first heard it at Neth Dun More.

"—And the spear pierced his side upon the instant, and the Holy Grail disappeared from the sight of men. And we blood of Saint Joseph have mournfully searched for our lost charge these four hundred years since. Now, is that not a tale of sad wonder, my lord Prince?"

"Fascinating," Peredur mused. "I mean, if it could be found."

"No, it is gone from mortal sight," said Lancelot. "I've searched, but with my—with our imperfections, we can't hope to see it."

Something unreadable flickered in Guenevere's eye.

"Galahalt!" Eleyne prodded her wriggling son. "Don't squirm so in your chair. Noblemen do not squirm before their king."

"He's tired, bless him. Dear Eleyne." Gwen was always oversweet to Lancelot's wife. "Don't you think we should put him to bed?"

"By your leave, my lady. It is history of the Grail that he should hear."

My wife vented on Eleyne the smile usually reserved for Pictish envoys. "Of course, dear."

Peredur's British soul loved the Grail legend though his Roman mind stumbled on its inconsistencies. "Not to deny miracle, but doesn't it strike you as impractical to search in place and time for something outside both? Forgive me, Ancellius, but there does seem a better way. For instance, I remember the abbey on Wyrral Tor. Built of stone."

"So it is, like Neth Dun More," said Geraint.

"And Lady Eleyne is sure of the details of the story?"

Eleyne sure? "Does the sun rise in the east? Am I a woman? Sure of it all, every word passed down by our forefathers one to the next."

"Then that's the place to start," Peredur concluded with a hint of satisfaction. "The highest hill, Wyrral Tor."

He caught Guenevere's hand. "Gwen, love: remember when we used to hide-and-seek in the church at home? The old altar to Diana in the cellar?"

"Yes. I used to hide behind it."

"And in the sub-cellar one even older, carved with a bull's head. The hill folk called him Herne the Hunter."

Even I caught some of his infectious excitement. "What are you onto, lad?"

"The story says Joseph of Arimathea visited Ynnis Witryn many times as a merchant in tin. Then he'd know our people and customs. So, when he built his church, wouldn't he do as our northern priests and pick a spot already known to the people as a sacred place? A *high* place?"

His excitement grew as he laid out his reasoning. "Wyrral Tor must be the highest hill around. The stone abbey would take an army to build, hordes more than Joseph had. If he built a church, he built it out of wattle and thatch, stuff that could be packed up the hill on a few mules. And just like the old bull-altar, I'll bet the remains of Joseph's church are under the abbey cellar. The disciples probably built their huts at the foot of the hill."

"Aye," Eleyne confirmed. "Where the old well is."

Peredur thought any search should start with the abbey cellar. "God punish me for pride if I give too much weight to human reason on a matter of faith."

But Eleyne wouldn't hear of that. "You are as Christian a lord as ever I knew." She hooked a possessive arm through Lancelot's. "Saving my husband. But only God can decide who has sufficient grace."

"Amen to that," said Peredur. "But we have only the world in which to look for His wonders, and one has to start somewhere. Geraint, I'll have my servants pack me to leave with you."

His decision was a quiet thunderbolt to all of us. Guenevere said, "You're going to Astolat?"

"That I am, Gwen. I've been father's eyes in the north, tracking this what's-her-name Faerie queen. Why not the south? If Cador asks, I'm off with Geraint to observe those few Saxons he deigns to leave alive."

"With me? And why not!" Geraint pounced on the frail prince to thump his approval on Peredur's less than sturdy back. "Good man that you are, my ship is yours. My ship, my home, my horses. Ask for them."

Peredur took refuge from the ebullience in a fit of coughing.

His British heart might brim with apostolic zeal, but his logic was pure Roman. Our church was anarchic and militant as our tribes. To present the bishops with the Grail in the name of Arthur and Guenevere would tend to rally them behind the throne now when we needed unity.

Something about the tale nagged him, though, something missing. Peredur knew several devout priests in Eburacum who still kept a wife or two without harm to their holy office. God pardon him, he couldn't believe the Grail would vanish primly at the first sign of healthy blood in its keeper.

"There *was* a cup," he reasoned to me later. "Wood or metal and not destroyed, it exists somewhere. Do you notice how Eleyne tells the story? As if she were singing by rote, not really aware of each word. She must tell it again while I write it down. I can't help feeling there's a half-lost hint in the tale itself." Peredur coughed into the blood-spattered linen. "And if there is, by God's Eyes, I will find it."

Geraint's premonition proved correct. Within three days, Marcus' courier brought news that Cerdic's scattered raiders had formed and were making for the rich port of Llongborth. Geraint charged to his ship in a flurry of kisses and orders to servants, trundling Peredur aboard in a last-minute whirl of love and disorder.

"Sister, good-bye, I'll bring Galahalt an heathen banner. *Mind those chests, you men!* They contain my best armor. Animals! Must I go naked into battle? Oh God, did they set my sword? Come, Peredur, I'll leave the boldest of the heathen to your lance and none other. Hurry now, hurry! *Gently* with that horse, God blight you all! Arthur, bless you for a king for bards to remember, and I'll be back when the south is set right again. Galahalt, kiss your poor uncle who has not even the time to love those dearest to him. Would there were more hours in the day, that's the sad truth of it. Good-bye . . . good-bye."

The ship moved out from the quay into the stream. Peredur waved from the deck, but Geraint climbed monkey-nimble into the rigging to hail me once again.

"Ah, she's lovely, Arthur. Lovely all!"

I shouted back, "Who's that?"

His arm wheeled out in a wide salute to all of God's Severn valley. *"Camelot!"*

Marcus Conomori, Princeps Dumnonii, to Artorius, Imperator: greeting and long life.

> *We are pleased to report complete victory against the
> host of Cerdic at Llongborth, costly as it was . . .*
> *Among the nobles lost was our loyal tributary, Geraint
> of Dyfneint, who fell in the last charge . . .*

Marcus' report is long lost in the dusty limbo of old court
records, but I still have Peredur's letter from Astolat.

> *—so drunk with battle, he didn't know how badly he
> was wounded, and always too far forward of the line
> for us to protect him. On the last charge, they sur-
> rounded and unhorsed him . . .*
> *I curse my ignoble mind even as it compels me to look
> at dear Gerry-fach without tears—God's eager assas-
> sin with neither the imagination to fear nor the intellect
> to doubt. We are shaped as the Lord needs, I suppose.
> Some men light an epoch. Geraint was for a moment.
> Rest him gentle.*

They tell me kings should have majestic memories. Mine are
smaller and warmer. There's no more beautiful way to remember
him: unfurling like a banner from the ship's high mast, sword
swinging about his legs, arm flung out to us, to life itself. *She's
lovely all!*
And yet they weigh on my heart, all the good-byes.

I went east with the *combrogi* and left Lancelot with Guenevere.
Lancelot and Guenevere. What is there about them that makes
bards reach for the harp and the prurient lick their lips? You'd
think they dove into bed the moment I was gone or, kept apart,
whinnied for each other like stallion and mare. It was never that
simple. As Peredur did for Geraint, look at them fondly but
without tears.
You can say that Lancelot loved Guenevere when he allowed
himself to love anything at all. Never mistake him for a Trystan.
There was nothing dark or complex about Ancellius Falco, only
that he burdened his uncomplicated nature with complex absurdities
too heavy to bear.
The most popular Christian philosophy in our youth was that
of the Anchorites, who believed the way to heaven led through
denial and mortification of the flesh. Lancelot embraced it but
thought himself too frail in spirit to persevere. In truth, he was

too much a part of life, a fine soldier who needed to settle down with a wife and children. But Lancelot never in all his self-punishing days realized that. When he left the monastery, he saw it as personal lack of worth, as failure rather than incompatibility. All his life he remained a twig caught between opposing currents, whirling in futile circles.

He didn't marry Eleyne, he allowed her to marry him but never rested content with the arrangement. Whatever the consequences, the healthiest act of his life was reaching for Guenevere. Of course he would be punished for it. He couldn't bear not to be.

Guenevere now—and a far greater complexity. Christian she was, but of the ancient Parisi, whose royal women were always associated with fertility goddesses in times not far removed. This attitude survived conversion. Bishops like Anscopius might mutter and warn, but if the princess's bed was no longer an augur of fertility, it was at least her own business.

Promiscuous? Hardly. Grant to any affectionate, well-governed wife that she won't commit adultery on sheer impulse alone, how much less likely for the most public of all women to succumb? If and when she does, it follows that more than one day prepared her for it. When Lancelot came back to court, Guenevere had worked at statecraft daily, girl and woman, for many years.

Daily, I said.

For a moment now, you are Queen of Britain. Try on the crown.

You rise near dawn. While your women dress your hair, you're already reading half of the day's first dispatches while your husband reads the rest. You discuss the most urgent over breakfast while other business is already crowding in on you. The morning audiences: which are important, which not? You oversee all negotiations with Cador, who still uses the blood tie to further his own aims. Where do you bend, where draw the line?

You think on your feet, you listen and judge from waking to sleep again. Which of your household can be trusted, who are spies for Cerdic? Marcus Conomori? Your own father? Some must be. You maintain people to do the same for you, because the name for a trusting and uninformed ruler is corpse.

Every waking moment has some strain on it, speaking in one breath Latin to one ambassador, British to another. How realistic must you be with your father? How idealistic with Dyfneint or shrewd with Cornwall? You command where your husband can't because he's somewhere else just as important. You sign documents that grant or deny, bring life or death, the dirty laundry and the housekeeping of kingship.

And when you wake one day to find yourself pregnant, the world doesn't stop to coo over your fecundity, nor can you. You go on riding, writing, judging, listening, commanding, working to exhaustion, charming this or that ambassador at table and not drinking half as much as you'd like because your ears must be open and your mind working.

For a few minutes before sleep perhaps you can share with your husband whatever is personal between you, this child in your body often forgotten completely through the hurtling day. And that day doesn't wash off at night but leaves a residue, the thickening grime of state that comes to bed with you, lies in your arms and your dreams.

The child, the one thing that was yours, is torn from you in a last effort to save your life, and with it any hope of another.

The sadness and the state lie between you and your husband in the big bed. Not that you love each other less; but so much lies with you now. As a queen, you know the first bright dream of a golden state will never be—your best will be a compromise with barbarity. Better than nothing; you're no longer an optimist.

Or that young, says the mirror. If some part of you is wanton, it's only that renegade *I* that wants something, some little thing for itself alone. Somewhere. Something always put off and denied for lack of time. Not petting or flattery, that was distrusted and bred out almost before it seeded, and you're too ironic for vanity. Still, something is drowning in your mirror with a silent scream.

And as you sink, a hand is held out to you.

It might have been anything else—a different life, healthy children, less of a talent for rule, more for love. It might have been Trystan, who could have handled the whole bloody mess better.

But it's Lancelot, whom you once called wretched and honorable. Uncomplicated, undemanding. Where do the strong go to be weak? Perhaps a moment comes when *must* is too damned tired to fight and *want* breaks free to cry *I am* just once before the sun goes down.

Not who came, but when.

Perhaps after years, you realize that what drew you to Lancelot has aged along with you. But the habit outlives the pleasure.

And then your husband—not the most comprehensible of men—shames you like a common criminal before all Camelot, and for

another woman. For a Faerie slut, half devil and all dirt, everything you hate. But she gave him the one thing you couldn't.

Queen of Britain, what would you have done?

Thus the triangle. The aging queen, the adulterer, the royal
husband wounded to the heart by betrayal—God, it looks mawkish
on paper alone. Do people actually think that way?

I guess so. It's a simple picture, but not what we meant at all.

The Ghost Dancers

Cador died finally, or rather gave in and allowed God to take him, no doubt scheming for a new kingdom on his way up. Peredur was crowned by the Parisi and Brigantes, and we breathed easier that our back door was still securely locked. Good to know one of them was. Feeble and near death, Marcus yet hoped to make a separate alliance with Rome, still tottered to the Council on Yseult's arm. The aging queen was more nurse than consort now, fussing over Marcus' meals and medicines, seeing to his soiled linen, matching her step to his faltering walk, no longer bothering to conceal her weight. Guenevere rejoiced that age didn't thicken her own delicate frame, but even as she chortled over Yseult's corpulence, the lines deepened and the flesh wrinkled about her own mouth.

And I was forty-five. Vanity tempted me to think I looked younger, though the illusion needed a little charity now and then. My hair dulled from yellow to whitish sand, my sword belt let out a reluctant notch or two. I tended to weary earlier in the evening after a hard day. Grain by grain, time sifted down the glass until, one autumn day, even I noticed it passing. Standing on the parapet with Bedivere, I watched a procession of young people along the riverbank, singing as they went to gather late flowers for Samhain night.

They were all young enough to be beautiful with youth alone, but their leader was a dazzling girl. She rode a white horse led with great ceremony by two youths in green, her hair unbound and shining in the sunlight. And as she passed under us, she looked up and blew a kiss.

"Why, the little flirt's waving. Hallo! Love and long life to my lady of the new year! Bedwyr, look. She's not half beautiful."

"She's my love," he said wistfully, gazing down at the girl. "Myfanwy's some old-religion ways yet. And the lass would know the fun of Samhain night."

It struck then, a treacherous hammer called Time. "My God, is that—?"

"Aye, Rhonda."

I felt flustered and oddly upset. "But she's just an infant, not near old enough to go off with that randy lot."

Chin on folded arms, Bedivere watched his radiant daughter as the procession wended toward a hilltop. "Sixteen, Artos. Some of her own friends are married, but I hoped she wouldn't. Not just yet."

A whole new generation, and where did they spring from? Where were we so busy we didn't notice? I felt like saying to the world, "Slow down, this is much too fast." For the first time in ages I thought of my own son, wondering if he leaped through the fire and danced this Samhain on some hill with a Prydn girl.

Not likely. Peredur's last letter reported Morgana and her people moving boldly toward the Wall in such numbers no village dared stop them. Bedivere was at Camelot to ride north with Gareth for observation, but now his worry was all for the splendid girl on the white horse.

"Bedwyr-fach," I invited, "would you care for a drink?"

His eyes never left her. "At least one."

I bade him farewell a few days later when he rode out with Gareth. He was still bemused and now a little bewildered, muttering absently as the grooms cinched straps and tucked away his sword. Suddenly his hand slammed down hard on the saddle.

"Damn! The cheek of him!"

Rhonda had come tripping home to announce herself betrothed to one of the lads who led her horse at Samhain. And next night hadn't the boy come to speak with her da, and himself all of raw eighteen?

"You were an officer at eighteen, Bedivere."

"That was different. We grew up quicker then, we had to. This boyo, where's he been, what's he done? Comes in all proper-dressed and scented, a Silure tongue so thick I could cut it like cheese. Shifty lot, the Silures, never trusted one of them."

My friend fretted over his gear while I hid a tender smile.

"So this cub tells me they were proper plighted at Samhain night, and he would now speak of the marrying, if you please."

Well, Bedivere just wasn't ready for that. Sometime, yes, but
not yet. He made an awkward scene of it, Myfanwy and Rhonda
waiting expectantly in the background and the boy nervous and
eager but trying to put a manly face on it. Saying Rhonda's
father was a man of great honor and responsibility with state
matters that weighed on his advanced years, and he might overlook a daughter passing the right age for marriage.

That was the wrong tack. Bedivere squared him off sharp. The
visit ended with the lad embarrassed and incoherent, Myfanwy
furious—"She's not a *child*, Bedwyr"—Rhonda in rebellious
tears and Bedivere feeling wounded and guilty all at once.

"That little pup. Advanced years. Oh, did I give him something to think of as he went *un*plighted home. Did you hear that,
advanced years? When I was his age—when I *was*—and I can
still ride all day and night, and—Artos, I don't find this funny at
all."

Neither did I, though I smiled. Not a boy but the hand of time
touched Bedivere, and he was only just feeling it. He hauled
himself into the saddle with a grunt as much disgust as effort.

"*Ach-y-fi*, the boy's barely placed in the world."

"You're right to make them wait." I took his offered hand.
"But for myself, I found no better friend in all my life than the
son of a groom."

"It must be thought over, Artos. I don't hand my Rhonda to
the first Jacky comes sniffing by on Samhain night. By God, I
do not. And yet she barely spoke to me by way of good-bye. If
you had your own to raise, you'd know the worry of it."

One of my own. I thought about that long after Bedivere rode
out and in the middle of the thought, wished: Lugh, let me see
my son once before I die.

More love letters from Rome recalling our great days as the
jewel in their crown of provinces. The new king, Theodoric,
promised me an ambassador: Lucullus Aurelianus, who would
come like a dove cooing friendship. More likely Lucullus was to
note which British princes might be persuaded toward Roman
rule for love or money and how much of the latter. Business as
usual.

Lucullus waited at Brittany for my answer. On a gusty day in
late autumn with cloud shadows racing over the Severn, I was
framing a cautious invitation when old Prince Maelgwyn appeared
in the doorway of my small *scriptorium*, scarlet cloak flung

back, sword belt in his hand. He dropped the sword on a bench
and knelt stiffly to me.

"You old turtle, I've missed you. What's the news?" .

Maelgwyn dropped into a chair by the fire, clawing through
the white mop of his windblown hair. "Not good, Arthur. I
think they're coming."

That only meant one thing. "Cerdic?"

The old prince nodded. "Not that we weren't expecting it."

Maelgwyn knew well the Saxons who nibbled at his borders, a
thickening crescent of busy farmsteads to the east and south. Yet
since harvest most of them appeared almost deserted. His scouts
searched in vain for the men of the tuns.

"The whole border's dead. It's downright eerie." But then
Maelgwyn winked. "It was a whore set me thinking. One of my
young lords got in a row with this dox. Bleedin' shrew said she
was tired of stingy Brits, she'd go down Winchester where
there's enough Saxons to make her rich in a month."

I saw his reasoning. Why no men on the tuns and suddenly so
many in a sleepy stockade where dogs usually dozed in the
middle of the road?

"We questioned her, gave her a few coins," Maelgwyn recount-
ed. "She allowed they weren't in the town but up in the hills."

"The hills?"

Maelgwyn preened a little. "So, not to bother you, I sent my
own lads to look. They'd walk into a dragon's mouth to count its
teeth. For sure, there's the Saxons all in camps, neat and proper.
But nothing permanent, not even a ditch. They're going
somewhere."

I frowned over the intelligence. "How many men?"

"At least three thousand, more coming in all the time."

Sitting by the fire, we worried it between us. No war chief
would hold thousands of men together without moving. They
must be supplied out of his own pocket, and Cerdic was smarter
than he was rich. More, I was kept informed of all shipbuilding
and fleet movements in harbor on the Isle of Wight. Since
nothing unusual was reported, a sea venture appeared unlikely.

"Not a raid, Mal, not even a big one. It's the invasion."

The old Catuvellaun scratched his head. "That Saxon bastard,
I never could cipher him out. He shouldn't, Arthur. There'll be
snow soon or rain enough to drown the Ark."

No, he shouldn't. You don't push a large army through winter
country barely able to feed itself, but who said Cerdic wouldn't?
After all, the mud would hinder me as much as him.

And who said he couldn't?

Not how but where.

It nagged me to sleep and through the next chilly morning and then snapped into place so suddenly I stopped in mid-stride down a corridor in front of a startled servingwoman.

"Ambrosius!"

"S-sir?"

The old fox, he guessed it twenty years ago. "Where's Lord Ancellius?"

Confused, the woman didn't know for sure. "So please you, he may be with the queen's audiences."

"Find him, tell him to meet me at Prince Maelgwyn's lodging by the south gate."

I broke into a trot, rounded a corner and collided with a ruddy-faced young knight, Lord Bors of my *combrogi*. He stepped back hastily and bowed. "Forgive me, I'm sent to find you, sir. Bedivere and Gareth are back from the Wall."

"No time." I hurried on past him.

"But, sir! They said it's urgent news that you alone—"

"Take it to the queen."

"But, my lord, Bedivere *said*—"

I fixed Bors with an imperial forefinger. "To the queen, damn it, and send Gareth to me at Maelgwyn's. That's an order. Hurry!"

I burst into Maelgwyn's quarters, waving the map at him. "I know, Mal. I *know*."

He looked up, startled, from his breakfast. "Eh, what? What?"

I pushed the dishes aside and spread out the map. "Ambrosius was right. Look: forty miles from Winchester, two days' march. Mount Badon, the biggest fort in the south."

"But my own horse and infantry are sitting on it," Maelgwyn protested. "Four, five hundred men and two dozen catapults."

"Against three or four thousand? Old Cat, if Cerdic gets there first, he can spend twice that many storming it and as many cleaning it out."

And there he'd sit, as Ambrosius predicted, king of the highest hill in the south midlands, a day and a half from Severn, two days from the Catuvellauni, the same from Cornwall. Winter didn't matter now. A force that size could carry enough grain and meat to last a good while on measured rations. Cerdic knew just how far he had to march, and if Badon were his, he'd have no trouble convincing the other Saxon princes to push west

behind his spearhead. No doubt they were already poised and
waiting to swing on the hinge of his success.

"It's Badon, Mal. It has to be."

When Gareth came, still weary from his travel from the north,
I barely gave him a chance to speak, throwing the situation and
orders at him. He must set up a chain of post riders between
Severn and as close to Winchester as possible, touching at
Mount Badon. Lightly armed men on fast horses to report morn-
ing, noon and night to Camelot.

"If a dog takes out after a rabbit, I want to know, is that
clear? Where's Ancellius? What's the news from the north? Did
you take it to the queen?"

Intent as I was, I only then noticed Gareth's diffidence and the
flush like anger or shame on his face.

"That we did, sir. We tried to see you first."

Just then Lancelot's thick frame filled the doorway, and I
dragged my lord-milite to the map in a flurry of facts and orders.

"I want a workable plan of march based on *combrogi* as
point, the tribes behind. Before anything else, I want Badon
strengthened, and then—Lancelot, what is it? Gareth? Both of
you look like you've been spanked."

Lancelot sighed with Gallic pessimism. "Lord Gareth was
more involved. Perhaps he should tell you."

"Gareth?"

The little Irishman spread his hands, resigned. "We saw the
Faerie woman on the Wall. She sent a message, sir."

"A message? Morgana?"

Gareth still found it difficult. "We knew that the queen—Jesus
God, there's some things women just don't understand."

"Gareth-fach, we're going to be at war any day. I'll hazard
the queen's mood."

He said it with a hangdog duty. "She would come here with
all her people. To Camelot. She would show our king his true
son."

My stomach had the gray feeling of a bad mistake, like
indigestion. The news should have come to me, but everyone in
Guenevere's presence was stunned by the red, unreasoning fury
that swept my queen like fire in dry grass, lashing out at everyone in sight, heaping abuse on Gareth and Bedivere. I went first
to Bedivere who waited, alone and stoic, in the small chamber
where Yseult had parted from Trystan. He sat on the edge of the

dais in his mud-spattered mail, seedy and tired, a shabby bundle at his feet.

"We met her at the Wall, Artos. So small, from a distance I thought she was a child gauded up in her mum's finery, all copper and gold bangles jingling like a tinker's shop. She remembered me from Cnoch-nan-ainneal. Called me Redhair, said she was first wife to Artos."

I tried not to sound too eager. "Did you see her son?"

"Her folk stayed back on the hill while we talked." Bedivere wiped at the road grit under his eyes. "I mean, we laughed at her, absurd as it was and herself near impossible to understand. Then she said *look at his cheeks that are marked like mine*. And she gave us this."

He unwrapped the blanket bundle and laid out two garments. "The cloak could've been anyone's, but I wouldn't forget this."

Bedivere took up the filthy old jerkin, his voice soft with memory. "Long ago as it was. See this stain? It's my own blood where you carried me when I caught the Pict arrow. You said you took a Faerie queen to wife. And I thought you were having me on."

He folded the garments and brought them to me. "Well, we can't laugh now, Artos. She'd come to Camelot under safe conduct with her son and the whole perishing tribe. And I was to say—uh—'First wife needs land for her people that third husband must give out of respect.' "

The bundle was heavy with *fhain*-smell, recalling the brief, innocent time when I could live my own life like any other man.

"And this went to Guenevere?"

Bedivere's look was eloquent. "You know how she is about the bloody Picts. God knows we tried to come to you, but young Bors went galloping off to Guenevere, and she sent for us straight."

Guenevere had heard them out in a gathering cold, her eyes never leaving the stained old tunic. Then she rose and gave answer. How dare they? How *dare* they bring such a message? Her father would have sent two severed heads, the whore *and* her bastard. Before Lancelot, Bors and other lords, she reviled Gareth and Bedivere as peasant dolts that only my mistaken friendship raised to a semblance of honor. Then she flung herself out of the chamber, leaving them smarting in their astonishment and shame.

The gray feeling thickened in my stomach. "Gwen did this? Before the court?"

"Hell, we can live with that. We're not boys to brood over a tongue-lashing."

"Bedwyr, I'm sorry. I'll deal with Guenevere."

"Yes, you will." My friend looked at me with a searching, bewildered kind of sympathy. "I understand a bit of what she feels. All of a sudden there's a whole Artos I never knew. And bloody Christ, you never told her."

We hadn't shared the same bed for some time, and instinct told me to avoid Guenevere's closet until we were both cooler. When I entered her chamber, she dismissed her women brusquely but kept her back to me, brushing the faded auburn hair before her great bronze mirror. Silent but tensed for battle, the brush driving through her hair in quick, furious strokes. I sat on the bed, wondering how to begin.

"It's been quite a day, Gwen."

"Quite." She bit the words off. "Cerdic's future and your busy past."

"We'll speak of that."

"Yes, we will."

"Bedivere and Gareth deserve an apology."

"No." The brush snapped and crackled through the lashing hair. "I criticize incompetence in my own terms."

"Incompetence?"

"They should have killed the woman and ended her presumption then and there."

I said, "There was a time when we dreamed of something better."

The brush paused, the mirrored eyes winced. "And a time when you trusted my judgment, husband. You rule the north through me, and I say it's madness to let her come. Like disease, they're welcome nowhere, and we must say to the princes it's by your order because this animal calls herself your wife?" Guenevere whirled on me. "Not only wife but demanding out of respect some place for her rat's nest. What place? Given by what generous prince? Not Peredur, he'll go to war first."

"I have Morgana's word there'll be no theft crossing our land."

Guenevere laughed. "Thus the weasel to the chickens: don't get up, I'm only passing through."

All true, perhaps, but Morgana had my son with her. "I know these people, Gwen."

"Intimately, from the evidence."

"I'm family to them. They wouldn't steal a button from me." —

"Arthur, sentiment is a dangerous indulgence for a king."

"Don't tell me what's indulgence, Gwen. I've ruled twenty-two years without much of it. I'm letting her come with her son and just a few close—"

"No, Arthur!"

"I want to see my son."

"No, damn you—no!"

The force of it brought Gwen to her feet, quivering, arm raised as if to strike at me. But the anger melted into a cry. *Why didn't you tell me?*

"You knew I had a wife."

"Like I've had other men—past, gone, invisible—do you think that matters?" Suddenly she wilted down on the bed, face buried in the blankets. "But she comes with—with the one thing I couldn't have, and I must look at him? And you knew and never told me. I feel—"

It came out harder than I intended. "Betrayed?"

She looked away. "I didn't say that."

"No," I said. "I don't think that's a word for us."

Then the habit of closeness took over and I lay down beside her. After a moment she turned and pressed to me, mouth against my throat. "You never told me about him. I'm sorry about Bedivere and Gareth, I just couldn't stop myself. I've been a good queen," she breathed like a child confiding a secret hurt. "Is this all I get for it, dry old age spent looking at what I can't have? Don't bring him here."

I stayed with Gwen that night. You could call it love-making. We tried to join, but it was distant and sad like ghost dancers on long-abandoned ground.

Don't bring him here.

I had to, an old debt owed to my own heart. Something for myself, even as Guenevere took Lancelot. Not for a love but a bandage. Not as king but breathing man, I needed to know my flesh wouldn't die; above all, to touch him and say "my son" just once before I ended.

Weary or not, Bedivere must carry my message north again. Morgana would trust no other.

"Bring Morgana and my son," I told him. "And with them only these few, remember them: Cunedag, Urgus, Drost, Dorelei . . ."

I had a small house readied for them, warm and comfortable, but a good half mile from the palace out of deference to Guenevere. I fussed over the pile of gifts for each like a father hiding sweets for his children. When they arrived I was nervous as a bridegroom, fidgeting about my closet while Bedivere tried to fasten the rich imperial cloak about me.

"Stand still, else I'll never get this right."

"Who's with her? Did you have a good journey?"

"Na, I've told you twice over, and we're all nigh frozen." Bedivere closed the brooch at my shoulder. "Do you mind if I sit down, Artos? I'm perishing tired."

"Sit, sit. Tell me of them."

He collapsed onto a couch and seemed to melt into it like water. "Well, there's Morgana and her first and second husbands, devil if I know one from the other. Cooney-something."

"Cunedag."

"Right, and Urgus, and your son's cousin."

"Drost? Good lord, little Drost!"

"Not a bad lot for Picts," Bedivere owned.

"Prydn."

"Well, *I* can't tell the difference."

"Ask them. Picts have a place to go home. Tell me about my son, what's he look like?"

"Modred? Like his mother. Yes, very like her. Bonny as a girl. Not as friendly as the rest. Eyes in the back of his head."

I gave my robe one last tug in the mirror. "Is Guenevere ready?"

Bedivere hesitated. "Not quite."

"Where is she?"

"With Lancelot, I believe."

"Oh."

Bedivere cleared his throat. "Speaking of that . . ."

"Don't." Our eyes met in the mirror. "I know what you think you ought to say. Don't."

"It could be trouble, Artos. More than that, it could be used for trouble."

I chose the words carefully. "It could, but I've seen no proof. Nor would I be kind to anyone who brought it to me. Let's go."

I'd peopled the hall with enough of an audience to give Morgana a sense of importance, few enough to show my court that this was in no way a political occasion nor did I recognize Modred as any sort of heir. Morgana's "demands" were a thin mask over desperation. Her band was too large and predatory now for Erca, the new king of the Picts, to overlook. If she stayed in the north, she faced a fight to extinction with no place of her own to fall back on. I was her last hope and not at all sure what to do.

I took my chair on the dais as the small audience bowed to me. Maelgwyn and his chief men, Gareth and Lady Rhian, Bors and his young wife. Guenevere swept in, followed by Lancelot and three young knights, Parisi by the look of them. I barely knew one of them by name, Brocan. My queen was impeccable as always when in public, though I noticed her hair was drawn down to soften her face that bore just a shade more assistance from powder than usual. I felt a twinge of pity. It didn't wipe away her years, only commented on the attempt.

She wore an iron cross at her breast.

The kiss we exchanged before she took her place was largely for the court, the murmured words for me alone.

"I don't know why I endure this, Arthur."

"I want to see my son, is that so difficult?"

"You've heard Peredur's opinion."

"Your brother remains celibate and hears mass three times a day. I don't question his peculiarities. Leave me mine."

"Well." Guenevere sat. "Let's get on with it."

"We won't drag it out, Gwen. Remember, if one of them puts his hands on your stomach, it's a mark of respect."

"Like flowers on an old grave."

At my signal, Bedivere set the dragon ensign in its socket and crossed to the main entrance. He spoke briefly to someone beyond it, then announced in a clear voice: "Queen Morgana. Her son, Modred-Belrix. Her honored husbands, Cunedag and Urgus. Her nephew, Drost."

A sibilant reaction rippled through the hall as Morgana entered with her old energetic stride. Here and there I heard a choked titter. Her uncut hair was more gray than black now, the small body still lean and cat-agile. She wore a blue cloak, obviously cut for a man, that trailed the floor as she walked, overhung and jangling with far too many ornaments looted from God knows where.

She reached the center of the hall and planted herself, throwing back the oceanic cloak. Another gasp from the women of my court; underneath was an open sheepskin vest that concealed nothing at all, and a short skirt of fringes and tassels.

The men were dressed much the same, plain wool girdles and vests covered by mantles garish as Morgana's and an armory of bangles. I winced at the gaudy sight of them. Bedivere was right. They looked like children who robbed a parent's chest to play grown-up.

My attention riveted on the young man who hovered on Morgana's left. Twenty-three last Brigid-feast, my age when I took the crown. Modred was Morgana reborn—face, coloring, small bones, even the same pale gray eyes flickering watchfully about the hall. No resemblance to me at all.

I rose, moved down to Morgana and placed my hands on her stomach. "Welcome, *Gern-y-fhain*."

In a second she wiped away the years as her hands shot aloft in her old impulsive greeting. "Belrix!"—and she sprang to hug me tight, weatherbeaten cheek against mine, hard and strong as ever.

"Belrix, Belrix, so long a time. Oh, but . . . but must not cry in front of second wife. Here, kiss thy wealth who's named for thee."

Modred's head didn't top my shoulder, but close up I saw what distance concealed. Not his features but his expression sometimes hinted elusively of my own youth, some look that was not Prydn.

"Well, boy."

"My father. Morgana's told much of thee."

I pushed aside his vest. "Thee's scarred."

"Venicones," he remarked with some pride. "Dead ones."

I embraced him. Modred suffered it with dignity and reserve. "We will talk," I said, turning to the others. "Brothers!"

With a shout they descended on me as if we'd parted yesterday. Cunedag and Urgus, grizzled leather like Morgana, the look of those who spend their lives in the open. Broad-shouldered young Drost playful as ever—oh, dost remember our game, boy? Thy mother was the sweetest of women, do grieve she's gone. And look where Urgus still bears the burn scar from Bel-tein. Aye, what news of Nectan and Bredei? Oh, my good brothers.

They ringed me about, hooting and pounding my back while the court shuffled in embarrassment, a little put out at this raucous familiarity with the emperor's person. Only Modred remained aside, aloof and cautious.

Then Morgana asked, "Does not second wife come to greet me?"

I escorted her to the dais where Guenevere waited with frigid composure. "Morgana, here be Gwynhwyfar, *Gern* of Britain."

Morgana didn't even incline her head. The respect was due her, she felt, as first wife.

Guenevere drew on a lifetime of tact. "We welcome Morgana and her people."

Morgana assessed her openly. "Be fair enough, Belrix, but hast no wealth to show me?"

"And dost grieve for it," I murmured, glad Gwen couldn't follow most of the exchange.

Morgana beckoned in a jangle of ornaments. "Modred! Do greet and honor the *adaltrach* of Belrix."

Too late. It was said and everyone heard it. Many Prydn words are retained in British, though meanings have changed through the centuries. To Faerie, *adaltrach* means only a second wife. To moderns it has come to mean an adulteress. To Guenevere—I won't labor the point.

Her smile froze. She visibly shrank in the chair when Modred placed his hands on her stomach and repeated the word that sealed the tragedy of errors.

"May *adaltrach* have many years and child-wealth."

Guenevere rose with such revulsion I thought she would strike Modred, but her venom leveled at me. "You taught it to say that."

"Gwen, you don't understand."

"But I do." She swallowed hard, trying to control the fury. "Perfectly. And I will not dignify these animals or you any longer."

She hurried out of the hall, leaving me with my little *fhain* in the middle of shocked, disapproving Brits. Lancelot hovered among the Parisi knights, troubled but not stupid enough to compound the issue by following Guenevere. It was young Bors who bumbled forward to comment on the obvious.

"My lord! These people insult the queen."

An understatement. "Bors, please attend her."

He threw a huffy glance at Modred. "But really, sir!"

"Attend the queen, Bors. Say I'll be with her presently." I turned to the court, read the embarrassment in their averted glances. "The audience is ended. Thank you for coming. We give you leave to go."

The hall emptied quickly, everyone glad to be done with it,

hurrying past Bedivere, who leaned on his drawn sword at the entrance. Morgana knew something was terribly amiss, but not why.

"What ails second wife?" she wondered. "Well, do thee go love her. Will be well."

That's all it meant to her. She'd never see and Gwen would never see. Light and dark trying to understand each other. I lifted Morgana in my arms.

"Go to thy rath now. Will come later."

She gave my nose a playful bite. "Promise?"

"Promise. Redhair will take thee. Bedivere, come."

Modred darted a glance at the entrance as if suspicious of an ambush. "How safe be *fhain* here, father? And for how long?"

"Safer than north of the Wall, and thee knows it." Still, I felt proud my son was no fool.

I gave Bedivere instructions to stay with them until I came. He received the orders in silence, offering no comment on the shambles he'd witnessed.

As Morgana trotted out after him, she turned to gaze admiringly about the huge hall. "A braw big rath, Belrix." She hauled the voluminous cloak over her small shoulder. "But where dost byre cattle a-winter?"

Then she was gone and I was alone.

"My lord?" Lancelot was at the entrance, two parchment rolls in his hand. He advanced to me. "This just came. Lucullus Aurelianus is landed at Castle Dore and sends his greeting."

I glanced absently at the roll. Of course Lucullus would stop with Marcus first since he was most likely to defect. Much more interesting was Lancelot's suppressed emotion. He handed me the other roll.

"This as you asked: my suggested order of battle against Cerdic."

"Thank you. How does the queen?"

He shifted from one foot to the other. "She rode out with her Parisi knights. To take the air, she said."

"I see."

Lancelot still hovered, then said it. "My lord, I would like to leave court as soon as possible."

"Yes, that seems prudent."

"For Badon, sir."

"Of course."

He remained tensed in front of me.

"Something else, Lancelot?"

"What happened just now. This thing you have done—"

I pretended to peruse the schedules, keeping my tone casual. "You sound like a man about to say something acute regarding honor and shame."

I raised my eyes from the parchment and gave him time to read their silent comment. No, he wasn't ready to talk about that. "What shall we say about these things, Lancelot? Or not say?"

He was miserable, speaking out where he must and had no right, ambivalent as always. "You should not have done this to her."

"Lancelot, I've learned to be frugal about guilt. I didn't teach Guenevere to hate Faerie or them to be ignorant. If your own wife went to Morgana's rath, she'd be as clumsy. I see by this order of battle you've placed your Dyfneinters near the front of our march. Good, they're fine cavalry. Keep me informed. That's all."

He didn't move.

"You may go, Lord Ancellius."

He bowed and started away.

"Except, I dearly hope you find your Grail someday."

"Thank you, sir."

"Whatever it is."

When it grew dark I left to see my family. Preoccupied and troubled with feelings not yet sorted, I told no one, merely took a horse from the stable and departed by the west gate. Except for a groom and a sentry or two, the court thought I was still in Camelot.

The night was cold. I was chilled when I arrived at the small house along the riverbank, but my brothers had a healthy fire going in the pit. After the hubbub of greetings, I gave Bedivere leave to go home at last. No man deserved it more.

"Home to Myfanwy." I walked him to the door. "Rest tonight and take a boat in the morning."

"Shouldn't I wait on you, Artos?"

"No, I've kept you too long, and I intend to be unkingly as hell for a few hours."

"I'll be at the palace then."

A burst of laughter from my family. Bedivere looked back at them. "I know them better now. Sad in a way, such children. Well, sleep y'sound."

Children they were and unused to a house. They rattled loose in it, playing with their gifts, prowling like foxes in a coop, relieving themselves in the corners. No one thought to use the table for eating—Drost thought it was a bed—but squatted around the firepit, leaving a place for me at Morgana's left.

She told me how Prydn had grown strong since I left. First was only *fhain*, then two *fhains* together as they moved from pasture to pasture among the scattered Prydn, coaxing and convincing them to merge. Morgana led from the start. Cradda and Uredd were too old to argue with her, Dorelei too gentle. They bargained for cattle or stole them. They stole children, and when their numbers were large enough, they attacked openly by day, looting and burning tallfolk villages.

I watched her windburned face as she talked, stamped with that cast that leadership leaves on one who makes decisions for many years. No longer mercurial, surer of strength, the old anger held in check, her merest word to the men around the fire taken as command and answered or obeyed instantly. They followed her without question. And Modred idolized her.

"And should see the braw wealth grown tall as thee now!"

"New blood to make us strong," said Urgus.

Morgana swelled with pride. "Tens and tens now, to the count of two hundreds. As thee showed me in the picture on the ground."

As for tallfolk, now *they* could mourn lost children and taste the bitterness. How often in famine and blight did Prydn leave its own in valley cradles? Wasn't a sister of Cradda put newborn into a Roman house for lack of food in the crannog? But now there was plenty, meat and milk for everyone every night and tens of children to gobble it down, singing about the fire, and the day was at hand when Belrix would give Prydn a home. No more running then. Nothing but peace.

Cunedag threw up his hands in approval. "Yah!"

"Yah!" cried the others—all but my cool, detached son.

I listened to them, increasingly sad. Morgana talked of the promised land, but she was no Moses with a tablet of laws to bind her people to purpose. A place might be found, that wasn't the worst problem. The impossibility was in their lives, in the way they lived and the images they lived by. Morgana's stories were all fluid, all of moving on.

"And then did run like the wind out of Taixali land with a's sheep in our flock, looking for better grass . . . were gone before Erca's men could come . . . moving on, running . . . hiding.''

And so for countless centuries till the drifting became part of them, now suddenly they would stop and change overnight? Put seed in the ground and wait for a harvest while Earth and Lugh urged them onward in their ancient dance? Mingle with tallfolk when distance, fear and superstition were their only real protection? Become familiar where they were once fabled, let the world see they were not magic but only remnants from the morning of Man, unable even to make iron tools or a decent loom for cloth?

"And when Dorelei died," Drost was saying, "did bare have time to barrow a's body, running swift south . . .''

And would keep running until history ran them off the edge of time. Suddenly I pulled Morgana to me, holding her tight because all I could give her was a place to die.

It grew late. Drowsy with rich food and barley beer, Cunedag, Urgus and Drost stretched out on the comfortable pallets along the wall. Morgana drew me to the curtained bower at one end of the house, but I wanted to talk with Modred.

"Be pleased with him, Belrix?''

"As thee said, greatest beauty of all Prydn. Will be in soon."

Modred hunched moodily by the fire. The house was warm; he'd thrown off his sheepskin. His whole lithe torso was ridged with scar lines.

"Thee's fought, boy.''

Modred nodded. "All my life. First memory was Morgana lifting me to horse near a burned village.''

"At least you had a mother, Modred. Why so sad now?''

When he spoke it was with something close to gentleness. "Was thinking of my own wealth.''

I grinned rather foolishly. "Thee's got bairn?''

He was surprised I'd think otherwise. Of course there were children. A boy and girl by a woman of another *fhain*.

It was a shock being father and grandfather all in one night. "And did not bring them to see me?''

"Did leave them to wait at the Wall. Do not have *Gern-y-fhain's* trust.''

"In me, you mean.''

He returned my questioning look with no expression at all. "Mother's old. A thinks of thee like a god. Be always 'when Belrix came, when Belrix was here.' Did have fine husbands in

Cunedag and Urgus and could have more. But always Belrix. Belrix will give the land we need. Where, father?''

I countered with another question. ''And if I could, would Prydn stay on it who have never stayed two fire-festivals on the same graze?''

He looked up at the walls and roof as if they hovered to trap him. ''Always the same. No place be different for us.''

''Soon we take back land from the Saxons. Perhaps there in the east.''

''See?'' Modred thrust forward suddenly. ''In the east. Not here, not with *thy* folk. Always somewhere else.'' He buried his face in brown fingers, and I heard the passionate caring he had masked before.

''Mother be old, but a's done more than any *gern*. Made us rich, but not enough. Never enough. But, oh, must still believe in this and that. And Belrix. Belrix will give us land.''

Modred held out his open hand. ''She told me how thee once brought seed to the rath to show Cradda its magic. Did hold it in this hand many times, but a would not speak to me. Seed magic be not for us.''

''But still thee rides in search of a land.''

The passion faded, the veiled look came back into his eyes. ''Mother searches. Do only follow.''

''And not believe?''

''Only in her.''

''There are few like your mother, son.''

''None, father.'' He turned a little away. ''And do wish for some of that love a wasted mooning for Belrix. What did thee do but leave her?''

''That angers thee? Hast never left a woman out of need?''

''Anger?'' His girlish mouth twisted in a hard, ugly grin. ''Thee's too small for such an anger, Belrix. Nothing but Morgana's wish would bring me here, and only for a's safety. Any harm to my mother in this place, thee answers for it.''

Modred was what life and Morgana made him: a realist, but also a scrap pit for all the hate and anger Morgana laid aside in maturing. When he was young he sensed these things in her and aped them to please her until they were no longer aping but a part of him.

''Modred, I love your mother.''

''*Did leave her.*''

''And I want to love you. And you threaten me?''

"Prydn be dead already, here or somewhere else. Did know that from the seed when a would not speak to me."

I don't know what I expected of Modred. Something more human, a little glad of life, but when all your life has been running and fighting, perhaps glad has no meaning. For this I yearned so many years? This the small hand imagined in mine, toddling beside me as I taught it the music of Earth? Those scarred, powerful arms around my neck as he kissed me good-night? This cold, purposeful, subtly malignant, girl-pretty serpent of a son who'd cut my throat and walk away whistling?

No, I was a fool trying to warm myself by a fire long dead or never kindled. No use lying to myself. I couldn't love Modred. The time for love was past and Modred could not be blamed because I rode away.

"Modred, I'll do what I can for *fhain*. Your father promises you that. But whatever happened to you, let your own bairn be clean of it."

The ugly grin leered up at me. "Clean? My bairn say 'tallfolk' and spit."

No more to say; I needed to be away from him. "Sleep well, my son."

"Well is lightly, father."

Morgana considered it outlandish luxury to sleep in a bed so warm and soft. She yawned and stretched and wrapped herself around me when I slipped under the covers, still gristly hard while my own body had thickened. She patted my stomach and yawned again.

"Thee's fed well, Belrix. Must forgive me now."

"For what, wife?"

Morgana hesitated as if ashamed. "I *would* love thee," she whispered. I had to coax it from her in awkward fragments. She wanted to be all I remembered, but was too tired now to make love.

"The riding, Belrix. The long way."

I laughed into the tumble of her hair. "Fool woman, don't think of it now."

Relieved that I didn't expect miracles, Morgana relaxed, kissing my shoulders and chest. "Aye, tomorrow. Be so tired and the riding hurts my back now."

"Oh, where?"

She placed my hand on the spot. "Like knives sometimes, but must never show it."

I turned her over gently and massaged the sore area. Morgana lay with her cheek on one hand, a blissful smile curving her lips.

"Good . . . so good. Can sleep now."

But even in sleep, she said, there was no real peace. So many people now, so much to carry. In her dreams she led them up an endless hill while the sky got darker and darker and she felt lost.

"You can sleep. I'll hold you."

"Thee'll not go away?"

"Not a foot."

She sighed with contentment. "Could get used to such a bed. Thee talked with Modred?"

"I tried. Be no warmth in the boy. Does not trust me."

"Or anything."

"He's full of hate."

Morgana knew, but how to cope with it? She'd hoped through it all he'd grow to be like me or Melga or even gentle Cunedag, but it never happened. Too much running, too much killing. They were all a hard lot, these new ones growing up. She didn't know where the warmth got lost.

And there were gaps in her wisdom. She wished now she'd listened more to Cradda and Uredd. She had so few of the answers her people needed. Maybe Dorelei should have led them, or someone else.

"Ah, foolish, foolish." She snuggled against me. "Be tired to death, that's all. Who could turn back and change it now?"

"The same with me," I said into her hair. "Who indeed?"

We floated toward sleep in each other's arms.

"Second wife be not plain at all," Morgana drowsed. "Just a wee bit pale. But why dost hate us so?"

How in a lifetime to tell that? "Did never dance at Bel-tein or jump through the fire. Has never heard Lugh's music."

"Would much've helped," she grunted. "But say that first wife be *gern* too, and has tried hard for a's people. Do say as much, Belrix, and a will know me sure from that."

With the beer and Morgana warm in my arms, I relaxed and slept deeply. Too deeply to hear the horses approach at a muffled walk, or the rustle of a body at the stone casement. I woke only to Morgana's tortured shriek, rolling out of bed to grab blindly for my sword, hearing the door crash in, the shouts of my brothers.

Something moved against the dark on the other side of the bed, briefly silhouetted against the pale casement. My legs bunched and sprang. I swung the sword at arm's length, felt it bite deep into solid flesh that sagged away from me and fell.

Thuds and screams from beyond the curtain.

"Mother!"

"Modred, it's me!"

His dim form plunged past me to scoop Morgana in his arms.

The light was poor, but I saw her head and arms fall back limp.

"Mother!"

"Artos!" Bedivere's voice. "Artos, where are you?"

"Here!"

"Liar." Modred dropped the body and turned on me with a snarl. *"Liar."*

His knife slashed wide at me in the gloom. Then, without breaking his momentum, he bounded to the casement and cleared it light as a cat, head first.

I heard the hard clang of iron on iron, swung the curtain aside to see it all in the dying glow from the firepit. Bedivere against the wall, sword at guard, ringed by three men moving in on him. Even as I lunged forward, Bedivere sprang through one man's guard and struck. Another turned on me, raised his sword but paused fatally.

"Stop, *stop*. It's the ki—"

I drove the blade through him. "Bastard!"

"Hold, in Christ's name, *hold*!"

It was Brocan the Parisi. He dropped his weapon. Bedivere forced him to the wall, point against Brocan's throat.

"We didn't know," the stunned young knight stammered. "God's my witness, we didn't know the king was here."

"That was careless," Bedivere hissed. "I saw these pigs leave. Struck me an odd hour for Parisi to depart."

I lit a fat lamp and held it up, a sour sickness in my mouth. Cunedag had died in his bed. Urgus hung head down over the edge of his pallet. Halfway to the bower, Drost sprawled with his blood soaking into the earthen floor. Only Modred had escaped.

"Keep him still, Bedivere. One move and he's yours."

"I'd enjoy it," said Bedivere.

In the bower, the wounded Parisi lay at the foot of Morgana's bed, groaning weakly as I turned him over. Very deliberately, I placed the sword against his throat and shoved.

Morgana lay as Modred dropped her, eyes open and staring, the wide wound under her heart. Numb, not letting myself feel, I closed her eyes and straightened her arms.

"Is she alive, Artos?" Bedivere called.

"In a minute."

I began to shake. The trembling increased till I shuddered like a man with terminal fever, teeth chattering with the uncontrollable spasm. Through all this a name whispered itself again and again, persisting even though I tried to push it away.

I took Morgana's bronze knife from its sheath and waited for my body to stop quivering. After a time it did.

Good. The rest of this night must be spun out in cold blood.

I went back to the other room, lifted Drost's body and laid it on his pallet. The house was silent enough to hear Brocan's ragged breathing.

"Morgana?" Bedivere asked.

"No."

"The boy there?"

"Drost? No. He was so beautiful when I met him. Three years old. He taught me the world could be music as well as matter."

I stood up and pointed at Brocan. "Bring him here."

Bedivere flung him forward. Brocan stumbled to his knees in front of me, doomed and contrite. I believed him as far as that went. Whatever his mission, my death was no part of it. Not that it mattered now.

"We meant no—we didn't know—"

"On your back, Parisi."

When Bedivere pinned him, I took his wrists and sliced them neatly across with Morgana's knife. He stared unbelieving at the wounds as I tore two strips from a blanket and held them in front of his eyes.

"You're bleeding to death, but you can still stop it. Name who sent you."

Now it was done, Brocan got hold of himself. "I'm not afraid to die."

"That's your concern. We can wait."

The wind sighed beyond the broken door. We squatted by Brocan, waiting impassively. The blood collected in little pools at his sides. The color drained from Brocan's face and the sweat started. And the fear—not of death but something worse.

"You must not let me die unshriven."

"That's your choice," I said. "Who sent you?"

"Let me have a priest."

"That would take time you don't have. Say a name, you may not need one."

Brocan twisted his head to Bedivere. "You're a Christian. You can't let me die this way."

"Not much time," said Bedivere. "You're sweating already."

"Oh, Christ . . ."

"Men are different." I held up the blanket strips. "Some can last longer, some less. Perhaps it's too late already. One name, Brocan. Say it. You'll suffer no more than banishment."

Brocan groaned, no longer able to hold his head up.

Bedivere leaned over him. "Now it should be hard for you to see us clearly. Useless to die for nothing."

"God forgive me." Brocan gasped out a name.

It didn't surprise me at all.

Quickly binding his wrists, I gave Bedivere orders in a tone carefully washed clean of any emotion. "In your witness, tried and convicted of high treason. Put him in chains, then down Severn on the first galley out. Never to return on pain of death. What hour is it?"

"About four," Bedivere judged.

"Send a burial detail when it's light."

"It will be done." Bedivere kicked the panting Brocan. "Up."

"My brothers are to be buried with respect. In a new cairn with their names cut on the edge of the cover stone."

"And the lady?"

I had to think a moment. That was the first time anyone ever referred to Morgana by that title.

"She comes with me. When you've stowed Brocan, turn out the court. The whole palace, high and low, to meet in the great hall to hear a criminal charge."

When they left, I went back into the bower and lay down beside Morgana. Whenever the tears started, I willed them back, turning them to cold rage inside. After a time, I wrapped the body in a blanket and carried it to my horse.

Bedivere had already done his office when I approached the palace gate with my burdened horse. Lights flickered from the casements of the audience chamber.

"Who's there?"

"The emperor. Fetch a groom for my horse."

Across the dark courtyard with Morgana in my arms, servants holding torches aloft and murmuring fearfully among themselves. Up the stairs, hearing the rabble of voice from the great hall ahead, dozens of people milling about the chamber and sleepily wondering why. They knew only that it must be important to be waked so long before dawn. The emperor never imposed on them out of caprice.

Fires had been started in the pits at each end of the large chamber, but the great space was still clammy with winter morning, I shouldered through the crowd to the center of the hall, hearing the hushed whispers as I laid down Morgana's body.

"What's he got there?"

"Oh no, it's—"

"Make a ring about the room," I grated. "Everyone back."

They hollowed a wide space around me. No one gave particular note to Bedivere, who waited near Lancelot in the first rank, holding a pair of manacles.

"Lord Ancellius, a moment."

He came, still a bit hazy with sleep like the rest.

"I want to hear from your own mouth that you were no part of this."

No. When I uncovered Morgana's face, his pity and shock were too genuine.

"None of it, my lord. On my life."

"Then take heed, Lancelot. Don't try to be part of it now. Stand back."

I surveyed the court of Camelot. The flower of Britain.

"My lords and ladies, until today I deluded myself that I ruled a civilized land. The last and best of Rome."

Gareth seemed to sense the danger in my tone. "So you do, my king. Who says else?"

"I say it, Gareth. We shortly go to war against a man we presume to call a barbarian, and I find myself wondering why. To save what? I kneel here by this measure of our enlightenment, and I'm tempted to tell Cerdic he can have it all. *Where is the Queen of Britain?*"

"Here, Arthur."

Guenevere had entered and mounted the dais behind me, bleak but composed.

"We would not have you sit, Lady. You are not here in state."

She didn't flinch. "No."

I peeled the blanket from Morgana's pathetic form, hearing the reaction of my people. Whether for me or Morgana, I couldn't say. Perhaps for themselves. I'd brought a truth home to them, as if to say: "This is the sewer that runs beneath our ideals. Have a smell."

"She was killed tonight, my lords. Of course you may say she was only a Faerie, less than human. But let's pretend for a moment we're civilized, that we have at least the justice of Saxons, among whom the poorest farmer has some sort of redress. If a person under crown protection be killed, what is the charge?"

Bedivere spoke it sharp and clear. "Murder."

The whisper went around the hall, hesitant at first, then more positive. "Murder . . . murder."

"No. Justice," Guenevere snapped. "Royal judgment that must be absolute and above question if there is to be any law at all. My lords, why should I dissemble? This was done by my will."

Cador's child had cold courage, I gave her that.

"By my will and for reasons any one of you would approve. I begged the emperor not to let this woman cross the Wall. You saw her and her brood. Did you know there are two hundred more waiting to follow after, to inhabit the land she demanded of our king?"

Her force and resolution put a new stamp on it. My court looked less certain. Aye, after all, it was true. The woman was a danger.

"My people," Guenevere stretched out her arms to them. "Have I not been a just queen, just and merciful, for many years? Does one of you think I had this woman killed for the foul personal insult she gave me?"

"No, Lady."

"No, never."

"The queen is right!"

"She had ambitions in Britain," Guenevere went on. "Aims that she didn't trouble to disguise, she was that sure of Arthur. He speaks of the war with Cerdic, a war to be fought for much this same reason. If Cerdic came into this hall now and demanded the same land, would our answer be any different?"

"No."

"*No!*"

Guenevere urged, "Was it murder then, or execution?"

"The queen is right," said Lancelot.

"Never," declared doughty Lady Rhian. "The woman was under royal protection. By God, I stand with the king."

"And I with the queen," said young Bors. "We cannot have these people here."

Gareth answered that quietly. "I might agree, lad, but I've seen too much royal murder in my own land. *Daone sidhe* she was, but under the king's peace."

"And under a royal roof," Guenevere countered. "And who is to say what she was planning there?"

"I am, Guenevere."

I rose from the body to confront her. "I was there, Gwen. We were sleeping when your men came."

She didn't move, but the steel went out of Guenevere. Her mouth opened silently. Oh God, no.

"Since the court is mixed in judgment, I put a further case. If in that judicial execution the king's life be endangered so that only darkness and good luck preserve him—in such a case, whatever extenuation, what is the charge?"

Lady Rhian had not wavered from the beginning in her judgment. Perhaps there was a trace of grim satisfaction in her answer now.

"High treason, my lord."

"Treason," said Gareth.

"No, not the queen!"

"No!"

I whirled on them. "Lords-comites, draw your swords."

The blades hissed from their scabbards.

"Restrain anyone who tries to interfere."

"Arthur!" Guenevere broke and ran to kneel at my feet. "I didn't know you were there. I'll swear it on relics, I would not hurt you, not my husband." She looked at Morgana. "But for this, you'll have my head before my repentance."

I grabbed her hair and twisted. "Not your head, woman."

"Stop!" Lancelot sprang forward, but Bedivere tripped him neatly and slammed the iron manacles down on the back of his head. Lancelot sprawled like a slain ox.

"Your filthy *pride*." I forced Guenevere down to Morgana's body, to the wound, grinding her face back and forth against it until she was smeared and caked with blood, then let her up.

"Guards!"

Guenevere was stunned. She wiped at her cheek, unbelieving. "A real king would kill me rather than this."

"Bedivere, the irons."

Guenevere's hands were manacled to the chain that clasped to the heavy iron ring about her neck. The chains were absurd on her, but meant more as symbol than restraint.

"Lock her up."

Guenevere lifted her chains. "Is this what we come to, Arthur? We stood against the world together. When was I ever less concerned with justice than you? When did I ever do anything against the good and safety of Britain?"

"Don't add hypocrisy to your other talents, Lady. It would make you too dangerous."

"Kill me then," she flared. "You lack the courage?"

"I lack your facility, but I won't let you wear good intent like a butcher's apron. We said it years ago. Right is bigger than princes. If not, your Brocan deserves to be king."

"Then I won't be a hypocrite, nor should you." Guenevere's haggard glance drifted to the inert Lancelot. "Is it really for her, all for Morgana, that I'm in chains?"

"As sure as you are that her death was impersonal."

Her fists balled. "Damn you. When Peredur hears of this—"

"He'll know before anyone else. You see, Modred escaped. And I think Peredur will be the first item on a very long bill of charges. Take her away."

With Guenevere gone the tension shuddered out of my court. The knights relaxed, the women whispered back and forth. They all wanted to be dismissed. I went to sit on my audience chair, but it seemed much too far. I slumped down on the edge of the dais like a bag of sand.

"My people, it must be nigh time for matins. Before you go to pray for God's blessing on this jewel of a land, think on this. If this dead woman wasn't safe under my law, which of you is?"

Suddenly the white anger that had sustained me for two hours drained dry. I sagged, elbows on my knees, imperial dignity be damned. "You can all go."

Lady Rhian stepped forward from Gareth's side. "It must be said. Long life and God's blessing on our wise and just king."

"Please, all of you go now. Leave Lord Ancellius. I'll speak with him."

He lay stretched on his side, the blood drying on the back of his head. When the hall emptied, I got up heavy as an old man and went to flop down again beside Morgana, cradling her in my arms, fussing over the clumsy blanket wrap as one would with a baby.

I brought her to this. She came in trust, with no place else to run. Even now, at the Wall, they waited for Morgana to lead them into the land of the Firelord. Now Modred would lead them, doomed as his mother, but with less time. Someone would ride him to earth, but not before his vengeance took so much down with him.

Lancelot stirred and opened his eyes.

"It's over," I grated. "Get up."

He rolled over and blinked at me, then the empty hall around us. "What have you done with her?"

"Nothing yet."

Lancelot lurched to his feet. "Where is she?"

"In irons."

He didn't believe it at first. "God damn you, Arthur. If that's treason, I'll make it stick. God *damn* you. Do you know what you've done?"

"Do you see this? What the hell do you think she is, a dead cat?"

"She begged you not to bring them."

Christ, I was tired. "Yes. As you begged her not to commit murder, I'm sure. But you wouldn't prevent it, either. This woman—I know what you think, what they all think. But she touched my soul once and never let go. She was my wife, she had my son, she took her whole life and hung it on a belief in me. Yes, she was wrong. Narrow, ignorant and wrong, but she was looking for a Grail like you, in the only way we left her. And when she needed my help, she put on all her bangles and that big, silly cloak and—"

The tears wouldn't be held any longer. I choked on them.

"Go on, get out. Go to Astolat, say good-bye to your dreary little wife. I want you at Badon in ten days."

Lancelot nodded. "So I will be. And if I live through Badon, let me be far from you."

"Go to hell for all I care. Get out."

He shook his head slowly. "And I saved your life once."

"*Get out.*"

Lancelot walked out of the hall, leaving me with Morgana in my arms on the cold floor. No one dared to come near, so that my crying echoed alone from the stone walls until first light crept through the casement.

Morgana was carried to rest by Bedivere, Gareth, Bors and myself and laid beside her husbands and Drost in the new cairn, her name etched before theirs on the entrance stone. We placed her on the central bier with her husbands on either side. The shroud was of simple linen, but her small head was fitted with a bronze circlet inscribed in Latin and British:

This Is Morgana, First Wife to Belrix

Peredur was pressed between two painful choices, loyalty to me or to Gwen. Predictably, he decided for the blood tie.

—must insist that Guenevere be restored or at least returned to Eburacum. She does not deserve this, Arthur, and while she remains in prison, no Parisi or Brigante will march under your banner.

Even my stalwarts were dubious. Waiting for Cerdic at Badon, Maelgwyn kept his grim silence, but Kay wrote it for both of them.

You've made no friends with this, and it may be used against you. Among my western trevs, they say Artorius is become a tyrant too full of power . . .

Too full of power? When was there ever a leader in Britain who ruled enough of them at one time?

"His Excellency, the ambassador to Theodoric, King of Italy, Luccullus Aurelianus!"

Lucullus wafted into my *scriptorium,* a perfumed and tonsured vision in fur-trimmed blue and gold, no less than eight heavy rings on his slim fingers, the medallion of his office set in rubies and emeralds and suspended from a heavy gold chain. He looked the very manual for a fashionable prince, from his precisely crafted boots to the meticulously arranged black curls on his scalp. A little too black, I thought. At least my age, Lucullus should have sported a white lock here and there. But he was determinedly youthful, speech and movement of a studied grace as he knelt to me.

"Long life and prosperity to the Emperor of Britain."

"We welcome the ambassador from Rome. My dear cousin, how does your lord?"

"Most happy that he greets Britain through me."

"We receive him thus and hope our poor comforts please his embassy. Come by the fire and enjoy some Falernian with me."

While I poured the wine, I took the measure of my cousin, Lucullus Aurelianus. Close-set eyes over a long, severe nose. The mouth seemed incongruous, soft and sensual as Modred's. "We hear you stopped at Castle Dore."

Lucullus accepted the wine and sat, arranging the folds of his cloak like a great bird coming to rest. His exquisite hands fluttered away the negligent matter.

"Merely trade schedules. Lead, tin. The usual."

"And we further hear you put in at Wight. Forgive me, I've forgotten what Rome imports from there."

He didn't bat an eye. "An emergency anchorage, urged by the vessel's master. Fresh water only. The Saxons—as my lord *knows*—are at present quite outside our sphere of felicity. Our love in Britain is for Britons, whose blood flows richly in my own veins."

God, he was good. I could almost believe him. "Your beloved father was our teacher, and we remember you might have been emperor in our stead."

The hands danced again to the measure of his musical laughter. "Kingship is not among my talents. I've seen too many dicers lose everything on one throw. But I made a profit standing on the edge of the game and betting on the odds. That is my poor gift, to see how things will fall."

"Very prudent," I observed. "Sometimes I wish I had that choice. For convenience, ample quarters have been prepared for you and your consorts within the walls of Camelot."

Lucullus set down his goblet. "Touching that, I'd hoped to convey Rome's greeting to Queen Guenevere."

Not only meet her but find how the wind blew now over Britain. There was hardly a corner of the land where her incarceration wasn't known and discussed, and Lucullus needed to know every ramification. While we smiled and drank each other's health, that was his job.

The stop at Wight bothered me. It was not inconceivable that Rome's friendship could be balanced on a hinge between Cerdic and me. No one has fewer friends than a defeated king.

"The queen is unavailable though she will grieve to have missed you."

Lucullus draped himself in regret. "And I her. Is she not called unique as far as Byzantium? Not only beautiful by report, but a ruler worthy of legend."

Enough panegyric. I tried a quick jab through his guard. "And the only one currently in jail."

It caught him unprepared but Lucullus recovered quickly. "So we heard. Most unfortunate. May my poor efforts urge clemency and reconciliation."

"It is unfortunate, Lucullus, but let Rome see our true image in this mirror. We are the last undefeated province of the old empire. When it was truly Roman. We've held our borders against barbarism for an hundred years and don't intend to flag now. The emperor's word must be good and his peace inviolate. Surely a Roman, with his instinct for precise justice, can understand that. If the law and peace are not for all, they're for none."

"Most assuredly," Lucullus agreed. "Yet this estrangement in the royal house must—especially now—give rise to apprehension among tributary princes. The Parisi, for example."

I thought I would spare him Peredur's agonized letters and merely refilled his goblet. "Does the oak tremble at one stroke of the ax? Britain is sound as your father made it, Lucullus. And now I must meet your train, your consorts, and give order to set a dinner to honor Lucullus' return to his native soil."

He rose with a charming, deprecatory laugh. "Too much honor."

"Not at all. They tell me there's roast peacock."

"Peacock! Surely not."

"The absolute last in Britain, my stewards assure me. Pity. We have no more time to enjoy them esthetically, but we can still cook them to a turn."

"Ah—yes. And who adorns my lord's arm at table?"

"Tonight," I assured him, "my guests are my jewels."

Lucullus bowed and recovered with a knowing look. "Still, a king need not want for such comforts."

I gave him a light pat on the back. "Nor an ambassador with two such pliant consorts. However do you manage?"

"It *is* busy," he simpered.

"All those decisions."

"Ah *ha*! Right, right, but surely Venus' fire burns as brightly in a king's chamber."

"Ah, you flatter me, dearest cousin. If your bed is a busy crossroad, mine is a mere footpath: a pleasant ramble somewhat in disuse."

"My lord is a veritable wit." His jeweled fingers caught the firelight again. "Touching Ambrosius, there are letters he charged me long ago to deliver when I could. Letters to him from my aunt Julia, your grandmother.''

"Yes, he did mention them once. Shall we join the court now? After you, cousin.''

I breathed his strong perfume as he passed.

If you find all this sickening, remember that kings and scullions have much in common. We both get the jobs no one else wants.

I met his luggage at dinner. Lucullus might have aged, but his tastes did not. The girl was very young, willowy and vapid, the boy poutish and pretty. Conversation was a one-sided effort. Both spoke the vulgate of the Roman street, which was more than ample for any audible thought required of them. Lucullus chose his consorts as he might a garment or wine. Frankly, I missed Gwen.

That night, propped up in bed, I studied the packet of letters tendered by Lucullus. The brittle brown pages were parting along their folds, written more than sixty years ago by my grandmother Julia to her young brother Ambrosius when Britain's patricians were prouder of their Roman heritage than their British blood. Mundane letters describing travel with her husband Metellus Tiberius, embassy-at-large for harried Vortigern. They were seldom at home, life a dreary round of strange places and stranger people, bad food and worse weather. They longed for the sound of Latin, a hot bath, food seasoned with something other than wild garlic.

One theme wove through all Julia's letters, her need for children and her despair of ever having one.

> *Our physicians say the constant travel interferes with the natural urges of my constitution. There is no problem in conceiving, only in carrying the child. Our household gods are bored with my pleas as must be my dear, patient brother.*

She finally stopped pestering the gods and conceived once more. This time the crucial third month passed without mishap. Hardly daring to hope, Julia wrote from north of the Wall, where Metellus was on a mission to King Brude.

> *These Venicone are crude and superstitious. When I asked about the markers around this village, they said*

it's to keep out "Faerie," the stunted nomads who inhabit the surrounding hills, wild-looking creatures beside whom Germans seem positively urban. Once when I was waddling about just before my time, I saw one of the hill women watching me from just outside the pale. No proper garment, just some sort of animal skin wrapped around her.

Suddenly, when the child was due, Julia began to bleed. She was put to bed by her physician and forbidden to move; even so there were grave doubts she would deliver a live infant. Her Venicone servingwoman suggested that, with proper precautions, the Faerie women excelled at midwiving. Julia was ready to try anything.

The woman came next day.

—young and handsome enough in her wild way, but half starved, poor thing. They tell us this is a bad year for the northern cattle, and the nomads always suffer most when that happens. My servingwoman was frightened of her and wouldn't stay in the room. The creature set about bargaining for her services in a very matter-of-fact way, and I thought, well! She can't be too lethal if she's dickering like a fishwife. One of her conditions was that she be allowed to deliver me with no help from anyone else, that this would hinder the circle of power she raised about me—or something like that. Since my doctor gave no hope of a live child, desperate as I was, it was now or never. I said yes.

Julia offered a fair price in gold *solidi* and the woman seemed content. She gave Julia a draft to induce labor and agreed to return later when it took effect. The pains started—

—but I hardly felt them. I was really quite drunk and only wanted to go on floating in this delightful limbo. I hardly noticed the woman when she came back into my room with a big, covered basket.

The woman took something from a corner of the basket and mixed another draft. After examining Julia's dilation, she said that the child would come easily. My grandmother would feel no pain at all.

*—and I didn't—felt nothing, saw nothing, just floated
away into the silliest dream where I was an ocean and
someone was trying to take a fish from me.*

I put the letter aside, bothered by the inconsistency. Prydn
women never used drugs to induce labor or during it. She must
do her part, like Dorelei and Morgana. And to render a woman
unconscious was unheard of.

*This woman truly worked magic, Ambrosius, for
when I woke there was my daughter in her arms,
clean-washed with none of that angry red one sees in
newborns. The bed was a mess, even blood on the
floor. The woman was crooning to the child with soft,
weird sounds. Then, while I was still in a haze, she
placed the child at my breast—and oh, the dear little
thing tugged at me, so hungry! I could see the tiny
fingers that moved and toes and little legs kicking. The
woman said that since I was so generous with my gold,
she would preserve the umbilicus to make strong magic
for my child. Generous! Ambrosius, can I describe the
delirious joy! The foolish tears running down my cheeks,
thinking all at once to send for Metellus, then forgetting it to thank the woman again and again, thinking of
the sacrifices I would make to my gods for this gift. A
hundred doves! And maybe a little something for Jesu,
too.*

In unslaked gratitude, Julia wanted to double the fee, but the
woman seemed very anxious to be gone, barely bothering to
count her fee. Julia was determined some extra gift must be
hers. She sent for the woman repeatedly through the week.
Finally, the Faerie returned word that she would come only to
the pale. Julia must not under any circumstances bring the child,
for that would destroy much of the beneficial magic woven in
its behalf.

*Her two husbands were with her, wretched, scrofulous
beggars. She hardly looked at the gold coins I gave
her. She asked only did my daughter thrive and was
pleased when I said yes. I asked her name that I might
at least send the blessing of my gods to her tribe. One*

of her little husbands stepped forward with all the pomp
of an Egyptian minister, pointed to the woman and
said with a pathetic flourish, "This is Gernafane."

Then that would be part of the payment. The child must be
named for Metellus' mother Fulvia, but her second name would
be Gernafane.

My benefactress said nothing, just muttered at her
husbands, then hurried away with the men trotting
after. I'd swear she was crying. Odd little things, but
they do seem quite human at times.

Julia kept her promise about the name, though they shortened
it to the British Ygerna.

—which I like much better than Fulvia, but then you
know my opinion of Metellus' mother. Except for duty,
I wouldn't put her name to a dead cat.

The last letter was dated ten years later, when Metellus was
dying. Evidently the paternal bequest would leave his daughter a
wealthy woman, and what the family knew or guessed they kept
to themselves. Julia's last reference was rather cryptic.

I know what happened and why, but it matters so
little now. Fruitless to yearn for what might have been.
She is ours and beautiful and we love her.

Fulvia Ygerna. My mother.
I folded the letters carefully and put them back in their rose-
wood box, feeling—it's hard even now to write of what I felt
then, but the last piece of my fragmented life was cemented
firmly in its place.
Brother Coel is delighted, of course. He has the instincts for
drama, if not the style, and this fits his highest concept of a
British royal chronicle. After all, Saxon kings claim descent
from divine ancestors, and our own heroes are sometimes sprung
from the union of mortal and *boucca*. So Arthur, like ancient
Merlin, becomes the son of prince and spirit.
But they're people, Coel.
Hell, write what you please. We Britons tend to be lyrical

anyway, and it doesn't matter now. If the future cares at all, perhaps by then the running and the hunger and the tears will have faded so that only the magic remains.

We had no proper Yule that winter, there wasn't time. One blustery day I was drafting a letter to the Ordovices and Cornovii in the far west.

> *We hear you call us tyrant and compare our rule to the sterner days of Vortigern and Ambrosius. We put it to you, where is a family's strength when irresponsible children have none but an indulgent parent to lead them? As for my predecessors, one bargained for your lives and the other fought for them. Wherein tyrant?*

Gareth rapped on the open door. "My lord?"

"Yes, Gareth-fach?"

"Prince Kay's barge has docked on the quay, and will you receive him now?"

"Send him here to the *scriptorium*. Is the evening rider in from Badon?"

"A bit late, sir. Expected this hour." My stubby little captain jiggled with ill-concealed exuberance.

"With the news so bad, it's good to see one man so cheerful, Gareth."

He was smug with it. "King of a hundred battles, forget the news. Not all Britain's deserted you. You have friends of old, devil if you do not."

"That's good to hear. Tell the prince to hurry, I've missed him."

A few minutes later I heard voices along the gallery outside, Kay's and a deeper one I couldn't quite place. Then Kay hurried into the chamber, flinging his cloak and sword onto a chair before he hugged me like a fat, affectionate little bear.

"Damn, I'm cold. Let me get by the fire."

Kay presented his spreading rump to the firepit with audible pleasure. "Ah, that's good. We weren't half frozen."

We caught up quickly on family news. His wife and children sent their love and were coming by barge with Kay's entire household.

"Are you ready to march, Kay?"

"With a few hundred horse, all that are loyal. Mother's with me."

"Flavia? Why?"

"I couldn't leave her, not in conscience."

"Kay, what's wrong at home?"

My brother turned back to the fire and now I heard the strain and frustration in his voice. "I've only got half a tribe left, that's what. The rest are siding with the Parisi. They say it's because of Guenevere, but they're really paying you out for Pwyll."

"Pwyll? But that's years ago."

"Small minds, long memories," Kay growled. "Old ways, blood ties. They know Peredur's against you, and that senile shit Marcus is sitting on the fence as usual." He threw down his heavy gloves. "Cerdic will love this, right enough."

Kay turned to me, a chunky little man in the corpulence of well-fed middle age. Jowly, with more white in his beard than I remembered.

"I've shipped the family because if we lose the battle, the Dobunni will choose another prince. If I go down, I want to know they're safe."

"Fools. If we go down, the Dobunni won't choose anything, they'll be too busy running."

"Well." His round face creased suddenly in a sidelong grin. "It's not all black as night, brother. I've a surprise for you." He gestured to the door with a flourish. "Imperator, the King of Orkney waits on you."

"I turned. "The King of—?"

Gawain filled the doorway side to side and top to bottom, grizzled, dour as ever, squinting dubiously at me. It was a moment before I could speak.

"Well, now. Am I forgiven at last?"

"I would not say that entire," Gawain allowed, "but did think it was time to put in my say."

He lumbered forward and bent his knee before me, huger than ever if that was possible. He must have needed one of his little islands just for a throne room.

"Long life to the Emperor of Britain. The sovereign isles of Orkney place their sword in your hand."

I swallowed hard. "And we thank Your Grace for this—for— oh, get up. Get *up*, you great, lovely ox! It's too much happiness for one day."

I put an arm around both. "Brother and friend. By the gods, it's been ages since I felt so good. How many men, Gawain?"

"Five hundred horse."

"So few?"

"All I could ship round the north cape to Solway. They're with Kay's men up Severn, waiting the order. Did send to Agrivaine, but he stays with Peredur."

"And hates me still?"

Gawain shook his head. "Apples grow sweeter—my brother went from green to sour. There's no reasoning with him anymore. The hell with him. What's right is right."

Kay calculated. "There's us here and Lancelot and Maelgwyn sitting on Badon. What are the odds now?"

"Four, five to one," I hedged, guessing they were more.

"Why did I bother then?" Gawain wondered airily. "That's barely five apiece."

I laughed aloud; it was a moment when comet hopes and laughter went well together. "Right, old friend. Geraint said that once when the odds were much worse. And still we won, and we will again. Dobunni and Orkney? How can we fail?"

Gawain moved to the fire, spreading his hands to its warmth. "Not that I wholly trust the sly ways of you. You were a pain in my heart, Arthur. But did think and think on it and decided I'd deal with the Saxons once and for all. We can't have such rabble calling the turn. Rabble, by God! Mark me, Arthur, the commons can be dangerous, they do lack proportion and respect. Look you what they call a king. Cerdic, is it? Is he a nobleman? It is grave and getting worse, so I came to set it right, knowing you'd never do it alone."

Though he'd make three of Geraint, they were spirits of one breadth. "And I am grateful, Gawain."

"Well you might be," he snorted, "with your odd and liberal ways. Na, I've heard of this roil with Guenevere. You gave her too much power. You should have kept her in at door to knit with her women."

I clapped them both on the back. "My good lords, such as we are, we're full strength. No sense waiting. Send to your captains and tell them—"

An agitated trio of voices exploded in the gallery outside my *scriptorium*, two determined, one plaintive and resisting. Lucullus was shoved unceremoniously through the door by Bedivere and Gareth. The Roman was livid and shaken.

"Artorius, I protest. I protest vigorously. This is a breach of courtesy and an intrusion on my office."

I looked to Bedivere. "What in hell is all this?"

"Lords." Gareth ducked his head to Kay and Gawain. "Sir, the post rider's in. Cerdic is breaking camp."

"Readying to march?"

"Looks it, sir."

I spun on Kay and Gawain. "Send for your squadrons now, tonight. Give them a point to meet with us on the way to Badon. Hurry."

"Forget the barge," Kay muttered to Gawain as they pushed by Bedivere and out the door. "We'll send by fast horse."

I turned to the new problem. "Now, Lucullus?"

"I protest!"

"So you said. Why?"

Bedivere shoved him further into the room. "Artos, this bastard—"

"If you please, Bedivere. Our ambassador from Rome."

Bedivere bit the words off, slapping a folded letter into my hands. "If my king says so. Lancelot intercepted this on its merry little way to Cerdic."

"Hands *off*, sirs." Lucullus shook himself free of the restraint. "An embassy has some privilege."

"Yes, there's no need to clutch at him, my lords. He won't disappear."

I read the letter carefully as it was couched in extraordinarily careful language. A simple greeting from Rome to Cerdic, praising his repute and accomplishments. It promised nothing, compromised nothing, made no mention of me or any other Briton. On the other hand, it shut no doors in the face of Roman-Saxon accord. A masterly letter, the sort all ambassadors write as groundwork for the bargaining of powers. Ours is an amoral vocation. The sin is not in plotting, only in getting caught. Lucullus and I both knew this.

"Of course," I said to him, "no one could ever prove you advised him to attack now."

Lucullus made a scoffing noise. "You know that's absurd."

"Of course."

"Rome's friendship—"

"Warms me so that I would not be without it in winter. Lord Bedivere, provide Lucullus with armor, weapons and a good horse. I'm taking Rome's friendship to Badon so that, like a friend, he may share my fortunes."

Lucullus went a little pale.

"And Lord Gareth, tell my stewards that every comfort will

be provided the ambassador's consorts while he adds honor to his name."

Gareth suppressed a giggle. "The dears will be coddled like prize geese."

Lucullus moved forward. "This—is—intolerable! The first embassy to touch Britain in years, and I am treated thus? Cousin, you are not naïve. You can't view that letter as the work of a spy."

"I'm not and I don't." I snatched my cloak from a chair and slung it over one shoulder, moving to the door. "Since Rome is interested in Saxons, you will now have the chance to observe them minutely. When we've won, you're at liberty. Till then, cousin, I would not part with you."

Lucullus saw it was inevitable and with an effort retrieved some of his grace. "Let it be then. A good horse and the best sword, if you please. It's been years, but I know something of war."

"Good," I saluted him. "We're wretchedly shorthanded. Lords, I'll be at Prince Kay's."

But Lucullus called after to me. "How if you lose? How will Britain account to Theodoric for his embassy and close friend? How then, Artorius?"

The thought stopped me. "Frankly, I don't know. We've improvised so long, we'll think of something."

Gareth swept low in a flourishing bow. "*Dear* my lord—after you."

Kay's house was always kept ready for him, a large dwelling near the north gate, not unlike Uther's but notably lacking in some of its comforts. His servants were bustling about in preparation for Flavia's dinner when I arrived.

Nearing seventy, my stepmother still insisted on a Roman household, rather impractical in these declining days. As the years passed she retreated more and more into a narrow memory of the past, and drinking had become chief prop and solace to her illusion. Ill with nothing more than age, she directed the servants from her bed, one hand fluttering in imperious command, the other holding a goblet of costly Egyptian glass inset with pieces of jet, amber and onyx.

"The last of six." She set it down with a mournful pride. "Sent from Rome by Augustulus—my cousin, you know. Nice boy, but a ruinous emperor."

Flavia patted the edge of the bed for me to sit. "Come here, Artorius? Why in the world did you allow anyone to scar your cheeks like that. So unfashionable."

I eased down and kissed her. "Comfortable, mother?"

"Comfortable, what's that nowadays?" she fretted. "I want to be home in my own house, damn those Dobunni. Uther's family ruled them superbly for an hundred years, and *now* they want a change. Stupid animals. *Herds*, not tribes, the whole country."

I tucked the coverlet around her. "Yes, mother."

"They're forgetting everything Rome ever taught them. No wonder Lucullus feels a stranger. You won't deal too harshly with him? After all, he is a Roman knight."

"Not too harshly, no. A little fresh air."

"Poor Kay," Flavia mused vaguely. "He does try so hard for those savages. Why did you shave your beard?"

"It's gone all white and makes me look ninety."

"Vanity," she scoffed, holding out her goblet. "British vanity. You always looked a prince, though you never dressed it until that very clever girl took you in hand. Fill me up again, Artorius."

I poured more wine into the goblet and wrapped a shawl around her bony shoulders. All Flavia's plumpness had deserted her in age. She rambled now in the wine mist that was her only comfort.

"Kay has a talent for rule. He does, give him that. Who was it revised the tax structure for you when you were crowned? But . . . you had a genius for men. How oddly things turn out."

Flavia plucked at my sleeve with thin fingers. "You never hated me, did you? You never grudged Kay his birthright?"

"The Dobunni never had a better prince," I said truthfully. "I would have had them at my throat in a year."

Flavia settled back on her pillows, in control and pettish again. "I daresay. Talent is always more reliable than genius. A steady glow beside lightning. You're dark more often than brilliant, boy."

"Yes, so I'm told."

"I mean this mess with Guenevere."

"Let's not talk of that."

"Rot!" she said sharply. "I am a decade older than most of the gods, that gives me some privilege. Your wife is a fine ruler. What in hell is she doing pent up when she's worth five of the best ministers you could find? Yes, yes, I know what she did, a hasty decision perhaps, but after *all*—''

"Mother, I know who I am."

It caught her off guard. "What?"

"I know what I am. Where I came from. It answers a lot of things."

The news silenced her. She leaned over to set the goblet on her bed stand, but her grasp slipped and the glass toppled to the floor.

"Oh, is it broken? Artorius, I don't dare look. Is it broken? Oh, *no*."

I looked at it quickly and refilled the glass. "Good as new."

She closed both hands tight around it with relief and reverence. "Just that it's the last. Augustulus sent a set of six. They were exquisite. See how it catches the light? Vortigern drank from one that day he came to the villa. What . . . what were you saying?"

"Lucullus brought Julia's letters. About Ygerna."

"Julia," she murmured. "Marvelous woman. Long-suffering. Generous." She fussed at her shawl, suddenly tender. "I never held it against you, Arthur. Please believe that."

"I know, mother."

Her eyes ravaged mine for assurance that I did truly know. "Really?"

"No complaint. If I've lost Ambrosius from the family tree, I've also pruned Lucullus. It's a distinct consolation."

"Just that Uther was *my* husband, and it—it hurt so much. I was so frightened before he brought you home, frightened what you'd look like. Silly of me, you're a big, fair ox like Uther's father. But I couldn't help hating her."

The rain began again, the cold downpour of late December. Flavia's servants came in to latch the casements against the wind and poke up the brazier near her bed.

"Wretched country!" she muttered, grabbing the shawl tighter. "Poor Kay, having to campaign in weather like this."

"Mother, did you know Ygerna?"

She answered without relish. "Yes, it was unavoidable."

"Tell me."

Flavia dabbed daintily at her mouth with a napkin. "Ambrosius' so-called niece was a spoiled brat. No humility and absolutely no modesty. Unstable, but your father found that attractive for a while."

The bitterness in her voice was old as a faded scar. Her mouth curved in an arch smile. "And a positive gift for saying the right thing at the wrong time. You remember Caradoc, what a bore he was. Good man, but *such* a trial with that Grail story. If we heard it once, we heard it a thousand times. We could mouth it along with him."

"His daughter's much the same. Have you met her?"

"Eleyne? No." Flavia sniffed. "If I arrange my time carefully, I may never have to. Well, anyway, we were all at a banquet given by Vortigern . . ."

It seemed Caradoc trotted out the venerable story again on this occasion when Ygerna was a little drunk. She listened quietly, chin on her hands, until Caradoc got to the part about the young female pilgrim and her loosened robe.

Suddenly Ygerna broke in with a merry laugh. "My lords, I am nineteen years old, and do men lie when they call me beautiful?"

The table gallants assured her to the contrary.

"Then by all the gods and Caradoc's too," Ygerna vowed, "if I were undraped in public, I'd expect *someone* to take passing note without the crockery vanishing."

"The table laughed for a quarter hour. Caradoc never spoke to your mother again." Flavia's afterthought carried delicate venom. "She had all the luck."

I leaned over, laughing, to hug her. "Flavia Marcella, one more emperor is your slave."

"Oh, you big ruffian. There now, I love you too." She pecked my cheek. "And where's my supper, damn those people! Artorius, tell them to bring hot bricks, my feet are *blue*. Why have I lived in this miserable country all my life?"

The curtain thrust aside. Kay clumped into the bower, wet and shivering. "Filthy night."

He bent dutifully to kiss Flavia, stripping off the sodden cloak. "We heard you all the way to the scullery, mum. Your supper's coming."

I asked him if his messengers were gone north.

"An hour ago. Bedwyr says the *combrogi* are seeing to their gear and horses. They'll be ready."

"When must you go?" Flavia asked us.

"At first light," I said.

She held out a hand to each of us. "It has been so long since I had both of you under one roof, and here you go dashing off again. Oh, such times, everyone running, nothing permanent. And in such weather."

I kissed her hand. "Maelgwyn and Lancelot expect us. If Cerdic gets there first, they'll take an awful pounding."

She dropped my hand but held on to Kay like life itself. "Will you send word every day?"

"Every day," he promised. "By the post riders."

"Where must you go?" she pressed. "How far away?"

I handed Flavia her goblet. "Not far, just to Badon."

"Where is that?"

Kay grinned. "Nowhere really, mum. Just a silly big hill."

Flavia gasped suddenly. "Look!"

She held the goblet close to a lamp. "It *is* cracked. Look, a thin, thin line, but it goes all the way down. Look at it!"

She peered up at us in anguish, the sudden tears blurring her eyes. "It was the last. Augustulus sent me six, and this was the last. And it's cracked."

We hovered on either side of the old woman, trying to soothe her, saying it was nothing, just a glass, when it was really so much, and Flavia hugged the forever-flawed glass to her breast and cried with despair bottomless as a child's.

"It was the last . . ."

King of a Hundred Battles

You don't know misery until you've pushed yourself and horses through winter rain driven by a relentless east wind. I had planned originally to raise Badon in a day and a half. With the hampering muck underfoot and waiting for the men from Severn, we took three long, sodden days.

And Cerdic was there already.

Even now it's hard to believe he could do it. His entire force was infantry. He must have marched them clear through two nights with only short rest. A clever man with iron men behind him. Maelgwyn said they came on the field and stormed the hill with no rest at all. But then Badon was Cerdic's ultimate gamble. He wouldn't commit everything and then cripple it with half measures.

The rain limited visibility, but as we watched the embattled hill from a mile-distant promontory, we knew how late we were. Badon was under heavy attack, the lower defenses perhaps already breached, we couldn't tell. We expected to be outnumbered, but the juggernaut on the plain stunned us for its size.

"Ten thousand," Gawain whispered.

"More," said Gareth. "A deal more."

"I once saw some ants find a bit of pastry at the scullery door," Kay commented grimly. "That's what they look like. Hungry ants."

"Well, I made confession before we left," Bedivere consoled himself. "But I do wish I hadn't rushed it."

Gawain said urgently, "Let's charge them now."

"I'm for that," Kay agreed through chattering teeth. "The only way to get warm."

"Wagons!" Gareth said suddenly.

We stared at him.

Gareth jiggled with his inspiration. "That's it, high king! The wagons for the carrying of food. He can't have many yet. Can he push oxen so fast as running men? Nay, he cannot. And if that's so, are not most of them straggled out from here to Winchester?"

I beamed at him. The secret of being a brilliant general is to have men like Gareth. "You're my eyes, then. Get down close as you can, circle the hill. And count his wagons."

Gawain watched him depart, grumbling. "What he can see, indeed? What's to see but a pocky lot of foreigners? Why wait?"

I didn't bother explaining. "Your grace, will you see to your men?"

His craggy face broke into a sudden, warm smile. "A long time since Eburacum, Arthur. Remember what a clout of fools we were then?"

"You were brave ones, though."

"Haggling over who was to be first, as if someone might think we were afraid."

"If I remember right, Gawain, it's Orkney's turn."

The King of Orkney brightened. "So it is. And to think my brother missed it. Ah, well, did he not have his chance?"

"That he did." But somehow I couldn't grieve for Agrivaine's misfortune.

Take a wide disk and lay three disks over it, each smaller than the last, and you have the shape of Mount Badon. The hill is not terribly high but consists of four separate rings of defense all round with the inner redoubt at the top, each level ramparted with log and stone. There are timber halls at the top to shelter men and horses; narrow causeways join the levels to one another.

The earthworks were there before Caesar came and were perhaps used to repel him. When Ambrosius refortified it, he added little beyond the halls and cleaning off the levels. The hill itself is the fort. To take it, infantry must fight upward, level by level, as Cerdic no doubt planned to do.

But his men were tired as mine. They'd have to rest. They had to eat.

Decision: we could stay in his rear, make him split his force, but how far can a thousand horse push six times their number? Lancelot may have done it with eighteen men, but I suspect he was opposed by untrained, poorly armed troops without cohesive strategy or leadership. Against the sheer weight of Cerdic's disciplined force, I could only push them indecisively one way or another, like shoveling sand in a desert.

And we were too vulnerable on the open plain. Cavalry is formidable in attack, helpless when it rests. They seldom have time or equipment to dig defenses, and it's very hard to explain to an exhausted horse why there is no food or rest, and ours badly needed both.

We would smash through to the fort and then attack from it, rested and fed. Except for the *combrogi* who would do what Vortigern dreamed them for, led by the man born for it.

I formed my force in a wedge, Orkney first, a squadron wide at the head, the rest fanned out behind. While we waited for Gareth, I splashed through the cursing ranks as they milled into formation and then draped blankets over their mounts and rested between the beasts' legs, whetstoning razor points to their lance heads.

Waiting was worst. The rain soaked through everything, cloaks, mail and clothing, and then to our shuddering, clammy skins. After three days of this, we felt as if we'd never been warm or dry in our lives.

"Will it never stop?"

The irritation rose from a mound of damp misery under a cloak and several blankets.

"Ah, Lucullus! Ready to ride?"

He poked his head out and glared at me. The cowl of his mail was pushed back and some of the dye had soaked out of his hair, revealing a few white ones like pariahs among the black.

"You're a hard man, Artorius."

"One way or another, what we do here today will change a lot of tomorrows. You can tell your children you saw it."

Lucullus wiped the rain from his dripping nose. "My son is an Augustinian monk and far too lofty to care. Tedious boy, but then his mother was a Gaul."

"You saw service in Gaul?"

"As in this case, quite unwillingly. The court sent me with letters to Sidonius of Auvergne. The Goths surrounded us as soon as I arrived."

"So you fought with Ecdicius?"

Where most men would be proud, the Epicurean Lucullus was merely annoyed. "One of the tiresomely immortal eighteen, yes."

"Cousin, you astonish me!"

"And myself. I have always resisted heroism with all the moral fiber of my being."

"Why, when it's usually just dumb luck?"

Lucullus explained with the patience of a tutor. "It gets you killed, and death impairs the senses that are our only perception of existence. If I must die, let it be at the age of ninety-five, slightly drunk on a rare vintage, the best lines of Catullus beating in my head and a beautiful body taking my last love-cry to Venus."

I said, "That's not the worst way to go."

He snuffled wetly. "Nor the best, perhaps. But it's leagues ahead of *this*."

"Artos!"

Bedivere bounded down the line of men, legs scissoring wide over deep pools of rain. "Gareth's back."

"Good. Pass the word: Kay, Gawain and all commanders meet me forward."

With the commanders huddled around him, Gareth rendered his report, using his round blue-and-gold shield for illustration. The hill was totally surrounded and under continual attack. The first level was hard pressed but holding, manned by stone slingers and Maelgwyn's archers. His catapults were playing merry hob with the heathens, but they kept coming. Cerdic had enough men that he could rest them in shifts, retiring one to the rear while another came forward.

"How many wagons, Gareth?"

He struck his hands together with relish. "Scarce half a dozen, sir, east of the hill. It's as we guessed. He left them to catch up as best they could."

I walked away alone to a vantage point on the slope where I could see all Badon and the mile of muck we must flounder across. Under the rain came the other dull, unceasing roar.

Well, Cerdic, here we are. Committed. All of you and all of us.

I trudged back through the rain to where my commanders hunched against the downpour, disconsolate as grounded birds.

"We're going into the fort. The mud will slow us down, but keep moving. Anyone who stops is dead. Gareth!"

"Sir."

"Detach the *combrogi* and destroy those six wagons. Then ride east after the others, no matter how many or how far. I don't want one stinking mouthful of food to reach Cerdic."

Kay protested. "We're too bloody few already. Take out the *combrogi* and we're scarce seven hundred."

"But we'll be warm and fed, Kay. They'll shiver and starve. Who'll feel more like fighting then? My lords, to your men. Bedivere, advance the dragon to the front of our line."

They all moved out to execute their orders. I hooked Gareth's arm and drew him apart. "Leinsterman, it's a long cold ride I've given you. Orders clear?"

His monkey face peered up at me out of the cowl. "Like crystal, high king. No food to Badon."

"When you get back, don't try to make the hill."

Gareth's mouth dropped open. "But, Mother of God, sir, we'll be half frozen."

"Don't try to make the hill. Stay in his rear, keep moving. Wherever he's weakest, hit him and run. No pitched fights, you understand?"

Gareth smiled ruefully. "Sir, is that a warning for a man within a finger's width of fifty and a worrying wife at home?"

I took him by the shoulders. "You're the best. I'm counting on you. Every hour we keep him from Badon, he gets hungrier for food that won't come. It's you who'll win this battle."

"If I don't freeze." He looked away across the plain toward Badon and beyond. The weather would be his most remorseless enemy. "Rhian, now. Is she not one for the taking of notions? It's been thirty years in the sweeting's head that I catch cold easily. And here I'm out three days in Noah's own flood and not a sniffle."

"Stay out of wet drafts, Gareth. We wouldn't want you to go home ill."

"We'd never hear the end of that."

"Take them out, Lord Gareth."

He saluted in the old *alae* fashion, hand to his shoulder. "God with you, sir."

Bedivere had my horse ready at the head of Gawain's Orkneymen. I mounted and sat for a moment watching the *combrogi* file by twos down the hill after Gareth.

Behind me, lances raised like a deadly forest, the seven hundred Orkney and Dobunni awaited my order. I stood erect in the stirrups, glancing back at Gawain.

"It's a sorry Yule I've brought you, but I'm glad you're here."

"And a happy Christmas to you, Arthur!"

"Forward—"

"Orkney squadrons, fo-*wud*—"

"Dobunni, forward—"

My arm came down. *"Ho!"*

And so it began. We had a mile of mud to cross and kept the pace easy, saving the horses for the final run to the causeway. Cerdic was well prepared. Two files of men ran out toward us to form a wedge of shields. Behind them more spearmen broke off from the attack and turned to face us, a wedge facing a wedge. The deeper in we got, the thicker they'd be. The lethal wedge waited, spined with spears above and more below to thrust out between the legs of the shield-bearers.

I let up a little on the rein. We were still far, still at half normal speed because of the mud, struggling to keep formation as the distance narrowed.

Bedivere rode without lance, guiding the horse with practiced knees, dragon banner in his shielded hand, sword in the other. He vented a sibilant curse on the stones and arrows still flying from the fort.

"Hold off, hold off, damn it! Artos, they'll hit us if they don't stop."

But Maelgwyn knew his time. Almost as Bedivere said it the missiles ceased to fly.

"Couch lances!"

The forest behind me bent as under a wind.

We let out the horses to spend their last. The whole lumbering tide of us rippled forward like a wind-stirred wave, but not fast enough, nor near fast enough. I roweled my mount's flanks, keeping my lance centered on the point of the shield wedge. Toy figures grew taller, doll heads became leather-and-iron helmets over hard eyes. Bedivere raised his sword—and then we hit them.

The shield wall buckled, but it slowed us. I kept the lance forward until some thoughtful Saxon splintered it with a war ax, then drew my sword and began to hack at the men crowding about me, shield high against the vicious throwing axes.

Then they seemed to melt in front of us. I kicked the horse to greater speed—"Stay close, Bedwyr"—and the point of our wedge surged forward. A few spears whispered over me, one caroming off my sword blade as an ax grazed my shield. Another rank of men broke over us, men with shaven heads and no weapons but small round shields and short swords.

"Berserks, Artos, watch out. Get *away*, you—"

Bedivere's lean body went flat along the horse's neck as the berserkers snatched at him. We bucked and kicked, using not only swords but high-lashing hoofs that cleared them from our front and rear as our blades cut at the flanks.

Clear again for the moment, we shot forward into a triple line of shields that waited until the last moment and then suddenly appeared to quail, faltering open to let us plunge through. Yes, Cerdic was ready for us. He'd learned all the lessons with me at Eburacum and afterward. Across our path, too near to avoid, three staggered lines of needle-sharp timber stakes protruded from the ground to take our horses in the chest and belly.

I yanked savagely at the bit to pull my horse aside. The men behind, able to dodge the stakes, were still slowed enough for the waiting Saxons to leap and pull some from the saddle. My own mount took a long, ugly rip along its flank, stumbling under me as I pushed it faster through the yelling, close-crowding men.

The causeway lay only a hundred yards ahead.

The horse faltered, lost its gait. I punished it for the last few yards. Bedivere's sword streaked on my left, then I had to guard myself, parrying, kicking hard at the shaggy bear of a man who clutched at my leg, and then I was free and staggering on a blood-soaked horse toward the causeway, Bedivere close behind.

"Don't stop, Artos!"

I tasted the last of sticky saliva in my dry mouth, realized I'd been screaming all the time. Faces blurred past me as I struggled up the narrow road, level on level, past the cheering men and catapults, then there were Catuvellaun and Dyfneint knights milling around me. I caught a glimpse of old Maelgwyn running, arms out to me, then my horse gave a sort of retching cough and crumpled, sprawling me face down in deep mud.

More winded than hurt, I felt someone turn me over, lift me in thick arms as I spat out a pound of Britain and my horsemen thundered past into the redoubt.

Maelgwyn hugged me. "Kings have come more dignified, but none more welcome."

"Bedivere?"

He was at my side, breathing hard. "Here, Artos. Right as rain."

"Damned horse just fell."

"Just died, you mean." Bedivere jerked his head at the twitching carcass. "I still don't believe it. Carried you up this hill with its stomach trailing out. Those bloody stakes. The men couldn't stop. Like meat on a spit, they couldn't *stop*."

"Where's Gawain?"

"Made it right enough," Maelgwyn said.

"Where's Kay?" I rose, holding on to Bedivere. "Where's my brother?"

"Just coming in. There he is."

"Condition, Maelgwyn?"

The old prince was haggard and red-eyed. "Pressed but holding all round. Lancelot's down with the archers on the first level. No rest, no rest at all. Too ruttin' many of 'em. They just keep coming."

I lurched away from them to intercept the horseman who staggered abreast of me on a wounded horse and simply fell out of the saddle into my arms, all bared teeth, mud and battle-madness.

"Bastard. Bastard . . ."

"Easy, Kay."

Blind, deaf, he struggled futilely to draw his sword against nothing. "Bastard . . ."

I slapped him, not hard, but it stung. "Stop."

Kay shuddered; his eyes focused on me. "Half . . . half my men, 'torius."

"But we made it."

"No, the dear good men and the fine mounts . . ."

"Meat on a spit," Bedivere hissed.

I whirled on him. "Shut up, just shut up. Maelgwyn, we need hot food and a warm fire. Come, Kay. See to your men. We're here, we made it. We've come through."

He wept softly. "All the good men, 'torius."

I pushed myself the last few steps toward the most beautiful sight in the world, a timber hall that would have a roaring fire and something hot to put in my stomach, opened the door, dragged to the firepit and flopped down by its heavenly warmth. Only gradually did I stop shivering and blinking against rain that was no longer driving into my face.

Maelgwyn said none of them had slept much for two days. Lancelot looked it when he clumped up to the fire, shaking mud from sodden boots. His square face was filthy and unshaven, aged with fatigue.

"Cerdic's breaking off," he said. "Too dark."

"Lancelot. Thanks for catching Lucullus' letter."

No response. It was clear he had nothing to say to me.

"We brought him along to share the fun."

There is, alas, no humor in Ancellius Falco, not even a grim one. "Bedivere's tallied your losses."

"History repeats. You brought it at Eburacum."

"Yes." He would remember the day Guenevere first spoke to him. "Where is she, Arthur?"

"Better off than we are."

"What will you do with her?"

My turn to be testy. "I don't know, don't ask me now. I've ridden three days, I'm tired."

"I meant it, Arthur. When this is done, so are we."

"Cerdic may do it for us."

"Yes."

"How many did I lose?"

"An hundred and thirty-five."

Too many, far too many for one charge. We didn't have men to spend like that.

"Dobunni took the worst," Lancelot added. "Slowed down by the men in front when you reached the stakes. Surrounded."

"I see."

One by one, my captains dragged into the hall and slouched to the fire, shedding cloaks, wet mail and sword belts until we were a circle of half naked scarecrows around the miraculous warmth. The mud spattered over their blue-lipped faces ended where the edge of the mail cowling had covered them, leaving rounded life-masks of mire until they smeared it, rubbing with stiff fingers. Bedivere discovered a cut on his right hand, licking absently at the raw flesh.

My brother breathed harshly, a sound somewhere between shudder and sob. "Is there . . . someone got something to drink?"

No one moved or spoke. My brain was tired as the rest of me, but tried to focus on Gareth, wondering where he was. It took a long time.

"We'll move at first light," I told the captains.

Still none of them moved, staring into the fire and listening to the fading din of battle as if they already heard it building again.

On my order, Bedivere and I were roused two hours before light. He was to summon my cavalry commanders.

"Have them here in an hour, soon as they've eaten. I'm going to get the feel of this hill."

Cadging a mug of soup from the cooks, I left the hall to feel the cold east wind in my face. The rain had lessened to fine drizzle that cleared my head with its million tiny stings.

From the dark heights, I saw how we were encircled by Cerdic's fires winking in an unbroken band around the base of Badon hill. I started down the south causeway, passing our own fires here and there between the catapults, some men drowsing, others huddled in blankets around the sputtering flames or perched on piles of catapult stones. A few challenged me.

"Who's there!"

"The emperor."

"Who?"

"Arthur."

"Oh! God give you good day, sir!"

The battered first level was manned by Maelgwyn's archers and stone slingers, most of them still asleep, a few carefully greasing their bows against the dampness or flexing numbed feet in the mud.

"Ten thousand fornicatin' angels!"

I halted by the colorfully blasphemous young archer silhouetted against the small fire as he held an arrow shaft over the flame, cramming a world of disgust into the word. "Warped."

Another voice rose sourly from a pile of blankets. "What's thee hope in such wet?"

"Perfection," said the archer calmly, turning the shaft expertly over the flame, bending, inspecting, straightening little by little.

"What's your name, archer?"

He barely looked up at me. "Dafydd."

"As in the Bible."

"There now, there, stra-a-a-ight, you bugger," he crooned over the imperfect shaft. "Aye, Philistines enough, but no Goliath yet."

"You sound like the north. What's a Parisi doing here?"

"Damned if I know the shape of that." Dafydd sighted along the shaft, replaced it and began to worry at another. "There was I, harping at Maelgwyn's board when the war comes boomin' across my day like a discord." He shrugged, cocky. "So I came along. Prince Maelgwyn's a generous man and should have one harp worthy of the name."

I offered him some of my steaming soup. He accepted it eagerly.

"That's good, thanks."

"A bard, no less of a man?"

In the firelight his young profile stood out sharp and strong. He reached down into a heavy sheepskin bag at his feet and drew forth a polished harp. His hands caressed its wood and strings like old lovers.

"Not a bard, no. My da, now: he was one. Or so mum said. Not that she'd lie, mind, but she was known to bruise truth summ'at. There's few left with bard-skill and the thousand verses that must be learned. I play a bit. You get a feel for it like the drawing of a bow."

"Davy-bach," another voice chuckled out of the near dark, "while you're gawpin', give us a hint of that cup."

"That I cannot, it's his."

"Come round and share," I invited them. The hooded shadows crowded in around us, young men with bows slung over their broad shoulders. One looked closely at me across the fire and went rigid.

"Snap to, it's the king."

"What? Oh bloody Chri—"

They would have knelt, but I stopped them. "Easy, easy, not in this muck. Pass the cup round, Davy."

"Thank y'sir."

"God save the Emperor of Britain!"

"God save King Arthur!" Dafydd toasted with the mug. "It has a better ring for rhyme."

I felt a liking for young Dafydd. His bumptiousness held no insolence, only the high, thoughtless spirits Bedivere and I knew once. "You a harper and can't find a rhyme for emperor?"

Dafydd sipped at the mug when it came back to him. "If I could, I'd be the first. Let's see . . . emperor."

The other men shared the cup gratefully, a little embarrassed by my presence. Partly to relieve it, I climbed up on the log parapet and looked out across the fire-sown dark. Some of Cerdic's fires were very close to this lower level. We might talk to each other.

Then a scrabble and grunt close by as young Davy climbed up beside me.

"Temperer. Temperer, that's it, my lord."

"What's what?"

"Why, the rhyme for emperor."

"That's not a word, Davy-bach."

"It's not?" The poet's dismay, then the true creator's answer. "Well, it should be."

While he spoke his eyes never left the nearest Saxon fire. A shape moved across the light and back again, then paused. With velvet skill, Dafydd fitted a shaft to his bow, drew to the head and loosed. Down by the fire, surprised curses went up like flushed birds. My archer grinned white in the gloom.

"I do that now and again, sir. Keeps my spirits up and theirs down."

"Ever hit them in this dark?"

"Ah, who knows? Come light, they go down like wheat. We get sick of the sight." The cockiness deserted him for a moment. "But still they come."

"Listen." From the plain below I heard a muffled, rustling jingle, the sound of large numbers of men shuffling into position. Dafydd said grimly, "Getting an early start, sir."

I cupped both hands to my mouth. "*Cerdic!*"

"He wouldn't be so close, sir. Back taking his ease, that sort of style."

"He's been up this hour like me. Ay, Cerdic! You there?"

A pause; then, over the rustle of moving men we heard a loud rattling, the sound of spears and swords clashed rapidly against shields.

"There's someone of note out there," I told Dafydd. "Thane or earl. That's how they honor their leaders."

"Noisy sods, aren't they?"

The clear, vibrant voice came suddenly out of the dark. "Good morning, Arthur."

"Cerdic?"

The voice was full of careless good humor. "Yes. Horrible hour to be up."

Dafydd muttered savagely, fitting another arrow. "Just a gleam more light, just one. I could pick him like a cherry."

"We were just breakfasting," I called. "Thought I'd nod in."

"Good of you," Cerdic returned. "Looks like better weather."

"Colder."

"We're used to it."

A rapid exchange in Saxon gutturals and a burst of rough laughter.

"Arthur, we regret killing so many good horses. It's the best part of a British lord."

Dafydd howled, "*Bugger off!*" and my men roared behind the rampart, throwing a few sentiments of their own. I waited for quiet so Cerdic could hear every word.

"You'd better eat them, boyo. They're all you're going to eat besides mud."

He didn't have a ready answer for that. I added with honeyed malice, "Getting hungry, Cerdic?"

"Not yet, thank you."

"Well, breakfast is cooling. Till we meet, boyo."

"Till then, Arthur."

We jumped down from the rampart to warm our hands at the fire while Davy preened for his comrades.

"Imagine me, lads: up on the ramp nattering away with bloody Cerdic himself. Oh, I gave *him* summ'at. Hear me?"

"I caught every word of him," one of the men wondered. "Not half the proper Brit, is he?"

"That's just what he is, half," I said. "And a fine prince."

Dafydd gaped. "That trash?"

"Never knew better."

He was shocked as if I'd confessed a family of congenital idiots. "I thought you were just having him on, sir. But you know him?"

"And wish he were on my side. The trouble is, the man wants to walk where you're standing. And you were here first, Davy-bach."

At the first gleam of light in the east, our cavalry filed down the two causeways, Lancelot with his Dyfneinters, Kay and Gawain with me. We would operate separately with a single plan: drive through to Cerdic's rear, then prowl the fringes of the voracious ant-army in tight formations, darting in and out with the same tactics that drove him into the water at Eburacum. This way we peeled him like an onion while he could never exert full pressure on the hill.

That reads well; the military historian can diagram it neatly, the bard conjures flying squadrons as they batter into the shield-locked ranks:

> One blade out of many blades,
> Great scythe of Arthur and Gawain,
> Even slain, they slew as they fell.

It is neither precise as the one nor lyrical as the other, but give it a try. You are King of Britain and leading trained cavalry. Forty-five years old; still hard and strong, but the life-or-death dance of war takes your muscles an eye-blink longer than before and you pay more for it afterward. Couched under your right arm is an ashwood lance ten feet long with a needle point. On your left arm is a heavy shield of bull-hide stretched over wood, bronze-bossed and rimmed with iron.

You charge in line, hoping that line will stay intact, praying you won't go down with the next rank too close behind, because you'll be crushed or caught by the nimble Saxons who dodge between the horses to drag men out of the saddle.

You have a moment before the lance strikes a shield, one moment when everything seems frozen still and you can see with heightened clarity every detail of the death in front of you: shields locked under cold eyes, cone helmets with the broad nose guard that makes the wearer look remote and inhuman. You see the spears and the stakes suddenly thrust out from behind the shields like a wolf baring fangs.

At the last moment you brace yourself forward against the collision, head ducked in behind your shield, and then you hit with the composite shock of war—tortured wood and iron, jarred sinew and the scream of metal on metal, the explosive grunt of men slammed together like brutal lovers.

The line of shields buckles and gives. For a murderous instant, you feel like plunging on through, but that's folly. Your knees transmit their message to the trained horse and you swing aside, already feeling the rumble of the second line behind you coming to hit them again, and you'd damned well better be out of the way or become part of the landscape. But that's for green boys, beginners. You've been too long at this and you dance clear of the carnage as the second line goes in.

But there's four of them dashing out at you from one side— Jesu, where did *they* come from—at you, precious mortal flesh, *you*. Too close for you to get up any momentum in the hoof-sucking mud, and as you tighten rein for quicker control, you almost feel their unstoppable determination. They're going to kill you. Bleeding, cold, starved or crippled, they're going to kill you.

You stop thinking and let your muscles react. You back the horse craftily, apparently unsure, as if you're boxed, drawing them further and further out of their ranks. The vicious pleasure gleams in their eyes when they realize they've got you.

"Artur! Ha, Artur!"

And now they're unprotected, too far out and know it too late as the rider hurtles down on them, sword raised like an archangel's vengeance before it whirs through flesh and bone.

"Back to the line, Artos. I'll cover you!"

Out of the chaos the line forms again. You lift in the stirrups for all to see: you still live and while you do, so does Britain.

Your arm comes down. The great scythe whistles forward again. And again.

The rain falls, men fall. Again. And all through this, all through the screaming welter of fear and rage and agony petrified inside seconds like flies in amber that will be remembered in troubled dreams, you ride an animal mortal as you but, for all its endurance, remarkably stupid. As you execute the movements refined by a lifetime of training and intelligence, the brute under you may lose its footing at any moment or be hamstrung by a darting sword, may blunder into one of the myriad holes dug for the stakes that took so many of your men.

Stakes, where are they?

Then you know: the next time you hit, the stakes are thrust out suddenly, followed by an avalanche of spears. The horses go down; you don't look, don't want to recognize the men already good as dead on the ground. You swing the brute under you, kick clear, slash with the sword, dance away. Back to the reforming line. Your arm goes up—"Forward!"—and you dash in again. This time you're ready and wary for stakes or spears behind that shield-wall. But not for what happens. The wall opens suddenly and lets you through, and coming at you is another wall of long stakes, each driven by two leg-churning, long-haired men while two running files of them snake out along your flanks.

"Artos, they're getting round us!"

But the stake is coming dead at you to take the guts out of your laboring horse. You swerve at the last second and take half the head off one of the carriers as too many horses go screaming down into the mud, and screaming men, too, but you are free again, gasping, bent forward over the pungent foam on your horse's neck, looking desperately for the center of your line if there is one.

"Right wheel!"

And as the Saxons close ranks again, you're moving once more beyond their rear like wolves around a flock, looking for another weak spot, another opening.

There's an easier way to imagine all this. Put a ten-pound weight in either hand and run three miles. Take care to select only muddy ground and be sure to lose your balance and stumble dangerously on the edge of a hole now and then. Have someone run alongside to yank at the weights regularly, yelling all the time. Imagine the whole three miles that the next instant may never come for you at all. At the end, fall down between two men that you may or may not know, one crying and vomiting at the same time—very hard on the stomach—the other with no stomach left to vomit from.

Then get up and do it all again.

One last condition. Know, as your brother helps you up to start the horrible dance again, that it was mostly for nothing as his hoarse voice gasps in your ear, "Didn't stop them. They're taking the first level. Look at them!"

For all you've done, the ants are still moving on the hill, and the first level can never hold.

We pulled back to a good distance behind Cerdic's rear so that we could hit him with as much speed as possible. The horsemen limped into formation behind Kay or Gawain, balky and mean as tired children. Bedivere was unhurt, but there was no fight left in him. He grimaced at the leaden sky.

"Going to rain again."

I snarled, "What else would it do?"

"I wonder how Lancelot managed."

"How did we?"

He only stared back at my truculence.

"That's how we managed." I twisted in the saddle to glare back at Gawain. The bulk of him and his mount were one vast *corpus* of misery, blood on the horse's shoulder, blood on Gawain's leg and in his beard.

"Got to go in quick," I shouted. "They're losing the first level."

"Do I not have eyes?" Gawain grated, rubbed raw himself. "Don't tell me it's lost. I can see it's lost!"

I hauled erect in the stirrups, a weary ton raising a hacked and blunted sword. "Forward—"

"Orkney, forwa—for Christ's sake, straighten that *line*! What is it I lead, a clout of wounded nuns? For-ward—"

"Dobunni, for-ward—"

Once more we staggered toward the juggernaut. Once more the lumbering charge, the shock and tearing through, and then we swept up the causeway through a rain of stones and axes from the captured first level, on to the second where men cursed and oxen strained to drag the heavy catapults higher to the third. The causeway was crowded with double-burdened men as we clattered in, all carrying bundles of shafts and a catapult stone under each arm, still able to laugh as they trudged through pelting rain. Vital men of a youth that war requires, for whom age is still too far to see clearly and death unimaginable even when it happens next to you.

I reined aside, dismounted and gave my horse into Bedivere's keeping—"Go on, I'll stay here"—then perched on a timber to one side, looking back past the laboring men to the plain below where, in Cerdic's rear, men ran to collect in busy little clumps too distant for me to discern their purpose.

"Ay, Dafydd!"

He bobbed toward me, loaded down like the rest, the harp bag swinging on his side. "And a fine day to my king, sir."

"Tired, Davy-bach?"

In daylight, the young harper had a wide white grin and eyes that looked out in sardonic comment on a world full of music and only a *little* too serious for its own good.

"Not a whit, great king." He wiped his face, sweaty despite the cold, flinging his arm out at a world thick with Saxons. "But they don't know when they're beaten."

"Let's teach them."

"Won't we just, now!"

I pointed out over the plain. "You've an archer's eye. That lot in the rear, what are they about?"

Dafydd shielded his narrowed eyes. "It looks like—oh my! Yes, it looks like they're cutting up your downed horses, sir."

Time, that was the piece to move on the board now. Give Cerdic no hope but cold waiting and hunger and then Gareth on his back. While we held on. We had to hold on.

The Saxons lost no time in filling the first level. I found Maelgwyn watching them anxiously from a catapult platform.

"Can't let them take any more ground, Arthur. We've scarce room to move now."

"Tell your archers to keep sniping. Where's Lancelot?"

"Caught a nasty one. Went to rest while he'd time."

The timber hall was crowded with wounded now. I picked my way through them, passing a word and a joke with some, then pushed aside the heavy curtain that separated Lancelot's tiny bower from the main chamber. My lord-milite hulked on a low stool, clumsily wrestling the mail shirt over his head with one good arm.

"Here, I'll do it. Hold still."

Stripped to his thick waist, Ancellius Falco looked like an

aging, battered bull, once-powerful muscles blurred to shape-
lessness. The heavy chest and shoulders, crinkly with whitish
hairs, no longer rippled with excess power but sagged with the
toll of their exertion. Fleetingly I imagined that body covering
Gwen's, surprised that the thought could still carry a pang,
however faint.

"I'm glad you're back," I greeted him. "How many did you
lose?"

Sharply, out of his exhaustion. "Too many."

"That's not a number."

"Thirty, thirty-five, I don't know. I'll count later." The
words were barbed with aggression. I knew that tone. It wanted
to hurt something back for the pain it suffered.

"Give me your arm."

The wound was short but deep, the work of a throwing ax. It
bruised the whole forearm. Lancelot reached unsteadily to the
small dish that held a greenish-yellow salve of chicken fat and
decayed hyssop. He gobbed a bit on shaking fingers and tried to
work it into his right arm.

I knelt beside him. "Here, let me."

He submitted, hostility rising from him like rank sweat. "How
is it our valiant emperor has no wound?"

"Lucullus said he'd like to live to ninety-five. Down on the
field it seemed an attractive idea."

"Obviously."

"I'll be honorable tomorrow."

"Or surely the day after."

The naked scorn was a measure of his fatigue. Worn to the
quick now and always frustrated, Lancelot wanted to fight something, mostly me.

"Always in command, Arthur."

I went on working over his arm.

"I've always marveled at your lack of doubt," he probed.
"No, it's more than that. No consciousness of sin or error, like a
man who never bathes because he thinks he never gets dirty."

I rubbed more salve into the wound. If our confrontation was
to be here and now, then so be it. Even controlled and honorable
men like Lancelot needed an accounting sometime, and they may
pick their own moment.

"Why in God's name did she marry you? Why you when I
could have been happy all my life with nothing but her? She
proved that, she said as much. I loved her when you were still

running the moors with your Pict woman. I loved her even then.''

"Purely and perfectly, like your Grail. Bandages?''

"Over there.'' Lancelot hissed in irritation. "Stinking rain, it never *stops*.''

I uncoiled the linen dressing. "How's Lucullus?''

"Alive,'' he retorted flatly. "That lily, I thought he'd be the first to fall, but he was always a survivor. Like you.''

"We're a happy breed.''

"If survival means that much.''

I started to bandage his arm, feeling my own irritation rise. "Honor should be on the inside, not an iron shirt. A man can't grow that way.''

That grated him even more. "Good King Arthur, always sure and strong. Then why did she come to me?''

"I don't know, Lancelot, except that we all somehow get what we deserve. You got Eleyne. Gwen and I are so alike, good at rule, clever with words, shrewd with people. So stuffed with talents, the love got mislaid like something we just put down a thought ago and can't remember where. Don't ask for reasons. We've always had the whole Christly mess in bed with us. It gets crowded.'' I tied off the bandage. "There, you're wrapped.''

Lancelot hauled a blanket over his shoulders. "You only know her as a queen and consort. To me she was a woman.''

"That surprised you?''

"Gentle and yielding and full of so many needs you never—''

"I'd hoped you'd spare me this.''

His head snapped around. "Spare you hell!''

"I mean the mawk. A moment ago I was jealous because you'd had her. Now I wonder if you ever did. Deft and sure she is, but not gentle, and if she yields, it's like steel that will straighten again. She was raised that way.''

"Have you seen her with flowers, Arthur? That garden she tends like children?''

"Very like children.''

"Sometimes I'd watch her hands on a petal or a stem and know it worth my salvation to be touched like that by her. Then I'd turn away, say no, never. You see, I'd never have—she came to me.''

"I remember when, almost the week.''

Lancelot spoke now with a soft urgency, finally voicing the confession he'd wanted to make for so long. I couldn't deny him the painful pleasure.

"She came like a hurt child," he said, "and I thought, how could someone so cool and perfect need so much."

I sat down across the firepit from him, the warmth bringing my weariness to the surface like infection. "You're all so astonished at that. We were tired, we were empty. I searched a few beds myself, don't ask what for."

"It was a day in the garden among her flowers. A plant had died, something she tried to grow and failed. She was so disappointed. No, more than that. Suddenly she looked up—I'll never forget it—looked up at the ramparts and the walls as if she were stifled. Not beautiful then, but very plain and so damned helpless I had to take her hand, put an arm around her and say something like 'It's only a flower' when it seemed so much to her. She was beautiful all her life and I loved her all my life and the one moment I *had* to tell her was when she wasn't at all beautiful or perfect but pathetic. And all the closed doors just . . . opened."

His expression seemed to sag as something went out of it. "Wrong it was. Mortal sin, but she made me come alive where I was dead, and for a while . . ."

For a while; until a lifetime caught up with him and he found that guilt was all that ever defined him. I thought, I'm getting old, I've lived too long when I can know that much about an honorable man that bards sing of and common folk speak of as a god.

Lancelot studied me with puzzled loathing. "And you knew all the time and never did anything, never raised a hand."

"Perhaps I owed her something. Someone. You or something else. It would have come." I sagged toward the fire's heat. "I'm very tired, don't ask me to make sense now."

That wouldn't do for his bafflement and his ordered cosmos. He must have lived with the question from the beginning.

"Why?"

"Oh, think a little. Think, you tiresome man. Gwen is a ruler. Adultery for her isn't just another pair of shoes under the bed, it's high treason. Put her on trial and I lose the north and the Church that's always favored Gwen more than me, bishops who'd be forced to condemn her. And I open the door to every petty prince looking to take sides for his own gain. You'd be amazed at the grubworms who feel born to rule."

"So you put her in irons and lose them anyway."

"Yes," I countered, "but for something better than your twitching glands, thank you. Damn it, man, it's not all reasoned out or clear even to me. I love Gwen—that surprises you? You don't always need to be lovers to love someone. But she hurt me, can you understand that? She hurt me badly in the one small place that was mine. Those people you and she call dirt taught me to be alive, to be a man. They were my blood.''

"She had good reason, Arthur!"

"They were mine! They loved me. I owed them so much."

He waited some moments before asking, ''What will you do with her?''

I got up and went to the casement. The fresh air cleared some of the weariness from my thoughts. "What should I do? Pardon her, restore her to power? Let all the tribes know that imperial unity is a joke, that no man is safer than the Parisi queen allows? A kingdom's only an idea that men agree to, but tribes are people, and the idea'd better be stronger or the people will tear it apart.''

"Send her home," Lancelot urged. "Peredur would love you the more for it. You'd insure his loyalty."

"Do that and Guenevere *is* the north, a separate crown with Agrivaine as the willing royal sword. She won't give up power and neither will I. Then what? Civil war, patchwork treaties, all the muck old Vortigern had. I'm getting too old for that. Dying in bed isn't heroic but at least it's dry."

I listened to the dull racket from beyond the casement.

"Now you see why the earth didn't shake or the angels weep because Guenevere came to you. I can live with that, but *no one* carves up my country, boyo. Not while I'm head of the table."

"So Guenevere goes to prison."

"Yes."

"That easily."

"You fool. None of it's easy."

"For your stinking principles."

Principles. I thought about that. An idea not even mine, that only worked through Vortigern and Ambrosius and myself like a tool. One strong country welded from jealous tribes. None of us made it, but we had to try.

"It's got to be, Lancelot."

"How short are we?"

"Short of everything," Maelgwyn admitted. "Stones, arrows, even food. We didn't expect the attacks to last so long. They just keep coming."

We stood on a parapet at the south edge of Badon's crest. The

attack had been broken off a few minutes before for no apparent
reason, giving us a chance to assess our situation. Our catapults
still commanded the third level, archers the second, their ranks
thinner now. Below them on the first level, under a canopy of
shields, Cerdic's berserkers waited the order to advance.

We hung in balance today, equal forces opposed. The scale
would tip with Gareth, and where in hell was he? Our lookouts
sighted nothing, no movement at all east of Badon. I told myself
Cerdic had broken off to save hungry men and hoped I was right.

"Arthur, look!"

Down on the plain three horsemen broke out of the Saxon
ranks and trotted to the base of the hill. Cerdic and two of his
earls. One of the nobles wheeled his horse back and forth,
waving a large white cloth.

"I think the bleeders want a chat," Maelgwyn grumbled.
"What say you, Arthur? Hear him out or spit in his eye?"

"Let's go down. While he talks, our men rest and his get
hungrier."

Flanked by Bedivere with the dragon and Maelgwyn on my
other side, I met Cerdic at the causeway by the first level. His
men cat-called the dragon, but Bedivere ignored them.

Cerdic was accompanied by two of his earls, hulking, bare-
legged men in sodden red tunics who carried their heavy shields
as if they were made of feathers.

Cerdic had gained considerable girth in the years since we met
last, his face fleshier now though the charismatic smile still
transcended its heaviness, warming the blue eyes but never quite
masking their watchful calculation.

"Hail, Arthur. Or is it *Ave*?"

"Hail, Cerdic. Surprised to see you mounted. We thought
you'd eaten everything but the hoofs."

He ignored the jibe. "Prince Maelgwyn. Pray my friends be
valiant as my Catuvellaun foe. And Bedivere, still lean as scrub
oak. I hear you've a daughter betrothed at home."

"If I choose," Bedivere acknowledged stiffly. "Never mind
our children, go home to your own—if you know them."

Cerdic grinned. "The Gryffyn never changes. Few words and
all sharp. Well, Arthur, I propose a truce."

I had to laugh at his breezy crust. "Certainly. Disband your
men and render yourself hostage."

"Or cut your throat now and save us your keep," Maelgwyn
suggested.

Credic was unruffled. "I had something more sensible in

mind. Retire to Severn and leave me Badon. No treaty, no surrenders, no bargains. Just Badon.''

"I agree with Mal. Cut your throat. I'll loan you the knife."

His easy charm vanished. "You can't win, Arthur."

"If not, you wouldn't be talking."

"Perhaps. But how long can you hold me back? I have no demands in the west. Why can't we rule together?"

"I've many failings, Cerdic, but stupidity's not one of them. I've played the same game with the same map. Just Badon, yes. Sit on Badon and you hold the whole south at bay. Marcus, Maelgwyn, the lot. You 'protect' the trade of the southern ports, and suddenly you find what a friend you have in Rome while Arthur and his British shrivel in the west. Is this your bargain?"

I swept my arm up the hill. "I can't win, can't defend this hill against men already eating dead horse? You've got numbers, but you haven't got time. Where's the food you counted on? And where are my *combrogi*?"

He studied me for the slightest nuance of doubt or hesitation. "I know where they are."

He spoke to the earl on his left, who unhooked a round shield from his saddle and dropped it face up in front of my horse.

"Or where they were," Cerdic added, regarding the shield's blue field and gold figures, a cross and a sun blaze. "Gareth mac Diurmuid. A knight for scalds to sing of. A close friend, wasn't he, Arthur?"

Bedivere raised his glance from the hacked shield. "When you come up this hill, Cerdic, call my name."

I choked back the murder that welled in me at the thought of Gareth dead in the mud somewhere. This was a time to think, not feel. "He'll come hungry then. If I know Gareth, he did for the wagons before they got him."

"Some of them," Cerdic admitted. "But your archers quit the first level in such haste, they left much of their bread and cheese behind."

He barked an order to the Saxons watching along the first level. Some of them held up a loaf or a full stone of cheese, cheering in their gutturals.

"They thank you, Arthur. What about it? Will you retire to Severn?"

"Go to hell."

Cerdic acknowledged it with a little nod of his head. "Stubborn as Geraint, another immortal. He went down, though. You all have to go down." Cerdic pointed to his men on the plain.

"Know what they are, Pendragon? The future. And I believe in it. I know you, Arthur. I know what you've lost. Your boasted *combrogi*, your queen, half your tribes ready to revolt, the rest in doubt. What have you left to fight *for*, to believe in so much you'll die for it? Think about that until we come."

With a sharp command to his earls, Cerdic turned his horse and trotted down the causeway. Bedivere dismounted to retrieve the ruined shield.

"He could be lying about this, Artos."

Maelgwyn agreed quickly. "Anyone can lose a shield."

I didn't want to ponder it. "They'll be coming. Let's get back."

"Na, a moment." Bedivere hooked the shield to his saddle. "Rhian will want it if—when we go home."

Bedivere, Maelgwyn and I leaned over the edge of a platform used to direct the flight of catapult stones. The silence was broken only by the slingers as they found chance targets on the first level, a Saxon careless enough to move without his shield. Then the whu-whu-*whu*! of the sling and a hit, or the target scurried for cover.

The rain had stopped. No noise broke the soughing of the east wind.

"Waiting for something," Maelgwyn guessed.

Bedivere paused in cutting up a last hoarded turnip for his horse. "The word go?"

Maelgwyn cocked his ear. "Something else. Listen."

Around the west curve of the hill, a great roar and clash of swords to shields, the honor-sound of Saxons. The din went up again and again.

"Oh yes—hail Cerdic," said Maelgwyn. "Hail the Woden-son, begotten of many gods."

I was honestly surprised. "You know the language?"

He nodded. "I gave Tryst his start in it. Grew up with Saxon slaves in our hall."

Surprising, but why not? We of the west don't have much contact with Saxons, but to the Catuvellauni they're a daily fact of life.

"We always pretended ignorance when we dealt with them. It helped, a word here and there while we just looked blank. You can learn a lot looking stupid."

Among Saxons, he said, the power of speech and persuasion

was prized in a war chief as much as his word of honor, since he must sway men to his cause with powerful reason.

"I'd guess that's what he's about now," Maelgwyn said. "Stirring them up to the next attack."

"Bastards, they'll need it. Jesu." Bedivere spat downwind. "We should have finished him at Neth."

Distant horsemen rounded the base of the hill, approached the causeway and rode up into the first level amid shouts and clashing spears. Cerdic and his two earls. Behind them rode an old man on a mule, long white hair and beard billowing in the wind.

"The scald," Maelgwyn pointed. "The speaker of truths and poetry. See how the boy leads his mule? He's blinded early when he takes up his art, leaving his sight clear for eternity. There, listen!"

The old man's voice rolled out, cadenced and powerful, clear as a youth's. Maelgwyn strained to hear him.

"For man's life is the briefest day, coming from darkness only to return. A toy of the gods, the greatest of whom will fall . . . something-something the bridge to doomed Asgard. Therefore since life is a moment, let it be lived with honor among war-companions. Cry *hoch* to Cerdic Sword-Giver who feasts his brothers on spoil while ravens gorge on his enemies."

The spears and shields thundered. *Hoch! Hoch!*

Now Cerdic paced his horse up and down the first level, men kneeling in clumps as he passed them, and began to speak in a voice far-carrying and vital as the scald's.

"Clever bastard," Maelgwyn cracked a dry grin. "Oh, he knows how to use them. The berserkers are pledged not to outlive him if he dies in battle. It's lifelong shame if they do. A little thing like an empty belly? They'd die before complaining."

Bedivere and I listened as Mal translated the cadenced voice. Cerdic knew how to use words as a torch, simple, moving words that had a way of staying in the mind.

"If we must die, I could choose no better place than this mud of Badon and no better companions than you, the oath-brothers who have followed me here. But let dying go, let's talk of life.

"I'm a plain man as you, my feet as cold, my spirit so weighed down with Briton tyranny that I come to spit it back at them or admit myself a slave.

"I do not tell you to hate Arthur Pendragon. Why curse the snow that summer will melt anyway? He sits in a crumbling house and calls you barbarians because you love and husband the soil as Freya commands. How can *he* know what you are, he or his great lords who grind their own people underfoot, who count a man nothing who is not highborn. *They* are the barbarians, the rags of rotten Rome. They are the ignorant and the dead.

"You there! You look like a farmer. May I, even your chosen war-chief, take from you one hide of land without payment? Arthur can. May I kill your kinsmen with impunity? His lords can. Enter the poorest hut without permission? Arthur can. His *queen* can, the fabled Guenevere so like her father. We remember Cador, don't we?

"They cling like rot on the leaves of a healthy plant, and even Britons rise up against the foot on their necks, the foot of lords who say to them, 'Sweat in my fields, bake my bread, bow your head when I pass, listen to the monks when they tell you the meek will inherit the earth. Swallow *that* lie whole so you won't see that not the meek, not you, but *I* inherit the earth, and it will always be so. Live on your knees and I'll throw you my leavings.'

"You younger men, ask your fathers how they were driven out of the midlands, those that survived. Ask why there were so few women for almost twenty years, and almost no children. Ask *them* the kind of war Arthur waged in the Time of the Smoke when nothing could live but flies. Ask of the great British lords so honored and sung by their bards, the names so well remembered. Bedivere, the right hand of Arthur. He's here today. Ancellius, called Lancelot, the pious butcher of children. He's here today. Gawain who threw Saxon tongues to his hounds at Eburacum. He's here. All here—or all remembered, like Trystan, harp in one hand and a whore in the other, so *nithing* and bare of honor that his own kind rose up at last to cast him from Britain.

"Can such as these say to dawn, hold back? To spring, stay winter? To seed, flower only at my will? To the future, you may not come? No! They can only delay, this faded rag of Rome, only hide their heads and pretend *you* are not rising like the sun, but even as they squeeze their coward eyes shut, they feel your heat on the lids.

"Brothers—I do not move you to hate; how can you hate the mere husks of winter, bending dry in the wind and ready to blow away? Plow them under and plant again. Seeds and sons and tomorrows, for every man who follows me today carries tomorrow like seed in his loins. Every men—*every* man a pride in my heart, the equal of their father gods. Fated men. Horses, brothers to Baldur, follow me now and let our waiting women say we brought tomorrow like a gift."

*   *   *

"Oh, he goes *on*, that Cerdic," Bedivere complained as we trudged back up the hill. "*You* could say it in half the words."

Perhaps. But with the heart of my country eaten away in disaffection and distrust, could I have so believed as Cerdic did?

My cavalry were pummeled to pulp. I had to save them for the next foray out, knowing it would probably be the last. Cerdic's next attack, when it came, was a fierce clash between men on foot, archers and slingers against spear and sword, finally fist to claw. Small detachments of horse guarded the causeways, beating them back whenever they gained the beleaguered second level. Bedivere and I rode a wide circle higher about the hill, observing the mad dance of the slingers, the graceful, deadlier movements of the archers, all under the great dissonant bellow of war and the time-beating thud of the catapults. We saw the defenders tense for another effort as the yellow-haired men broke over the parapet only to be driven back as our own troops rallied or a few swift horse streaked along the ditch to trample the invaders underfoot.

Someone called as we turned off the third level into the causeway, a rider, plowing through a press of men. "Arthur? Where is Arthur?"

Bedivere thrust the dragon aloft. "Here, here. What news?"

The horse stumbled toward us, bleeding about the shoulders and forelegs. Lucullus bowed over the saddle horn, short of breath.

"Ancellius sent me," he panted. "We lost a part of the second level on the north. Trying to clear them out now. If we can't, just have to barricade and hold the rest."

"That's all you can do." I noted the bent sword in his grip. "You look like you've caught it."

Lucullus glared, wheezing. "Let Bedivere witness that once more I formally protest this callous insult to Rome. I've been nearly killed three times this hour."

"We regret the inconvenience, cousin, and will make full account to Theodoric."

"Account? What account?" Lucullus stared from Bedivere to me as demented children who drained the last of his mature patience, yanked the lathered horse about and plunged back up the causeway. "What account, you idiots? We're all going to be *killed*!"

The battle rose to a fever pitch as the high tide of Cerdic's men broke once more over the second level, hung in balance, fury against fury, then fell back repulsed while we crouched for the next screaming rush. It didn't come, but still we waited.

Old Maelgwyn leaned against a parapet timber, spent. "Now, d'you think?"

"Has to be now," I said. "They won't have the strength tomorrow."

"Nor we." Maelgwyn gazed about the battered second level where the dead and wounded were being cleared out to the redoubt. "Nothing left above but the catapult crews. All else is down here and scant enough. We can't hold, my king."

He jerked his white head toward the battered and dispirited men still on their feet. "Good lads, but they've taken the brunt from the first, and that bastard just keeps coming. Kill ten, thirty come running after."

His voice broke. The old prince's tears left lighter furrows down his spattered, wind-burned cheeks. He tore off his helmet and raked furrows of frustration through the snowy thatch. "I've led them, driven 'em, sworn to bloody well hang them if they fell back. That—that won't do anymore. They're too worn out to care, the best of them."

I saw what he meant in the listless posture of the youths around us, drained of vitality, moving as little as possible, the disjointed movements of men amazed that they were still alive, that their ration of courage was enough, their mortal fear not too great. This time. But what of the next?

Maelgwyn passed me a flagon of *uisge*. As he did, I noticed a familiar sheepskin bag at his feet and drew the dark-polished harp from its depths.

"Dafydd's?"

"As I said, Arthur. The best of them. He just left it there."

"Where is he?"

"Down the line. Hurt and trying not to show it, like the rest."

"Bring the *uisge*, Mal. Let's find a harper."

To know the face of war, you need look no further than Dafydd, who sprawled against a pile of logs, gray with pain, one shoulder of his buff leather jerkin torn and stiff with caked blood. Eyes closed, mouth shut tight around the misery, that unchanging picture of wounded men—not age, but the youth wiped out for a time before life calls it back again. Like a father

I wished I could keep him from this bleak knowledge, leave it to old men like Mal and me who have known it longer.

Dafydd's eyes opened, the only part of him that moved. I put the flagon to his lips.

"It's fitting for a king to serve a bard," I said, "for they stood high as druids and could call a chief to judgment."

He coughed as the liquor burned down his throat. "They almost did it this time, sir."

Maelgwyn laid the harp in Dafydd's good arm. "Here. What are the people of the cat without their bard?"

"Not a bard, and the thousand verses never learned. But my da was one. A bard and a great lord, mum said."

Another generous drink sparked a flicker of his old spirit. "God, that's good! A great lord, she always said—on one sweet night's acquaintance, mind—traveling from the south to the Wall, the lord of him half drunk and the bard all mad as it should be. He left in the morning with a smile and a rhyme and myself snug inside her, that sort of style. She always said I had his touch."

Another drink, Maelgwyn wincing only a little at my prodigality and the boy's thirst, but Davy-bach recovered more each moment. He nestled the harp into his good shoulder.

"And perhaps more than just the touch. Sometimes in your hall, Prince—oh, the glorious nights when the rhyming came like spun gold from my mouth and my fingers knew they could stroke and grasp and tear such music from these strings as no bard in the wild, wailing world has ever made."

The stiff fingers of his right hand splayed clumsily over the strings.

"Music just beyond me when I reached, but *there* and waiting to be found, so pure and perfect that no other song need ever be sung. And each night I'd try and tear and try and tear and drink too much because that sound is fire and a pain in the gut—until they'd lay hold of me and pull the harp away—'Na, Davy, leave off. You'll kill the poor thing like a sufferin' beast. There's no such music, no such sound in a harp!' But there is. Listen, my king!"

A chord sprang out of the strings, impaling the listener on a spear of sound. Another and another followed, sounds a harp couldn't make but did.

"Who says there's no such music?" Dafydd challenged. "When I've heard it all my life saying: find me in these strings or just beyond what they were strung to do by small-singing, small-dreaming men. Find me when you're brave, reeling drunk or whispering between a woman's breasts or in the midst of revel when you're all of a sudden alone. Find me in all things too far and too much and just further than a man can reach, but must. Oh, Davy, it says to me, you'll always hear the echo of where I've been and always follow. Is there no more cheer in that flagon, my lord?''

"There is that." I passed it to him.

Dafydd took a last huge gulp with a sensual sigh, lurching to unsteady feet. "I'm feeling deathly and mad as an owl in daylight, but by God, I—can—sing!"

He touched the strings again, no longer a sound of darkness and sharp angles but mellow and rich with remembrance. Dafydd the harper began a song, and what happened then was, perhaps, what this testament is all about. I can't ask you to understand it where I cannot myself.

It was the sort of thing I have seen and heard all my life among Britons, from lords to farmers: one man, one harper began a song. Within a few soft notes, another man had joined him in unison. And then another and another, the sweet clear line of "Bronwen in the Vale" that I've sung since boyhood. And then, as our people do, other men began to sing, not the melody but the harmony that deep-dyes and thrills through the sad, glorious music of my people.

Maelgwyn and I were rooted to the spot. "Listen to them, Arthur," he whispered reverently. "*Nefoedd annwyl,* listen to them!"

Then, with his helmet off and the wind whipping about his white head, Maelgwyn was singing yet a third part of the soaring, intricate music he'd learned in his cradle. And the music spread out from us along the trench.

> *Light the candles of evening*
> *And wait me, dear Bronwen*

And still another line of harmony rolled under the melody like a deep river, and I looked up, spirit thrust aloft by the swelling sound, to see our men on the third level, standing forward of the catapults, joining in.

> *Let the sweet sound of summer*
> *Call me home to the vale*

And more and more from God knows where the voices rose, until the winter air went warm with a beauty to burst the heart. Stronger and stronger the voices until I wondered how the drab world could hold so much of heaven and what god had set it down here just for me. And I cried out to them, "Sing it, you lovely men! Sing out clear! Let them hear what they come against."

No man not on his feet now all along the ditch, turning the song with the unexpected twists of harmony that sear the soul with its sound. I grabbed Maelgwyn, the two of us dancing like mad old bears in the mud.

"Ha-*ha*, Arthur. Just *listen* to my boys!"

"They'll hold, old Cat. They'll hold this ditch against God himself. Just stay with them, Mal. Now's the time. I'm going out."

The last chords were still rolling lovely about the hill as my cavalry trotted into line behind their commanders. Battered and weary, they still sang with the others, faces new-lit with an old joy. Even laconic Bedivere was ecstatic.

"*Och*, Artos, I never sang better, and the highest notes were mine, did you hear? Listen, some of them are at it still."

"No better time to go, Bedwyr. Advance the dragon."

There were beautiful tears in his eyes. "Aye, Artos."

"Kay, Gawain! Bless you all this day. I'm going out."

And then a kind of preparate stillness broken only by the leather-creak metal-scrape harness-jingle of men and steel and horses drawing together into single purpose. Once more the silent lines, the lances aloft, the ready men waiting, and under it all the whisper of the east wind, the snuffle of a horse here and there.

I couldn't speak for all to hear, but I needed no eloquence like Cerdic's, not for Britons who'd found their own in the song. Little need I say to the soul of them.

"My lords, I must go down this hill against Cerdic. And I would be honored by any man who cares to follow."

No command was given, not one voice, but the forest of lances swept forward in salute. I closed my eyes against sudden tears.

"*Alae*, forward—"

"Orkney—"

"Dobunni—"

"Dyfneint—"

"*Ha-oh!*"

* * *

It was the beginning of the end for Cerdic. His men would still fight, but no longer as a savage tide. Most of them hadn't eaten for two days, fighting almost continually in wet muck and cold with no shelter. Strong men with the spirit of gods, but mortal bodies that could not be pushed any further. Several attacks hit the second level, but they were sporadic and easily beaten back. When we smashed through and began to tear at them, Cerdic was forced to face his men away from Badon, forming them into squares and diamonds of locked shields.

"Gone to defense," Bedivere hissed between bared teeth. "Gone to ground and it's my turn now. Cerdic, where are you?"

Defensive but hardly beaten, the Saxons held their ground. They held, they went down, they fell back craftily only to close about the unwary, run in slaughtering and then reform, each square its separate redoubt torn by our attacks. Cerdic's berserkers forsook the hard-won first level and streamed down the causeway to reinforce their comrades. Some never reached the bottom, pelted and crushed by the last of Maelgwyn's catapult stones.

I reined in beside Gawain, screaming through the noise. "We've got them, got them. Take your Orkney, hit them on the right. Kay! Kay! Dobunni forward to me."

"*Cerdic!*"

The horse and rider hurtled past me. Leaning from his saddle, Kay punched my arm. "Look!"

It was Bedivere, bent forward behind his shield, sword whirling in his right hand, galloping alone straight at a shield wall. Cerdic was behind it, the great war ax resting for a moment on his shoulder. Searching since we dashed off the causeway, Bedivere found him now.

"*Cerdic, you pig—*"

We had seconds or less to support him. I snapped the order to Kay and his men. "Couch lances, follow me."

My own lance was long gone. I drew my sword and dug heels into the horse's flank, plunging forward. We smashed into the outermost square only a few bounds behind Bedivere.

It was a mistake and almost our last. I had eyes for Bedivere and Cerdic alone and never stopped to realize how few Dobunni ever heard my order. Only Kay and a handful followed me into the square. As we plowed through the shields, the Saxons cut off and surrounded us. A moment of whirling about, then someone hamstrung my horse and it went down under me. I managed to get free of the stirrups before we fell, but my right leg was pinned. Helpless, I saw Cerdic's head go back in a roar of exultant laughter, then a blur of horses as the Dobunni circled me about while I struggled free of the crippled mount. Bedivere was on foot now, leaping free of the horse that fell dead with a throwing ax in its brain. As three of Cerdic's men closed in on him, he screamed with maniacal joy, a high-pitched song of mayhem counterpointed by the *swoosh* of his longsword cutting a great, murdering arc in front of him.

The fools were coming at him with swords alone. No one does that and lives, not with Bedivere. His feet were cat pads, the feet of a dancer, the sword a mere extension of long, ropy arms as his body twisted lightly under the clumsy blows and came up killing. I saw him spin out of a slice that shattered one man's arm and lunge forward against Cerdic's ax before another man cut across his path. Cerdic strode down on me, raising the ax, but even as I dragged free, a horse shot by me and Cerdic, with his ax poised to kill me, was blotted out by a body that dove from the saddle to tumble him in the mud. Only a moment's scrambling, then Cerdic's hand snaked to his belt, out and back, and the body lay still. But I was clear, rising to my knees, groping for the dropped sword.

What happened then was a blur of shock and sound. I saw Cerdic wobbling to his feet, shaken, then suddenly both of us went flat again out of sheer self-preservation as a roaring storm broke over us. Horsemen from God knows where, a solid line of them that shattered the Saxon square like kindling and swept the survivors away from Cerdic and me. It was stupid, comical. We stared at each other like pummeled clowns in a farce—*What happened?*—while the iron line of horse ground Saxons into the mud. Then Cerdic reached for the ax. I couldn't find the sword—no, there it was, but too far, not enough time, and Cerdic was raising himself, the ax already swinging high.

"Now, Arthur!"

Before the swing reached its peak, I dove at him, the instinctive last-first weapon in my hand. The old bronze knife that marked me *fhain*. I closed with Cerdic under his raised arm and drove the knife through his eye deep into the brain behind.

We teetered together like statues, then the ax dropped behind him and Cerdic fell away from me. I remember stabbing uselessly at the body again and again with Bedivere coming and then suddenly dodging aside with the same comic desperation as a fresh line of horse damn near ran him down. Filthy, stubble-

bearded men on spent horses that still hit the remnant of Cerdic's
near men with the force of God's own lightning, scattering,
trampling before they wheeled in formation like urgent autumn
birds to charge the next square.

Then Bedivere clutching my shoulder, hoarse and jubilant.
"*Combrogi,* Artos! They got back!"

I wiped the mud from my eyes, trying to make out faces in the
scrofulous pack. "Who . . . who's leading?"

"Don't know, the fool's got no shield."

Suddenly Bedivere lifted me off my feet with a massive,
savage joy. "It's Gareth! It's the macDiurmuid."

Bedivere was twenty again, leaping up and down like a child.
"The Goddamned horrible macDiurmuid! You beautiful man,
you darling. *Gareth!*"

"Give . . . give me your sword, Bedivere."

I severed Cerdic's head and lifted it by the thick hair as a rider
wheeled away from Gareth and lumbered wearily toward us. A
fine head, a king's head.

The horseman stripped off his helmet: Lord Bors, pig-dirty
and red-eyed but sustained by that vitality that comes too early in
life and leaves too soon.

"My lords, I saw the dragon fallen, and I thought—"

"Na, I dropped the bloody thing," Bedivere growled. "We
thought *you* were dead."

Bors grinned. He looked tipsy. "And if I didn't die this week,
I never will."

"Hell, at your age it's impossible," I said. "Lower your
lance."

He dipped the point, and I impaled Cerdic's head on it.
"Throw this to his earls. Let them see it's over."

"Aye, sir, will I not." Bors swung the victory high. "And
God give you long life, sir."

He yanked the tired horse about and galloped to where the
combrogi and Orkney were combining in a deadly phalanx,
driving the Saxons further back. Some of them were running
clear away from Badon now. It was over.

I sagged down in the mud by Cerdic's hacked trunk, shrugging
off Bedivere's arm. "Leave off, leave off. I'm not hurt."

"I know that. It's Kay."

He pointed at the muddy little pile not far away. My brother
Kay, the body that hurtled between Cerdic and my death, and he
lay in the mud with the stain widening over his torn mail coat.
The *combrogi* had run right over him.

"Give him water, Bedivere."

Kay opened his eyes, the only thing he could move. "No water. Half blood as it would be."

My little brother Caius, my Kay, so eager to keep up with me, so much of his life lived in my fast-running shadow.

"Did . . . did y'see me land on that b-bastard?" he choked.

"Didn't I now? I'd be dead without you, Kay."

"Ah . . . mum always said so."

Bedivere tried to ease him, clumsy with caring, but it hurt Kay to move at all. "We're nothing without you, Kay."

My brother sighed as if he were suddenly tired of the whole thing. His breathing was broken, hollow. "Great louts, both of you. Should have stayed home." He tried to smile; blood trickled out of his mouth. "Can't feel my legs, 'torius."

"Don't try. The men will carry you."

Kay gagged suddenly. "You'll see I get back? You know how mum worries."

His fingers closed feebly around mine, and then Kay was gone.

Bedivere and I couldn't look at each other. We straightened the crumpled little body and I closed the eyes. Bedivere tried to speak, an odd, strangled sound. Sitting in the cold mud, suddenly he buried his face in dirty hands.

"Oh, Jesus."

"I know, Bedwyr."

He lashed out desperately. "You don't know. Nobody knows anything ever, Goddamnit. Jesus rutting Christ, where does it end? I'm old and shivering cold and I want to go on living and breathing sweet, and I've already lived too long to look at this, and—"

He lurched to his feet, glaring at the plain and the enemy streaming away in defeat from Badon. Suddenly he lifted the sword and jammed it into the ground with a dry sob.

"Burn in hell," said Bedivere to no one and the world. "Burn in hell, burn in bloody, rutting hell!"

My small bower had room only for a firepit, a cot and a stool, but Maelgwyn's cooks brought hot water enough in an iron caldron for me to bathe luxuriously. Wherever the water touched my skin, the over-strained muscles melted like butter until I had to sit down or fall on my face, washing and dragging off my clothes piecemeal. When the small, bedraggled man pushed aside the bower curtains, there wasn't much royal dignity left that I couldn't cover with a towel.

"King of a hundred battles," Gareth wheezed, "no food has come to Badon."

I beckoned him to the stool and rose. "Come rest, Gareth."

He stumbled forward. "If I do, will I ever get up again?"

Gareth collapsed on the stool, clawing the mail cowl from his head. It seemed a lifetime since we said good-bye. Never, of all the men in all the battles of my life, have I seen a man so pitiful as Gareth. Without hot food or warmth or dry clothes since Camelot, his short, bandy-legged body shook with a chill deep in the marrow of his bones. Under the incredible grime his lips were blue and cracked with exposure. He'd lost his shield on the way out, he said, skirmishing past Badon. After that it was a long cold run from wagon to wagon. Let the bards sing what they will, Badon was won by a mite of a Leinsterman miles away from the battle.

"Plenty to eat," Gareth slurred drowsily, yawning as the warmth invaded him. "They make good beer, heathen though they are, and I was forced to drink great quantities against the cold. All (yawn) for naught, though, for I've caught the devil's own chill."

A great, rattling snuffle. Gareth dragged a dirty paw under his chapped nose. "And Rhian'll be at me now (yawn) with her stinking onion poultices . . . and telling me I should . . ."

My back was turned for a moment as he spoke. "Yes, Gareth?"

He never answered, fallen dead asleep in the middle of a thought, head drooping, swaying slightly on the stool. Before he fell off, I picked him up like a child and carried him to my cot. It didn't wake him. Nothing could.

Not for months did we realize what a staggering thing was done at Badon. Of ten thousand Saxons, half never left it. Another two thousand, fleeing from Lancelot's cavalry, never reached home. For the surviving chiefs it would be years, even decades, before they could dare such an effort again.

More than defeat, we broke them. They can't take the west, not now, perhaps not ever. Whatever history says of Britons—arrogant, treacherous, jealous and self-dooming—with all of that, we've somehow learned to be a country.

I leaned out the casement. Getting dark now; our fires were bright jewels hung on the night. Somewhere on the parapets, someone plucked limpid melody from a harp. I hoped it was Davy-bach playing.

*   *   *

The news of victory sped before us to Camelot where a dozen messengers waited—obsequious, over-hearty men already claiming their share of glory. *Artorius, Gloria!* The map of Britain was stable, the future assured. Once again the fractious tribes were my dutiful children, pledging that loyalty from which (in their true hearts, of *course*) they never departed. Wordy letters from old Marcus with the same felicity: we *must* stand together, we *are* Britain, et cetera. Business as usual.

Fires of celebration blazed all over the Severn valley, flared up in Camelot's courtyard. Horns blared, dancers leaped, flagons broke and emptied, pipes squealed, drums boomed in jubilation, and a certain percentage of the next generation were joyously conceived.

Victory! Victory!

But from honest Peredur only silence while Guenevere waited for exile.

She was still confined at Camelot with one servingwoman and under close guard, in a small house near the south wall. She and her woman rose when I entered. Gwen appeared nervous, bundled in a shapeless robe, obviously neglectful of her appearance. The once meticulously plaited hair was merely combed out, hanging loose with gray wisps streaking the dull auburn. Her cheeks fell in more sharply around their bones. She looked haggard.

"My royal lord."

"Lady."

"Welcome home. You may withdraw, Imogen."

Her servingwoman bobbed up and down to me and retired behind the bower curtain. Guenevere made a vague gesture at her hair, then gave it up.

"It's the wet. I can't do a thing. Would you like some hot wine?"

"Yes, thanks. How is it with you, Gwen?"

She offered me the drink. "I don't seem to need much nowadays. Imogen sees to me. Poor Arthur, you look so soggy."

"Tired to death." I sagged onto a bench. Still Gwen hovered close. We hadn't spoken since the night of Morgana's death and that distance stretched between us now. From outside we could hear the orgy of celebration.

"You're their darling again." She wandered away to sit, her movements oddly vague and directionless, a bird born to soar suddenly without a sky. "It's been very bad without you."

"Yes."

"Odd. I mean we weren't all that much together before."

"But it's worse now," I confessed.

"Having you here and not—why did you come, Arthur?"

"I don't know. To tell you we won. Maybe a pat on the head, well done."

Something glistened in her eyes. She ducked her head over a scrap of sewing to hide it. "Somehow I feel like an afterthought. No matter, I hear the court's full of comforting women now."

"Gwen, don't. Not between us."

"That's true," she reflected. "Two hypocrites in hell roasting each other's sins on the same spit."

"Just that I couldn't imagine not coming to tell you."

The needle plied through and through the cloth. "I hoped you'd come before you left. I waited here thinking of how I'd receive you and what I'd say, warm or cool, injured or repentant. You didn't come and didn't come and then I opened the casement and hung out of it shameless as a brothel sign, just hoping for a glimpse of—oh—hell!" She snapped off the thread angrily. "There's a lot to be said for the convent life."

"I missed you, Gwen."

Her fingers paused. "You do know how to hurt."

No, it was raw yet. Too painful. I changed the subject. "We lost Kay."

"Oh, no!"

"I have to see mother and I dread it. There's no way to make it easy."

"Poor little butterball," she murmured. "I loved him, everyone did. We—you must comfort Flavia."

"The rest are back. Bedivere didn't take a scratch."

"Indestructible peasant."

"And Gareth. A little frozen but fine. Rhian got him roaring drunk and he fell asleep in the middle of making love."

Gwen's laugh lilted in its silvery arc. "Lord, was he that tired?"

"Dead. And Rhian's in her glory bullying him back to health."

There was a question I wanted to answer before I saw it in her eyes. "And Lancelot. I sent him east to mop up."

"Yes." Gwen busied her hands with the cloth. I saw how thin they were, the veins like cords with small brown spots between them.

"Why him, Gwen?"

"I thought we didn't talk about that."

"He doesn't know you at all, never did. Why him?"

Guenevere answered, still and bleak, talking of something long dead. "Why not? There was nothing else. I wasn't used to needing."

"What was there you couldn't bring to *me*?"

"That would be going back into the pain, where it came from. You were always so sure, so self-sufficient—"

"Oh, God damn it, Gwen!"

"Oh, you were. Love is needing and we aren't needers. I used to wonder in bed with you where a monolith learned to make love so well. Then I found out. You trotted her out for me. The little pig still had her figure, I'll give her that. She must have been a grimy jewel at eighteen."

"Did you love him? Do you?"

"Does it matter now?"

"Not to the king, just your husband."

She worked the needle jerkily through the linen. There was no thread on it. "I've thought about it. You've given me time for that now. Did I? Once. For a while."

"Of all the men in Britain."

Her head snapped back, tense. "Yes, of all the men. Don't you understand? Anything else hurt too much. I failed."

"Failed how? You never failed in your life."

"*I lost it.*"

"The baby."

"And I'd never failed before and I didn't know what to do. My soul can pray, but what do I do with this empty, useless body?"

Guenevere recovered herself with a terminating sigh; the subject was dull as it was painful to her. "What's it matter anyway? Sometimes at night when I'm tired enough to imagine death and remember my catechism, I think: What manglers we are, Arthur. The lives we've stretched and pummeled and twisted to our own shapes. People that never really lived except through us. We're creatures of a kind, hatched from the same egg. That's why— funny, but after all the years and all the beds—you're the best friend I ever had."

It was true. "I guess that's why I'm here."

She raised her head slowly. "Then, damn you, why am *I* here?"

"Don't start that. You made me put you here."

"Good God, you gave me reason. You gave the whole north reason to rise against you."

"Don't come the martyred patriot. Not to me, woman. You didn't have to kill her. She was helpless. Why did you have to hurt me like that?"

"You hurt me."

We were on our feet now, squared off, the wound raw and open.

"I didn't want to. I only wanted to see my son once. I never meant to hurt you."

"But you did. I never meant to, but *I* did. But I loved you, Arthur. Damn you, *I don't want to love that much*. My life is mine and you took up so much of it. You . . . attract people like . . . I don't know. You change them. And I said all right, I'll be changed. Now I can trust, now I can give, there's the child. And I fought for it in that sweaty, bloody bed, but it would not be born and it ripped me apart in its dying."

"Gwen, I know that fight and I know that loss. Prydn folk, *my* folk. People you step on like roaches, they fight and lose like that every day, but they don't throw life in a corner like a toy that won't work. I've heard flatterers call you Guenevere the Wise, but I tell you this: If you'd lived one year or even one season with them, you'd know one hell of a lot more about the guts of what you call a peasant."

"They're not my people, not them. They're not my kind." Guenevere was trembling now. "But you brought them here. You had to track your dirt into the house."

"Like you with Lancelot."

"I was discreet, Arthur."

"Christ, yes. The best-kept secret since Noah's Flood. It wasn't discretion that kept the Commandments off your back, but me. Don't look dense. Lancelot didn't understand it either."

"Oh, Lancelot, Lancelot." She flung her hands out, sick of it all but shaken. "What does it matter who, when, where? He got so little and he was satisfied because little was all he ever got from that nun he married. But you . . ."

Guenevere advanced on me, voice trembling, fingers curved in and spread apart. "You could behead me, hang me, rack me, lock me in a convent for life. But no, that wasn't your way. You put me on my knees and rubbed my face in it like a naughty dog. Bad dog, Guenevere. *Bad* dog. Put her back in the kennel. You bastard!"

Her nails raked suddenly across my face, stinging, drawing blood. "I despise you, I—"

I caught her arms, but she still came at me, kicking, butting with sharp knees, spitting like a cat.

"Stop it, you bitch. You're not God, no matter what you think. What you are is rotten with the power I gave you, and it stinks. Worse than the people you hate."

"You should know, you're one of them."

"*Yes.* And if I rolled in shit for a year, I wouldn't smell as bad as the murder on your hands."

The word *murder* unlocked something vicious, something that leaped from its prison into my hands. I shoved Guenevere away, slapping her back and forth, again and again.

"Murder! Murderer!"

The last blow knocked her over a bench and onto the floor. I was on her in an instant, hands about her throat. "Kill you—"

She twisted in my arms to hiss it in my face. "You *did.* When you brought him."

"What do you mean?" I pulled her roughly to her feet. "Him?"

"I screamed a warning God could hear and still you brought him."

"Gwen, stop. Him?"

She gave up then, hugging herself to me, face buried in my throat, sobbing. "And he was so beautiful—"

"Gwen, he's not. He's a twisted little monster."

"—And when he touched me, it was like you touching me, and I wanted to kill him and kiss him and—"

"I hated you, too. I hated you and had to hurt you back, wanted to hurt you all the days since."

She relaxed slowly in my arms. Her body swelled against me in a long, shuddering breath. "And only the ache in our bellies to call us liars."

"Only that. I feel hollowed out."

She spread her hands over my throat and chest. "So bruised. And your face is raw as an oyster. And I can smell those clothes, when did you change them last? You're sopping, Arthur, you'll catch your death."

My wife broke off and pulled away. Guenevere again, the queen. In control. "And why should I care? You've got it all and I'm being packed away like last year's fashions. And I'm comforting you? Go to hell, Pendragon."

No chance that spirit was broken. My love, my enemy, my equal. "You don't really want me to go?"

She presented her back to me, straight and adamant. "Try me, dear. But get me a drink first. I feel a bit mishandled."

"You deserved it."

"So did you. Pour."

I filled a cup, righted the bench and motioned Gwen to sit beside me. Under my arm she was still shaking with the residue of emotion. For a while we only drank and watched the fire.

"This is how it started. Gwen. Sharing a cup. Remember?"

"Oh dear, yes. That day at Eburacum. The Saxons coming and the women hysterical and myself wondering what to do—and in strides young Arthur Pendragon, male as a yearling stallion and alive as a toothache. You took a clout of frightened women and made them feel needed and important. You cried over them."

"I did, didn't I?"

"You were beautiful." Guenevere kissed me, licking her tongue over my dry lips with some of her old pleasure. "Love's such an easy word. I've never said it without wondering what in hell it meant. But just then I saw someone that I couldn't hurt. That shouldn't be hurt. And that's all we've done for years."

"Guilty," I admitted.

"Not even ignorance for excuse. I am going to miss you, Arthur."

"We've done that for years, too. People like us, Gwen." I realized in the middle of the thought that what voiced so simply now was so true. "Why are we so lonely? Why am I?"

"Why did you have to say that?"

"You're still shaking."

"A little chilly, that's all. I've just a linen undershift on."

"Didn't Imogen bring your woolens?"

"I hate wool next my skin, you know that. It scratches."

"Wear it anyway. And eat more. You're a stick."

Guenevere shook me off, gruff. "Oh, I'm nothing of the sort. Not sick nor this nor that, just not eighteen anymore. We wear out, you know. I'm even looking forward to it a little. Heaven or hell, at least there are no decisions to make."

She kissed my ear. "I am glad you're here. And what's to become of us?"

I didn't want to think on that. "Here, drink up, To Victory."

"To us," Gwen toasted me. "Long life to Arthur and Guenevere."

"Fabled as far as Byzantium. If they could see us now."

We watched the fire-shapes dance, listened to the hounds of victory baying beyond the casement.

Gwen murmured against my shoulder. "Nice, isn't it? Pretending we're somewhere else and years ago. I love it, but the world keeps coming back. Where will you enshrine me?"

"Caerleon. I was thinking of Trajanus' old house. You'll be comfortable there."

"And almost extinct, the dear gray Lady of Britain." Her mouth set stubbornly. "I was right to execute them, and all Britain knows it."

"Until I won at Badon, love. Now they couldn't care less."

Her smile turned sweetly acid. "Neatly put as usual. I'll be no end of trouble. Wherever you put me, that's the firepit of Britain."

I sighed: intelligent but thick. "Gwen, forget it. Neither you nor Peredur nor anyone else is going to rule in the old way. Cerdic had our measure all right, and it's not going to be any longer."

This was always a blind spot to my queen. "I was born to rule, Arthur. My blood was crowned when yours was shivering in a straw hut. And affection has nothing to do with it."

I ruffled her hair vigorously. "Listen to the Burning Bush!"

"Don't *do* that, I hate that!"

"Four hundred years of royal blood, the iron tits in the silken kirtle. Yes, yes, yes and bloody amen. We've done what we dreamed, love, made something better than just we two. It's beautiful, and I won't let you put a halter on it because Boudicca slept with one of your randy ancestors. Come on, now."

We walked toward the door. "So, eat your hot soup and put on a woolen shift before you start sneezing. Tell Imogen to start packing. Plenty of warm clothes."

"So soon?"

"I'll come to say good-bye."

"Thank you for coming. I prayed you would."

"As if I could stay away."

"How long will I be in Caerleon?"

"I don't know, Gwen." And I didn't.

"Don't make me beg. You owe me that much."

"I don't know. Until I can go to sleep without the north coming down around my ears. Until all of them realize we're big boys now."

She hugged me suddenly and I felt her tears on my own

cheek. "It's either monstrous or a proof of God," she whispered, "but I love you, Arthur. I don't suppose that's worth a pardon."

I held her. "No, but it goes a long way toward parole. I'm lost without you."

Gwen chuckled. "Most of the time. We love like seasons. It's the rest of the year that kills us. There now, kiss me."

"Good night, love."

"And Arthur?"

"Yes?"

"Fair warning. Just try to keep me in prison."

"Fair. Rest you gentle, Gwen."

My queen bowed with inscrutable dignity. "Sleep you sound, my lord."

I sent for Lucullus to attend me in the *scriptorium*, dark now but for two candles on my writing table and the glow from the firepit. The victory celebration, born in the courtyard and sprawling now into the palace, beat on my surfeited ears.

Lucullus appeared, transformed by a perfumed bath and considerable artifice, cinched at the waist, hair freshly dyed, once more the glittering bird of youth.

"You sent, Artorius?"

"Come in. I must say you look fit. Our climate agrees with you."

Lucullus winced in distaste. "Your climate is abysmal. When wayward Christians die, they must come here. You have my safe conduct?"

"And my report to Theodoric. *Mea culpa*, of course, and some mention of your good service at Badon."

Lucullus' distaste darkened to actual suffering. "This for a man who only wants to make love and grow grapes. Disgusting. One night of pleasure is more positive than a thousand heroic deaths."

"You're a philosopher, Lucullus."

"No, only one to smell the wind and which way it will blow next."

He moved to the casement, contemplating the celebration below with detached amusement. "When may I sail?"

"With the morning tide. Your ship's fitting on the quay now."

A great shout of *Victory* sprang out of the courtyard din.

Lucullus smiled wryly as my name rose again and again. *Arthur! Ave!*

"The wind blows for you now," he observed. "But how tomorrow?"

"That's tomorrow's problem." I held up another parchment. "A policy letter to Theodoric. I was just about to sign it. I want no more weepy nostalgia for the lost children of Rome. Rome's a memory, a grave. Its children are grown and gone. And we keep our own house."

The son of Ambrosius spread apologetic hands. "Forgive me, that does sound arrogant. There's no life, no anything without Rome. It's a contradiction in terms."

"Thus Pharaoh to Moses, but the Jews went on packing."

I reached for my stylus and signed the parchment: *Artorius, Imperator.*

"You see?" Lucullus indicated the signature with quiet certainty. "You even think in the language of Tiber. How will you forget us?"

With one stroke I lanced through the Latin and wrote under it: *Artos, Rix Cymri,* sprinkled the sand, blew it off and thrust the document at him. "Fare you well, Rome."

Lucullus went down in a courtly bow. "You know, my lord, I really ought to test the wind in Byzantium. Subtler breed of men, one hears. Civilized. They might use me to advantage, don't you think?"

He paused for a moment at the door. "Fare you well, Britain."

Lucullus gone, I turned reluctantly to less pleasant work, an order to the lords at Caerleon for Guenevere's incarceration. The writ needed careful wording and detail. She was to live in ample comfort with a good household, guarded night and day, with no visitors not personally authorized by myself.

and shall remain at Caerleon until—

I hated the end that must be written, pausing while the roar rose again and again from the courtyard.

Arthur! Arthur and victory!

The fire had died down, one of my candles was guttering. My eyes burned with fatigue. I dipped the stylus and completed the sentence.

—until we deem fit for the safety of Britain.

Cerdic with a knife, Gwen with a bloodless line of writing.
We do grow old.

Arthur! Arthur!

"Be still," I groaned. "Let me alone."

"They won't, Arthur. Ever again."

"Eh? Who's there?"

"Only me."

I made out the tall figure in the gloom beyond the firepit.
"Merlin?"

"Yes."

Merlin rose and crossed to the casement. Silhouetted against it
and gazing down at the firelit celebration, he was very still, still
as marble or oak. The imperial garments did not move or rustle,
the graceful drapes of a noble statue. Still as strength itself that
had borne much and would bear more. The profile was heavier,
craggier. Still audacious, ready to dare as well as dream. His head
lifted to search for something else beyond the ramparts and the
river, perhaps as far as stars.

But I felt peevish and in no mood for eternals. "What do you
want? Another lesson for Druith? You're only myself, a shadow-
me. But you always looked more the king. They should have
crowned you."

Arthur! Ave, Arthur!

"Won't they ever shut up?"

Merlin moved slightly. "I asked you once did you love them.
You didn't know."

"Love? What else have I given them all these years? And
Gwen, for that matter, and Bedivere and all the other heroes they
conjure with and wouldn't know for one second as humans?
What else did we do with our lives? They take everything and
give nothing back. And what's left for me? One love gone and
another going and I've nothing left and no place to go. Be still,
you *leeches*!"

"No more," said Merlin. The profiled lips barely moved.
"You're the golden grist of bards, boyo. They'll cram the sprawl
of you into song, use your name to inspire dull children, frighten
enemies, hearten the faithful and even cure warts. They've made
you a god for all the usual reasons. If they can't be something
higher, they want to believe it's there."

I snorted at him. "Rot! Go away, you can't help anymore.
I'm not the pliant genius I was. I make mistakes. I let my heart
get the best of me. And I'll be talking to shadows soon enough

without their nattering back. Vanish, why don't you? Vanish, go, all of you and leave me alone.''

Merlin was gentle but inexorable. ''There's a pattern they won't have broken, Arthur. It's very old. You've given them the chance to hail you, love you—''

''Balls!''

''—Denounce you, feel remorse with the twice-crowing cock, and come home at last to your redeeming bosom.''

''You're an old bore, Merlin. You were more fun as a juggler.''

''I only see what is.'' Merlin moved at last, fading from the casement back into the shadows. ''That's what a god is for, Arthur. Who cares what he feels?''

Arthur! Arthur and victory!

''Shut up!'' I flung myself at the casement where Merlin had stood, leaned out over the sill, virulently hating their upturned faces. ''You've got it all. Victory, peace. There's nothing left. Do I have to die for you as well?''

Do I? Is that really what a god is for?

Modred and a Grail

So we come to the end, the Gordian knot in which all skeins meet. You may say *that's not what I thought,* and perhaps it's not what we meant. The difference is history and possibly literature.

I drank from a heady cup after Badon. Formerly rebellious chiefs fawned on me with bad grammar and worse breath, would-be bards flocked like fleas, recalling my deeds at Neth Dun More and upping the odds even further. Camelot received a gaggle of highborn daughters to be polished at court, preferably in my private chambers. The climate had changed: sad about Guenevere, of *course*, but Cador's line was always too proud, and we must think of the future.

Is that you laughing, Ambrosius?

With the ominous exception of the north, the country was united. My people breathed easier, looking forward to an untroubled planting and harvest. The trade of the southern ports flourished again without fear of raiders. Rome's galleys came, stuffed themselves with our export, paid our price, and went home. I took time without misgiving for personal things, seeing to Kay's funeral, keeping Gawain as guest at Camelot while prudently quartering his men with the Dobunni. So placed, they were an assurance of order while the Dobunni chose another prince.

Peace. I let down my guard and made a mistake—three, in fact.

One, I delayed Gwen's exile out of a frank loathing for its necessity. She made ready to leave twice before I finally gave the order to Bedivere.

Two, the post riders reported that Lancelot, harrying the Saxons far into the east, had passed beyond contact. I assumed he was still there.

Three, I told Guenevere where she was going. She said she'd be trouble, and my wife is not given to idle threat. A word to Imogen who spoke to someone else along the web of blood loyalties always ready to strangle Britain. The word got to Lancelot, who, when I thought he was still east, appeared suddenly in Eburacum at Peredur's ear with the Dyfneint cavalry behind him.

The tinder: two men of conscience joined to free a woman they loved. The flint: Agrivaine—vengeful, vindictive, canny and courageous. The daring plot bore his stamp: one fast squadron, enough for the task, few enough to avoid suspicion, traveling peacefully south with their prince toward Camelot.

The spark: any one of a hundred in Camelot personally loyal to Guenevere, poor enough to have that loyalty spurred with gold. "Just the day, that's all we need to know. Here's for your pains and God reward your faith in the best of ladies."

The fire. On a cold, clear day, Guenevere set out for Caerleon with Bedivere and ten *combrogi* who expected no trouble.

"I'm shamed, Artos! I should have been brought back dead rather than live to tell you this."

Bedivere's exasperation and disgust were classic. He stumped up and down the chamber, favoring a lacerated thigh.

"Bedwyr, light somewhere and give me the facts."

He dumped his long body onto a bench, clawing the dull copper hair out of his eyes. "A full squadron of Orkney. We weren't two hours out when they hit us."

"Agrivaine?"

"And Peredur, and thank God for him. Agrivaine would have slaughtered the lot of us. Peredur made them take Guenevere and run."

Their mission completed, the raiders ran against time in hostile country. They didn't expect pursuit by stubborn Bedivere. A few of their wounded turned to make a stand while the others escaped with Guenevere. A brief, whirling skirmish and all the rear guard lay dead except Peredur, long sick and in no condition for a venture like this. The Parisi had swooped across the board only to trade a knight-prince for a queen, but the outcome would be the same.

"Civil war." Bedivere fiddled with his hands, troubled. "We've spent our chances like the prodigal son, you and I. We should be playing with grandchildren, not running to one war on the heels of another."

Barely listening, my mind raced over the ramifications of the raid; tomorrow's move, next week's. Guenevere's mind and those she now commanded. Lancelot would follow her without question, but Agrivaine would goad for war.

"Where's Peredur?" I asked.

"In the house where you kept the queen," Bedivere told me. "He never wanted any of this. Shouldn't have come, he's weak as a kitten. But he loves his sister, he honors Lancelot and he's Cador's son."

Civil war. We could keep Peredur from it but not Guenevere. Unless, just possibly . . .

"Gwen's got sense," I said. "She doesn't want a battle any more than we do."

Bedivere grimaced. The pain in his leg eroded his small hoard of tact. "Well, if there is, you asked for it. By God, you begged for it."

The blunt honesty stung. "Not now, Bedwyr."

"Bloody hell, not now. Artos, I'm your man, I'm with you. When the flags go up, I'm there to say the king is right. But after forty years, who knows better when the man is wrong? I mean bringing Morgana. I can understand it, a man's mistake, not a king's. But a mistake."

He was right and that smarted most. "That is the studied opinion of my lord Bedivere?"

He wagged his head in disgust. "Don't lord me, Artos. I put the irons on Guenevere myself and turned the key on her. Ride against her now, I'll be there with the dragon. But I say you should know a mistake and learn from it."

"This is one country with one code of laws!"

"That again?"

"You think I don't know by now it was insane? The last thing I need is you for a conscience."

Bedivere rose awkwardly, still favoring the bad leg. "As my king says."

"None of that, either. When you turn respectful, I know where to get off. Get out of here. And send someone to poke up this fire."

Bedivere studied me with sharp concern. "Artos, Artos, you're tight as a nun's—have you been sleeping well?"

"Not much, no."

He knew me far too well. "And alone."

"Mostly."

"With all these women about?"

"I've—tried that. You have to talk to them sometimes." And what does one say to a vacuous twit with nothing to recommend her but youth and virtue? Who is, ultimately, not Gwen?

"You could marry again. That'd take the horse out from under her."

"Gwen would still fight. Harder than ever."

"With less support," Bedivere noted. "There's a difference between a wronged queen and a rebel."

"Bedivere, I think you're actually becoming a statesman."

"Defend me from that." He turned at the door. "We'll be north then?"

I relished it as little as he. "Yes."

"I'd dearly love to see Myfanwy and the girl first. I'm thinking perhaps I should let Rhonda marry that scamp of hers. Give me a grandchild to play with."

"You have leave. Take them my love."

"And if I was too sharp, let my king forgive me."

"Ah, let be." I snatched up my cloak and joined him at the door. He was an unmitigated pain in the arse sometimes, but every king should have a Bedivere. "Come, I'll see you out."

Peredur was thinner than ever, fish-white with a blood-spitting cough, hair and beard sparse and neglected, the habitual pilgrim's robe stained with dark spittle. The image of the monk was belied, however, by urbane poise and hands that caressed books with the intimacy of Lucullus stroking a lover. I found him by the fire surrounded by a pile of parchment rolls. The eager hand he gave me had no warmth in it.

"Good of you to visit, Arthur. Forgive my not rising, I feel a bit fragile. And one hopes I'm more guest than prisoner."

Peredur put aside the book he was enjoying. "Gwen left her library. Marvelous style, Luke. And look, here's Augustine. Narrow man, but what a hunger for God! How are you, Arthur?"

"At war with your sister, damn you both. Comfortable?"

"Quite." His pallid hands waved away any notion of inconvenience. "The guards are courteous, but they needn't look in all that much. I couldn't make it to the gate."

That was true. It hurt to look at him. "Idiot, why'd you try this?"

"A large gamble," said the Prince of the Parisi, "a large profit."

"I'll send my doctors. They're bored with my own infallible health. You'll be a novelty."

Peredur shrugged. "They'll tell me to eat more meat and onions and avoid chills. They won't say what I know already. No matter. Gwen is father born again. She'll rule better than I."

"No, she won't. I'm going after her. You've made me."

Peredur's head snapped around. "I had to, Arthur!"

"You're not going to be a separate crown, whatever excuse you give."

"You had my loyalty, Arthur. If you hadn't brought your filthy Picts. My God, what were you thinking?"

I sighed; twice in one day. "Obviously, I wasn't."

"Nicely put. The modest admission of the philosopher king. But what you did here, we pay for at home."

"What do you mean?"

"You wouldn't have heard yet," said Peredur ironically. "Your firstborn in whom you were well pleased. He raided Cilurnum last week. Corstopitum the week before. Doesn't take children anymore. Just pieces of them."

I sat down, not able to look at him. "Modred."

I knew it would happen. Modred, who saw so clearly his own doom, who courted it perversely in the name of twisted love, taking the world down with him.

"They call him the firelord," Peredur said. "And he'll sit back and laugh while we kill each other."

His dry laugh tore into a fit of painful coughing. I held him as his thin body convulsed. When it passed, I poured him some of the herb tea kept hot on the hob and helped him to his couch.

"Absurd," he panted. "You and I and Guenevere. We'd rather be racked than fight each other. And I'll sit it out here. What a magnificent failure: not quite a prince, not quite a priest. I couldn't even find Lancelot's Grail."

"You did try."

"I was so sure we could find it." A hint of life returned now as he spoke of his quest; how they ferreted the monastery at Wyrral Tor top to bottom, pored over its fragmentary records, questioned the monks, set men digging in the cellars. Peredur wanted nothing from his remaining days but to find the Grail. Not to own it, not for any glory. Let it blaze up in light and vanish once more—if it ever did—that didn't matter. He wanted to see the completion of something, an assurance.

"A sense of continuity, Arthur. Christ to Joseph to us. Something that won't change, that says we *are* His children no matter how we muck up the world. That's all I want. All Eleyne wants, really."

"She could never put it so clearly."

Peredur coughed into his linen. "Eleyne never put anything clearly. I've listened and listened to that Grail story, and it still makes no sense. They say listening's an art. With Eleyne it's an ordeal. She talks in circles, I listen. Always the same."

Only fair to tell him he had not suffered alone, as it were, under Pilate; that Ygerna had often been subjected to Caradoc's version of the venerable tale.

"There was once at Vortigern's table when Caradoc dragged out the old story. When he got to the pilgrim girl, Ygerna vowed if *she* went undressed in daylight, she'd expect to be noticed too."

Peredur gasped. "*Ach-y-fi*, she didn't! She actually said that?"

"My dear mother."

"To Caradoc of holy Dyfneint? Oh dear. Well." Peredur broke off, giggling over the image. "Well, actually, she's right. I suppose. If a woman did go un—"

As I watched, Peredur's expression changed from twinkling good humor to revelation.

"God love us, she's right! That's *it*."

Peredur swung off the couch, swaying on thin legs. "That's it, that's what's wrong. Arthur, look."

He burrowed into a leather bag by his couch, retrieving a tattered parchment roll. "I've carried this for years. Each person that's told the story, I've set it down close as possible to their words."

The parchment rattled through his fingers, a river of Latin script.

"Yes, here. Quote Eleyne: 'It was hot summer. Her robe was loose.' " Riffle, rattle, the script-river flowed. "Quote Galahalt: 'It was the high summer and her raiment was loosened.' Quote the Abbot of Wyrral Tor: 'As she came close, he perceived her robe was loosened.' The rest much the same."

I was not terribly impressed and a little confused. "Well, it was summer. Beyond the weather, what does it prove?"

"Something so simple, anyone could miss it. Would a pilgrim approach the holy of holies without some thought to propriety?"

"No, I suppose not."

Peredur plucked at his garment. "This is a pilgrim's robe, the same for men and women, winter and summer. Now I kneel before you." He did. "What falls open? Nothing."

Peredur was already in a light sweat from excitement. I tried to coax him back onto the couch, but he resisted.

"Bother that; don't you see?"

"Perhaps she wasn't wearing a pilgrim robe."

"Your crown against a radish, she wasn't." One finger raised like a debating scholar, shaking at me. "And she bloody well wasn't on pilgrimage, either. A plain peasant girl? What do they wear in summer? Something that fastens snug over one shoulder or ties at both. Neither likely to fall open to the carnal eye—unless she loosened it herself."

I thought I followed his reasoning. "You think they were making love?"

"Oh, good God, no!" Peredur rocked with high, excited laughter. "But you've seen peasant women in summer. About as modest as cows. They strip to the waist and bathe outdoors. Bathing, Arthur! Not on Wyrral Tor, but at the well. *At the bottom of the hill.*"

Well, you could argue it. The Grail could be there, so far as that went, or in a hundred other places if any at all. But seeing Peredur's joy of excitement, tinged with terminal desperation, I would have been cruel to dampen it. The enthusiasm only brought out more starkly the pallor of his illness and how close Peredur was to the end.

"The well. Yes. Brilliant, Arthur." His spurt of energy burned out, Peredur wilted back onto the couch. "Worthy of me and as useless. I am your prisoner. But," he looked up at me urgently, "you might get word to Eleyne. Perhaps . . ."

He let it trail off into silence. As I stood watching him, I made another decision from the heart rather than my head, but one I've never regretted.

Shortly before three, the guards admitted me again to Peredur's quarters. I gave him no smile, let him see only the apparent heaviness of my spirit.

"What is it, Arthur?"

"Peredur, certain conditions have become too dangerous." I let him reflect on that. "Do you understand?"

He eyed me closely. "I am dangerous?"

"While you live."

Peredur stood up. The natural fear flickered in his eyes for a moment before the habit of a lifetime quelled it. "I see." A pause. "May I have a confessor?"

"Peredur, a life like yours never earns more than five minutes in purgatory. You have time to pray."

He couldn't believe it. "Not even a priest?"

"I'm sorry. This must be done quickly. You might do the same thing in my place."

And indeed he might. Peredur knelt in front of the small altar installed for Guenevere and made his contrition in a low voice that never faltered. I opened the door to see Lord Bors striding across the courtyard toward the house. "Come in, Bors."

Inside, the young knight glanced curiously at kneeling Peredur. "Sir, Lord Gareth sent me. You have orders?"

"Questions." I put my hands on his shoulders. "When I charged my queen with treason, you spoke out for her."

"Yes, sir," he admitted hesitantly. "I—I did feel in my conscience she was right."

"How then are you loyal to me?"

Bors flushed and corrected me straight. "Sir, I rode with Gareth at Badon. There's fingers and toes that still have little feeling from the long cold. With respect, sir, that's not a question to ask me."

I nodded in approval. "Then I'll ask one more to the point. Is there an edge to your sword?"

"That a hedgehog could shave with, sir."

"Then draw it now and strike off Prince Peredur's head."

His mouth dropped open. I took advantage of the shock and pushed it.

"Come, he's under my sentence, shriven and prepared and kneeling for the blow. Draw your sword."

He still hung back; for a moment I wondered if he would obey. Then Peredur helped him.

"Come, boy. Don't keep a prince waiting."

Bors extracted his sword from its scabbard like something unclean. "My lord," he mumbled to Peredur, "forgive me my duty."

"I forgive it. Take my blessing."

Peredur bowed his head forward. Bors stepped to one side, set himself and raised the longsword.

"Hold," I said.

Bors froze. The look of death was still on Peredur as he straightened up slowly.

"I never meant it to be, Bors. But I had to know you could."

Bors shook. "Thank God."

"Get up, Peredur."

Instantly Bors was there to assist the frail prince. "Let me help. If you knew my admiration, sir. There's no more Christian prince than you."

"And none more relieved." Peredur patted his arm. "Arthur, you can be cruel."

"Right." I clapped my hands sharply to dispel the sepulchral mood. "Bors, impress ten *combrogi* with good mounts, order a galley at the quay. You are to escort Prince Peredur from here to the mouth of the Brue, thence to Ynnis Witrin. You'll afford him every courtesy except the chance to escape. And you will assist him in his mission."

Gratitude and confusion. "Aye, sir. And what might that be?"

"Tell him, Peredur."

"The Holy Grail," said Peredur. "I know where it is."

Bors crossed himself. "With my life, sir."

"Attend me outside. I'll be a moment."

Dazed, Bors stumbled out the door. Peredur waited with arms crossed and a wondering smile.

"You're a bit of a saint, Arthur."

"And you're still a prisoner. Try to escape and he'll bury you at Witrin."

"And something of a bastard. But heaven will reward this."

"Just let them spare me the fervent. You true believers are no end of trouble." I hugged his wasted frame to me. "There, now. Go find your silly cup. And no trouble, mind."

"I'm too sick for trouble."

"Sick my royal butt. I wouldn't trust a son of Cador two weeks after I buried him. Come, get ready. We'll dine together before you go."

I left him collecting papers in his leather bag, eager, happier than I'd seen him in years.

"It's got to be there, Arthur. It's got to be."

Yes, I prayed. Someone who heeded fallen sparrows might take a moment for Peredur.

Outside, I hooked my arm in Bors' and walked him toward the palace. "Help him all you can, lad. It's still cold, make him wrap his chest."

"For the Grail, sir? Anything."

"Just be gentle with him and believe with him. He doesn't have much time."

*   *   *

Gareth became my new lord-milite, his first task to inspect the fitness of the *combrogi* for a new campaign. He rendered a sorry report. Some horses were lame, others too sick or wounded to rise in their stalls. Some men were abed with wounds, others still hobbling on crutches. Almost all suffered the aftermath of exposure and frostbite. Gawain's Orkney were no better off. A letter to Maelgwyn brought the reluctant promise of a hundred fit men, no more.

We might have drawn on the other allied tribes, but they'd be more hindrance than help against Agrivaine's cavalry. We had numbers on our side, but the superiority consisted of six hundred worn-out men on half-lame horses. Desperately, hour by hour, I searched for a way to avoid it, to find a compromise where, miraculously, Britain lost nothing. How to deal with Guenevere. She was the key.

The days melted into weeks while we waited out the mending. Winter dissolved to sudden, early spring with brilliant sunshine and a warm wind over Severn rich with the scent of flowers. Fishing boats bobbed and tilted on the river, the smell of new-turned earth wafted from the fields. Boys and girls ambled hand in hand through the trees or along the riverbank. Men and women stopped sometimes just to smell the air, eternally surprised at the new life hidden in a cold, dark world.

Bedivere came back on such a day, fresher, the set of him fuller and softened from the too-keen edge of war. He brought news of his family and one of Myfanwy's fresh-boiled puddings for me. I held the halter while he dismounted, and together we walked the horse toward the stables.

"So, are the young ones married?"

He glowed. "Are they not? And what a wedding. Part Church and part old ways. Such cakes and wine, and the doves sacrificed!"

"Doves, no less!"

"The priest would've had a fit if he wasn't too drunk by then to see them. *Och*, Myfanwy goes to mass, sure, but you know. When it comes to a wedding, the old way's best."

Oh, and his jewel, his Rhonda! Like a sprite come fresh from the woods, barefoot and with the flowers worked through her hair. The groom was nervous and Myfanwy cried and came close to war with the servants over the laying out of supper, and Bedivere hovered about the edge of it all, feeling superfluous.

"But now there'll be grandchildren. I wanted that."

He sounded wistful and reflective, only grunted when I mentioned Peredur's mission.

"That doesn't fret me half so much . . ."

"As what?" I prompted.

He started to speak but changed his mind. "It's not my place, Artos."

"When did that stop the Gryffyn?"

Bedivere halted, patting the horse's nose, avoiding my eyes. "Well, have you thought who's to follow you?"

Frankly, I hadn't. I didn't yet really accept growing older, if the truth were known, much less a successor even if the choice were wholly mine to make. I gave Bedivere the easy answer.

"There's only one could, and she's at war with me."

"Aye, and who else? Kay dead, Peredur who won't see another year. Maelgwyn a good man but too old, Mark in his dotage."

"Nor this one, nor that," I agreed. It wasn't a thought I liked. Who would come after? Where was there another grubby young tribune with a Merlin at his ear?

Bedivere called for a groom at the stables, gave him the reins, and sat down on a mounting block. "I've thought of going home soon. To stay, Artos. I mean if . . ."

The unfinished thought dangled between us.

"If what, Bedivere?"

He spread his arms, let them fall at his sides. "I don't know."

"There is something."

"Na, foolish," Bedivere shrugged it off. "I'm not one for second sight. But I've a bad feeling about the going north."

"Omens?" I asked.

"Na, na, but it keeps coming back. I want to see Rhonda's children. And yet so many years, so many battles without a hurt. Kay lying in the mud at Badon, and the thought was on me. It *is* on me, wakes me sweating at night."

I sat down beside him, concerned. "What thought, Bedivere?"

My friend looked away across the courtyard. He considered the words before he shared them. "I don't think there's any luck left in me, Artos."

And then the rider out of the south pounding up to the gate, into the courtyard, off the winded horse and dashing up flights of stairs, his news spreading before him like a wave to wash over lords, ladies and servants alike before he fell on his knees to gasp it out to me. Lord Culwych, one of Peredur's escort.

"It is found, sir. The Holy Grail is found!"

"I can see the sun on their lance heads." Bedivere leaned out over the parapet. "Gareth, how many?"

"A great, long snake of them," Gareth bubbled. "Two hundred at least. And look at the Bors, will you now! If he reins that nag any tighter, he'll break its suffering neck."

Bors was indeed the picture of pride—head high, lance socketed and rigid in his stiffly straightened arm, the horse controlled to a swaggering trot that was almost a dance. I called down into the courtyard.

"There by the gate! Tell Lord Bors we wait him in the great hall."

I clapped my friends by the shoulders. "Come on, you two barnacles, let's make him feel important. It's a great day."

Camelot came alive with the news. While Bors dismounted in the courtyard, the great hall was already filling with lords and their wives, priests, eager servants and, trailing last, mortified and frantic, Bors' young wife, Lady Regan.

"Oh, he *would* come like this with no warning," she wailed. "No decent time to change or groom. What will he think?"

"That he married a treasure." I beckoned her up to the dais with Bedivere and myself. "Stand here by me so he can tell us both."

A hubbub at the entrance, an eddy of people moving aside, and Bors strode down the long chamber, sweating in full mail, to kneel before me.

"Long life to my king." One brimming glance at Regan. "Praise God who lets me be His poor messenger. I am to say the Grail is found, and it comes even now with Prince Peredur."

For all the portent of his news, there was something hesitant in his manner, an ambivalence.

"Praise God," Bors mouthed dutifully.

"Amen," I said. It was echoed by a number of the eager company hanging on his words. "But you might include Regan here."

She skipped down from the dais—when you're sixteen and in love, you can skip. "Welcome, husband. Forgive my hasty dress. I was about some mending, and—"

"Oh, lass, I don't *care*." Bors squeezed her tight as if she might disappear if he let go. "Just hold me. My head's not big enough to know the half of this."

"Come up beside me," I ordered. "Bring Regan and tell all of us."

Facing the expectant throng, Bors was even less certain of himself. The odd manner contrasted so sharply with his tidings. Unused to oratory, he took a moment to collect himself, unbuckling the heavy sword belt, turning it in his hands while he spoke.

"My king and lords, the Grail is found. That is, Prince Peredur says it is found."

And Peredur was the meat of his story. They made camp by the well at the foot of Wyrral Tor. Day by day as they dredged the bottom, a larger and larger crowd gathered to watch the work. Monks from the monastery, the folk of Ynnis Witrin. Word spread and eventually even Lady Eleyne came from Astolat to fuss over and nurse the failing prince who would not rest but sifted with his own hands through the muck and centuries' debris in the growing pile. Old pots, rusted bits of iron, rotted bucket staves and hoops, slime-green stones.

Then the workmen said they'd dredged nigh to the bottom and the well had nothing left but water in it. And Peredur held up a small object he'd been cleaning.

"It was a coin," Bors went on. "Hardly used by the look. When it was burnished clean, you could see the image of a man's head with his name on the back. Emperor Tiberius, Peredur said. And that meant we were probably as close as we'd get."

But it was no Grail and there was little left at the bottom. The workmen were shivering blue with going down and filling the buckets, and the monks themselves suggested most tactfully that folk *did* need the well for water. Lady Eleyne turned on them all like an iron judgment. Was she not of St. Joseph's own blood? Did she not rule here in the absence of Lord Ancellius? Quickly on with the work and let these commons fetch their water from River Brue.

"They went down again and came back empty-handed. Nothing but sand and loose stones at the bottom. The divers were pure spent from being under cold water so long. Then it was that the prince took off his robe and, all in his drawers, with the folk looking on, started to climb down the well."

Bors protested, of course. It wasn't fitting for a prince to labor so. Bad enough in private, but with commons looking on—but Peredur would have none of it.

"I alone," he said. And he went down the rope into the cold water.

He came up once to say that they weren't bottom stones, but loose rocks thrown in to raise the water level. The second time, he sent up a large load of them, pausing only to fill his lungs, and dove again to dislodge another bucketful of the greenish rocks.

"He was down so long, we began to worry and then to pray outright. He was much weakened and the water like ice."

Then Peredur's arm broke the surface, coming straight up with something dark clutched in its fingers. His head bobbed up; Peredur sputtered and gasped, "Hu-haul me out! Quick, I'm starting to cramp."

"And we did," Bors reported baldly, voice sunk to a halting whisper in which there was still more puzzlement than reverence. "There it was in his hand."

An old priest stepped forward, eager. "What, Lord Bors?"

"Something. I know not what. All caked with green weed and God knows what else."

I pressed him. "But what?"

He only bowed his head, miserable. "The prince can tell of it."

"But you saw something, boy?"

"Yes, sir." Bors sounded only weary now. "But I have no words. You see, all my life—I mean, it doesn't . . ."

Bors looked down at Regan pressed against his side and tightened his arm around the girl as if to comfort her, comfort all of us.

"I have only my faith," he ended doggedly. "But it is not what we thought."

If the Grail was an anticlimax for Bors, the procession of honor was not. I suspect Eleyne had a hand in its elaboration. First came Bors' detachment, stiff and proud, then a dozen trumpeters with *bucinas* rummaged from the shards of Trajanus' old camp. The players were not keenly proficient with the obsolete instrument; they distracted the horses more than they stirred the heart. Immediately behind them came a burly monk holding aloft a great silver cross. More monks then, a dun clump of them, hands clasped and singing *Hallelujah* and *Nova gaudia*.

Before Peredur's litter strode a young priest, chanting sonorously, "The blessing of God on Prince Peredur who has restored to us the proof of Christ in Britain. Praises to his name which shall be called Venerable."

Peredur swayed limply with the motion of his litter, wrapped in blankets, head propped on a pillow of rich fabric, one bloodless hand resting on a jeweled reliquary in which, I assumed, lay the triumph of his quest.

And then in state came Lady Eleyne, carried in a chair and wearing the ancient crown of Dyfneint. Close behind in their moth-eaten finery followed the elder nobles of Dyfneint. A few Caerleon lords rode after to keep the rear in some kind of order. In their wake, the holy procession trailed off raggedly into jubilant and curious common folk, larking children, dogs and beggars who followed any royal progress for alms.

It was a brave spectacle, goggled at and cheered from every casement and rampart in Camelot. With their huzzahs and the monks' singing and the dogs' woofing, it was quite a racket, but I suffered it. If God himself sent down an order for quiet, no one would have heeded.

The glittering, hosanna-ing parade entered the south gate of Camelot and filled the courtyard before we shut the gates against the commons still cheering outside. I sent two servants with a hoard of small coins to distribute and several more to clean the cold leftovers from the kitchens, so that the country around the palace looked like a huge, holy picnic, not far off the mark for definition.

As I took Peredur's hand, a faded picture came to mind: Ambrosius coming to Eburacum, his death hanging on him like a dingy garment.

His eyes glittered with fever. His head barely moved on the pillow. "Thanks, Arthur. For the chance."

"Call it an investment. I suppose you're the holiest prisoner since Jesus. Welcome, Perry-fach."

A great, swelling *Hallelujah* and *Amen* went up from the monks around us as I lifted Peredur from the litter. His mouth was close to my ear and, with the last of his energy, Peredur whispered, "I do hope God likes music. They've not let up since Caerleon."

Eleyne hovered over Peredur, grimly solicitous. She was sole ruler in Dyfneint now, though she referred to Lancelot's defection as a mere absence and acted as if she expected him momentarily. Guenevere she mentioned not at all.

She was thirty-nine. Her brief bloom had faded rather quickly, leaving the immutable, leaden seriousness etched deeper as she settled directly into middle age, convinced as ever of her place among the angels. Harder, bleaker. She'd wrapped her life around Lancelot. When the truth filtered at last through her granite sensibilities, she must have been very unhappy in her submerged soul, but never spoke a word against the husband to whom she was forever bound by God.

Peredur lay on his couch in the small house that he would never leave again. You could say he killed himself. He needn't have gone into the well. Bors and the others scolded with tender exasperation to no avail. He would go down; that's a note on his character. Only Eleyne approved and encouraged what was, in effect, his doom—a note on hers.

The reliquary rested on a small stand before his couch, closed and locked.

"Bors is confused," Peredur labored in a broken whisper. "They all are. They wanted so much more. A miracle. Open it, Eleyne."

She unlocked the chest and lifted its lid. Since it was expected of me, I knelt and crossed myself.

What rested in the box seemed hardly worth a genuflection. An ordinary shallow bowl of pitted bronze. Someone had taken great pains to scrape away the crust of centuries, working with the ardor of reverence, hoping the spiritual light of Christ would eventually blaze forth. Their industry produced a clean but pockmarked surface that shone with less enthusiasm than a common flower bowl. Frankly, I was disappointed. The palace dogs ate from more impressive service.

I asked obliquely, "What do you think, Peredur?"

Eleyne answered for him. "The Church of Britain has acknowledged it. We have found the Grail."

"And who are we to say them nay," Peredur added significantly. "Does that answer?"

"Not really. I know you, Peredur. How you think."

"How I thought. And whatever we thought, this will be the Grail. For all of them."

So mundane, so shabby. "You really think—?"

"Arthur, what I think matters very little."

"Or I," Eleyne agreed. "So says the blood of St. Joseph of Arimathea, amen."

I reached for it. "May I?"

Peredur gestured slightly. "Of course. With your other inordinate titles, you are now *good* King Arthur, patron of the Grail quest."

Peredur's frail, reedy voice went on as I studied the object. "It's the reaching, the hope and the faith that really count. How can any reality shine like the dream of it? They're all confused, but they believe. That's enough."

He glanced up at Eleyne. I read the understanding between them.

"A common bronze bowl," Peredur said. "Not very well made. Test the weight: more tin than copper. Must be thousands like it. Cheap enough for peasants and inns that catered to men of limited means. Look at the bottom."

I turned the bowl over. There was no design at all tooled into the age-dark metal at its manufacture, but someone with a crude point had scratched two simple arcs, one inverted, that crossed to form the rude outline of a fish.

"The earliest symbol of Christ," Peredur breathed. "Interesting coincidence. But if there was a Grail, it would look like nothing so much as this."

Nothing to say, then. Peredur and Eleyne were silent, arrived at a stillness of wisdom. I passed the bowl to Eleyne who locked it in the reliquary which she brought to me.

"My lord king, when he greets my husband, will please say that Eleyne of Astolat has lived and lives still in the sacred charge of her blood. And in the sanctity of my marriage vow—"

Something haunted her eyes for a flicker of time, like a shape moving under dark waters.

"—From which there is no loosing even in heaven. I send him the Holy Grail to heal his heart. And I will bide here by his friend whose feet should be washed by saints."

I hoped it would heal more than Lancelot. Going north I needed all the help I could get.

Peredur held out his white hand. "You'll be going soon?"

"In a day or so."

His fingers spidered over mine, the grip of an infant. "I love you all. I'd see you at peace but for the absurd things we have to do. What do you think God does most, Arthur? Laugh or cry?"

He died in his sleep the night after I left. The Bishop of Caerleon said the mass himself and the requiem was sung by a choir of several dozen monks. Masses were ordered for each anniversary of Peredur's death. The prince lay in state two full days, and I think more of the faithful knelt at his bier than will ever weep over mine. Why not? He touched an enduring need in their hearts. They saw him rise like a spirit bird, molting mortality, ranks of angels guiding him to paradise, *dona eis requiem*, armies of welcoming seraphim, ranked saints eager to make him one of them, his head suffused in holy light.

Peredur would have thought it all a bit thick. I knew him. His faith might have sent him down into the well, but a keen, critical mind led him there. And he always hated crowds. As for veneration on earth or apotheosis in heaven, he would be distracted by the noise and embarrassed by the adulation. Perhaps one friend to be waiting, the only one he ever wanted, at ease and casual, ready to take him home with a good chat along the way: "Come *in*, Perry-fach! What a mess they've made down there, when I meant it all to be so simple. Oh, the *ideas* were good but I've done so much better since. Come—walk with me."

I rested my horse on the hilltop, looking out over the moor southwest of Eburacum. Bedivere whistled softly as he appraised the distant squadrons arrayed against us.

"All neat and proper, Artos. I thought Agrivaine would go for an ambush."

"Guenevere has more sense. She wants results, not blood. Tell the commanders to join me here."

Awaiting them, I scrutinized the terrain we might have to fight on. Agrivaine was not so eager to kill me that he chose his ground carelessly. Behind his forces the moor rose in a low, scalloped hill, the earthworks of an ancient fort. If necessary, it would give him good cover.

My commanders trotted up to me to take their places: Gareth, Gawain, Maelgwyn and Bedivere, each estimating the force in front of us.

"They're all bunched up," said Gareth. "Was not Lancelot drew up that order."

Obviously not. Agrivaine was lord-milite of the Parisi and the more experienced Lancelot was too modest to assert himself. The squadrons were drawn up in blocks; impressive but not the best starting position for an attack. We'd deploy in a wedge headed by Gareth's *combrogi*, narrow at the head, wider than Agrivaine's line at the rear so we could turn his flank if we must.

If he attacked without warning, we'd be in the better position. I gave my orders.

"Make your dispositions and turn the squadrons over to your seconds-in-command. Tell them, once we're on the field, I'll draw my sword if Agrivaine tries to shift his position. On that signal—and only that—they'll attack in formation."

"And we?" Maelgwyn asked.

"Up front with me. Guenevere will see we're ready to reason first."

They cantered away to transmit the orders. A few minutes later, when the first of the *combrogi* approached, I slapped Bedivere's arm.

"Up the dragon, boyo. Let's go to work."

When we reached our position on the level ground, I smiled a little at the sight of the three figures waiting in front of the northern forces. Guenevere in the center, Agrivaine on her right, Lancelot to the left. My queen sat a heavy gray, dressed in a long mail coat that must have dragged cruelly on her thin shoulders. Over the mail was draped the purple robe she wore in state at Camelot. Her head was rounded with the coronet of the Parisi. A clear and formidable statement: she would have all her rights. I would strip her of nothing without dispute.

I turned to view the precise movements of my own squadrons, mindful that the impression was not lost on the forces opposite. The wedge formed with sure, economical movements, no noise or milling about. The finest weapon in the world.

Then, my commanders behind me, I paced forward until only a few yards separated me from Guenevere.

"Before any speaks," I began, "let me say I'm in a better position to attack. And if there's any shift in yours, I will."

I caught the silent I-told-you-so Lancelot vented on Agrivaine.

"I came for my rights, Arthur," said Guenevere. "Not for a fight."

Trust Agrivaine to amend that. "But every bit of a fight if you want it. And Gawain, I'll have no mercy on a brother."

"Nor I, brother," Gawain answered with still conviction. "The price is too dear now."

"Hear, Pendragon!" Agrivaine shouted. "No bargains. The north will—"

"*I* will speak for the north," Guenevere reminded him with cool authority. "Arthur, will you hear me out?"

Gladly. It was time to listen. Gamblers, we knew each other

too well to bluff. I might impress her men and had the means for it in my saddle-purse, but Gwen? Where was her weakness?

"I am here to listen, Guenevere."

"The Parisi are to be sovereign again as they were under my father. And no reprisal for this honest rising."

"No reprisal," I agreed. "As for sovereignty, we've argued that for a hundred years. It's never been codified but always depended on who was stronger, emperor or tribe. Let's end it. Let there be a writ between us as to the legal rights of the Parisi under the crown."

"All rights?" my shrewd queen asked.

"All rights saving separate treaties."

"Not yet agreed," Guenevere frowned, digesting the offer. "Hear me further. With my royal brother dead, I am to keep the crown of the Parisi and Brigantes if they choose me."

If indeed. With Agrivaine and Lancelot behind her, it was a choice for the Parisi of being cooked or eaten raw. A good move, since Gwen assumed I would never restore her as queen. She knew the game and the board.

But she'd given me the opening I needed. I knew Gwen; she'd always trade good for better and both for best. I muttered to Bedivere, "Cross your fingers. The fat's going in the fire."

I flicked the reins and moved out alone, beckoning Guenevere to come forward. We met alone in the open space between our commanders. Poor Gwen was sweating and miserable under the hot mail and heavy cloak.

"I've a better idea, Gwen."

She lifted one eyebrow, wary. "It'd better be good. Right now I *am* the north."

"Give it up."

A little gasp of disbelief. "You are off your form, Arthur. Give it up for what?"

"A crown at Camelot."

Stunned surprise. She wasn't ready for that. "What—?"

"One or the other, Gwen. A little crown here, a big one at home. But not both."

She'd recovered, her guard closed again. "Under you?"

"With me."

"My power restored?"

"All of it."

"In writing? Sworn on relics?"

"In marble if you like. But no more north as a family toy. Let someone else have a chance. They'll think you're gracious as hell while we rule them together.''

''Well,'' Guenevere admired. ''After all these years, you can still surprise me.''

The charm didn't fool me. That quick mind was sifting choices and the value of each. Guenevere lifted a gloved finger. ''And total pardon.''

I bowed my head to her. ''Total and humble. An apology here and now and to be published later.''

Guenevere was still not completely convinced. ''You always did humility well. It's the peasant in you.''

''Wait till you hear me today. I'll make the Sermon on the Mount sound like arrogance. Bargain?''

''Oh, don't rush me. I'm uncomfortable enough as it is.''

I pushed it gently. ''Come on, lass. You were always an advocate of the bird in the hand. Bargain or bloodshed?''

Guenevere looked around at the forces poised against each other, biting her lower lip in concentration. A gamble, yes. Her wise instincts as a ruler against the personal habit of power. Opposed, we were a threat to Britain. Together, a fortress.

''Bargain, husband.''

I took her offered hand. ''So be it.''

''Poor Agrivaine,'' she remembered. ''He'll be so disappointed.''

I backed my horse. ''Break the good news and watch me.''

Guenevere turned the gray and raised her voice to Agrivaine and Lancelot. ''Rejoice with me. The king has satisfied my demands. There will be no war.''

Some of the knights on both sides sent up a ragged cheer of relief and approval through which lanced Agrivaine's piercing dissent.

''I don't trust his bargains.''

''You're not required to,'' Guenevere squelched him. ''Only to obey.''

''We came to fight.''

''We came for justice.'' My wife's voice turned suddenly hard as a whiplash. ''And we have it. To your men, my lords. The king in his own words will exonerate me and all my cause.''

While I fumbled at my saddle-purse, Bedivere and Gareth surrounded me with their doubts.

''High king, it all seems too easy. What happened?''

''You've got ears,'' Bedivere growled. ''He gave away the

whole pasture, he did. The north free under Guenevere. We'll be fighting till we're too old to ride.''

I sighed, leaning on the saddle horn. ''You two are worse than old women. The north goes nowhere. Guenevere will give up the Parisi crown and return to Camelot.''

Bedivere shook his head. ''To Caerleon, I say. But when did you ever listen to me?''

''With Agrivaine and Lancelot in the north? We've tried that and it doesn't work. Without the Parisi crown, it'll be in her interest to hold the new prince to us—and I can keep an even closer eye on *her*.''

''But, Artos, you told her—''

''Ah, Bedwyr, don't be thick! I promised the Parisi a writ.''

''That you did,'' he maintained. ''All their old selfish rights.''

''And if Gwen drafts this writ, how much power is she going to give away?''

He's a straightforward man, my Bedivere. The dawn broke slowly but the light was beautiful to behold. ''Oh-h-h, yes.''

Kings can learn much from a merchant. When a man doesn't meet his first price, he doesn't bash the bugger over the head. He merely pretends great sacrifice and offers the price he intended all along.

''And now, lads, I have to make a few angels blush. Bear with me.''

I drew Peredur's Grail from the saddle-purse. Instantly Gareth and Bedivere dropped to one knee and crossed themselves.

''Jesus God,'' Gareth flustered. ''The Holy Grail, and he carries it like an oatcake.''

Gawain sat his horse, at ease but intent on his brother across the field in huddled conclave with some of his lieutenants.

''Go you out alone, Arthur?''

''It's better.''

''Take me with you,'' said Gawain in a low tone.

''No, it will be well.'' I mounted, the Grail in one hand. ''But be ready. It's about cooked but not out of the oven yet.''

I started forward over the moor, veering toward Lancelot and halting where most of the men could see and hear me.

''I speak to all of you! Orkney, Parisi and Dyfneint. Since Guenevere has shown herself as wise and selfless a ruler as ever I hope to be, I give her full and unconditional pardon for the execution of Morgana which was, but for my personal anger, an act seen by all as done for the good of Britain.''

Cador was right. You have to be a king to lie with that kind of style. Guenevere sat straight and proud in her vindication, and I wondered how long before my queen realized that, benevolently and for the good of Britain, she'd been had.

"I, Arthur, ask her forgiveness and that of every lord who stands in support of her cause. Let you now support us together. My queen will take her throne again, and the Parisi will choose a new prince according to their ancient right."

I thrust the Grail aloft for all to see. "I sue to you all for peace among Britons and bring in token this Holy Grail, lost four hundred years and only now found by a saintly prince whose life was spent in reclaiming it."

The wave of awed whispers spread through the Dyfneint knights. "What is it? . . . Let me see. Does it shine? Nay, it does not. But he says . . ."

"Surely its revelation now is God's wish that there be peace between us. Why, if not, did God let me win at Badon against odds of more than six to one? Why did good Peredur fall my prisoner until the weight on my conscience sent him free to Ynnis Witrin? Why then his own last words that he loved us *all*, dear sainted man, and would have us at peace?"

"It must be true; the prince would speak so. He was ever blessed . . ."

"Witness this company. I am not worthy to hold this best treasure of heaven and earth. And I return it to him who was Peredur's friend in life, who himself carries the charge of the Sinner King."

I held out the Grail. "Lord Ancellius, take this holy vessel from me, for my sins make it too heavy to bear."

Profound silence. Then leather creaked and mail rattled as men among the Dyfneint and Parisi dismounted, kneeling in respect. No other sound broke the tranquillity of the still, warm afternoon. Lancelot moved out to meet me, slipping from the saddle as I did.

"Thank you, Arthur."

I passed the Grail into his reverent hands, saw the familiar disappointment cloud his eyes.

"This?"

"I know it doesn't shine. But Peredur found it and Eleyne sent it to heal your heart. She wants you to bring it home."

Lancelot turned the shabby old vessel in his hands. "This?"

"It could be, man. It could be. If not, then where and what?

Take it back to Eleyne. Peace you can find; that's not holiness, just growing up. Finding what's really meant for us.''

Then Bedivere: *"Artos, mind out!"*

We both spun, saw Agrivaine start forward, the Orkney squadron behind him. Straight at us. Lancelot tossed me the Grail and flung himself into the saddle as my commanders moved quickly to cover me. *Jesus, the bloody fool, he's starting it* and in three more seconds our men would attack, signal or no. Two seconds. One. The orders rang out behind us as Agrivaine's men rumbled forward, still too close-packed for speed.

That alone saved us. In that fraction of time before my men put spur to flank, Guenevere's horse streaked out in the path of the Orkney, halted, and my queen planted herself like a rock. Her back was to me, but her voice carried to every man with withering fury. She stood erect in the stirrups, one imperious arm raised. Magnificent.

"You dare," she quivered. "You dare, Agrivaine? Without my order, you attack your king?"

He hadn't expected this and lost the initiative. Behind him the Orkney milled and shuffled in confusion. In that vital moment, Lancelot was at Guenevere's side, lance couched and bearing on Agrivaine.

I muttered to my captains: "Quick, let's get up to her. Let them see us together. No, Gawain, wait!"

I grabbed his bridle, stopping him before he plunged dead at his brother.

"He's shamed me, Arthur, shamed me all my life. He's no blood of mine. Nor the rest of them."

We eased toward Guenevere, careful not to make any sudden move.

"This comes of my brother's lenience." Guenevere pointed at Agrivaine. "The dog let into the hall and petted until he thinks he has a right."

"I have a right," Agrivaine fumed. "We came for a war and the war is just. I say finish it, with Guenevere or without her."

"You're a watchdog, Agrivaine," my queen said casually. "Kenneled and fed until we need your teeth. But when the cur turns on its master—"

"As you have turned," Agrivaine threw it back at her. "Using your brother, your husband. Your Lancelot."

But Guenevere knew she was in control again. "It's absurd to think of you as the son of a king, Agrivaine. You have no feel for state, you never did. Brave, yes, that you are. But an unbroken hound hinders the hunt. What will you do now? Run me down to get at Arthur? Your lances are crouched, but the Parisi will not point theirs at me.''

"Nor Dyfneint," said Lancelot. "Don't be a fool."

"You're alone and you've chosen," said Guenevere. "You are no longer lord-milite of the Parisi."

"And no more of Orkney!" Gawain roared. "Come you no more home.''

It was too far to see Agrivaine's expression as he turned on his brother. "You had to be born first. My perfect, protecting brother.''

Gawain's great, thick body slumped. He was crying. "God help you, Agrivaine. No more."

"Quit this field," Guenevere ordered. "And the land of the Parisi. I will not look on you again."

The hate wasn't worth it, but Agrivaine still clutched his ounce of right. An ancient right, out of style, but it cast the shape of his few remaining days.

"And where can a man go," he shouted, "where it will not be the same? All of you, listen to me. Not a man on the Wall who does not know the service of Agrivaine meqq Lot. And I say this: Have I not seen it coming since Ambrosius? No more free and sovereign crowns, but mere magistrates again under the tyrant and the *adaltrach*. They are not for us, they only use us. Who has Arthur not juggled? Who has Guenevere not promised and lied to and used? Even each other.''

His men roared back, "We serve Guenevere no longer!"

"Nor Gawain!"

"No!"

"Then go your way!" Gawain howled at them. "My islands are small and no room for the like of you."

"We follow Agrivaine!"

"Do so." Guenevere accepted it. "But hear this. Hear, all of you, all the nobles of Britain."

With a warm glance at me, Guenevere turned the horse and paced slowly along the ranks of the Parisi and Dyfneint.

"All men have a piece of truth, Agrivaine no less than others. Arthur the king has made mistakes. Arthur the man has here confessed them. Can I do less? We were both wrong. But his came out of love, while mine masked jealousy behind the good of Britain. But we have made composition, and there will be peace."

I felt the general easing of tension in all the ranks and marveled at the woman I married.

"A king asks forgiveness. A queen grants it." Guenevere stepped down from the saddle and sank to her knees, arms outstretched to me. "And Guenevere asks her husband for like grace."

I choked a little. "Stay here, my lords."

She waited on her knees as I walked my horse to her, dismounted and pressed my face into her hands.

"God, I love you, Gwen."

"We love *us*, darling. It was *our* dream."

I felt suddenly light and happy. "It's like our wedding day."

Gwen winced. "Not quite. All this on and off a horse and this damned mail. I don't bend as I used to. Help me up."

I thrust out my arms, high and welcoming. "I see two armies here. Let's have one. And celebration and music."

Then the happy sound of men freed of a fight they never wanted, laughter and jingling harness as the sundered causes drew together, each greeting each. Only Agrivaine and his rebels stayed apart, retiring from the field toward the north. Only one man watched them go: Gawain, who helped his brother take the first limping steps but could never make him walk straight.

For me, it was the happiest moment of my life: Guenevere and I, arms linked as as the captains approached to attend us. And Gwen, of course, was always Gwen.

"You could smile a little, Bedivere, I'm home. *Sut mae'r mab*, Gareth-fach! Have you caught up on your sleep? And Maelgwyn! Come, kiss me. Dear God, you're a good-looking man. It's been ages."

Maelgwyn suffered her embrace awkwardly. "A long time, Lady."

"Too long, and you'll dine with us straight. And give me a man to see to this poor, disgusted horse who will not believe women should ride."

The prince turned to search among his milling knights. "Ay, Davy-bach!"

The young man swung around, the bow and quiver slung over his shoulder. "Here, prince of the cats. What's to do?"

"Come look to the queen's horse."

I should have known Maelgwyn wouldn't travel without his harper. Dafydd saluted us in his cheery way and took the reins Guenevere gave him. "Bless you, Lady."

"And you, young man. Take—" Guenevere broke off as she took a good look at him.

Dafydd asked, "Something else, Lady?"

"No," she murmured. "No, nothing."

Dafydd led the horse away. Guenevere watched after him. "Arthur, for a moment, I thought—"

"I know."

"The resemblance; it's uncanny."

"And wait till you hear his harp," I said.

There on the moor we had a kind of holiday fair in the beautiful spring weather, all together, singing, hunting, making feasts out of simple food and happiness. Gwen and I found time to stroll alone in the hills. We found a secret little brook and stripped down to the skin like truant children, swam, played and made tentative love that turned suddenly deep and fierce with the need we always tried to deny. And walking back to camp, hailing this or that lord, Gwen swung along on my hand, radiant and young as Regan. The glorious weather, Gwen and I listening to Dafydd's harp at sundown, the laughter of my men at peace, all of this was like a new beginning.

But Bedivere went on watching the hills and stoning a keener edge to his sword. "My luck's gone dry, and I want to go home."

"Pessimist," said Gwen and stuck a flower in his hair.

The holiday couldn't last. Gawain departed for Solway, Maelgwyn saddled his weary hundred and came to us with a farewell gift from his heart. He pushed Dafydd forward.

"A harp to gladden the soul, and deserving of a king."

So Davy came to me and, through me, to that service you might say he was born for. Say that I owed it to two old friends.

There was another good-bye, more final. When he stood before us, Lancelot, like Bors, had lived to see something less than his hopes and was bewildered.

"Take the Grail to Eleyne," I urged him. "Summer comes early on Neth. She'll have the hall full of flowers."

Yet he hovered. "Guenevere?"

"Yes, dear?"

"Must I?" A little shaking of his head. "Must I go?"

"You've heard the king."

Stubbornly, "I will hear it from you."

Gwen made an impulsive movement toward him, then checked it—not because of me, because she was Guenevere and knew it. "You must go, then. What was before is no longer."

"Not so," Lancelot choked.

"Truth, Lancelot."

He stabbed her with an anguished look. "You know I have nothing then."

Full of compassion, she said, "You have everything."

"No. I should have died before this. To reach for one perfection all my life and be given tin. To find another and be sent off like this. Nothing."

"Everything." Gwen wrapped him in tender arms. "Dear man, will you never be happy? You have a wife who'd never be false like me. Who bore a son I couldn't. You can close your eyes in peace at night while Arthur and I lie down with serpents. Everything."

"I'd give it up. All of it."

"But I wouldn't," Gwen said. "And that's the difference. Everything Agrivaine said of me is true. I use people. I know my price and I give away nothing without a profit. I'm what he called me, a whore."

The frankness startled that upright, honorable man. "You were never that."

"The shoe fits," Gwen said with a wry glance at me. "I was born to it, but at our rank they call us kings. Go home, Lancelot."

Lancelot couldn't accept it. He backed away a few steps, then it tore out of him.

"Is there no place left for honor?"

"If there is," I charged him, "find it. Peredur found one Grail. I know in your heart it isn't yours. Find your own."

He rode away toward the waiting Dyfneint knights, out of our lives.

"Find it," I called after him as something swelled in my heart. "For all of us."

Guenevere slipped an arm through mine. "What a bitch I am. He was quite a man when he managed to get the saints off his back. Loving, eager, grateful as a boy. I shocked him sometimes." My queen considered her wish with cool hope. "When you and I go to hell, Arthur, will they please leave us together?"

I couldn't imagine them not. If they have any feel for government, they'll put us in charge.

* * *

I was preparing to depart with the *combrogi* early next morning when Bors galloped in from picket duty on our north to report: one man on foot leading a horse with what looked like a body strapped across its back, apparently making for us.

With Gareth and Bedivere, I followed Bors back to the picket hill to have a look at the still-distant figure. Gareth noted that the man was in mail.

"And hurt," he concluded after a closer scrutiny. "Not badly, but he feels it."

Man and horse inched toward us over the moor. "I make out his shield." Bedivere narrowed his eyes. "But I don't know the blazon. White horse head on a black field."

"That's Tara," said Gareth, who knew them all. "Cumaill of Tara, one of Gawain's men."

"That *is* a body on the horse," I said. "See how the crows stay overhead? Let's go down."

Seeing us come, Cumaill stopped and waited, one arm over the body protectively. An Irish lord, he took service in Orkney a few years before Badon and went through every day of that muddy hell. A huge, burly man, he glowered at us from under beetling brows and told his tale in a Gaelic accent twice as dense as Gareth's.

"The finest king I yet laid eyes on," he glowered. "That I should have to put him so to horse."

We gave him water. Cumaill brooded murderously while Bors washed the wound on his scalp. The moor shimmered with heat barely relieved by a light southern breeze. Not a man among us without respect for Gawain. No one had much to say.

"I have seen treachery in my time, King of Britain. But this of a cut to shame Judas."

The body of Gawain was battered to a pulp as if he'd been trampled to death three times over. I wished we had something to cover it with.

Cumaill told the bald, ugly tale. It was Gawain's intention to make straight for Solway where his boats were moored. They expected no trouble and camped in a happy mood, glad of peace, eager to be going home.

"Good, loyal men," Cumaill mourned, "and every one behind you at Badon, is that less than truth?"

The horsemen hit them at first light when they were scarce out of their blankets. Cumaill fell next to a gored friend and was left for dead. All his squadron were.

Gareth queried in Irish: "*Daone sidhe?*"

"No Faerie, not them." Cumaill growled in disgust. "Agrivaine it was. And pray for the Orkney Isles. There's not a lord old enough for a beard left to support Gawain's son-regent. Will they not have to accept Agrivaine, and that on their knees? May God regret the day He gave Gawain a brother."

I stroked the lank black hair hanging down from the crushed skull. Gawain had been my most impoverished chief and perhaps the most honest. Against me when I played him false, but at my side again when his heart found me right and putting his life in the scale to attest it. I looked at the glowering, eloquent faces of my lords. They knew something was owed to Gawain.

"Agrivaine has to get there first," I said.

"He'll make for Solway and the boats," Bedivere guessed.

"No mercy," Cumaill begged.

"No. Gareth, when we get back to camp, bring me the maps of the Wall. Gareth?"

My lord-milite was gazing fixedly at the northern horizon and now uttered the most uncharitable sentiment of his life.

"I've hated the insides of that scant man since we rode the Wall."

I thought he hadn't heard me, but then Gareth vaulted into the saddle with a sudden, massive energy.

"Shall be done, sir!"

News of the treachery spread through my *combrogi* like a disease, the anger personal with each of the many men who knew Gawain. None wanted to be left behind. To find an escort for Guenevere, I had to remind them of their personal oath to me and, after some arguing and delay, assembled Lord Bors and twenty of my younger knights.

Bors still objected morosely. "It will be dishonor that I'm not there."

"Nonsense. The Church has named you a knight of the Grail, you and the others who went with Peredur. With whom is the queen safer? Who hinders you goes against God. You could almost travel unarmed."

Bors accepted his duty reluctantly. "I'd be a fool to try. Please the queen, we'll be waiting."

Guenevere walked to her horse on my arm. "What a mess. Just when we thought there might be quiet again."

"Agrivaine's not war, it's sanitation. Now listen: When you get to Camelot, issue a general proclamation of our peace and send it to the Saxons as well."

"Won't I just." She stretched on tiptoe to kiss me good-bye. "I want those savages to know who's back. And that Britain intends to remain"—another lingering kiss—"*very* British."

"Fine. Then I want you to write Gawain's wife at Orkney with—"

Gwen stamped her foot. "You *maddening* man, you'd think I never governed so much as a cow pasture. I've been at this longer than you."

I grabbed my wife by her narrow waist and lifted her off the ground, suddenly happy. "List to a's pride! A's got a mouth like—"

"Don't talk like one of them!" She pulled viciously at my hair in revenge. "I hate that."

"Then would my lady be so good as to belt up and get mounted? I hate to think of the work waiting at Camelot."

Guenevere put her foot to the stirrup and I gave her a leg up. "You never trust me, Arthur."

"Up you go! And long life to the Lady of Britain."

My hand rested on the saddle horn, and Gwen covered it with hers. "*Do* you trust me?"

"You always ask that. I need you, Gwen."

"Of course you do. You didn't become great alone."

"And you need me—"

"I've always suspected it."

"—To keep you honest. Don't proclaim your divinity till I get home."

Guenevere leaned down to kiss me again and bit my lip. "Peasant."

"Bitch."

She waved Bors forward to join her. "That I am, and the best in Britain. God wouldn't waste a nice girl on you, Pendragon."

Bors cantered up, the escort in formation of twos behind. Guenevere took a deep, pleasurable breath of the scented spring air.

"It's our time, Arthur. I feel it. We could do anything now. We could take back the east, even civilize those Saxon bastards."

"Next year, love. Next year, by God, we'll do it."

She blew me a kiss as she moved off. "Don't be long."

We let Cumaill lead the chase until we raised the ambush site where heat and the crows were doing their work, pausing long enough to pray for Gawain's men, then off again following

Agrivaine's easy trail that led straight north toward the Wall. He obviously wanted to cross before running west for Solway. By the map that meant he'd come up on the Wall a little east of Camlann. We tracked until it was too dark, unsaddled and slept by our horses with a careful watch and were up with the first light, eating on the move.

The chance of ambush seemed small. We rode over bare, bleak moor with hardly a stone to hide behind, yet Gareth and Cumaill rode ahead with Dafydd's bow for cover. They began to sight a good many crows.

Gareth found the first body about ten miles short of the Wall. One of Agrivaine's men, neatly speared with an arrow. When they found two more a little further on, I had Davy retrieve one of the arrows and showed it to Bedivere.

"Bronze head. See how it blunted a little on the mail?"

Dafydd inspected it critically. "Too soft. Who'd make an arrow that way?"

"People who can't make iron," I said.

My cold little premonition was confirmed less than a mile later. The trail was very fresh now and the crow-ridden bodies still warm. Tracks showed where Agrivaine's men dashed off this way and that to nose for their invisible stalkers, then doubled back before the harried squadron pushed on faster.

But they'd searched mainly to the south where there seemed better cover for archers, if any at all. Perhaps a few dogged his rear, but the main party would be *down* the wind, which had blown all day from the south. You can hide from a man's eyes, but rarely from a horse's nose. Agrivaine didn't grow up with this knowledge but Modred did. I gave the order.

"From now on, look sharp. Don't ride three breaths without a look left, right and behind."

The hills grew even barer as we approached the Wall, difficult for even a hare to hide in, but Agrivaine's trail was punctuated by three more bodies. And on either side of the fly-buzzing clump, someone had gouged two straight lines in the earth.

Bedivere licked his lips. "Think it's Modred?"

"For sure. That's our *fhain*-sign. He wants me to follow."

We moved at a swift but watchful gait now, no one daring to straggle, until we raised the line of the Wall less than two miles off. Gareth rode back to report, pointing north.

"They're across by now. That's their dust."

Cumaill's eyes glinted with satisfaction. "We'll have them before dark. Close now," he urged. "Let's finish it."

Instinct said no, not too hastily. It was no longer Agrivaine's game but Modred's. He toyed with the Orkneymen in a manner calculated to taunt their tallfolk pride. No doubt he started out merely to decimate Agrivaine, but once he knew I was trailing, the game had a more deadly relish.

Gareth's instincts agreed with mine, but that wasn't good enough for Cumaill. "Will we not *lose* them?" he wailed.

"Lose what?" Bedivere answered coolly. "Modred's doing it for us."

We hallooed the sentry castles when we drew up to the crossing ramp. Everything seemed normal. A few men walked the top of the low parapet. Others leaned out of the mile castle's upper level, worried at first, and very relieved to hear I had no quarrel with them. Yes, Lord Argivaine had crossed scarce an hour before with all his squadron. They didn't stop but turned west on the north side at a full gallop. No, nothing else had been seen. The Orkneymen had shouted something about Picts, and the sentries were ready, but they hadn't seen hide nor hair.

We were right, then. Agrivaine would pass near the abandoned village of Camlann.

But where was Modred? The Faerie might yet be south, but I doubted it. More likely they had crossed to the west to be waiting for Agrivaine. In country like this you follow three things: tracks, dust and crows. Where men have passed you find the first two; where they've fallen the third come quickly.

The sky was white as I scanned the west where Agrivaine's dust settled slowly. He wasn't that far ahead, and he wasn't moving.

"Gareth, give them ten minutes' rest. And make the most of it. We're going to close."

"Down, you lovelies!" Gareth bawled. "Give 'em a breath. We're going in."

He drew his sword and jammed it upright into the ground, drawing a line along its shadow edge with his dagger. Our column dismounted, filling buckets for the horses from their water bags, easing cinches.

Bedivere and I sprawled out together in the shadow of his mount.

"Cnoch-nan-ainneal," he mused. "That's where I lost you, wasn't it?"

"The hill of the fires. You waited and we were under you all the time."

The sword-shadow crept over Gareth's mark. Bedivere took small, measured sips from his water bag, always watching the hills.

"Still worried about your luck, boyo?"

He stoppered the bag, nodding. "Since I saw Kay dead." My friend rolled over on his lean stomach, squinting up at me out of a seamed, weatherbeaten face. "You've got the luck, Artos. They said at Badon you couldn't die, but me . . ."

"You?" I scoffed. "Who charged a Saxon square alone and walked away from it? And the same at Eburacum and Neth Dun More and the midlands and where else? You've survived poisoned arrows, Irish *uisge* and legion food. You'll probably live forever."

Bedivere rolled over with rich laughter, kicking long legs in the air. "That muck they called soup at Cilurnum, remember? Thickened with dust and seasoned with flies. And that dirty Brigante cook saying, 'Don't mind the grit, it'll clean your teeth.'"

I remembered it too well. "Take away the grit, there was nothing left. And Tryst throwing the bowl at him and screaming, 'You're not a cook, you're a bloody assassin!'"

"I remember," my friend chuckled. "Clear as yesterday. Odd, but I daydream more and more now. I think of Tryst a good deal and the old squadron, the old days. I look back more than forward. That's age for you."

Gareth sat up and consulted his sword sundial. "Time, sir."

"Get them up. Column of threes behind the dragon."

The men formed quickly. We moved forward at a trot, then a canter. When the rested horses were warmed to their stride, we lengthened it to a gallop, eating up the long valley leading to Camlann and the hill of the fires. Head on a swivel, as when we learned our soldiering in these same hills. Be alert, don't go to sleep. Is that a rock? Did it move? You won't get a second guess. And Agrivaine's dust loomed nearer. Too near. He could see our own now, probably hear us.

"Artos, the birds!"

The moor scavengers were descending just beyond the next hill. I shot up my arm for a halt and signaled Gareth to me, studying the ground to the west and north. There was the familiar hill of the fires crowned with its ancient stone circle where I went home to *fhain*. Camlann lay just beyond the next hill. Agrivaine must be there, halted still, though that was hard to believe. The gathering crows indicated a different possibility. I wheeled my arm overhead, one hand over my mouth, the *combrogi* signal for quiet, as Gareth reined in by me.

"Lord Gareth, who is your best scout?"

Without a pause, "Myself, sir."

"But among the younger men."

The question gave him some umbrage and Gareth let me know it. "Well, if it's a novice you want, high king, there's a glimmer of talent in Culwych."

"Send him forward. And don't sulk, Gareth-fach. You're lord-milite now and much too important to go poking around alone."

Young Culwych was a Grail knight like Bors; his shield was already blazoned with the cup symbol in one corner. He carried it proudly and always turned it so that a newcomer or someone who didn't know him couldn't help noticing the golden cup.

"Go forward," I instructed him. "Around the hill to the north, not over it. Take a look without being seen."

We waited then in the dusty, fly-buzzing heat, no one talking. The south wind dropped to nothing. The air sweltered. When a freshet of breeze sprang up for a moment from the northwest, my horse tossed his head nervously and snorted. I didn't try to quiet him. He was my guide now. When the breeze came again, I smelled it myself.

"Gareth, alert the men. Stay silent, ready to move quickly. There's something besides Agrivaine out there."

We waited. Bedivere trickled a few drops from the water bag over his sweaty red face, rubbing it in. "What's keeping Culwych?"

I was still tasting the air for the *fhain*-scent. There it was again: wild garlic. Prydn ponies fed on it.

Bedivere pointed. "There he is."

At the top of the hill in front of us, Culwych sat his horse at ease, waving us on. He pointed urgently beyond it and waved again. I started to signal the column forward when something—I don't know what—said no. With a wary glance at the hill of the fires, I motioned Gareth to me.

"You're in command. Seems clear ahead, but Bedivere and I will go up for a look. Watch that hill to the northwest, the Prydn may be there. And send me Dafydd."

Culwych waved us on again. When I trotted forward with Bedivere and Dafydd, he turned and disappeared down the opposite slope.

Bedivere was a little in the lead when we topped the hill. He reined in sharp. "Jesus!"

Dafydd set an arrow to his bow, trying to look everywhere at once. I was right. Agrivaine had chanced a brief rest here, just long enough to dismount and breathe. It must have been a slaughter swift as Gawain's. The men lay scattered from the base of the hill over a hundred yards. A few might have escaped but no more. Far out on the moor, three horses staggered clumsily about, dragging the weight of men who'd made it as far as the stirrup.

We couldn't feel sorry for them, the justice was too poetic. Still I wondered at the awesome efficiency of the attack. Such a thing must be done quickly. Men don't just stand still waiting to be targets. Dafydd instructed me tersely.

"Done it myself, sir. A hundred bows massed, one man forward to sight. Second flight ready while the first's still falling. If the men know their craft . . . and these did."

No other explanation for what we saw. The archers hidden, perhaps behind this slope, bows angled up, loosing in a deadly rush, the next in flight while the first is striking. Perhaps a few lucky men escaping, and then the eager crows, resentful now of Culwych dismounted and stalking among them.

"North, Artos. There!"

I followed Bedivere's point. The line of small riders dashed out from around the north slope of Cnoch-nan-ainneal, a hundred and more, streaking away to the east. Modred's first mistake. He could hide from *combrogi* but he couldn't outrun them on open ground.

"*Gareth!*"

He saw them too. His head swerved to me.

"*After them!*"

A sweep of arm, and the column shot out in a galloping arc to overtake the Faerie.

"I'm sorry," I said to my son and the men of my blood. "I didn't want this, but it has to be."

The distant figure of Culwych pointed urgently to something on the ground. I wondered if I should take the time.

Yes. Gareth could catch them, and rather him than me. I had to know Agrivaine was dead.

"A few paces behind, Davy, and keep that bow nocked."

We started down the slope, raising a cloud of crows at the bottom. They flapped away to settle again at a distance, waiting.

"Culwych should stay mounted," Bedivere worried. "They could still be watching."

Our horses threaded through the arrow-pinned bodies toward Culwych, who waited some distance beyond. I paused by the red mound he'd pointed to. Only by the shield blazon could I recognize it as Agrivaine. Cumaill would want that for Gawain's widow.

"Don't get down," Bedivere warned.

"I just want the shield."

As I hooked it to my saddle, I saw Culwych bend and retrieve a bow at his feet and called to him, "Ay, who dropped that now?"

Still looking away across the moor, Culwych fitted the shaft. "None."

He swung around in a fluid motion, drawing the bow. In the flash of realization before the arrow hit me, I saw the changeling's face. Tall as Culwych, able to fool us in the mail, but the cheeks were darkened with years of weather and scarred as mine.

"Did make it, Belrix."

I stumbled backward with the shaft deep in my gut, jolting in a grotesque dance as the second arrow hit me in the back. Shock before the pain, and through its glaze, I saw it all happen at once. Dafydd bent and loosed on the changeling, the arrow finding its mark in the sun-browned throat, Bedivere off his horse and at my side to cover me with his own body. When the arrow hit him, Bedivere went taut with the shock, grabbing at me. The whine of another shaft and Dafydd's cry of pain.

"Down," I hissed to Bedivere. "Down and still."

We collapsed together in a bleeding, shaken huddle. I felt the warm stickiness under my mail and clothes. "Down, Davy, it's our only chance."

The startled crows settled down again while the heart-thudding seconds passed with no sound but our ragged breathing. Bedivere lay with his face close to mine, the arrow protruding from his left shoulder. It was painful—he panted with it—but not as deep as the two in me.

"Bad, Artos?"

"Worse. Don't move. Davy, are you hurt?"

"S-summ'at," he wheezed. "M'leg. How is it with you, sir?"

"Managing." What else to say with one arrow in my vitals and another in my back? I was beginning to die, but fought to stay conscious, willed myself not to writhe with the pain settling into a steady throb.

Bedivere choked on pain and strangled fury. "God *damn* it, let them come down. We shouldn't go like this."

The crows hopped closer, interested, no doubt wondering when we'd be ready.

"Is there anything they won't eat?" Bedivere wondered.

"Let them get close. You'll look deader to the Prydn."

"Where d'you think they are?"

"Waiting."

And so did we, motionless, while the sun crawled across the white sky and the half-gorged crows lurched drunkenly about us. One lighted on my back, and I felt a tentative peck at the rent in my mail, fighting the revulsion with all my will. One wave would have scattered them, but we couldn't afford that.

Bedivere sucked in his breath. "There they are."

"Can't see. How many?"

"Two."

"Modred?"

"Could be. And a bigger one. Not coming down yet. Not yet, the bastards. Just looking. Christ."

"What?"

A little shamed, Bedivere admitted, "Damned thing hurts."

"Oh. Davy, how is it?"

"Bleedin'," he husked.

"Bow to hand?"

"Aye, sir. But I can't last much more of these crows."

Bedivere's voice was tight and cool now. "Coming down, Artos. Slow. Aye, it's that sweet bairn of yours."

"See 'em, Davy?"

Dully: "I do that."

"On Bedivere's word . . . steady. How close?"

"Twenty paces," Bedivere said and then stopped breathing.

Ear against the ground, I detected the first faint vibration of bare feet. Flies buzzed around my face. The seconds stretched out like eternity while I waited for Bedivere's word that didn't come and didn't come—

"*Now!*"

My eyes shot open to see Dafydd rear up, drawing and loosing all in a blink, his right hand already fitting the second arrow. I hauled up painfully on one elbow in a flurry of cawing, flapping crows as Bedivere roared to his feet, saw the tall changeling go over backward with the shaft in his heart.' Startled, Modred lost his chance in that trice, shooting a hair wide as Dafydd's second arrow ploughed into his naked middle just over the wolf-hide girdle.

Bedivere strode down on him, sword drawn. "Now, you little—"

"No, I croaked. "No, wait—"

Dafydd sent another shaft into Modred's shoulder. I heard it grind against bone as he staggered back. The bow dropped from his fingers. The wound would have been fatal, but Dafydd was wounded and shaken, far off his best. There was still time.

"Hold," I screamed at them, struggling up to my knees. "He's done. Leave him, he's *done*."

So was I, with the blood seeping fast and sticky from my stomach and down my back. The four of us poised like figures in an interrupted dance, Bedivere's sword raised, Modred swaying on his feet but never taking his eyes from me. I tried to read them before it was too late.

"Let me kill him, Artos. Don't be a fool."

"*No!*" I couldn't. At the end I couldn't let them, could only say his name. "Modred."

His near-naked body shook with something beyond pain as he clawed the bronze knife from his belt. Bedivere's sword lifted in warning.

"Don't, Faerie."

"Modred." It was a prayer, a plea. "Don't, they'll have to. Please."

My son looked at the knife, then at me. "Did leave her. Did kill Prydn."

"Son, don't."

He lunged forward, straight at me. Dafydd's arrow caught him under the heart.

"Don't—"

He could have lived, could have lived, was all I could think. It doesn't make sense, purely instinct. I snapped off the shaft protruding from my stomach.

"Help me up. Take me to him."

Bedivere and Dafydd lifted me and set me beside my son. Awkward and clumsy, blurred with tears, I lifted his head and shoulders and cradled them in my arms. His girlish mouth quavered open.

"Dost come to hold thy wealth, Belrix?"

"It didn't have to be this way. I tried, I tried for all of you."

The hate was fading from Modred's eyes with the life of him. "*Gern-y-fhain* said . . ."

"What, boy?" I couldn't bend close for the wounds, but I tried. "What?"

The delicate mouth twisted into the scar of his mocking grin. "This."

My son spat in my face and died.

Rest You Gentle,
Sleep You Sound

And so this place the monks call Avalon, the scratch of Coel's stylus, the smell of apple blossoms, the hum of bees beyond the casement, the quiet end to the clangorous song. Lucullus' notion of an exit might be more fun, but this isn't at all a bad way to go.

We're finished, Brother Coel.

Bald? For an ending, perhaps, but then there are two schools of thought on literature and love-making. Some say the climax is all. I think it's not so much the end but the getting there. Give me the stylus, let me sign.

Artos, Rix Cymri

There. And now the letters. Just two, and then we're done. And make them part of the record.

Arthur to his dear Yseult, Queen of Cornwall—

(Write larger, boy. Her eyes aren't what they were.)

> *Dear Yseult. I send to your personal service Dafydd of Eburacum, a soldier of proven worth and a harper who has served both Maelgwyn and myself with honor.*
> *When his music falls on your ear and your eye on his face, I know you will treasure Dafydd's qualities as no other woman could. Long life and music, sweet.*

360

Now to the queen. *Dear Gwen*—no, not formal, Coel. The sword will be solemn enough.

> *Dear Gwen*—
> *Bedivere brought your message. If he returns with the imperial sword, don't waste time mourning when there's work to do. And please don't come to Avalon, but stay where you're needed.*
> *The princes may call for a new king, though I don't know where they'll find your equal. They could do no better.*
> *And though it shivers your patrician soul, listen to Bedivere and Gareth. Ask their mind and don't be surprised when you get it. With them and the combrogi at your side, you are Britain.*

(We two, so clever at words and so clumsy at meaning. We did it, Gwen. Something bigger than ourselves. I sit in the north writing what you will read in the south while every prince and peasant between waits for word and asks of travelers: "What news of Camelot? What word from the crown?" Being a circlet of metal that hopefully encloses an idea.)

> *I can't help noting how dry and hot it is this spring, and that always means a cold winter on Severn. So conquer your dislike of wool shifts and wear one or even two—you know how drafty the chambers get. And you mustn't work too long at one time, but take your nap in the afternoon and sit down to regular meals. Tell Imogen I order and again order her to be a bloody nuisance until you finish everything on your plate at every meal. You can't rule from a sickbed.*
> *And you mustn't forget to write Gawain's family and make it clear we support them against all pretenders. And get the Demetae to pay their taxes, even if you have to go in after them. They've always felt that distance from Camelot equals an exemption, you know that.*
> *It's quite lovely here. I wish you could see the trees blossoming—*

(I wish I could say now what I mean. What we mean. Did I love you, do I? What does that word mean, thief and tyrant that it is? I know that I saw you one day at Eburacum and you touched my life and shared it, and even if we walked apart sometimes, it was always on the same road. People should remember you, Gwen. Not the crown or the trappings, but *you*. How you loved flowers and making love in the afternoon, and that idiotic garden hat you wore till it fell apart, or that shirt you knitted for our child and could never give or throw away. Why is it always that these dear things get lost?)

Yes, I've started bleeding again. Rather badly, I think. We'll make it short. It's all said anyway.

> *There's work as always and I must be at it. Remember about the woolen shift or don't blame me when you start sneezing. And we must start planning for the east, because next year we're going to take it back. None but us, Gwen.*
>
> *Rest you gentle.*
>
> Arthur

Thank you, Brother Coel. If God has your patience, I'm halfway home. Yes, of course you may pray for me. Often, I hope. And insistently. You never know, I may need it.

Please send in Lord Bedivere.

Bedivere comes in. My friend tries to give me his old world-as-usual air, but he could never hide an emotion.

"Sit, Bedivere."

But he falls down suddenly on his knees by the bed, head against his clasped, trembling hands. Stiff with the wound in his shoulder. I try to touch him, but it's a long way to move. Even speaking is an effort now.

He keeps his face averted from me. "Long life to my king."

"Now what's this? Ceremony?"

"My beloved king."

"Victory at last. I've been hoping for years you'd address me like one sometime."

"Artos, I . . ."

"But don't go wet on me. Up, man, there's work to do."

He wipes his eyes, snuffling and awkward. He doesn't cry prettily, my Bedivere.

"Listen, now." Jesus, so weak. "I don't see what you're

boo-hooing about. You were wrong about your luck, and you're rutting well wrong about mine. I'll be back.''

"I know that, Artos."

"Well, then."

Our words are carefully said, like something polished and put out for show. Bedivere glances to the table where the imperial sword rests, and there's a truth we don't want to speak of.

"Still, it might be best to take Guenevere the sword. She'll need it till I get back.''

Bedivere turns his stubborn back to me. "Let someone else take it.''

"There's no one I'd trust."

Pleading: "Not me."

"Bedwyr, don't."

"Someone else, damn you." Then muffled, "Don't make me go now.''

"God, you're thick," I snap with no strength. "You don't think I'm finished, do you? Take it.''

After a moment he lifts the sword from the table, wrapping the broad belt about the scabbard. "Till you get back.''

"Well enough. Like pulling teeth getting you to just *do* something without an argument.''

"Well, I'm not educated like you. I have to think things out.''

He's found something out the casement to watch. I can't see his face. "Good weather here.''

"Yes," I agreed eagerly. "I've been enjoying it."

"Good the last time I was home, too. I was wondering, Artos. Why stay here when you could rest with Myfanwy and me?''

"Good idea. Splendid. As soon as I can travel."

"Yes, then."

"And Gwen can rummage those gardens of yours."

My friend comes to the bed finally. His hurt arm is stiff, but he makes a stab at arranging my pillows. I keep the covers up so he can't see the stains.

"Then it's done," he says softly. "I'll tell Myfanwy you're coming.''

I touch his hand. "Tell them all, Bedivere."

The monks begin to chant in the oratory. Flat as usual. You'd think with all their practice they'd get it right now and then. Bedivere the singer suffers with me.

"Who let *them* in?''

"Nor do they improve," I advise. "I'd leave now and avoid the worst.''

"We'll be waiting then, all of us." Bedivere raises the sword in good-bye. "Up the dragon, Artos."

"Up the dragon, boyo."

Well now, all done. A little nap until the doctors come. Not that I'm really sleepy, just those monks go on for bloody ever.

My dream was involved and ridiculous, the usual refuse emptied by the mind at the end of a hard day. In my dream, the doctors and the abbot and dear little Coel came and stood about my bed. The lot of them looked very solemn while I felt uncommonly good.

I said to them, "Go away, all of you." And they went, except for one I hadn't noticed at the door, a golden-haired boy in a tunic of brilliant spun gold under a green cloak.

"Hail, Arthur."

Merlin produced his three colored balls and began to toss them casually—up, over and down, never missing a beat. I sat up, feeling better with every breath.

"Hello, Merlin. I told you juggling was your real talent."

"Part of my trade," he admitted. "I came to say good-bye."

"Where are you off to now?"

The colored balls soared higher, four of them now, five, six. The shimmering boy balanced and timed their flight so skillfully that they moved in a smooth circle like the sun. "Don't they shine, Arthur? Shaped from the finest tomorrows. Not an easy job, you know. Another dreamer to be born in the same old place: where he's needed."

He was my genius, this juggler, always the more impressive part of me. Or was I merely a facet of him, designed to lead and care for men?

Merlin caught the high-arcing balls one by one and tucked them away, reading my thought as usual. "By the way, when did you know you loved them?"

There was an answer now. "I thought I knew once in the midlands when I was disgusted with the flowers and loved the fruit. But I'd only just come from Morgana."

Merlin spun toward the door on dancer's feet, restless to be away, doing and changing. "We all feel pastoral now and then. When were you sure?"

"When I heard my men singing on Badon hill."

"Oh, yes!" Merlin hugged himself with delight at the memory. "Was that not the sound of angels?"

"The sound of love, Merlin. That's when I knew how needed the flowers are. The dreamers. They give reason to all the rest. They grab life by the collar, make it shine and boot it into tomorrow. Life's a sweet, terrible wonder, Merlin. A mere king can't be expected to understand it all."

The golden boy hovered at the door. "You didn't do badly at all, Arthur. If I hadn't been at this for ages, I might even boast a bit."

"Thanks." I stretched and yawned. "But now I really ought to get up."

"Up!" Merlin sang, opening the door. "You're still king and people are waiting to see you. You don't think you're finished, do you?"

Finished? I was just starting. I jumped out of bed as Merlin disappeared, struggling into my harness as Ambrosius strode in energetically.

"My lord Ambrosius! Oh, now I *am* dreaming."

My king and teacher planted himself in the middle of the floor, dressed in his plain field harness, the imperial robe slung carelessly over one arm.

"Get dressed, Artorius. You're posted with me."

"Good, sir. Where?"

"To safe keeping." The old emperor bit off the words, never one to waste time. "Now snap to and try to look like an officer."

"No more Roman uniforms, sir. Not for years."

Ambrosius grunted. "Hell, we've run out of Rome itself. I've got to keep you safe, Tribune. I'm only a fact, but you're going to be a legend."

"What? Balls!"

"That's what I say." Ambrosius drummed his fingers on the hilt of his shortsword. "I've got to save *some* of you for the historians."

I finished buckling the harness, set the helmet on my head. "Ready, Imperator."

"Good, let's go." Ambrosius struck his hands together. "It won't be too bad. Historians take forever but they do get you squared off in the end. Organization, by the gods! People get fuzzy without it. And who cares if they don't love you? They *need* you—and they never seem to forgive that. Come on, Tribune, and don't slouch."

And we hurried off to work.

And in the dream, I watched the young tribune go off with

Ambrosius. The door was hardly shut on them when it was flung open again.

"Hail, my comet!"

Trystan, arms folded, lounging against the door, graceful and insolent in his best finery, the harp slung over one shoulder. I jumped out of bed to greet him.

"Tryst! My God, it's the most extraordinary luck, but I met your son at Badon."

"My son." Over the old supercilious smile, his brows arched in mild curiosity. "*My* son?"

"His name's Dafydd. He's an archer."

Trystan considered. "Forgive me, I've rather forgotten things like time. Can't seem to place his mother."

"In Eburacum."

"Oh, yes!" with a finger snap. "Tawny hair, marvelous figure. A common archer?"

"Most uncommon, lad. Like his harp. She said he had your touch."

"Then someone did remember me." His superiority softened to something finer. "Well enough. Are you ready to go?"

"I just did. I mean, I'm not sure. Where?"

"Where?" Trystan raised his arms in dramatic invocation. "Arthur, my comet, my king, you have no idea what a legend you're going to become. You, me, all of us. Magnificent!"

"Yes, Ambrosius warned me that—"

"The founder of Camelot! Palace of the mind that will endure as long as men dream. The Grail, the great deeds, the battles, the songs. I've been writing some of them myself. Ought to have something tasteful before the Christians get hold of you." He unslung his harp, eager to play for me. "Here, listen."

"No, wait. Tryst, where are you taking me?"

"A long way," my friend said, lyrical as always. "Long as time, swift as memory, to saddle scrolls and sharpen pens to lances, ride patrol on a hundred books to keep them shining with life and not *too* ordinary."

I finished dressing in the strange, impractical armor. Trystan fastened the purple cloak and set the gaudy crown on my head.

"I know," said my legend-wise friend. "It's not what you were, but what they'll think you meant. Ready?"

I doubted it.

"Let's be off!" Trystan dragged me to the door, looking marvelously vital, twenty again. "Geraint is waiting for us."

"Geraint? Oh, bless him, how's he been?"

"Volcanic as ever. A day's talk to a minute's meaning, and a positive desert for conversation. But he's part of the legend."

But he wasn't, none of us were. He was real as myself.

And real he was, peacock-florid in his brilliant armor and flower-decked helmet, sitting one of three magnificent white stallions whose saddles and harness sagged with the weight of jewels. Geraint drew his sword and swept it out in a lavish salute.

"Hail, Arthur! Where you go, so do I. What else for the friend who stood with me at Neth Dun More, three against three hundred!"

I winced. "For shame, Geraint. As I recall, there were no more than—"

"Oh well." He shrugged blithely. "Of course you've lived longer and your memory, look you, may not be keen as mine, but they were at *least* three hundred and many say more, including my sainted sister who has always had naught but charity to speak of you, save for your carelessness. Arthur Pendragon is a *good* man, says she, but . . ."

Trystan sighed philosophically. "As I said, doomed to legend. What historian would believe in *him—Hi!*"

With a shout, Trystan spurred the great improbable charger to a gallop. I suddenly felt I could ride forever and called after him: "Then we'll make it a good story, Tryst. By God, a great one! Come on, Geraint. I'll race you!"

And in the dream I watched from my bed as the three of them rode off, preposterous in their gaudy trappings, on horses bigger and in armor more ornate and impractical than anyone ever wore.

A light, rapid tap at the open door. "May I come in?"

Guenevere in her state robes, a new gold crown set firmly over the plaited auburn hair.

"Come in, Gwen! I don't know what they put in that last medicine, but this is the most delicious dream. You look ravishing."

She came to fuss at my pillows, leaning over, teasing my mouth with hers. "You were always the most illegally handsome king, Arthur."

"And very relieved. Thought I was gone for a minute there, riding off with all those memories and futures."

"You'll never die, Arthur, you're not the sort." Guenevere sprang up, not a moment to waste, deftly smoothing her hair under the crown. "I only have a moment. The Council's waiting."

"Don't try to do it all alone, Gwen. Listen to Bedivere and Gareth and don't scold them too much when they tell you off. The people can deify you all they want, but start to believe it and you're in trouble."

"Don't tell me how to rule, Arthur Pendragon. My blood was crowned when—" Her dagger-look of impatience broke suddenly in a smile. "Oh, you're right. Oh, Arthur, I could have been such a wonderful little tyrant but for you. Now I don't have the ego for it; just the job and the habit."

"Keep at it, love. And mind out for Trystan. He's stuffed the lot of us into some overdressed legend."

"A legend?" She has the most beautiful laugher in the world, my Gwen. "That's *so* like him. He can't resist an audience. There, I'm late, but I do love you, sweet."

She came to kiss me again in her cool, lingering way.

"Most of the time, Gwen?"

In a queen's hurry, she paused one last time at the door, vital and full of destinies. "A grand time, Arthur. We didn't win it all, but we gave it a fine try. The two of us in a legend: I've always fancied it, but won't we shock them?" She blew me a final kiss. "Rest you gentle."

Sleep you sound, Gwen.

Well now, I do feel a bit subtracted with all those selves flying off and no telling where they'll light.

But I'm still here and feeling marvelous, feeling twenty like Tryst. Alive? I yearn toward the open hills beyond the sunny casement, want to fill my lungs with air and run for the pure joy of being. And by God, I will—

But there's a movement in the corner of my eye, and a smothered giggle. The dark little head rises up from the foot of the bed where she's been hiding all along, and—

"Yah!" cries Morgana as she springs up, arms shooting high in her eager child-greeting, and then she ducks down again quick as a thought to hide from me.

Sly, mouse-quiet, I slip from the bed and down on my knees, and—

"Yah!"

—grab her, laughing, as she leaps up into my arms, kissing and nipping at my mouth and ears and chin.

"Belrix, Belrix, did wait for thee."

And holding Morgana, I look back at the empty shell in the

bed and know it's time to go. This is the last and best of me.
Morgana's mouth is next my ear as she kneads my shoulders
with brown fingers that slip down over my back and thighs. She
pulls her sheepskin vest aside to push her small breasts against
me, rousing me like new Bel-tein flame rekindled from old.

"Do thee come home now," she whispers.

She kisses my mouth, a long kiss sweet with the magic that
passes from her to me. The old hollow place in me is filled with
Morgana, and I
>   feel
>   myself
>   waking,
>   *growing*
to my true self joined with hers as we spring light as deer over
the casement sill and out into Lugh's sunlight, and Morgana
takes my hand to pull me after her.

"Summer king, summer king, come with me! Will dance on
the hill of the fires."

And in the dream we run like the wind, run home forever
under the hill.

ABOUT THE AUTHOR

PARKE GODWIN is coauthor of *The Masters of Solitude* and the forthcoming sequel, *Wintermind*. He has been a radio operator, research technician, professional actor, advertising layout man, dishwasher, and *maître d'hôtel*. Recently he traveled to Scotland to participate in an archaeological dig.

*Don't miss any of these works by
World Fantasy Award-Winning Author*

PARKE
GODWIN

☐ **THE LAST RAINBOW** (Available July 1, 1985) (34142-1 • $6.95/
$7.95 in Canada)
A novel of the young Saint Patrick in Celtic Britain—a moving,
magical, richly textured saga of the end of an era . . . and the
beginning of a legend.

> "THE LAST RAINBOW is a book to treasure . . . every one of
> Godwin's characters is memorable, and his vision is
> dazzling."
>
> —Morgan Llywelyn, author of LION OF IRELAND

☐ **BELOVED EXILE** (24924-X • $3.95/$4.50 in Canada)
King Arthur is dead. Now, surrounded by traitors and usurpers, his
queen struggles to defend the dream of Camelot. Here is one of the
most dramatic portraits of the great queen Guenevere ever created.

> "A blockbuster."
>
> —Marion Zimmer Bradley, author of
> THE MISTS OF AVALON

☐ **FIRELORD** (25269-0 • $3.95/$4.50 in Canada)
Here is the magnificent saga of Camelot and its glorious leader,
whose name is forever inscribed in the golden pages of history. A
man called Artorius Pendragon—Arthur, King of the Britons . . .
Firelord.

> "With its superb prose and sweeping imagination, FIRELORD
> brings to life a realer King Arthur than we have ever seen
> before."
>
> —*Chicago Sun-Times*

☐ **MASTERS OF SOLITUDE** (with Marvin Kaye) (24726-3 • $3.50)
A modern science fiction classic, the haunting epic of humanity's
descendants . . . and humanity's will to survive.

All are available at your local bookstore—or use this handy cou-
pon for ordering:

WEST
of
EDEN

Harry Harrison

From a master of imaginative storytelling comes an epic tale of the world as it might have been, a world where the age of dinosaurs never ended, and their descendants clash with a clan of humans in a tragic war for survival. . . .

"An astonishing piece of work." —Joe Haldemann

"A big novel in every sense . . ." —*Washington Post Book World*

"Brilliant." —Phillip Jose Farmer

"Epic science fantasy." —*Playboy*

"The best Harrison ever—and that's going some." —Jerry Pournelle

"I commend this rich and rewarding novel to those who know and love Heinlein, Asimov, Herbert and Clarke; they will find no less than what those masters provide here." —Barry N. Malzberg

"This is the way they used to write them, high adventure with lots of thought-provoking meat." —Thomas N. Scortia

Don't miss Harry Harrison's WEST OF EDEN, available in paperback July 1, 1985, from Bantam Spectra Books.

Announcing a new publishing imprint of quality science fiction and fantasy:

BANTAM SPECTRA BOOKS

Science fiction and fantasy have come of age—and there's a whole new generation of readers searching for fresh, exciting novels, fiction that will both enter- tain *and* enlighten. Now, from the house of Ray Bradbury, Samuel R. Delany, Ursula K. Le Guin, Anne McCaffrey, Frederik Pohl, and Robert Silver- berg comes the first full-spectrum publishing im- print that delivers all the excitement and astonish- ment found only in imaginative fiction. Under the Bantam Spectra Books imprint you'll find the best of all possible worlds: from serious, speculative nov- els to the most lighthearted tales of enchantment, from hard-science thrillers and far-future epics to the most visionary realms of magic realism.

Look for Bantam Spectra Books—we've rediscov- ered the wonder in science fiction and fantasy.

SPECIAL
MONEY SAVING
OFFER

Now you can have an up-to-date listing of Bantam's hundreds of titles plus take advantage of our unique and exciting bonus book offer. A special offer which gives you the opportunity to purchase a Bantam book for only 50¢. Here's how!

By ordering any five books at the regular price per order, you can also choose any other single book listed (up to a $4.95 value) for just 50¢. Some restrictions do apply, but for further details why not send for Bantam's listing of titles today!

Just send us your name and address plus 50¢ to defray the postage and handling costs.